gilded lily

STACI HART

Cover by **Quirky Bird**
Editor: **Jovana Shirley, Unforeseen Editing**
Proofreading: **Love N Books**

Playlist: https://spoti.fi/2D9FwyJ
Pin Board: http://bit.ly/2s1eBCW

gilded lily

To those of you
seeking perfection:

It's here—
Right here, in the palm of your hand.
For nature doesn't make mistakes,
and you, my darling, are already perfect.

AUTHOR'S NOTE

Many of us can claim our love for Jane Austen, but only a few of us are foolish enough to retell her stories.

I have taken some liberties with *Pride and Prejudice*, and I hope you'll allow me to imagine the Bennet sisters as unruly men (less our Lizzie) and Longbourne as a flower shop in Manhattan. And I hope beyond hope that you enjoy my nod to the Bennets, who we love so well.

A Spade's a Spade

KASH

Heaven existed within the walls of our greenhouse.

The shuck of my shovel against the iron wheelbarrow was the second hand on my day. Rich soil mounded on the spade, and I transferred it into the bed of black-eyed Susans, turning it to feed the sleepy dirt already gathered at the flowers' feet.

I caught sight of the snowy top of my father's head between stalks of amber amaranth down the row where he knelt, hands in the earth. He hummed along with the music playing from the portable speaker on our work cart, and with another shuck, I drove my shovel back into the wheelbarrow.

It was peaceful and familiar, the rhythm of our day, the slanting sun, the humid air and smell of flowers. I'd worked in my family's greenhouse during high school—as had all my siblings—but where they'd made their way into the world, I'd hung back, content at Longbourne with Dad and unable to leave Mom without anyone to fuss over. And if there was one thing Mrs. Bennet required from life, it was someone to fuss over.

I found myself smiling at the thought. She'd see us all married off—in fact, she played the matchmaker like it was her full-time job—but I had to wonder what she'd do with herself once we were all gone. Press us for grandchildren and divert her attention to them, if the rest of the Bennet brood were lucky.

The crack of the swinging metal door against the wall wiped that smile off my face. I shot up from my task with a hard look, appalled and accusing, prepared to smite whoever had disturbed our sanctuary.

Lila Parker blew in like a gale—just like she had almost daily for the last two months—heels clicking like hammers against the cement floor. At the sight of her, my fury abated, replaced by a curious wonder and the incremental slowing of time that always accompanied her entrance.

She was a study in white, pristine and stern in a pantsuit that belonged in some fancy lady's luncheon, not a greenhouse. Her legs were ten miles long in those white pants, the matching jacket cut low. A sliver of silken nude fabric was the only thing to mar the line of her cleavage, which my eyes followed before climbing up her lily-white skin, up the long column of her neck, to the set of her uncompromising little jaw.

God, she was pretty when she was mad. Shame she had a boyfriend.

I'd known Lila since high school, the notorious rule-follower and teacher's pet, thumbing her nose at the trouble the rest of us got in and refusing invitations to parties in favor of SAT prep. Her sister, Ivy, worked here then and stuck around like I had, and though Lila'd had every opportunity to join the gang, she'd happily declined. She'd ignored me then, and she ignored me now, outside of storming into our flower shop to get onto us—or *me* specifically—for whatever wedding we had, were, or would provide flowers for. As a high-profile wedding planner, I supposed that was her right.

The only bearable thing about it was the chance to give her

just a little hell, simply because I knew she could take it and I could take whatever she gave back.

As she approached, her lips set in a firm line, red as blood against the milk of her skin. The bridge of her nose was short, though long enough to look down at everyone from her high horse—or high heels, as it were—but her eyes always struck me beyond all else, cool and gray as a winter's afternoon, tight with suspicion, hard with the bite of demand. Incongruent to the impeccable, pallid shades of snow was her hair, a shining crimson too bright for all that ivory. It was as perfectly right as it was utterly unnatural, the only indicator that she ran on hot coals and gasoline, just waiting for a match to strike so she could ignite. Just as she had once a week—typically in my direction—since she started using Longbourne's flowers for her events.

That red hair bounced with every click of her heels as she rounded the corner of the aisle and marched toward me, her eyes narrowing another tick when they met mine. Tess, our lead florist, followed with an apologetic look on her face.

My lips tilted higher on one side. And with a shield of calm, unaffected charm in place, I leaned on the handle of my shovel, ready to catch whatever Lila threw at me.

"Coral," she snapped as she approached. "You were supposed to give me *coral* chrysanthemums for the Berkshire wedding, and you sent *pink*." She stopped a few feet in front of me, crossing her arms.

I offered an easy smile. "I cut those flowers myself, picked the best stock from our Gigi mums, just like you asked."

"Then why were they the *wrong color*? Do you have any idea the tantrum Johanna Berkshire threw over those flowers? She tried to get me *fired*."

A chuckle through my nose. "Sounds like she needs to get some real problems."

She eyed me as she drew a breath to fuel her furnace. "For years, my sister has begged me to bring Longbourne business, and I refused for exactly this reason. If it wasn't for all the press you've gotten, I never would have put my ass on the line. But if I say coral, I expect *coral*. Not pink. Not fuchsia. Not goddamn watermelon or flamingo or anything but *coral*."

"Sorry, Ms. Parker," I answered lazily. "Won't happen again."

"You're damn right it won't."

"How about we issue the Berkshires a partial refund for the trouble?"

Suspicion sparked in her gaze. "I'm sure that would help."

"Then consider it done."

Those cool eyes narrowed even more, but she changed the subject. "I need someone to come to a venue in Midtown to measure for arbors and garlands. They've requested an archway, and one of you needs to come take the measurements."

Dad cast me a glance that said *not it*. The way Tess glared at the back of Lila's head, I figured she'd just as soon claw Lila in the back with a hand rake than help her measure anything. Lila's sister, Ivy—another florist at Longbourne—was entirely too pregnant to measure anything but her uterus, and Wendy, our newest addition, just wasn't experienced enough.

My brother Luke might have done it, but something told me I wanted to be the one to handle Lila Parker.

"Sure. When and where?"

"Tomorrow, if you can manage it. I can meet you at three, Forty-Ninth and Fifth. I'm going to need an archway long enough for the wedding party to stand inside, and the arbor will need a special design built in the shape of a triangle. It's at the—" She paused, lips flattening. "Shouldn't you be taking notes?"

I tapped my temple. "Got it all right here."

Color rose in her cheeks as she drew a slow breath through her nose. "I really think you should write it down."

"What, don't trust me?"

"I don't know what instills more faith—that you can't tell the difference between shades of pink or that your shirt says *Can You Dig It?* on the front."

I glanced down at my chest, flicking at a streak of dirt like I gave a shit what she thought. "Listen, Priss. I'll be where you say, when you say, ready and at your service."

A pause while she stared me down, seeming to weigh her options. "All right, Filthy. Can you at least wear a clean shirt? This venue books for two hundred thousand per event, and I don't want to have to get you in through the service entrance."

"Deal," I said, extending a hand in challenge. It was as filthy like she'd said, with crescents of dirt under my nails and enough soil in the creases of my palms to grow zucchinis.

Her eyes dropped to my hand, and for a moment, I was positive she'd refuse. But somewhere in that pretty little head of hers existed *some* form of manners and a healthy helping of pride, so she slipped that spotless, manicured hand into my dirty, calloused one.

It was soft and warm, though her fingers were strong, gripping my hand and pumping it once, firm and definitive, before taking it back.

Instantly, I felt guilty for daring her—her skin was spoiled with streaks and flecks of dirt. To her credit, she didn't even dust it off. Instead, she held up her chin and gave me a quietly confrontational glare.

"I'll give Ivy the exact address. At least I know she'll write it down."

"Whatever you have to do," I said, returning my forearm to the handle of the shovel, not missing the flick of her eyes to my shoulders and the cross of my arms.

"Tomorrow then. Don't be late."

She tugged the hem of her jacket, straightening it to match the yardstick that was her spine, and once again, I lamented taking her hand. A scuff of dirt now sullied the very edge of that white tailored coat.

Before I could apologize, she turned on her heel to walk away.

What she didn't realize—the cat had taken up post directly behind her.

The moment stretched as she tilted in a successful attempt to avoid impaling Brutus with her heel, and when that heel came down, it caught in the seam of concrete. Her long legs twisted, arms shooting out for balance but finding none. Fast, but not fast enough, I moved for her, the shovel hitting the ground with a clang as that pristine white ass of hers landed flat in the black-eyed Susans and that fresh coat of soil I'd just laid down.

Brutus took a seat next to Tess's feet, curling his tail around himself and watching Lila with what I swore was a wry smile.

My urge to laugh was so intense, it caught in my chest, frozen by the sheer outrage on her face and utter hysteria of the sight of her, so clean and white against the browns and greens and golds of the flower bed. A slow heave of her chest as she breathed fire. The pink of her cheeks flaring to red. The gray of her eyes igniting into a cruel shade of blue, illuminated by the inferno of her thoughts.

I stepped up, unable to school my face as I extended a hand, this time to help her up.

But she scowled, slapping my hand away. "I've got it," she shot, planting her palms in the dirt to push herself up.

As I backed out of the way, I watched her swipe at her ass, too furious to realize she'd only smudged the dirt around.

Tess removed her hands from her mouth, unable to right her face any better than I had. "Here, let me help you—"

"I said, *I've got it.*" Lila's voice was deadly calm, and at the sound, Tess pinned her lips between her teeth and stepped out of the way.

"Tomorrow," Lila snapped over her shoulder, smoothing the shining waves of her hair, which remained undisturbed by her tumble.

"See you then," I answered with a nod.

And then I watched that dirty ass stride proudly out the door.

The second it swung closed, laughter bubbled out of Tess, and at the sound, there was no containing my own. Even Dad joined in, shoulders shaking gently.

"Oh, the poor Susans," Tess said, swiping at a tear. "Look, her ass print is still there," she squeaked before succumbing to another bout of laughter.

"The look on her face," I said with the shake of my head. "I don't think I've ever seen anybody so mad. Not even you, Tess."

"And that's saying something," she added, resting her palm on her belly like she'd just done a hundred sit-ups. "God, if Ivy and Lila didn't look so much alike, I'd never believe they were related."

"I didn't remember her being this …" I started.

"Bitchy?"

"I was gonna say bossy, but okay."

Tess sighed. "She wasn't kidding about sticking her neck out. She's handling this huge celebrity wedding on her own, and her senior is a total asshole, breathing down her neck and micromanaging her at every turn. Addison is constantly looking for reasons to throw Lila under the bus, and if we screw up, Addison will blame Lila. But even though she's a pain, the business is good for us. Archer Events handles the biggest weddings in the city, and that's putting us in their eye line. We've just gotta deal with all the stress that comes with doing weddings."

"Like bridezillas and entitled wedding planners?" I asked.

"Exactly." Tess sighed. "Although I don't know what we're going to do with Lila when Ivy is on maternity leave and isn't here to manage her. Today was bad enough, and Ivy was just at a doctor's appointment."

Dad dusted off his hands. "If she got past you, Tess, I fear for us all."

"I tried to tell her it wasn't your fault," Tess said, her eyes full of apology. "Those flowers went through three florists before it got to the wedding—which I told her—but she stormed right past me to yell at you about it."

I shrugged. "Don't worry about me, Tess. I can handle her." At the disbelieving quirk of her mouth, I added, "I mean it. She can get as mad as she wants, I won't get riled. I'll hold the bucket so she can dump all her rage into it, and when she's empty of it, I'll get whatever done that she needs done. Trust me when I promise you this—Lila Parker cannot get to me."

At that, Tess laughed. "Famous last words."

And oh, if I'd only known how right she was.

By Design

LILA

A whistle split my lips, my dirty hand in the air to hail a cab.

Eyes were on me, likely marking the filth on my suit. Or perhaps my height or my red hair, the latter calling regular attention. Not that I minded. I wouldn't wear so much white if I didn't want to be seen.

White, I'd found, called more attention than red ever could.

Of course, it also fell prey to every surface it touched, especially when I went to that goddamn dirty greenhouse where that goddamn dirty gardener always found a way to get under my skin. And his stupid cat, too.

A taxi screeched to a quick halt in front of me. With the snap of the handle, I was sliding into the back, digging in my purse for my phone.

"Twenty-Third and Sixth," I said with more bite than I'd meant. With a sigh, I added, "Please."

With nothing more than a nod, he took off.

In the fifteen minutes I'd spent at Longbourne, my phone had become a mess of messages and calendar alerts. And while I absently cleared them, Kash Bennet dug his way through my brain with his shovel and that smirk and his idiotic T-shirt.

I could have told you his every flaw. Like his hair, which was thick and lush, black and gleaming and far too long, brushing his ears in waves too perfect for a man that sweaty. Or his nose, which looked like it had been broken once, the perfect line a little bent, flat on top like a Greek statue. Maybe his beard, which was too long to be considered scruff, dark as his hair and thick enough to barely see any skin through it. Or his size, which was far too big. Beastly. Roped and corded with muscles that gleamed with sweat and a peppering of dirt. He was dirty. Filthy and dirty and in desperate need of a manicure.

I could still feel the scrape of his calluses against the un-worked flesh of my palm when we shook hands. Mine had disappeared into his, making me feel dainty, delicate, which was a feat of skill. I was no pixie, and my hands were proof—my fingers were slender and longer than my palm. Witch hands, Ivy called them, elegant and with the potential to wreak ruin or riches, depending on my mood. Which, of late, had been less than pleasant.

A pang of guilt niggled at me for giving Kash Bennet such a hard time. It was just the pressure of my job. Now, I loved my job—warts and all, as it was its own form of witch—but until I got a promotion, I worried I'd be impossible to endure.

We'd just landed the wedding of the decade. One of the Felix Femmes had met former-actor-turned-emo-rockstar in Aruba a month ago, and they were getting married. In eight weeks. Which meant I had a lot to do and not enough time to do it.

The Felix sisters were a quartet of socialites starring on a show titled *Felix Femmes*, a reality show documenting the daily lives of the infamous sisters. Their parents were one of the *it* couples from the nineties—Romanian supermodel Sorina Felix and her husband Adrien, a French socialite and retired playboy—and as such, the girls had been born with impeccable bone structure and an obscene wealth that afforded them a charmed life. And by charmed, I meant they were spoiled, entitled, and an absolute shitshow.

Alexandra and Sofia, the eldest, had been married and divorced half a dozen times between the two of them. Angelika was the third—and our client. And Natasha, the youngest, was every bit the party girl, gracing every tabloid in America with her beautiful face and-or beautiful vagina, depending on her outfit of choice. They were inhumanly gorgeous, with hard cheekbones and full lips and sweeping blonde hair, none of which were real. They had created fashion and makeup lines, perfumes and designer handbags. In essence, they were a household name of astronomic and notorious status and the clients that would likely test the limits of what I was willing to endure for my job.

For instance, at their engagement party last week, Alexandra had given a tipsy, passive-aggressive speech, halted by a glass of champagne in the face—courtesy of Angelika. Natasha, drunk, pelted them with pistachios while Sofia tried to wrestle them apart, resulting in a broken heel.

When she'd fallen, she'd taken Angelika's strapless dress with her.

Like I said, I had my work cut out for me, and until this wedding was over, I was likely going to be a nightmare, one fueled by my boss's breath on my neck as she waited to push me in the fire to keep herself warm.

Speak of the devil . . .

One of my texts was from Addison Lane, the senior coordinator in charge of ruining my life.

Johanna Berkshire was just in here with her lawyer. I told them I was handling it, so I hope for your sake that you fixed the flower issue.

A sharp inhale and flex of my jaw accompanied the tap of my fingers. *It's handled.*

Of course Addison had and would continue to take credit.

This was the crux of our relationship: I did all the dirty work—particularly dirty today—and she got all the kudos. I also got blamed for everything that went wrong whether I'd done it or not.

God forbid Addison actually owned up to a mistake. She was so far up our boss Caroline Archer's asshole, she'd taken a bag of Doritos up there with her and made a nest, and the last thing she would ever do would be to tarnish her perfect reputation, especially with our high-powered boss. Addison lied easily, manipulated without thought, and held the keys to my career in her evil, ambitious talons.

So, I took all the garbage she dumped on me with a smile and an internal promise to someday ruin her. Someday, we'd be equals. Or—if I played my cards right—I'd be *her* boss. I smiled at the thought of her retrieving my dry cleaning and picking up coffees that I could send back for lack of proper foam. She could take the fall for *my* screwups. It'd be so nice to be infallible.

But as satisfying as that might be, I was all talk. I defaulted to honesty and fairness to the point of personal injury—mine or others, depending. But the impulse sometimes made it hard to get things done.

Never was a fan of the easy way.

With a glance down at my screen, I cleared out the rest of my notifications and sighed, looking out the window as the city slid past.

Honestly, I had everything I wanted. I had the perfect job planning weddings for the biggest firm in Manhattan. I had the perfect apartment in the Flatiron District on the perfect block with the perfect coffee shop downstairs. I had the most perfect boyfriend—who would propose any day now, I was sure. We'd been saving to buy our own perfect home together. And once we moved in, I'd have the perfect wedding to kick off the perfect life.

As I stepped out of the cab and into my building, that thought had me forgetting all about my spill into the flower bed or my filthy pants or my stupid boss or the myriad brides hell-bent on making my job as difficult as possible. Because I was on the threshold of all the beautiful and wonderful things. All I had to do was walk through the metaphorical door.

I slipped my key in my very real door and opened it, touched by the familiar scent of home and the sound of my perfect boyfriend fucking Natasha Felix against the wall of our entryway.

I didn't feel my fingers let go of the keys, nor did I hear them hit the ground. I was too busy listening to the huffing and puffing and grunting as Brock drilled her into the wall, pants puddled at his ankles, shirttail covering most of his ass as he thrust. It was a small ass, I noted distantly, smaller than I'd realized. That ass was foreign to me, as were the noises he made and the sight of his hands on the twenty-year-old reality star's waist.

Natasha opened her doe eyes and smiled at me like a porn star, twisting her fingers in his hair.

And yet, I felt no pain. I felt a number of things, like a sad sort of pity for the pathetic visage of the man I'd thought I loved pumping her like a Chihuahua on a throw pillow. I felt a raw fury, mostly at the audacity that he'd deceived me, accompanied by a rush of shame at my stupidity for placing my trust so carelessly.

But there was no pain, a realization that dawned on me like sunrise over a mountain peak. In fact, under all that fury, I noted the dim sense of relief that I'd moved out of the way in time to miss getting hit by that particular train.

I hung on to that half-truth with the same tenacity with which I grasped a candlestick and hurled it at the wall, and when I walked through the door once more, it was with a slam that shook the stars.

Bawdy by Nature

KASH

The shower cut off with a squeak. Steam had gathered in tufts and whorls at the ceiling, diffusing the light and fogging the mirror as the dirt from the day, muddying the banks of streaming water, slipped toward the drain in cloudy eddies.

My mother would insist that her filthy Bennet boys were the reason she required a maid service three times a week, but we all knew a cover-up when we saw one. Truth was, Mrs. Bennet was a terrible housekeeper, as evidenced by the piles of orphaned things lining the walls as I exited the bathroom in a towel, propelled by a pulse of steam. Piles of books leaned into each other between the occasional cardboard box filled with more things with no home. Glancing into one might reveal a whisk, several lost socks, a stapler, loose photographs, a pair of shears, floral wire, fabric scraps. Mom needed places to stow things like a magpie, lost things, extra things. Things without status but not unimportant enough to throw away. She always held hope she'd find that extra sock or that she'd remember to return the whisk to the kitchen, not knowing why she'd brought it up two flights of stairs in the first place.

The Bennet home—a five-thousand-square-foot Victorian brownstone—had been in our family for a hundred and eighty years, passed down through generations of women. It occupied the space next to and above the flower shop, purchased along with four properties on Bleecker Street in Greenwich Village, behind which my predecessors had built our greenhouse.

We were a novelty in the Village, the only greenhouse of its kind and size in Manhattan. It had once brought us fame and fortune. My grandmother had sold the properties adjacent to ours in the seventies, which had previously been rented out to fund the expansion of Longbourne to include a handful of shops throughout the city. But under Mom's rule came the internet boom, the introduction of 1-800-ROSES4U, and the rise of Bower Bouquets, our rival flower shop. The Bowers bought into the internet bouquet business, and as they flourished, we withered, retreating slowly until only our flagship remained.

We only stayed afloat because Longbourne was a staple in our community, supplementing our income selling wholesale flowers to local shops. None of my siblings knew how bad it was, only me. I was here in the trenches—literally—and knew. Or suspected at least. It coincided with the progression of Mom's rheumatoid arthritis and the gradual loss of her hands, her duties sliding on a slow scale into Tess's lap. It was easy to ignore, as I spent my days in the greenhouse with Dad, avoiding the shop. But my brother Marcus figured it out when the deposits into our trusts dwindled. And when he really looked, he found the shop was in ruin.

So everyone came home to help save Longbourne, and at the lead was my little brother, Luke. He and Tess had given the shop the makeover to end all makeovers, and just like that, we were back on the map. Of course, that was just one step toward recovery—Marcus, the moneyman, assured us we'd be in debt for half a decade. But it was a start.

Luke had seen to that. We were twins of the Irish variety—though we looked it too, harboring the trademark Bennet blue eyes and black hair—born in the same calendar year and in the same class in school. Our old room was a time capsule of our boyhood, complete with bunk beds and baseball posters. The desks were still topped with relics, like Luke's Batman paperweight and a row of classic Hot Wheels I'd lined up next to my lamp. When Luke came home, we shared this room again—I'd moved into our sister Laney's room when she left, and she reclaimed it on her return. But Luke had moved in with Tess, leaving me alone again.

Of course, solitude never bothered me like it did Luke. He couldn't stand to be alone. I could just as easily not see another human for a week as I could share bunk beds with Luke without committing homicide.

I was pulling on my shirt when I heard the thunder of feet on the staircase and the word, "Dinner!" from Laney's mouth, two syllables stretched infinitely as her voice faded away and up the final staircase.

We all had our jobs around the house, and Laney's was the town crier.

I raked my hand through my damp hair to put it in place before exiting my room, making my way down the old, creaking staircase. Just before I reached the landing, I heard Laney coming and braced myself—a wise move. She jumped onto my back like a spider monkey, clamping my neck in a puny excuse for a sleeper hold.

I hooked her legs and kept going. "You're gonna have to do better than that."

"Meathead."

I trotted down the stairs with an exaggerated bounce, squeezing the giggles out of her with every thunk of my feet. I put her on the ground when we hit the main floor.

"How's the garden?" she asked.

"I'm digging it."

A chuckle. "You're going to make the best dad, you know that? You've already got a treasure trove of jokes on hand."

"I learned from the best," I said as we turned for the dining room. "How's social media going?"

"Well, we just hit thirty thousand followers on Instagram, and considering we had no presence a few months ago, I'd say it's going well. That article was the ticket, and Tess's pictures are just too good. Really, she's made my job easy."

Like I said, we all had our jobs to do.

Laney—Elaine, named after our grandmother—had come from a high paying, stable job in Dallas to run Longbourne's social media. Jett, or Julius if you were itching to get popped in the nose, had been working the last few years managing a bookstore bar, Wasted Words, on the Upper West, but came home to help around the house, since Mom could no longer cook, her hands too gnarled to manage anything requiring fine motor skills. Marcus—who sat at the table across from Dad in a suit, scrolling his phone and watching the Dow, no doubt—was our independently wealthy financial genius, having abandoned his Wall Street job to day trade, then to manage the shop. Luke and Tess managed design and production in the shop.

As for me, I worked in the greenhouse, as I always had. Because some things never changed, and I was one of them.

I wandered into the kitchen behind Laney to find the rest of the brood—Jett at the stove, Mom at the breakfast table talking Tess's ear off, Luke sitting on the counter, watching Tess with a goofy, lovesick smile on his face. Honestly, he took up the entire counter, the edge hitting him mid-thigh. He was a beast, the tallest of all of us, which was saying something. The Bennet boys were well over six feet of muscle, sharp jaws, and irreverent smiles—well, except for Marcus. His smiles were hard-won and reserved for only the most patient of women.

STACI HART

I followed my nose to peer into the sizzling pan around Jett. "Smells good, *Janie*," I snarked, flicking Mom's ruffly pink apron tied around his neck, dotted with big red begonias.

His elbow fired into my rib cage, knocking the wind out of me. "Been slaving over it all day, *Kitty*."

My hand clamped his shoulder as I caught my breath. "Don't let me stop you," I croaked, using the distraction to sneak a piece of chicken out of the pan, spinning away before he could grab me around the neck.

"Hope you burn your mouth," he shot.

I'd never admit that the chicken was molten lava, covered in cheese that I swore was a trillion degrees and razed every tastebud in my mouth. Instead, I smiled and gave him a thumbs-up, heading to the breakfast table.

"I don't care what Lila Parker says," my mother started, nose in the air. "You all have done an exemplary job handling the demands she's put on you. Really, to come in and complain about the shade of flower that *she* chose? Wedding planners are notoriously difficult, I'll admit, but she takes the cake."

"The business is good," Tess offered in Lila's defense. "It's the best kind of publicity for the shop, and there's *so* much money in it, far more than we can make just on the storefront or deliveries."

Mom sighed. "Weddings and funerals—the bread and butter of any flower shop and work we haven't seen much of in the last decade."

"It's taken years for Ivy to convince Lila to use us for weddings, but she wouldn't even entertain the idea until the article came out in *Floral*," Tess said. "It probably doesn't help that Ivy's her sister. It blurs the professional boundaries normally in place, leading her to believe she can march into the greenhouse and bawl Kash out about the color spectrum."

I chuckled. "She can bawl me out all she wants. Won't bother me."

Tess shook her head. "I don't know how. If she talked to me like that, I'd talk right back."

"I'm sure you did before she trucked into the greenhouse," I said.

"I tried," she answered with a tilted smile.

"Let her get it out of her system. I'll be the family dog."

Tess's brow quirked. "The family dog?"

"Yeah, you know, Dad has a bad day at work, comes home and yells at Mom for burning dinner. Mom yells at the kid for spilling milk. Kid kicks the family dog."

She frowned. "That's so sad."

Another soft laugh. "Oh, it's not so bad ... I've got nothing to complain about. Sounds like Lila's getting it handed down to her and she's gotta vent it off. It's not really about us. It's about her." I shrugged again.

Tess shook her head. "You're so laid back, you're practically horizontal."

"It's genetic. You've met my father, right?"

The room laughed.

"You do your fair share of fighting, Kassius," Mom said, turning to Tess. "Don't let him fool you. I've broken up too many fights to harbor any illusions about who's starting them." She gave me a pointed look.

"Luke starts them. I'm the one who *finishes* them," I noted.

"Because you cheat," Luke added.

"Cheat or outmaneuver?" I asked.

"Cheat," Luke and Jett said at the same time.

"Kassius, how was your date with Verdant Osborne?" Mom asked eagerly. "You're the only one who entertains my match-making with enthusiasm. Which is why you're my favorite," she said archly, glancing at my brothers.

Luke and I shared a meaningful look. Mom had a knack for matching me with the easiest of lays.

"We went to dinner and a movie," I said, not mentioning the fact that I couldn't tell you a single thing that'd happened in the show. We'd spent a hundred and nineteen minutes finding various ways to get each other off in the back row of the theater, fully clothed. "It was educational," I added.

"Well, she does have her PhD from Columbia. I'm sure she has a thing or two to teach you."

"You have no idea."

Luke coughed to cover his laughter. Jett just shook his head at the cheesy chicken. Tess rolled her eyes.

Mom, however, beamed. "She's such a nice girl. Her mother was just telling me at garden club about how she works weekends, volunteering at the library. Isn't that lovely?"

"Lovely," I echoed, nodding.

Verdant was nice, well-read, and educated, just as my mother had said, but neither of us had any interest in another date. She was the kind of girl who was in the market for a doctor or lawyer, not dirty gardeners their rich moms found for them at garden club.

The ability to remain naive of her audience was truly one of my mother's greatest qualities. She had no idea she was the odd duck in the blue-blood garden club she attended, grandfathered into attendance simply because my great-grandmother had *started* the club in the first place. My mother was innocent, blissfully unaware that they looked down their proud noses at her, humoring her with dates for her sons with their daughters, knowing full well that their daughters wanted nothing to do with the unrefined Bennet brood. Well, with the exception of Marcus. He was a prize stud—and utterly unattainable. He'd humor Mom by attending the dates with clinical detachment and polite endurance, just as he handled the rest of his life. I didn't think he'd slept with a single one. It was easy for me and Jett to fool around— none of the rich girls wanted a gardener or a retail manager for anything more than a night. But Marcus knew he was firmly in the marriage market, and as such, those girls would take a turn in his sheets as a sign of impending nuptials.

Lila rolled into my mind like a fog, licking at my awareness until forming fully, a vision in white, the stark red of her hair, the stern line of her mouth. Ambitious and in control was Lila Parker, a woman who wanted the best of the best, the top of the rock, the cream of the crop. She was luxury embodied, luxury and blatant power. It sounded in every tick of her heels, held up by the square of her shoulders and the stiffness of her spine.

I wondered what she would look like soft and languid, imagining that the only chink in her armor, her only vulnerability, was when she was being loved down, silky red hair on expensive white sheets, those cool eyes liquid silver, molten with desire behind heavy lids. Her alabaster skin flushed with pleasure, those lush, wide lips of hers bruised and swollen from insistent kisses.

A sight I'd never witness, judging by the unending well of disdain she held for the dirty gardener giving her lip at the flower shop. There weren't many people I flat-out didn't like—I got along with everybody and, other than my siblings, avoided conflict unless it was over a thing I had passion for. Lila Parker was my exact opposite. Where I was unruffled, Lila shook her tail feathers like a peacock. Where I'd rather have a beer together than argue, she seemed to argue as her primary mode of communication. And yet, here I sat, wondering over her, curious as to the fire that had forged her and the person who'd lit it.

But it was just as well. I didn't need her priss in my life, and she didn't need my filthy. Not for more than a night.

Though what a night that would be, I thought with a smile before burying the notion like a flower bulb in winter, not thinking how it might bloom come spring.

Tally-ho

LILA

Ivy gaped at me, hand still on the doorknob of her apartment.

The silence stretched, and when I realized she wasn't going to respond, I asked, "So, can I come in?"

She blinked and stepped out of the way. "Of course."

The plastic bodega bag, brimming with toiletries and stamped with a handful of *Thank Yous*, rustled against my dirty pants leg as I passed.

Ivy frowned. "Is that … dirt?"

"I fell in the flower bed at Longbourne," I answered matter-of-factly, plunking my bag on the couch. "Can I borrow some pajamas?"

Ivy closed the door and waddled in. "Yeah, sure—as soon as you tell me what happened."

"I told you—"

"*I caught Brock fucking Natasha Felix, can I stay with you,* is not an explanation. Now, sit. On the coffee table, please. I can't vacuum anymore without needing a three-hour nap," she said, hand on her burgeoning belly.

I did as she'd requested, sitting straight-backed, crossing one leg over the other, and clasping my hands on my knee. "What do you want to know?"

Ivy sank into the couch next to my bodega bag, her face softening, eyes wide. "Are you okay?"

"As okay as I can be. It did a lot for my ego when he tripped and fell trying to catch me with pants around his ankles just as the elevator doors closed. I hope he broke something. Can a dick break?"

"Penile fracture is a thing, though I don't think he'd get it from falling."

"Shame," I lamented on a sigh.

Ivy's lip slipped between her teeth, her eyes on me like I was a lost puppy.

"Don't look at me like that. I'm fine. I mean it."

"Lila, you've lived with him for two years, shared your life with him, your achievements. We've all been waiting for him to propose. You're allowed to be not-fine."

A flash of emotion shot through my ribs, gone as soon as I felt it, scared off by sheer force of will. "I know," I answered gently. "I'm fucking furious and embarrassed and ..." I took a breath, unsteady, then steady again. "I am upset, I'll admit that. But I'd rather think about all the ways Brock lost out. I'd rather recount all the things I just won by him nailing a *Femme* in my hallway."

"Like what?"

"Like I get to come stay with my sister and help with her baby, if I can crash for a little while."

"As long as you need," she said softly, reaching for my hand.

I smiled, squeezing it. "I get to take all that money I've saved and buy my own place, one where I don't have to deal with Brock's Sunday work calls or piles of sweaty gym clothes in the entry. I don't have to share a shower with a guy who has more hair products than me or clips his beard in the sink without rinsing it out. I don't have to cook for a vegetarian anymore. I'm going to eat all the meat straight off the bone with meat juice all over my face and imagine him gagging."

She laughed.

"It's true," I admitted, my voice losing its edge. "I thought … I thought this was it. I feel like a fool, Ivy. I trusted him. I accepted what he showed me as truth. *Me*."

"You don't trust anyone."

"Except you. And this is why. People lie. They have their own agendas, and we can't trust them not to manipulate us."

"Not everyone, Lila. Not everyone."

I gave her a look. "Everyone in my world."

"Then maybe your world is the problem."

I frowned. "This is everything I've wanted. I fought my way into this world. My career, my social life, all of it. Brock is just an asshole."

Her eyes flicked to the ceiling. "He really is. I've never heard someone bitch about a wine list like he can. Remember when he made the waitress cry at Delmonico's?"

"Entitled prick. I hope he and Natasha are happy together. They deserve each other."

"The entire planet knows she's a homewrecker. She's practically built her brand around her knack for stealing boyfriends out from under people. I suppose we should have seen it coming."

I ignored the sting of that truth. "But she always goes after *famous* people. What the hell does she want with Brock?"

"I can't imagine. He's hot and rich, but he's definitely not famous. And he hasn't even given you an orgasm in months."

I groaned. "It's tragic. Really and truly tragic."

"I mean, could anyone really consider him a catch?"

"I did," I answered quietly. "But now, I can't help but think that I was only settling. It's only been an hour, and I'm already struggling to remember one reason I was with him."

"You loved him. It's a marvel how much we can overlook for the sake of love." She sighed. "Lila, when this really hits you, I'm here, okay? Get mad. Cry. Come crawl in bed with me, and we'll talk shit about the preemptive hair plugs he got last year and his calf implants."

An unladylike laugh snorted out of me. "To be fair, I didn't know about the implants until we'd lived together for a year, and he swore me to secrecy." I paused. "I should tweet it."

"Hey, no need to defend. I'm not judging your choices in partner."

I gave her a look.

"Anymore," she clarified. "But I mean it, Lila. I'm here for you. Okay?" she insisted, making sure I understood the invitation was open and waiting.

"Okay," I answered just as Dean strode in, smile on his face.

Ivy's boyfriend—and baby daddy—was six and a half feet of muscle swathed in ochre skin. "Heya, Lila. What are you doing here?"

Ivy looked over her shoulder. "She's going to be staying with us for a minute."

"If it's no trouble," I added.

He rolled one massive shoulder and sat next to my sister, his smile fading. "Sure. I mean, the baby will sleep in our room for a while, so her room is free. What happened?"

Coolly, I answered, "I just walked in on Brock and Natasha Felix."

His eyes widened, the dark irises ringed with white. "You're kidding."

"Fortunately, I'm not."

That earned me a frown. "You mean, unfortunately?"

"No, fortunately. I feel like somebody just ripped open the veil. Maybe he's been cheating on me all along. Maybe I never knew him at all. He was a stranger in a familiar mask, and when the mask slipped, I saw the monster underneath. I've never run so fast in my life. Figuratively. I'm not running anywhere in these." I wiggled the crossed Louboutin.

"Wait, there wasn't a camera crew there or anything, was there?" Dean leaned in, brows drawn.

Surprise shook me. I hadn't even considered that possibility. "No, thank God. I … I can't even imagine what I would have done. As it stands, I chucked a candlestick. Lucky for them, my aim sucks."

"What are you going to do about Natasha?" Ivy asked carefully, noting the unfortunate fact that I'd be seeing Natasha almost daily for the next eight weeks.

Another flash, this one hot with rage. It didn't die so easily as the last. "Nothing."

"Nothing?" she echoed in disbelief.

"Nothing," I insisted. "She's not worth my job, and the Felix wedding is the biggest event I've ever handled. If Addison wasn't slammed with a Hilton wedding of her own, she never would have given me so much responsibility. And I'm not going to waste a shot at impressing my boss just because Brock can't keep his pants on."

Ivy chuckled.

"I mean it. Without a belt, I think his pants would slip right off that tiny ass of his and hit the ground. Why didn't anyone tell me his ass was so small? It looks like the end of a hot dog bun. Maybe he should have opted for butt implants instead."

Another laugh, this one hard enough for Ivy to rest her hand on her drum-tight belly.

"You don't think Natasha came onto him, do you?" Dean asked.

"Oh, I'm sure she did," I said on a tight, humorless laugh. "She's taken home somebody from every meeting we've had. Angelika brings her sisters—and the *Felix Femmes* camera crew—everywhere with her. But it's not her fault Brock is a shit-bag. If he'd loved me like I thought he did, he would have walked away from Natasha without a second thought. Like you two. I'm guessing you don't even have a Hall Pass list, do you?"

"Hall Pass?" Dean's brows quirked.

Ivy smiled sideways. "You know, a list of celebrities you could sleep with without consequences."

"That's weird," he said, lip curling. He turned to Ivy. "You're not allowed to sleep with anybody else. Even Zac Efron."

Ivy's expression turned all goopy as she cupped his jaw. "Aw, see? He even knows my celebrity crushes."

"I'm not kidding," he said, his face as serious as his tone. "If Zac Efron came here right now, begging you for just one night with a check for a million bucks in hand, I'd crumple it up and punch it down his throat."

"This," I said, gesturing to them. "This is a prime example of why Brock and I were all wrong for each other. I'd just convinced myself it was perfect, and he played the part of the perfect boyfriend. But he wouldn't take a bullet for me. He wouldn't sacrifice what he wanted for my sake. Not in a million years. I just wish I'd figured it out sooner." My throat tightened, and I swallowed to open it up. "Thank you. For letting me crash."

"Always," Ivy said.

Dean stood, making his way around the couch. "I'll get the bed ready and make sure the closet's cleaned out."

"Thank you," I said with a weary sigh and a grateful heart. "I didn't want to go to a hotel," was the most I'd admit.

But my sister knew the truth: I didn't want to be alone.

"You're always welcome here. As long as you need." She shifted to try to pull herself off the couch, but without abdominal muscles, she didn't make it far.

I stood and offered my hand, hoisting her off the couch. But once standing, she didn't let my hand go. I could tell she wanted to hug me but curbed the impulse.

"You deserve better than Brock," she said, her blue eyes earnest.

"I know," I answered, and I did.

But it sucked so bad that I felt like I didn't. The pain I'd so proudly noted as absent wasn't absent at all. It trickled under the surface, beneath the bedrock of will and anger. As Ivy gathered up some clothes and shepherded me into the bathroom, I considered that pain, the deceiving smallness of it.

When she closed the door and I was alone, it cracked open like the earth, spreading in a rumbling chasm. The hiss of the shower covered the hitch in my breath. The steam from the stream masked the tears in my eyes. And I stepped into its scalding rain, welcoming the punishment as pain swallowed me whole.

Pinging, stinging water against my scalp, rolling down my back, singeing my shoulders, teasing my skin to a dangerous shade of red. And every second brought another wave of memories. Brock in his tux, spinning me around a dance floor, my hand in his, his eyes full of love and a joke on his lips. His face, beautiful and tender across our pillows. The easy way he laughed, the easy way he loved.

But it was a lie, every moment, every kiss.

And I was a fool for believing him.

The water cooled by the time my tears slipped down the drain. I stepped into a pair of Ivy's sleep shorts and a tank, washed my face, and brushed my teeth. The mist on the mirror receded slowly until my reflection sharpened. The girl peering back at me looked equally like the fresh-faced teenager I'd once been and a woman older than me, more world-worn and cynical. Gray eyes, bright from tears, sunken from grief.

So I reached for Ivy's eye cream and did something about it.

Because that was who I was—a woman who did something about it. I was a fixer, a problem solver, a perpetual motion machine who only moved in one direction. Forward.

And forward I would go.

After tidying up and gathering my things, I exited the bathroom and stepped into the quiet, dark house. The sound of their voices were muted by distance, the light from their bedroom slanting into the hall. Ivy laughed, a soft burst, followed by Dean's deep baritone, and a sudden longing struck me, a fissure in the patch I'd mended the chasm with. But I smoothed it, turning for the nursery and my solitude.

The baby's room was shades of heather gray and white, marked by the occasional shot of coral in the way of the blanket hanging artfully on the crib wall or the throw pillow in the rocking chair. The velvet loveseat had been converted to a twin bed where I'd lay my head for a little while, and Dean had made it up, complete with sheets, two pillows, and a downy comforter that looked like a heaping pile of cloud fluff. Ivy had left a neat pile of clothes for me on top of the changing table, and on the pile sat a phone charger and a note.

Good riddance to bad lays.

Love you. Sleep tight.

—Ivy

I laughed as I picked up the charger and plugged it in. Brock really was a terrible lay, which I'd seen from a new, horrible perspective today. I'd settled in so many ways, convincing myself that he was perfect. A wealthy, beautiful doctor, charming and smooth. A man who had never had to work for a woman, present company included, which meant he'd never had to impress a woman in bed. He got what he wanted and never cared to learn the topography of a clitoris. Given that he had a medical degree, the oversight was as gratuitous as it was grievous.

Curse of the Adonis. Why would he be bothered to care? An endless supply of women was apparently at his beck and call.

I clicked off the lamp—a sweet, star-studded thing—and slid under the comforter, sighing the weight of the day into the comforting confines of the nursery. I'd have to find a way to be around Natasha, and there was only one plan: ignore her and pretend like nothing had happened. Business as usual, tally-ho, onward we went.

Of course, I also knew Natasha to be manipulative—the youngest of the Femmes had a penchant for drama that her sisters paled beneath—and wondered if she'd be trouble. I couldn't imagine a reason for her to sleep with Brock unless she wanted to get to me. Maybe for the sake of their show and any excuse to spark a fight in front of the cameras. I tried to tell myself she'd probably never see him again. He was too old and established for her, as her taste leaned more to the latest breakout DJ, other celebrity offspring, and whoever was making the most trouble in the media. She didn't want anything to do with Brock other than to humiliate me.

The best—and perhaps only—revenge would be to don my armor and show her just how unaffected I was. It would likely drive her insane, and if that was to be my only recourse, I'd wield it unflinchingly.

And with that happy thought clutched in my fist, I closed my eyes and sought sleep, though I never quite found it.

Labradoodle-dee-doo

KASH

I saw her the second I turned onto Fifth, standing at the foot of a flat-fronted onyx building.

There was no way to miss her.

She wore white again, stark against the glossy black wall she stood before. This time, she'd donned a tailored dress, the sleeves capping her shoulders and the hem brushing the top of her shins. Her profile was elongated, straight out of a fashion illustration from the fifties—hip cocked, chin high, that vivid red hair swept into a bun at the nape of her swan neck. With the phone pressed to her ear, her lips alternated between clipped words and a thin line, a slash of red against creamy skin.

Lila Parker was unhappy. I wondered if she existed in any other state.

Subsequently, I wondered if anyone had ever tried to make her happy.

With the hitch of my leather messenger bag, I picked up my pace just as she met my gaze. She stilled to unnerving stone as I approached. My brows notched—I'd dressed up as she'd asked, or implied. I'd worn a pair of navy slacks, for God's sake, and ironed my pale blue button-down. I couldn't be bothered with a tie, and I'd rolled the sleeves, unable to stomach the confines at my wrists. But I'd *ironed*. And if this wasn't good enough for her, I didn't know what was.

If I was to be the representative of Longbourne, I was going to show up for it in full.

Lila blinked, a flash of dark lashes and cool eyes, ending her call before I reached her. She frowned.

"You're early."

I gave her a look. "Sorry to disappoint."

A huff through her nose, the arch of one auburn brow. "Come on. This way."

She clipped her way into the Skylight building, and I followed. A tendril of hair licked the back of her neck. The impulse to reach out and tuck it into place curled my fingers in anticipation.

I shoved my hand in my pocket to curb the thought.

Lila reached for the brass handle of the massive door, long fingers wrapping around it to pull. I extended a hand to help, but it opened with more ease than a door of that size should have, so instead, I grabbed the edge to hold it open.

"Thank you," she said brusquely.

As we walked through the entry—a marble, mirrored French affair—I wondered over the suspicions of Lila Parker. What did she expect that left her so wary? She seemed to be waiting for something to go wrong, and I mused as to whether the cause was getting burned badly enough to scar or if she just harbored a compulsion to fix things. Lila was the type to thrive under pressure like a coal turned to diamond. That was where she shone—in bringing order to chaos. The act hardened her, sharpening her to a fine edge.

She'd expected me to be late. I'd wager she expected me to say the wrong thing in front of someone important, screw up my measurements, and-or disappoint her otherwise. I had the suspicion that if she could have done the job herself, she would have.

The thought made me want to do the job to the best of my ability, if for no other reason than to prove her wrong.

Into a gilded elevator we stepped, and the doors closed, sealing us in silence.

"Did you actually bring a pad and pen this time?" she asked, eyeing me.

"Nope."

Her brows clicked together, her lips opening to speak, but I headed her off.

"Pencil."

She gave me an unamused look, but the smallest curve at the corners of her lips belied the expression. "Clients are set to meet me here in a few minutes, so try to stay out of the way."

"Whatever you say, boss."

Her eyes narrowed. The elevator dinged.

I swept a hand toward the door. "After you."

She strutted out, nose in the air. "Thank you for putting on an actual shirt," she said over her shoulder and without an ounce of graciousness.

"I'm not an animal, Lila," I said with a lazy smile on my face.

"Oh, I don't know about that." She cast a teasing smile over her shoulder and pushed open the grand golden doors, revealing rows of white chairs with a dais at the end of the aisle where countless couples had promised their lives to one another. I mourned the muffled sound of her heels on the carpeted row. "A dog maybe, digging for bones?"

"You must be a cat person," I guessed.

"More of a Betta kind of gal."

"Not a goldfish?"

"They crap too much."

I chuckled at the thought of Lila Parker dealing with feces of any species. "And how about you? A poodle maybe. All that white, long legs, snobbish, with a pedigree, for sure." I scanned her form clinically.

She came to a stop at the dais, turning to face me. "If I'm a poodle, you're a lab—big, dumb, and with too much mouth for your own good."

One of my brows rose in challenge, though my lips gave her a cavalier smile.

At the sight, the tension in her shoulders eased. "I'm sorry. You'll have to forgive me. I didn't sleep very well last night."

"It's all right. I'm a Bennet, remember? I can take it."

When she rewarded me with a quiet laugh, I realized she didn't look as *together* as usual. Something about her eyes, dulled and smudged with shadow. Her hair wasn't as flawless as was her norm, evidenced by that stray lock of her bun I'd fantasized about and the copper glow of occasional flyaway hairs.

She hadn't slept, and I wondered why. Wondered *who*.

Her boss maybe. The mass of high-profile weddings and the pressure that came along with them. Dealing with the Felix sisters alone was a full-time job, I imagined, and she had dozens of other clients to tend to on top of it. And with her boss breathing down her neck to boot? Anyone would crack under that kind of pressure, maybe even Lila Parker.

Or maybe something else had happened. Her boyfriend, perhaps. I'd heard enough from Ivy to know he was a hoity-toity douchebag with a fake smile and too many stories to tell. If he'd hurt her, my first thought was that I hoped she'd strutted out the door. My second thought was what it would feel like to punch him in the nose for being an idiot. My third was that I hoped she was okay.

Lila launched into what she needed me to measure, and I listened dutifully, taking in the space while she spoke. The ceiling soared thirty feet to the domed Victorian atrium that gave Skylight its name, the only solid thing the walls around us. Beyond the glass stretched Midtown, steel and glass cut against the crisp autumn sky. The room was golden and cream, soft and bright, a place that breathed hope and happy endings.

I pulled out my notepad and pencil, which seemed to both please and relax her. She sprang into details, opening up her imagination. The arbor shape, the color scheme, musings on flowers she might want, depending on the palette they chose. Giving me notes on the garland, asking what kind of greenery and berry would be available. The tunnel, which would be built in pieces and placed in the ballroom where the reception would be held.

She was mid twinkle-light monologue when the doors opened, and a couple walked through, tall and rich and smiling.

Lila glanced at me, lips parting to speak, but I said, "Don't worry. I've got it."

A smile I actually believed, higher on one side with snark. "Good." Her attention clicked down the aisle. "Charles, Madison. I trust you found us without trouble."

And then, she was off.

I listened silently, measuring the dais and sketching in my notebook as she recounted the details of the building, the venue, amenities, and photography options. She spoke with utter certainty, with absoluteness, her word law and fact, indisputable—even her opinions. She was impossible to deny, and it didn't seem the couple wanted to.

I wondered what it'd be like to truly disagree with her. The sparring we played at was strictly for sport. But a true confrontation? I had a feeling she'd come to life with a defensive spark. I both shied from the thought and craved it, like the danger of setting off unmarked fireworks that might or might not be dynamite.

Measuring the aisle brought me closer to them as Madison interrupted Lila.

"I think this space would do nicely, don't you, Charles?" He started to speak, but she kept talking, his answer immediately dismissed, "A fall wedding next year with the gold of this room would be beautiful with mauve and peach flowers, dark greenery."

"We might have trouble finding flowers those colors in the fall," Lila stated. She didn't say or suggest—the words were a directive.

Madison frowned. "I'm sure we can find something. Greenhouses grow all year, don't they?"

"They do, but—"

"Peonies," Madison continued, her eyes sweeping the glass dome above. "I've always loved peonies."

Lila's face was a steel trap, her smile plasticine. "I thought you wanted creams, champagnes, golds?"

"Well, I *did*," Madison admitted without seeming at all apologetic.

"And before that, it was marigold and rose," Lila continued.

"But now that we're here, I'm thinking something more bold. *Peony* bold."

My measuring tape zipped, snapping into its housing with a pop that echoed in the massive room. "Actually, peonies are out of season in the fall, but cabbage roses bloom to look close enough. Dahlias would make a good option too, if you really want to go that route."

Madison's brows quirked, but her smile was a little too enthusiastic. She extended her hand, her eyes dragging down my body. "And who are you?"

I took her offered hand and shook it. "Kash Bennet. I work in the greenhouse that supplies flowers for Ms. Parker's events."

"A gardener? Or maybe you're a florist?" She tittered. "How modern."

"Mr. Bennet is a gardener at Longbourne," Lila said, her voice too tight to be considered casual, though it lilted smoothly past her lips. "If you're interested, I'll take you down to the greenhouse to see. It's the largest in Manhattan, right in the middle of Greenwich Village." She cut a look at me that said to get back to work.

"How charming," Madison said. "Isn't that charming,

Charles?" Again, he tried to answer, and again, she kept talking. "Maybe you could educate us on what will be in season and the kinds of colors we can expect from your garden. That would be such a treat."

I cleared my throat, nodding once, stifling a smile. "I'm sure Lila will be able to set something up. Now, if you'll excuse me, I'm just finishing up."

Lila watched me as I walked back up the aisle, and I heard Madison say under her breath behind me, "I bet he knows his way around a hoe, don't you?"

Lila made a strangled noise that should have been a laugh, but it caught in the trap of her throat, garbled and tight. I couldn't even find it in me to be offended for myself, only poor Chuck, who'd agreed to be yoked to Madison for life.

We make our own choices and live the consequences, I thought to myself, kneeling at the front row to measure the chairs.

Lila took charge, ushering the couple toward the door, directing them to the reception hall and bar, excusing herself for one minute, promising she'd be right behind them.

The doors closed, and I made it a point not to look up despite the feel of her eyes drilling me to the floor. Slowly, deliberately, I measured and marked, seemingly absorbed in my work and unaffected by the heat rolling off of her.

"If I need your opinion, I'll ask for it," she said.

In my periphery, I could see her visage—white curves, arms akimbo, hands hooked on her hips, hair red as the tip of a match.

I looked over as if I hadn't known she was standing there. "Just seemed they had a simple problem. Thought I was helping."

"She's already indecisive, Kash. Don't confuse her. I'll never be able to talk her out of cabbage roses now."

"Why should you?"

"Because I'll shift everything, form a new plan, build everything around it, and then she'll change her mind again. She's suggestive—"

A snort of a laugh escaped me as I stood, through with her looking down at me like she was. "You can say that again. I didn't realize you'd be pimping me out, Lila."

"Pimping you out?" she huffed, color smudging her cheeks and eyes tight. "You weren't supposed to talk to her."

I shrugged. "Sorry. Guess I forgot I'm just the help."

Her eyes rolled hard enough for her to get a good look at Fifth Avenue behind her. "Oh, please. Don't be dramatic."

I folded my arms across my chest, tilted smile in place. "Look, if it makes your job easier, by all means, pimp me out. And I'm sorry I opened my mouth about the flowers. I really was trying to help get her off the peonies. If she'd insisted, your life mighta been hell trying to deliver."

The simmering rage behind her eyes eased to a hot steam. "It's not your fault," she admitted shortly.

"Wow, that was *almost* an apology."

One brow rose with the corner of her lips. "Take what you can get, Kash." She turned on her heel and strode away.

"Always do, Lila," I answered, watching her until the golden doors closed behind her.

LILA

I toured Madison Wendemere and poor Charles Peterson through the venue—the guy couldn't get a word in. At least he was marrying a Wendemere. With all the money he was about to inherit, he could hide on his yacht or the golf course or the men's club where she couldn't nag him.

It had taken me a minute to recover, to flip on my charm and woo Madison after my outburst, which wasn't so much an outburst as it was a tremor. I just hated for anyone to have seen it. And I hated that Kash had irritated me by butting in even if he was right *and* had been trying to help me out. Which made me feel like an asshole, thus making me feel wrong.

I hated being wrong too.

But by the time Madison and I said goodbye at the elevator—let's be honest, sweet Charlie wasn't saying anything—she pressed her cheek to mine, her eyes fond and pleased. She was sold on the venue, and the deposit check was in my possession.

As I walked back to the chapel, I smoothed my dress, then my hair, then my dress again, pulling open the door with my spine straight as an arrow to face Kash.

He sat on the steps to the dais, dark head angled to the notebook in his lap and face narrow with concentration. Long legs were spread at the knee, ankles hooked, his hand so big as it scribbled, the pencil looked comical.

God, he was massive, a brute made of muscle and sinew. He belonged to the earth he tilled, cut from stone, hair black as a raven, eyes blue as the sea. Beautiful in the rugged, wild way, unpolished and unrefined and unquestionably right just the way he was.

In that tailored shirt and slacks, he looked like an uncut gem in a glass case—confined and incongruent, as if he'd somehow been bridled. Of course, he also looked utterly brilliant, the shirt tight enough to see the rolling cords of muscles comprising his biceps down to the smattering of dark hair on his forearms, fluttering as he drew.

I made it all the way up the aisle to stop in front of him, but still, he didn't look up. He knew I was there, and he didn't look up, and for some reason, I wanted to kick him in the shin just to get his attention.

"One sec," he muttered, hand moving.

I leaned in to peek at the page where he'd sketched the arbor, just as I'd described—a perfect triangle on a frame, touched with greenery and roses. Under it, he'd drawn a couple, the man square-shouldered and the woman wasp-waisted, gazing at each other, hands clasped. The proportion was just as I'd envisioned, the sprays of florals right where I'd have put them, had I drawn it. Which I couldn't have.

He'd heard every word I'd said, stored it all in his dumb puppy brain, and drew it up with the ease of a long-practiced artist.

"There," he said, finishing the lacy hem of her veil. "That look about right?"

He held it up, and I found myself smiling—really smiling, not that fabricated stretch of lips I'd been wearing since I walked into my apartment last night.

"It's perfect," I answered, my voice softer than I'd intended.

And then he was smiling too, an expression to match mine, genuine and earnest. It did something to his eyes, which were a shade of blue so bright and dense and deep, I was surprised I hadn't noticed before.

"Thank you," I said. "For coming here and measuring for me."

"Even though I undermined your clients?"

"Client. Charles isn't allowed to have opinions."

"Poor sucker. Gelded already, and he hasn't even walked down the aisle."

"Well, we can't all be lucky in love, now can we?" My tone was cool, bitter.

And he instantly knew. I could see it on his face, which disguised nothing.

"I suppose not," he mused without pressing. "But I've seen enough of love to know if you hold out, it'll find you whether you want it to or not."

I chuckled, folding my arms. "In all your worldly experience, that's your take?"

"You have a different one?"

One shoulder flicked in an impatient shrug, my heart a tight, closed thing. "That everyone's hiding something, and it's only a matter of time until the truth is exposed."

At that, his lips turned down at the corners. Broad forearms fanned across the tops of his knees, dusted with dark hair, threaded with veins like rivers running down to square hands. "You don't think honesty is possible?"

"People conceal what they don't want you to see, to control what you know, to manipulate you. Everyone does it. It's just human nature."

Dark brows held together with a crease over those striking blue eyes. "Ivy and Dean?"

"They're different," I snapped dismissively. "Most of us can't expect something that honest."

He stood, so much taller than me from his perch on the step. His brow smoothed, his smile easy, but I saw something behind his eyes, a challenge maybe. A sadness but not pity.

"I like to think we accept the love we think we deserve, like the old adage says. If you meet as equals, there's nothing to hide. And if you're so certain everyone's out to hurt you, you'll probably end up hurt."

I shifted, stepping back with a derisive laugh, affected by his nearness. "If only it were that easy."

Kash bent, snagging the handle of his bag, slinging it across his body. "It's only as hard as you make it."

I wanted to scoff, to tell him exactly why he was wrong and argue my point until he agreed with me, or at least pretended to. But more than that, I wanted to exit the conversation, my hurt too close and sharp and new to defend or dissect.

"Whatever you say, Kash," I said on another laugh, hoping I sounded carefree.

"I like the sound of that," he teased.

I rolled my eyes without any heat. "Send me the quotes as soon as you have them so I can get them approved."

"You've got it," he said as he passed, pausing just beyond me.

The scent of him—earth and flowers and knotted pine—slid over me. "Walk you out?"

"I've got a little more to do before I go."

A curt nod of his head, that square jaw of his hard, wide lips angled. "All right. See you later then."

With the tip of an invisible hat, he turned for the door. And shamelessly, I watched him until the massive doors closed, leaving me alone.

For a moment, I sank into that solitude, embraced by the quiet of the room. I'd been unkind to Kash, treated him like the help, just like he'd said. And all he'd ever done was lend a hand with the offering of that smile, letting whatever I threw at him bounce off like he was made of rubber.

It was shame I felt, and I wondered over what had trained me to be so severe. Years of failed group projects ,perhaps. Lack of trust that anyone could perform to my standards. Dating men like Brock, who berated waiters and complained over wine lists. I generally thought myself a kind and gracious woman, but I wondered if I looked it to the average eye and had my doubts.

But I'd entered into a season of change, a new era, one rife with possibility. And I'd do my best to embrace it.

Starting with Kash Bennet.

Nine Lives

KASH

My pencil moved of its own accord, directly connected
to the vision in my brain, my hand and fingers nothing
more than a conduit, a channel with which to broadcast.
The light in my childhood bedroom was low, but the old
reading lamp hooked to the bunk slats shone on my page, illu-
minating the graphite sketch, black against white. I'd used my 8B
pencil, the softest and blackest, to cover the page, all but for the
shape of Lila, long and white, in the negative space. She stood exactly as I remembered her in front of the onyx wall of the venue,
shocking and bright against the darkness. She jumped off the
page, the angle of her shoulders, the curve of her waist, her legs.
The point of her heels to the point of her chin. Her eyes were
scaled too small for the definition I wished I could give, but the
line of her brows and the shadows they threw were enough.

She was strength and power, determination and will.

I wished for my oil pastels, needing just one color—the red
of her hair. But the color didn't exist. Nothing could be quite

right—not quite red, not quite orange. Not burgundy, nor was it copper. It was a singularity, a thing that only existed in her. She was a tree aflame with autumn. The strike of a match, embers and sparks. A sunset that set the sky on fire.

Since we'd parted ways, she'd slipped in and out of my thoughts. Quietly, gently, she would be there in the replay of a moment, the vision of her at one point or another through our meeting. But always, my thoughts came back to this moment, when I'd seen her standing in front of the building like a feather on black sand.

I'd had to draw her. It was my only hope to get her out of my head.

It was said that everyone was the hero of their own story, and the reason was *context*. Everyone, regardless of honesty or truth, showed people what they wanted to see. In that, Lila was right. But every heart had a story to tell. A reason. A series of events that, when strung together in the right order, created a person's self, their motivation and fears.

For instance, take my brother Luke. As the baby in our indelicate family, he was naturally the family jester, the exhibitionist, the one who would do anything for a laugh, because how else would anyone see him in the Bennet fray? Jett and Laney were twins, but Laney had adopted the role of the eldest. She was a force of nature, headstrong and prickly as she was loving and giving, especially when it came to our family. And Jett was her converse—quieter, gentler with a penchant for self-sacrifice—because no one could compete with Laney.

Granted, Jett could still beat the shit out of me, but that was just Bennet conditioning. One had to be able to scrap with five children so close in age.

Marcus, the middle child, was reserved. Where Jett and Laney had each other and Luke and I were an inseparable unit, Marcus had gotten lost in the shuffle and decided that was fine by him. He retreated to books, was the silent partner to my father, the two of them content to never make a sound when the rest of us couldn't shut up.

And then, there was me.

Being so close in age with Luke, we were together always. In the same class at school. In the same sports. Worked summers in the greenhouse together. Luke's personality was so big, so vibrant, that I was swept up in his wake. I didn't mind. Luke was a beacon, calling attention and manifesting happiness, reflecting it back on everyone around him. Every crazy idea, I was there for. All the parties, all the girls. All the sneaking onto rooftops and into bars. He was the ultimate wingman, making sure I had someone to take my hand before he found someone to take his.

But here was the thing—I was so tethered to Luke that who he was became who people thought I was. I didn't know who, if anyone, knew me out of the context of him, and I never corrected them. It was easier that way. Let them think they knew me. I had no desire to prove them wrong.

Just like Lila's view of me, I was sure, was colored by her assumptions.

As was my view of her. But I knew there was more to her story. A person wasn't just born with that much of a penchant for control. Something must have happened to make her that way, and I longed to know what. To understand her. It had to be that curiosity that drove me to consider all she'd said, all she'd admitted, with the flippancy of someone who didn't care but the tone of someone who did.

She cared, but she didn't want anyone to know she cared. Lila Parker was covered in head to toe dragon scales, impermeable to mere mortals. At least, that was what she wanted everyone to think.

But I knew better.

The bedroom door opened without a knock, announcing Luke's entry strictly by lack of respect of privacy. I closed my sketchbook as he entered with a smile and took up residence in his old desk chair, leaning back lazily. He propped his feet on the old trunk at the foot of the bunks.

"Whatcha drawing?" he asked with a nod to my lap where my sketchbook lay.

"Just something I saw when I was out," I hedged. "How'd it go at the Long Island farm today?"

"I wish we got out there more instead of ordering what we don't grow online. Tess went nuts, over-ordered by half." His smile took over his face. "I don't even know what we'll do with all of it. We filled up the entire delivery truck."

"Oh, I'm sure Tess will figure something out."

"Me too. How about you? Lila give you any shit?"

"Nah, it wasn't so bad. She's like a toothless dog. All bark, no bite."

"I dunno. I've seen those choppers, and I'm pretty sure they could do some damage."

I shrugged. "Just gotta have thick skin, little brother."

I reached for my sketchbook, opening it further back to find the sketches and measurements I'd done. The pages ripped with a crack of sound, and I leaned into the room with them extended, and he met me in the middle.

"Measurements for you and Tess."

Flipping through them, he nodded. "This arbor is cool. Ask her if she wants to keep it—otherwise, I think Tess might want it. We'll just charge them for a loan instead of the piece plus labor."

"I'll let her know."

Luke shook his head. "How the hell did you become the point person for Lila Parker?"

"Ivy's about to be gone, and none of you babies have the constitution for her."

"You always were the better Bennet."

"Better or dumber?"

"Maybe both."

I huffed a laugh. "I can handle her. Don't worry about me."

"I never do." He watched me for a second with that X-ray vision one obtained simply from knowing someone so well. "You like her."

I made a face. "Now who's dumber?"

But he didn't falter. "You do. Look at that."

"I don't even know her. Plus, she's not my type."

"Oh? And what *is* your type? You've gone on twenty dates since we came home this summer. Twenty *first* dates."

"Because they're all with girls like Verdant. You know how that is."

At that, he backed off a hair, nodding. "Fair enough. But what about somebody else? Somebody *you* choose?"

"When do I have time? Mom has me booked out until I'm forty or get married, whichever comes first."

"And Lila is right up there with Verdant and Charity and all the rest of them," he stated, understanding the dilemma.

"Girls like that don't want second dates with gardeners who sleep in bunk beds in their mom's house. Blue collar guys without degrees. Or pedigrees."

"One superficial, privileged princess doing you dirty doesn't really constitute the whole bunch."

I shot him a warning glare. "Don't talk about Ali like that."

"After all these years, you still defend her? I don't get it."

"It's not her fault it didn't work out. It's mine."

"How so? For not being able to predict that she wouldn't call you her boyfriend unless your trust fund was over five million?"

"Goddammit, Luke, I said—"

He held up his hands in surrender. "I know, I know. I'll quit it. But listen, she might have set the gold standard for what you think women want from you—"

"I don't think. I *know* what they want. Ali was just the only one I was dumb enough to care about."

At that, he fell silent.

I knew my place when it came to dilettantes, and it was not

by their side. The summer after high school, Ali and I fell into each other and didn't find our way out. She'd been accepted to Vassar, close enough that it'd be easy to see each other on weekends. Even now, nearly a decade later, the thought of her brought a familiar pain. My first heartbreak. One I'd done everything to ensure was my only heartbreak.

In truth, she'd never promised me anything. We never spoke of our future, and I assumed too much—things were so happy, so easy, so seemingly perfect, I foolishly thought it was the natural course of things. We would carry on exactly as we had all summer, because who would be willing to put an end to something so undeniably right?

It was on the day that she left for school that I realized my folly. And even then, it wasn't until she uttered the words with a disbelieving and pitying look on her face. She'd first laughed—not with spite, but with genuine surprise—at my asking to come see her the next weekend. And then she grasped my hand and told me slowly that there was no future for us, that there never had been. That even if we lived the same sorts of lives in the same sorts of circles and even if she were able to look past that we didn't, her parents would never approve. That we'd had fun, hadn't we? And that she'd text me when she came home for holidays, so we could *hang out*, which was code for *hook up*.

And then, she'd left me there on the sidewalk with a broken heart, one I built a wall around, using her words as mortar. It was a truth I should have already known, one I would have seen, had I been wiser. But I'd wised up quick, realized my place, and I'd never strayed again.

Instead, I went on all the dates my mother planned—which was plenty to keep me busy—and my reputation preceded me. I let every date be what it was—fun and free of feelings. Soon, I found I didn't know many normal girls, only a selection of rich girls who were on the market for a good time. Nothing more.

Not for me, anyway.

Truthfully, it worked out. I really was too busy with Longbourne for a relationship—the older Dad got, the more responsibility I had. Single-serving companionship was convenient and safe. Sometimes, we enjoyed each other enough to make a regular thing of it. Even with Ali.

It was selfish to indulge myself with her. But I couldn't seem to say no even if I always left a little emptier than before. Not because she took without giving, but because I remembered all I'd wished for and lost. And yet, I'd go back again and again. Part of me wondered if I was expecting new results. Part of me knew I was. All of me knew I should stop. But none of me would.

I brushed my melancholy away, smiled like the rogue I always pretended to be. "Listen, little brother, it's not so bad being the king of first dates. I've become an excellent conversationalist."

He snorted a laugh, the tension gone with the sound. "Is that what the kids are calling sex these days?"

I chuckled. "Anyway, it's not like I can bring chicks here to bone on the bottom bunk, surrounded by posters of Hellboy and Sin City and Queens of the Stone Age."

"With Mom downstairs."

"With *Mom* downstairs. Can you imagine if I brought someone in?"

Luke perked up, screwing his face into a comical impression of our mother. "Why hello, and who are you?" he said in a warbling falsetto, pressing his hand to his chest dramatically. "Kassius is such a good boy, and I hope you'll consider him. You know, for marriage. He always was my favorite, loves his mother so much." He pinched his own cheek, glancing angelically at the ceiling. "Give me grandbabies!"

Laughter burst out of me and didn't stop. He wasn't far off. "Doesn't matter. There's time for all that. I'm only twenty-seven. It's not like I've got an expiration date or something."

"Maybe Lila's biological clock is ticking. She and Mom can talk about ovulating and uteruses. Uteri?" His brows quirked.

"She has a boyfriend," I said. "And again—she's the opposite of my type."

"So your type is short, prefers to wear black, has no opinion, and works in public service?"

"Maybe it is," I answered without answering.

"Right," he said with a roll of his eyes. "Just admit it so we can move on, Kash."

"She's hot, and I'd go on a first date with her. Does that make you feel better?"

He sighed, a content smile on his face as he folded his hands on his belly like he'd just had the meal of his life. "It does. It really does."

Thumping footfalls grew louder, along with the wail for dinner like an ambulance siren from Laney's mouth.

Luke snagged the papers off the desk and held them up as he stood. "I'll get these to Tess. I'm sure she'll have questions. Want me to send her to Lila or you for the answers?"

"Send her to me. I'll take care of it," I said without thinking. I could take them to Lila myself.

When he smiled, it was clear I'd stepped right into his trap. "I bet you will."

With an answering smile on my face, I punched him hard enough in the shoulder to make him yelp.

As I followed him down the stairs, I reminded myself that curiosity killed the cat. Of course, the cat couldn't help but be curious. Maybe that was why it had nine lives.

Somehow, I didn't think I'd get so many.

Anubis

LILA

Nearly a week passed, and I found myself too busy to think much about Brock. I had dress fittings and bridal showers to coordinate. Caters to direct and musicians to book. Far too much to do to be bothered with thoughts of that asshole or the way my life had been spun around.

During the days, at least. The nights were a different story.

I'd work myself until I could barely stand, let alone have time for idle thoughts. I'd be dead on my feet, dragging myself into bed, and the second the lights went out, my mind came alive with every choice I'd made and ever lie I'd accepted to bring me to that moment.

I wondered if it would get better after I went to the old apartment today to pick up a few things, like my dignity and hopefully the closure I hoped I'd left there.

Of course, today wouldn't be any less busy than the last week had been. I'd found myself in Longbourne almost every day. Ivy had cut back her hours so deep, she was rarely there when I came.

But rather than deal with Tess as expected, I'd been foisted upon Kash in full, it seemed.

A week ago, I might have minded. But after everything that had happened, Kash was the least of my problems. In fact, I'd started to look forward to the dirty gardener with the shaggy hair and the broad shoulders. I could give him all I had, and he'd take it with that lazy smile he always seemed to wear, unaffected and easy as a rule. Somehow it was a comfort, to know that even when I was at my biggest and loudest and most barkey, he could handle it. Handle me.

And I had to admit it was nice to be handled just a little.

I slipped out of my cab, looking up at the Perry building where I worked.

Archer Events was *the* event company for the New York elite, handling weddings, charity dinners, release parties, and a dozen other events the rich and famous could dream up. When I'd come out of college with my public relations degree from UCLA, Archer was at the top of my list. My résumé catered to their specific needs, my job through college—interning with event planners in Los Angeles—chosen so I could learn from the best of the West in order to get into the best of the East.

It had paid off. Caroline Archer hired me on the spot, impressed by my confidence and proficiency—and my white suit, which was the only expensive thing I owned, a splurge I couldn't afford. Living in LA, the vast majority of my business casual came from H&M—between my wardrobe, my studio apartment in Culver City, and my ramen noodle budget, I was strapped for cash. Our clients in Beverly Hills said volumes with nothing more than a lingering, silent glance up the length of my body regardless of the fact that I merely filled coffee orders and answered phones.

For a full year, I scrimped and saved, shelling away birthday money from my parents, housesitting, dog walking—any side hustle I could get my hands on. And then I drove my little black

Honda Civic to Rodeo Drive, walked into Armani, and bought a white pantsuit that cost almost four months of rent.

That suit, I was convinced, would be my ticket, the fulcrum of my success. I believed so wholly that if I had that suit, I could do anything, achieve everything. I could walk into Archer Events with my head high and back straight, feel their eyes on me as I passed. They would believe I was competent, capable. Someone to be respected.

And I'd manifested my destiny the day I walked into Caroline Archer's office in my Armani suit and landed my dream job.

Wonder still struck me in unexpected moments, like today, as I walked through the glass doors of Archer's offices, which resided on the forty-fifth floor of a towering building in Midtown. Shades of pink and creams colored every wall, set off by touches of gold and the occasional pop of navy. The offices were feminine and classic, somehow both soothing and crisp, welcoming and elegant, rich and luxurious.

The front desk was an opaline tiled affair with Caroline's logo—a silhouette of the Greek goddess Artemis, crescent bow drawn taut, her eyes on the sky—shining and gold on its front. Two receptionists sat behind in matching navy suits, headsets on and smiles in place.

"Good afternoon, Ms. Parker," Juliet said, standing. "Ms. Lane requested you come straight to her office."

I stifled a sigh, locked it painfully in my lungs against its will. With a thin smile, I thanked her.

Her dark eyes were full of apology.

Everyone seemed to know of the ritual mistreatment Addison Lane bestowed on me—everyone except for Caroline, who I could see in her office at the back of the building through the wall of glass bracketed by velvet curtains of palest pink. Beyond her stretched the city in layers, visible only in slats and rows of windows, towering in slivers granted by the maze of streets. I turned for the glass houses lining the galley of interns and assistants, the offices of the coordinators, including my own small space adjacent to Addison's. A dozen senior coordinators worked at Archer, and I had been yoked to the worst of them all. Addison Lane had a reputation for being ambitious and self-serving, her motto something akin to, *Whatever it takes.*

My blood pressure rose with every beat of my heart as I made my way toward her office, seeing her long before I cared to. She sat behind her desk, elbow on her armrest, hand closed gently, elegantly in the air next to her face. Her hair was black as pitch, pulled into a ponytail, sleek and inky. She was a jackal of ancient Egypt, her skin fair, the rest of her dark—dark dress, dark hair, dark eyes, dark heart. Blood-red lips, wide and humorless, were the feature to note after the bottomless depths of her eyes, then the line of her jaw, the soft point of her chin. She was sharp angles and contempt, fueled by arrogance and superiority.

In short, she was the devil, Anubis reborn in a wedding planner, and my goddamn boss.

For now.

I didn't bother pretending to smile when I walked into my space and stowed my things. Addison watched me coolly from the other side of the glass partition, nothing moving but her eyes as she tracked me.

"I'm sending Lila to approve it," she said, her eyes on me but her face tilted toward the phone on her desk, "and if it's not right, I expect you to make it right."

"Of course, Ms. Lane," the man on the other end said with a nervous edge to his voice.

Without a word of parting, her hand fell to disconnect him.

"What am I approving?" I asked shortly.

"Menu changes for the Hilton engagement party. You have enough events at the Skylight building to work it into your schedule, don't you?"

It was a challenge, not a request.

"Of course," I said, not afforded an alternative as I made a mental note to add her task to my calendar. "You wanted to see me?"

"Update me on the Felix event." Her eyes flicked to the chair in front of her desk, the only invitation I'd get to sit.

So I did. "I got the call this morning that Skylight had a cancellation, so I booked it for the Felix reception."

At that, her smile curled at the edges. "I'll call and let her know."

"Already done," I said with an answering smile and the delightful satisfaction I always felt when I was able to claim my own successes. "Dress is settled and with the tailor. Flowers and colors have been chosen, and Longbourne is already working on everything we'll need. Cake tasting is on the books, and we have a tour of St. Patrick's next week, thanks to the Felixes' donation."

It was obscene, the money they'd thrown at the church to secure a date. The tour and meeting with the priest was a formality, which was fortunate. Who knew what the Femmes would do to embarrass themselves—and by proxy me—when we were there.

"And Natasha's birthday party?"

A sharp tear split my chest at the sound of her name, cold and unexpected. I swallowed. "We're on track. Just putting the final touches on the family banquet. The club for her real party is rented out, and the waivers and liability paperwork are in hand."

Addison's office door opened, and Caroline Archer stepped in, smiling. She was a vision—shining blonde hair, silken tailored shirt and pencil skirt, graceful smile and kind eyes.

"Sorry to interrupt," Caroline started, offering me a smile before turning to Addison.

Addi*satan*, the shapeshifter, morphed into an unrecognizable thing. Her eyes brightened, smile broad and lined with perfect, vividly white teeth. "I was just giving Lila some guidelines for the Felix events," she said, her tone breezy and light.

Faker.

"One of our big ones," Caroline said with a glance in my direction. "It's going well?"

"I've got it under control. Don't worry," Addison said, laughing lightly.

"I'd never expect anything less, Addy."

Addison didn't even flinch at the use of her hated nickname. "Are we still on for dinner?"

"God, I hope so. I'm ready for wine. I was just coming to confirm. I had Lisa make us reservations for seven. We can share a cab."

"Can't wait!" She really did speak in exclamation points when Caroline was around.

It was one of the most unnerving, unnatural things I'd ever witnessed—Addison Lane being nice.

And yet, she sold it flawlessly, though I knew better. Caroline was at the top of the pile of bodies Addison had climbed to get where she was, and I was the poor sucker giving her a boost.

Someday, you'll be her boss.

I smiled placidly as they chatted as if I wasn't there. Sometimes, I wondered how I tolerated it all—the disregard, the disrespect of being undermined and used—and could chalk it up to two things. The first: I knew the devil by name and thus knew her motives. I saw her coming a mile away, and as such, I didn't get fired up about the injustice of it all. Addison was a tool for me to use just as she used me. The second: I'd learned early on that the only thing you could do was a good job. I couldn't control Addison any easier than I could control the orbit of the moon. But I could give her a length of rope and wait. She'd hang herself with it eventually, and when Caroline figured out Addison was largely full of shit, I'd come out of it fresh as a daisy.

Of course, it'd been years, and she had yet to falter. As an exercise supplied by my therapist, I kept Nag Notes in my phone where I noted every infraction, big or small. If I was upset, hurt, humiliated, it went in the notes. I archived them weekly and never read through them, never even been tempted. But I couldn't bring myself to delete them like my therapist had said. I could let it go—mostly. But I wouldn't forget.

Caroline said goodbye, barely glancing in my direction, and I wished she knew just how much I was doing. Honestly, I should have won a major award just for keeping my mouth shut. The high road sucked, but I'd worked too hard for anything less. My integrity was too important to risk on behalf of Addison Lane. And anyway, I had a feeling that was exactly what she wanted—to push me until I broke.

I wouldn't give her the satisfaction.

"Anything else?" I asked with the patience of a saint, hands folded neatly in my lap.

"I want you to really consider this florist you're pushing. We won't tolerate another incident like the Berkshire wedding."

The royal *We*, as if she were speaking for Caroline and all of Archer.

"Don't worry," I assured her. "They're the best florist in Manhattan, and our brides love the charm of using a shop that grows its own flowers."

"Bower Bouquets is the best florist in Manhattan. No one had even heard of Longbourne until a few months ago."

My lips flattened. "Bower is a big-box corporation without the charm of Longbourne. Just today, Madison Wendemere requested a tour of Longbourne's greenhouses, and if you don't think she'll tell her friends, you've never exchanged words with her."

Addison regarded me for a moment. "Just be sure, Lila. It's your ass." She turned her attention to her laptop, opening it before beginning to type, effectively dismissing me.

I stood and left without a goodbye, sliding into my seat and opening my own laptop to file away her threat and work through my notifications. Emails first, then my calendar. I went through my following day, making a mental checklist of everything I'd need to get done to match the expanded calendar, adding the Hilton menu to my next visit to Skylight.

Busy, busy, busy I kept myself, surprised when I realized the sky was on fire with dusk.

Swearing to myself, I closed my laptop and packed up my things. It was far enough beyond our normal hours that I owed Addison no explanation, and she didn't ask, just watched me with those jackal eyes as I left the office.

And almost ran straight into Caroline.

She laughed, an easy sound, and grabbed my arms to stop us both from falling.

"Oh my God," I breathed, heart pounding, though I smiled in response to her laughter. "I am so sorry."

"It's all right. I was actually coming to find you. I just received a call from Iris Berkshire."

I stepped back, stiffening for the blow.

But she kept smiling. "Don't look so worried. She called to apologize for Johanna's behavior last week and mentioned that she'd received a partial refund for the flowers. When she called Longbourne, they said you'd told them of the mistake, so they took care of it. Well done, Lila."

Relief and pride brought a flush of heat to my cheeks. "Thank you, Caroline."

"No, it's me who should be thanking you. We knew Johanna was going to be difficult the second she walked in, and she lived up to her reputation. You handled it beautifully. Keep up the good work," she said before cupping my elbow and breezing toward her office.

I floated to the elevator, though I felt Addison's eyes on my back. She'd seen the whole exchange, and like a petty bitch, I hoped it ate her alive not to know what had been said. When I turned in the elevator to face the doors, our gazes snagged for the briefest of moments before getting cut by the closing metal.

It was a win—a small one but a win nonetheless. And I needed a win.

Because my next task would be utter bullshit. I only hoped Brock wouldn't be home when I completed it.

The very last thing I wanted was to go to his apartment. I'd much rather head straight to Perry's and grab a slice of pizza on my way to my sister's. I'd lose myself in her life, in her and Dean's easy conversation, in their company. It was so much easier to be alone if I wasn't actually alone. But before I was awarded pizza and distractions, I needed to pack a bag. I wanted my own shampoo and my own makeup. I needed clothes and shoes and my book, which was sitting on his coffee table. Funny, how I'd already divorced myself from that place, from my relationship. But finding him *in flagrante* as I had was the snapping of a cord, immediate and unsalvageable.

Nerves rose with every block the cab rolled through. I should have left earlier to guarantee he wouldn't be home, and I hoped he had a late night at work. Or maybe he and Natasha were out. Maybe she was there.

God, I hoped she wasn't there. Though I might have nearly murdered them in the conservatory with a candlestick, I hadn't said a word. Today, I wouldn't keep my mouth shut. And the last thing I needed was a complaint from a Felix Femme to Caroline.

The doorman let me in with the tip of his hat and a look that said he knew something. I didn't have the courage to ask if Brock was home or if *she* was there, didn't want him to pity me. I'd find out soon enough. The elevator beeped slower than I ever remembered, filling the metal box with its countdown. And when the doors finally opened, down that hall I went. Emotion swept over me, fresh as it had been when I'd last been in this place. My busyness was a facade, thin and temporary over the truth.

I was not okay. And this was not okay.

My keys rattled in my hand, slick as I unlocked the door and opened it, my eyes clicking to the wall where he'd fucked her last night, catching on the nick in the sheetrock from my outburst. The empty space was thick with ghosts. The apartment was quiet.

I sighed my relief and closed the door.

"Lila?"

His voice, tired and worn, from the dark living room. A shock, cold and sharp, down my spine.

"Of course it's me," I said, my acerbic tone shellac over my pain. "Who else would it be? I didn't figure you'd given Natasha Felix a key, but you're just full of surprises these days, aren't you?"

The shadows shifted as he stood and turned on the light. I didn't wait to hear him out. Instead, I marched toward the bedroom to do what I'd come to do. There was no backing down, nor was there any running away.

"Let me explain."

"Explain what?" I asked dryly, flipping on the light before opening the closet.

He stopped inside the door, sliding his hands into his pockets, leaning on the doorframe. I didn't chance a look at his expression. My periphery was enough.

I thunked the suitcase on the bed and turned for my dresser.

"I didn't mean for this to happen," he said quietly.

A bitter, severe laugh shot out of me. "That's what you're going with?" I loaded an armful of panties, bras, and chemises and dumped them unceremoniously in the gaping suitcase.

Ignoring the jab, he continued, "We met at the engagement party—"

"I know when you met, asshole. I introduced you." To the closet I whipped, trying to calculate outfits and shoes with the tiny percentage of my brain that wasn't consumed with Brock the Cock and his excuses. I gnawed my lip so hard, I could feel the throb of blood at the point of contact.

"She's just … she's *different*, Lila. I've never met anyone like her before. Natasha is unpredictable when everything in my life seems planned out until I die."

It was then that I finally turned to him, a painfully slow twist. Our gazes met. He didn't look sorry, but he wasn't happy either. There was no regret, but there was no defense.

"Like me," I finished his thought.

"You and I are comfortable, easy. On paper, it makes sense. But that's been my whole life. My parents had my application to Columbia filled out when I was in diapers, and I went along with it. I've done everything expected of me. I made them happy, but I won't become them. Sleeping in separate rooms, never speaking beyond what's required of them. Cold and loveless. I need more. I need *passion*."

Fury. It was fury, unbridled and wild, lashed through me sharp enough to draw blood. "No," I said on a shaky breath.

His fine brows drew together. "No?"

"You don't get to break up with me. You don't get to blame me, to make this my fault." I stepped toward him as I spoke, my voice deadly calm and my body tight as a bowstring. "You weren't happy? Fine. But don't pretend like fucking a twenty-year-old *child* in the apartment we shared was the way to handle it. Self-destruct, if that makes you feel in control of your life. But you don't get to break up with me. Because I'm leaving *you*."

His face was still as he watched me approach, unafraid and unfazed. Pity flashed behind his eyes, and I resisted the impulse to grab the closest inanimate object and brain him with it.

"I don't give a shit why you did it or what revelations you had when you had my goddamn client nailed to the wall of our foyer. Just leave me alone so I can pack my things in peace and go."

A sigh, thick and deep, set his chest in a rise, then a fall. "I should have expected this," he said, pushing himself upright. "But deep down, I thought you might actually show some emotion. Be vulnerable. Be *honest*. I always was a sucker."

And he turned and walked away.

"That makes two of us," I said quietly to his back, my tears caught in my chest, in my throat, in the tip of my nose and the corners of my eyes.

I turned back to my closet in a haze of thought, a fog of emotion, blindly gathering suits and my garment bag, then shoes and silken pajamas. Into the bathroom I went, grateful it was joined to the room so I wouldn't have to venture out until I was ready. The light was too bright, overly harsh, and I avoided my reflection, afraid of what I'd see. And when the counter and medicine cabinet were half empty in ghostly equal, I walked out of the bathroom, then our room like a stranger.

He thought me invulnerable. Unfeeling. Dishonest with my emotions.

For all the years we'd spent together, it seemed he really didn't know me after all.

Brock glanced up from an armchair when I entered, scotch in his hand and brow smooth.

"I'm keeping the key until I've gotten the rest of my things. I'll be here Saturday from noon to three. Please, don't be here."

Another nod. "For what it's worth, I'm sorry."

"For what it's worth, I don't give a damn."

I turned before he could speak again, before my tears fell, racing down my cheeks the moment I was shielded. I didn't move to wipe them away, not wanting him to know, content to leave him thinking me stony and cold. The truth—that I was molten pain, pooling lava, white-hot and searing—was none of his business.

Not anymore, whether I liked it or not.

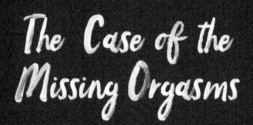

The Case of the Missing Orgasms

KASH

I should have known I was walking into trouble the second I saw Ivy and Tess eyeing each other across the work table the next morning.

"Kash," Ivy started, arms folded, "settle something for us."

I set down the buckets of zinnias on the table. "Lay it on me."

"How many times would you let your girlfriend go without an orgasm before you upped your game?" Ivy said without batting a lash.

A surprised snort. "Zero."

"See?" Ivy gestured to me. "Good guys don't let their ladies go orgasmless."

Tess laughed, rolling her eyes. "You don't think Lila at least faked it? How do you know he knew she wasn't orgasming?"

The knowledge that we were talking about *Lila* struck me like a bell, reverberating down my spine. I caught myself frowning and schooled my face.

"Because she told me, you ninny. He's a *doctor*, Tess. He should understand female anatomy."

"I mean, in theory," Tess answered.

"Lila thinks it's because he's too hot to have to try," Ivy noted.

"Is that a thing?" I asked dubiously.

"Oh, it's a thing," she assured me. "The really hot ones go one of two ways—either they're gods or complete duds. There is no in-between. Size of ego usually has something to do with it. Any man who would take a woman to bed thinking *she* was the lucky one has it all wrong."

"I think you're just mad at Brock," Tess said, turning back to the arrangement she was working on.

"Damn right I'm mad at Brock. She came home last night a mess, and it's his fault. He wasted her time and her love. I shudder to think what he said to her to have shaken her up like he did."

"You don't even know if he was there," Tess argued.

"Oh, he was there. I know my sister." Ivy huffed. "Stupid jerk. Of all the low down, dirty ways he could have played her, that was the worst."

This time when I frowned, there was no stopping it. "Brock?"

"Her stupid boyfriend. *Ex*-boyfriend." Ivy sulked, grabbing a zinnia and snipping its stem like it was Brock's inattentive member. "She walked in on him nailing a Felix Femme in their entryway last week. After she busted her ass in the flower bed."

I leaned a hip on the table, folding my arms. A flash of rage burned through my chest like a meteor. "Which Femme?"

"Natasha. And worse—Lila has to see her practically daily, what with her sister's wedding and all. God, you should have seen her when she came over after she caught him, still covered in greenhouse dirt."

"She must have been furious," Tess said.

"The opposite. She was matter-of-fact, completely calm and collected and in fixer mode. But that's Lila. Whatever she felt, she kept it locked up or reserved it for when she was alone. In fact, she insisted it was a *good* thing. That she'd somehow learned something vital, thus saving herself. But I know she's hurting. She thought they were going to get married, for God's sake." Ivy shook her head, brows drawn with concern. "I've always hated him, but now I could rip his face off and shove it down his throat like baloney."

"How long were they together?" I asked carefully, hungry for details and shocked that any man could be so ungrateful.

"Two years. I always thought he was a douchebag, but I never suspected he'd sleep with a girl who couldn't even drink—and right there in their apartment."

"And what makes him such a douche? He sounds like a stupid asshole, but not exactly a douchebag."

"Let me count the ways," Ivy said, ticking off points on her fingers. "He's a poor little rich boy, obsessed with status. Constantly talks about himself. Tells bad jokes. Didn't give my sister the orgasms she so clearly deserves. Wears too much cologne. Cheats on her with reality TV stars. His name belongs to a weatherman—Brock Bancroft," she scoffed. "Should I go on?"

I chuckled, imagining some weatherman type with a booming voice and too many teeth. I couldn't picture Lila with a man like that. She was too immaculate, too enterprising to settle for anything less than equal to her. Not that I knew her, I reminded myself once again. But the woman she chose to show the world was solid and unflinching. A woman who took no shit and accepted nothing less than the best.

How she'd ended up with some shitbag who didn't even give her orgasms was beyond me, a nonsensical concept with no grounds in reality.

To have something end like that was brutal, unforgivable

Ivy continued on her teardown of Brock the Cock, as she lovingly called him. Lila'd moved in with Ivy for a little while, I learned as Ivy went on, and was sleeping in the nursery. Last night, she'd gone back to get her things, and it hadn't gone well.

Ivy didn't know what had happened though, and Lila hadn't clued her in. This was apparently Lila's modus operandi—she gave nothing away, played it close to the vest.

Several pieces of the puzzle clicked into place as I turned the knowledge over in my mind. When we'd met at Skylight after her tumble into the black-eyed Susans, she'd looked like she hadn't slept, and now I knew the who of it. Her ideas about love and liars, the fury with which she spoke about relationships, all made sense. And now, Lila Parker was single—and heartbroken, if Ivy was to be believed.

A familiar sense of protectiveness bloomed in my ribs, common when I came across someone being mistreated. Lila seemed indestructible, and to think that someone had found a way to hurt her felt obscene, sacrilegious. I wondered how she might ever mend her heart, knowing time would help, distance. But her job required her to be around the very object of their demise—Natasha Felix. I could only imagine how painful seeing her would be, and to have to bottle it all up in order to perform? It seemed too much burden to carry, though I had a feeling that Lila shouldered it with grace and determination.

"What she needs is a rebound," Ivy said to the tops of the zinnias. "Somebody to pound her into oblivion, but someone disposable. Someone who she won't catch feelings for. Somebody to make her forget Brock the Cock ever existed."

A lightbulb flashed over my head, and I blinked at its brightness.

"When in the world does she even have time to meet someone like that?" Tess asked. "She works eighty hours a week. I'm not even convinced she does such human things like eat and sleep."

Ivy sighed. "I don't know. She doesn't believe in dating apps."

Good, I thought to myself. Because I knew a guy who might fit the bill, someone who checked all the boxes.

Pound her into oblivion—check.

Make her forget Brock existed—check.

Disposable—check.

There was no danger of Lila Parker catching feelings for me. I couldn't be convinced she didn't actually hate me. But maybe I could help her move on.

She deserved to be appreciated by a man. She needed to know her ex was the anomaly, not the norm.

And if she was interested, I might just be the man to prove it to her.

A Good Smiting

LILA

I woke the next morning with a renewed optimism and Brock firmly in my rearview mirror, and for a full week, I maintained that attitude with the white-knuckled will of a Spartan.

Ivy and Dean had let me slide into the apartment that night without pressing me for details, and I offered none. I'd gone to sleep in the comfort of my own clothes and the scent of my soap on my skin, the only familiar things about my circumstance.

Truth was, I was glad for the company. It forced me to retain my civility and togetherness, to pretend I was fine. I found that the longer you pretended a thing, the sooner it became reality. And I wanted to be fine, to be over it. Pretending was useful that way. And as long as I kept myself busy, it'd soon be a speck on the horizon at my back.

For a whole week, that was exactly what I told myself, repeating it again as I stood on the steps of St. Patrick's Cathedral, the sweeping neo-Gothic church casting me its shade.

I saw the cavalcade of black Escalades the moment they

turned onto Fifth, a string of them with opaque windows and drivers in suits, screeching to a halt in front of the church.

Doors opened almost simultaneously, and the retinue of the Femmes poured out. Camera crews first, then assistants, then bodyguards. Paparazzi materialized, flashes bursting. Five vehicles for five Femmes, who stepped onto the sidewalk nearly in blonde, leggy unison.

Sorina, the matriarch, took the hand of a bulldoggish giant wearing wraparound sunglasses, a suit, and a stern look. She had recently celebrated her fiftieth birthday but had not aged past thirty, thanks to advancements in plastic surgery. The five of them converged, heading toward me like a military chevron, all fashion and grace and unearthly beauty. Flanked by bodyguards with menacing looks toward the paparazzi, they carried on unaffected, two cameramen in their wake. The groom, Jordan Holt, was at Angelika's side with nothing but smoldering looks and Jesus hair and a suit he wore as easily as a regular guy would jeans and a T-shirt.

I smiled, creating a blank spot in my mind where Natasha stood.

"Lila, darling," Sorina said with a perfect smile, and we air-kissed in greeting. "Are they ready for us?"

"All set. Sister Marilla is waiting to show us around the church, and then Angelika and Jordan will meet with Father Dickman."

Natasha snickered. I wasn't the only one to ignore her, though Angelika flicked a glare in her direction, full lips set in warning.

"Come then," Sorina said, linking arms with Angelika, the picture of mother-daughter joy. "Let's have a look, shall we?"

I led them inside, past the brass doors carved with saints where Sister Marilla waited, hands in the pocket of her habit, her face bovine and kind. She wore an innocent sweetness that made me wonder if she'd relocated to New York from somewhere more remote. Like North Dakota.

"Hello," she said cheerily, extending a hand to Sorina. "It's so nice to meet you. You can call me Sister, or Marilla, or Sister Marilla, if you'd like. And," she said with a flush of her sagging cheeks, "forgive me, but there are so many of you, and I've forgotten your names."

A derisive sound came from Natasha at the slight—the vast majority of America knew them on sight—but Sorina, ever gracious, only smiled and introduced her daughters, oldest to youngest, who stepped forward one by one like the Von Trapps to shake the aging nun's thin hand. Alexandra, Sofia, Angelika and Jordan, and at last, Natasha, who pumped her hand theatrically and made a condescending show of things.

"Oh, I just can't wait to meet Father Dickman," she said snidely. "Does he handle all the new *members*?"

Sorina leveled her with a glance. Her sisters' expressions shifted from condescending boredom to a cruel twist of attention. Poor, sweet, unaware Sister Marilla tittered.

"Usually we sisters do, but aren't you just so kind to ask after him? I'll be sure to let him know how thrilled you are. Do you all have any questions for me before we begin?" she asked, smiling that sheep smile of utter trust.

"Would you say Father Dickman is shy? Or does he prefer an audience?" Natasha asked.

Sorina and I snapped our gazes to her. She smiled back unapologetically, her eyes sharp with challenge when they met mine.

"Oh, he's an accomplished orator," Sister Marilla assured. "World renowned."

"World renowned at oral education"—Natasha paused—"of *faith*."

"Yes," she insisted, smiling broadly. "You should come to mass, my child, and see for yourself. I think you'll leave quite pleased by Father Dickman. All of our parishioners do."

Natasha choked off her laughter, pursing her lips once Sorina's presence got too hot for her. How Natasha Felix had not been struck by lightning was beyond me. If anyone deserved a good smiting, it was that slag.

Marilla continued, unaffected, "Let's start here, in the chapel."

We followed her down the carpeted aisle as she spoke softly, gesturing to the sweeping ceiling of white, the rib vaulted ceiling joined by blood-red keystones carved with ivory designs, no two alike. She told us of the stained glass and how the collection was extensive and made all around the world, many from master crafters in France.

I listened only on the fringes, having heard the details a dozen times. Instead, I marveled over the architecture, feeling small and humbled, as I supposed was appropriate for a place of worship. She walked us through the broad strokes of a wedding ceremony, told us the story of the bells and listed their names, all nineteen of them. Even the cameraman was drooping by the time we made it to the pulpit. Sorina had a placid smile on her face, her eyes distant. The other sisters were on their phones, and my eyes lingered on Natasha, leaving me wondering if it was Brock she was texting with that vicious smile on her face. And Angelika was …

Missing.

Angelika was missing, as were Jordan and one of the cameramen.

My eyes widened, heart lurching. I melted back, putting myself behind the Femmes, my head swiveling as I looked for the other cameraman, my only clue as to where they were.

I found him perched outside a confessional booth, lens pointed smack at one of the carved wooden doors, and I swore under my breath, palms blossoming with sweat. Because I knew exactly what they were doing in there, and if one of the clergy found them defiling the hallowed space, the venue was off. And if the venue was off, I would be the one to take the fall, guaranteed.

The Felix Femmes were, quite literally, the fucking worst.

And their indecency, irreverence, and utter disregard for anyone but themselves was likely to get me fired over something so stupid as a stunt for their reality show.

But not today.

I clipped across the church and to the niche where confessional booths stood. The cameraman politely backed up to get me in the shot, then stepped behind me. Placing my body where I could shield the view of the box's contents, I took a painful breath, held it, and opened the door.

A giggling tangle of limbs greeted me, a flash of nipple, Angelika's naked ass, dress hitched up to her waist and G-string held aside by Jordan's broad hand.

"What the fuck are you doing?" I hissed, closing the door but for a crack, camera lens over my shoulder.

"What … the fuck … do you think?" Angelika breathed between humping.

"Put your clothes on and get out."

"One … second … *oh!*" she squealed before moaning into his mouth to the soft pat of skin on skin.

I closed the door with a snick and put my back against it, palms flat and damp against the wood, my mind flashing with solutions. It was one of the many moments when I'd regretted all the waivers and contracts I'd signed making me an accessory to such indignities, and the butt of jokes for their show to boot.

What I wanted to do was fling open the door, grab those walking publicity stunts by their entitled, disrespectful ears, and throw them half-naked into the cars outside. What I wanted was to dress them down, not that they had many clothes on to start. What I wanted—

Didn't matter because before I could figure out what to do, a nun approached, brows quirked and eyes suspicious.

I flashed my most charismatic smile. "Hello, Sister," I said overly loud, stepping away from the booth to greet her in the hopes that she wouldn't hear the fornication happening right there in the sacred place of her home. "I was just wondering, what time is confession?"

Relief smoothed the lines in her forehead. "After every mass and most afternoons. Are you with the Felixes?" She glanced at the cameraman.

"I am. Lila Parker, their wedding planner." I thrust my hand in her direction, speaking before she even took my hand when I heard a thump from the booth behind me. "We are just so pleased you found time for us in your calendar at such short notice."

Her eyes shifted behind me, but at the tangential mention of the outrageous donation that had made the booking possible, she settled her full attention on me. "Well, we seem to always find room for our most valued parishioners."

"And aren't we fortunate for that?" Another thump, and I scooped the nun's shoulders under my arm and turned her in the opposite direction. "I wanted to light a candle while I'm here. Could you show me where I can do that, Sister ..."

"Eleanor. Yes, certainly, child," she answered gently.

"My sister, she's having a baby soon," I started, following her lead.

"What a gift," Sister Eleanor cooed. "The welcoming of a child is a joyous thing indeed. If you just go past here and turn, you'll see the candles there. I'll say a prayer of my own for your sister and her baby. May God bless them and keep them."

"Thank you," I said, turning to face her so I could sneak a look back at the confession booth just as the door opened.

Angelika slinked out, adjusting her skirt, followed by Jordan, hands adjusting his pants. In the midst of rehearsing the brimstone speech I was about to lash them with—I mean, serious, scorched earth, end of days tongue lashing—she reached back for his hand with the deepest affection in her eyes. And he returned it with adoration, the connection between them visible, palpable, even from across the room.

Stunt or no stunt, sinners or snakes, those assholes had

found love. Real, honest love. A deep thrum of longing plucked in my chest. I sighed, the sound heavy with dreams lost and wishes I'd never have fulfilled.

Sister Eleanor watched me, worried. "Are you all right, dear?"

"I will be. Thank you, Sister."

She patted my arm. "Of course," she said before shuffling away.

Angelika and Jordan stepped up to the back of the Femmes, their absence unnoticed by everyone, except Natasha, who wore a look of disdain. She had something equally disdainful to say, judging by Angelika's reaction to whatever she muttered. Sister Marilla was still going on—if I had to guess, about the organ. And with a quick moment to spare and the sense that I needed a beat, I ducked into the nook where the candles waited, glimmering in the dark.

Flickering flames in amber glass, a vision from a dream, the quiet to calm my screaming nerves. It took only a second, maybe two, before calm washed over me.

An absent hand slipped into my purse, returning with a bill I folded and slid into the donation box. A taper in my fingers, I stepped to the row, finding an unlit candle. I wasn't a religious woman, ruled more by logic than anything, and faith seemed far away, a fanciful feeling. But there in reverent silence, I lit a candle, watched the wick catch fire, felt the tranquility of intention as I wished for peace of my own. And then, I placed the taper where it belonged, smoking in wait for the next soul who needed saving.

Sausage, Please

LILA

My sigh weighed a thousand pounds as I paid the cabbie and stepped onto Bleecker. The day had been eternal, the fiasco at St. Patrick's exhausting. We'd made it out of the church without further incident, and no one was the wiser. The priest had given his blessing, just like we'd known he would, and I'd parted ways with the Felix Femmes with plans to meet for lunch in a few days to go over finishing touches on Natasha's birthday party.

The way Brock had talked last week, they were still seeing each other. He'd probably be at the party, as would I, and there was no way for me to pass the task to someone else. I couldn't admit what had happened to Addison without her using it against me, and although we had access to interns, there wasn't a single one I'd trust with a Felix event.

So I'd endure it. I'd compartmentalize my feelings, pack them up, stow them away, and get on with it so I could do my job. So I could *crush* my job. I'd throw her the best goddamn birthday party to ever come out of New York despite the fact that she'd fucked my boyfriend.

Post-church, I'd gone on with my day, meeting with a caterer, stopping into the office for a meeting and to answer to Addison. And my last task of the day was to pop into Longbourne, where I'd become a regular fixture.

My purpose was twofold: take a look at the flower crop for a wedding this weekend and escort my very pregnant sister home. I'd been thinking about that pizza all week, and I'd convinced Ivy to let me get her a slice on the way home. Not that it took much convincing—pizza was her number one craving. I swore she was going to actually birth a pizza roll or a giant pepperoni. Or just a chubby little baby with doughy thighs and cheeks to pinch and fawn over.

And with that thought putting the first genuine smile on my face of the day, I walked toward the turquoise door of Longbourne and stepped inside, greeted by the dinging of the ancient bell over the door.

It really was something, what they'd done with the place. I'd been in and out of the shop since we were teenagers, when Ivy started working here. It used to be drab and dark, untouched by time, but when the Bennet children came home last summer, they came home with purpose. The makeover was brilliant—the shop was bright and cheerful, the windows inviting with gorgeous installations that had become a Village spectacle. I'd seen the crowds waiting on Sunday morning for the unveiling, and I'd heard from Ivy about the massive increase in business.

I was honestly happy to help by bringing them the wedding business I had to offer even if it was risky and even if I'd been a monster about it. As a rule, Archer Events used Bower Bouquets, but I'd gone over Addison's head, taking it straight to Caroline, who had agreed, loving the charm of the small shop and their greenhouse. I found I much preferred the one-on-one interaction I had with Longbourne. I never saw the same florist twice at Bower. Here, I felt like Longbourne was part of my team. Granted, my sister worked here, but still. It was nice using a small business, and it helped the flower shop make their money. Thus helping my sister make hers. Everybody won.

My heels were noisy on the black-and-white-tiled floor, the shop still busy with the rush hour crowd looking to grab something on their way home. I waved at Jett behind the counter, one of the beautiful Bennet men, and he offered me one of their signature smirks, a cavalier tilt of wide lips.

They were shockingly handsome, the whole lot of them—tall and raven-haired, crisp blue eyes and solid frames, square jaws and brilliant smiles. My favorite of those smiles wasn't Luke's, who took nothing seriously, or Jett's, who seemed to be just being kind. It wasn't Marcus either, as hard-won as those smiles were—he was a little too brooding for my taste. I preferred a man with the serious air of Marcus but the charm like Luke.

Which was Kassius Bennet.

As much as I hated to admit it, he really did have the best smile, and I felt like Goldilocks about it—not too happy, not too quiet. Not too forthcoming and not too shy. His was just right—a perfect mix of quiet weight and wry humor. It was a smile of secrets and surprises.

Your blood sugar must be low, I scolded myself. *Waxing poetic about the gardener? Get yourself a slice of pizza before you do something stupid.*

I saw him the second I stepped into the workspace, before my sister, before Tess. He leaned against the worktable with his enormous arms folded across his wide chest. He seemed the ideal blend of the Bennet qualities, from his stupid, irreverent T-shirts to his unflappable, solid support. Granted, his T-shirts were a little more bearable since seeing him fill out tailored clothes so nicely. Nicely enough that I'd made excuses to get him to come to a few venues in the hopes he'd show up in a tie. He cleaned up well, though his jaw, which had been smooth and clean just a few days ago, was already smattered in dark, thick stubble. I wondered what he'd look like with a full-blown beard, imagining it would be as lustrous and luxuriant as his hair. I wanted him to shave his face and cut his hair just as badly as I wanted him to let it run wild despite my wishes.

Today, his shirt read, *Sow Cool*, bordered with a silhouette of wheat beneath it.

I wanted to laugh, but then our gazes tangled, and I forgot what was so funny.

Something had changed in him over the last week or so, something I couldn't place. Something about his eyes or the set of his lips that smoldered serious. I'd caught a glimpse of it when he'd asked me about relationships—a personal tone we sadly hadn't slipped into since—but today, the expression was unprompted, existing before my entrance and seemingly likely to remain when I was gone.

He didn't move but for the uptick of one corner of his lips, framed by that square, utterly masculine jaw.

Caught off guard, I defaulted to my work smile.

"Lila!" Ivy sighed, smiling. "If you're here, that means it's almost pizza time, and thank God. I'm starving."

The room chuckled.

"I'll buy you all the pizza you can eat."

"The cruelest part of that joke is that I can't even finish one slice. I'm too full of baby," she said on a laugh, running her hand over the swell tenderly.

"Well, half a piece it is, and I'll get you one for the fridge. You can eat it in a couple hours when you're hungry again."

"Deal. How'd it go with the Femmes?" she asked.

"Well, Angelika and Jordan fucked in a confession booth, and I had to divert a nun who almost caught them."

The three of them blinked at me, mouths hanging open, before they burst into laughter.

"I know." I set my bag on the worktable, bending to smell the lilies in Tess's vase. "If they weren't totally goo-goo over each other, I'd have figured it for a stunt."

"I mean, it probably was a stunt," Ivy noted.

"Probably," I agreed. "But still. At least something about the ordeal was genuine."

"And at least one of the Femmes is actually in love," Tess said. "I'm convinced the others are in marriages of convenience."

"I wouldn't be surprised." I changed the subject to avoid talk of Natasha's romantic interest, lest I lose my appetite with pizza on the horizon. "Ready to walk me through the flowers for the Statham wedding?" I asked Kash.

"Born ready." He pushed off the table, flicking his head toward the back.

I eyed him. "Don't you need our paperwork? The concept designs Tess came up with?"

"Nah. I got it all up here," he said, tapping his temple like he did.

I resisted the urge to roll my eyes and said flatly, "If you say so."

"I say so. Come on," he said, and I had no choice but to follow.

His back was a landscape of muscle in shadows and highlights, the topography clear, even swathed in his dumb T-shirt. The fleeting thought of what those rolling muscles would look like undisguised by his shirt made me salivate. Actually salivate, a hot rush of slobber like I'd been offered that pizza I'd been daydreaming of. I swallowed hard, shifting my gaze to the greenhouse the second we'd passed through the swinging doors.

The greenhouse was humid despite the brisk autumn weather, a wall of thick air that absorbed me, pulled me in behind Kash. It smelled like heaven, of wet earth and perfumed blossoms, of leaves and moisture. It was alive, the heady fragrance so elemental, it seemed to call to something deep in my chest—*remember me?*

"Statham wedding is the one Tess is most excited about," he said as we walked. "It's rare we get anyone who trusts us enough to incorporate cabbage in their floral arrangements."

I chuckled. "Well, the bride is an interior decorator, so she's a little more *avant-garde* than most."

He stopped in front of a series of planters suspended from the wooden rack that ran the length of the greenhouse. In each planter sat row after row of blooming cabbage—purple and white crane cabbage that looked like delicate roses, the green crane reminiscent of succulents. A feathered varietal, veined like coral.

"They're coming in nicely," he said, thumbing a leaf before rooting around in the dirt to free what had been caught under a fresh dusting of earth.

"They're beautiful. I can't believe they're not flowers."

His smile tilted. "Nature's a curious thing. Sometimes it disguises one thing as another, hides its nature to protect it."

"Indeed it does," I agreed quietly, struck by the sentiment.

Kash jerked his chin toward the back of the greenhouse. "I've got the greenery we ordered for you, if you want to see."

"I do, thank you."

I followed him, the two of us pausing at the marigolds to peer at their lush amber heads. *Sometimes nature disguises one thing as another.* How true it was. There was more to Kash Bennet than I'd realized, a revelation that struck me like a match.

There was more to me too. And I wondered what he was hiding to protect himself. I wondered if he knew what I didn't say, what I didn't show, and got the distinct impression that he did.

It was as thrilling a thought as it was terrifying.

Once at the black buckets lining the workspace in the back, he guided me to the relevant greenery.

"Rose hips," he said, gesturing to the red and green berries, fat and shiny. "Sedum." He reached for a stem topped with a plain of tiny flowers of white and dusky lavender. "Is this lavender too pink? I promised somebody I wouldn't screw this up, and I'd hate to go back on my word."

I chuckled, ignoring the tingle of warmth in my cheeks. "They're perfect."

"The succulents came in too." He stepped to the table where trays of succulents and vibrant mosses waited for my approval. Tenderly, he scooped up a succulent that burst from deep purple to vivid green, center to tip. It sat in his broad, cupped hand, roots in its dirt in his palm. "For the centerpieces," he said.

"They'll look brilliant."

He smiled, returning it to its home and dusting off his hands. "There were other flowers we don't have space to grow, but they're in the cooler. White anemones, tulips, and hyacinth for the bouquet and touches in the centerpieces. Tess made the garland mostly out of purple amaranth, strung it with feather tops and sprigs of dusty miller." He reached for what I thought was a pile of furry lavender falls, pale feathery yellows, and silvery-green leaves dotted with buds, but when he spread his arms, the garland hung before him.

I drew a slight breath of surprise. "She is a genius," I said, eyes trailing the details of the strung grasses. "The bride is going to cry, and we'll all get a raise."

At that, he laughed. "I don't need tears. I'll accept anything, except for her coming after you like the Berkshire girl."

"Well, they *were* the wrong color," I noted, but I couldn't help but smile. "Anyway, you got yours—I ended up planted in the greenhouse."

"Should I be expecting a dry cleaning bill?" He smirked as he folded the garland, spooling it onto the table.

"Without a doubt. Consider the flowers officially approved. And thank you for letting me micromanage you. I know it's not typical for an event planner to come second-guessing your work."

"It's more common than you might think. And I don't mind, Lila."

Something in my chest snagged at the sound of my name from his lips. I laughed it off. "Not much ruffles you, does it, Kash?"

One of his shoulders rose and fell in a shrug. "You've met my family. It's no place for someone who's easily annoyed. We all learned early how to irritate each other and weather each other's irritations."

"Fair enough, but you're particularly unflappable."

"A trait I inherited from my father. I don't think he's ever been in an argument a day in his life even though my mother seems to argue with him daily. He just sits and listens and nods, and in the end, he imparts some deep and poignant wisdom on you. It's his special skill, aside from this." He swept a hand toward the greenhouse, wall to wall.

I looked over the rows of color and life, smiling to myself through a stretch of silence, not realizing he was watching me until he spoke.

"I'm sorry. About your boyfriend."

A shot of pain, and my smile was gone. I turned my gaze on him. "Excuse me?"

He had the decency to look at least a little cowed, but he crossed his arms and leaned against the edge of the worktable, the picture of amiability. Nothing about him seemed dangerous. But every warning bell rang, setting my spine stiff.

"Ivy and Tess were talking about it. Ivy wasn't gossiping or anything, just venting. She's not happy with him."

"That makes two of us," I said shortly.

He watched me for a beat. "He's a fool, you know."

Another jolt, this one hotter. "So am I."

His brows flicked together, more concerned than put off. "It's not your fault," he said. "What happened … it's not your fault."

The words hit me like a battering ram, freezing my lungs and holding the breath there. For a moment, I said nothing, just stood there, tracing those words with my heart. I hadn't realized until he'd said it that was exactly how I felt beneath my armor of rightness and false certainty. That even if I hadn't driven him to cheat on me, which I probably had, I hadn't known. It was my fault if for no other reason than I was blind. Stupid. Wrong.

A squeeze of my throat prompted me to swallow. And Kash just watched, his face touched with concern and earnest care. There was another edge too, singed by anger. Anger at Brock, I realized.

He pushed off the table and stood, busying himself with various unimportant items on the table as he spoke, changing the subject. "I've got the concepts for your spring weddings and planted what you'll need. As soon as I have something blooming, you'll know. And I'll see you this weekend for the wedding."

"You'll be delivering the flowers?" I asked, surprised.

He shot me a sideways smile. "Don't sound so disappointed."

"I'm not. It's just that it's usually Luke."

"He and Tess are busy with an installation, so it'll just be you and me. Unless you have any objections."

The thrill I felt shocked me. Maybe seeing him all cleaned up over the last few weeks did something to my brain, because the truth was that regardless of how gorgeous he was, we were nothing alike. I spent my weekends at events that cost four thousand a head. He spent his playing in the dirt. I had a bottomless well of ambition, and he had worked in the greenhouse since he was a teenager. I was uptight and closed off, and he was easy and open. Where I wore a mask, what you saw with Kash was exactly what you got.

The longing and quiet envy I felt struck me in the softest of places.

So I put on my work smile to cover it. "We'll have a grand old time."

"Plus," he started with that cavalier smile of his, "this way, you can follow me around and tell me what to do. I know how much you like that."

My eyes gave a turn, but I was still smiling. "Don't pretend you don't enjoy it."

That smile climbed as he stepped toward me, then into me as he passed, my space and senses invaded. "Wouldn't dream of it, Priss."

And then, he passed, leaving me in a whirl of his scent, musky and sweet.

"Come on," he said over his shoulder. "I'll show you what we've got in the cooler."

And blinking, I followed, straightening my thoughts as I straightened my skirt, pretending my wits were in perfect order too.

Into the workroom we went, Ivy and Tess chatting idly over their arrangements as Kash showed me the other flowers. We leaned into the open door of the cooler, shoulder to shoulder, close enough to smell mint on his breath and feel the heat of his body against the chill of the cooler.

"They're exactly what I asked for," I said.

"Can I get that in writing?"

I bumped him with my shoulder before we backed out. Ivy and Tess looked up from their arrangements with strange expressions on their faces. I felt bald and exposed under their gazes, and so, I offered Tess my absolute best smile and strode toward them.

"Tess, the garland is out of this world."

She flushed prettily, her brown eyes soft. "Thank you."

"I mean it. I've never seen anything like it."

"She's got a knack for that," Kash said, offering her a fond smile.

"It's a certain kind of magic she possesses," Ivy added. "Sometimes she walks into the greenhouse and stands there like a savant, staring at the flowers, calculating her creation. We sell out of market bouquets every day, and I swear she's never quite done the same thing twice."

"Cut it out," Tess said on a flustered laugh, reaching into a bucket of mauve hydrangeas.

"It's okay. I don't take compliments well either," I admitted.

"It's true," my sister added. "Last time I complimented her hair, she went on for ten minutes about how it was all thanks to her hair products and did her best to convert me to using them. She forgets I work as a florist and not a hot-shot wedding planner and can't afford Sephora anything."

"Assistant coordinator," I corrected. "And I told you, you could use mine."

"And get addicted to something I can't afford? I have enough vices, thank you very much."

"Are you about ready?" I asked, looking over her arrangement to see if I could determine that answer myself.

"Just about. You and Kash get everything approved?" she asked.

"We did," I said with a glance in his direction, catching him watching me.

He didn't look away, boldly locking eyes. They were a deeper, darker shade than the other Bennets, shot with a burst of blue so light, it shone silver around his pupil like an eclipse.

"Can we get that in writing?" Ivy joked.

"That's what I said." Kash's lips were tilted, wide and inviting.

God, what was it about that sideways smile? I'd always found smirks to be lewd and a little salacious, but he made the expression feel intimate, like a secret we shared. Except I didn't know what the secret was.

That smile promised to tell me everything and then some.

A wave of heat brushed my skin at the notion.

Mercifully, Ivy stood. Well, it was more of a cautious slide off the stool, then a waddle to her bag.

"See you guys tomorrow," she said in parting.

"Don't have that baby yet," Tess warned.

A snort from Ivy. "If she decides to show up, I'm not arguing." At Tess's frown, she added, "Don't worry, you'll all survive without me. In fact, I'm betting you'll get more work done without me here to distract you."

"Fat chance," Tess answered.

Ivy pressed a hand to her belly. "Watch it with the fat talk, Tess Monroe."

With a laugh, Tess and Ivy embraced, and I watched with a smile and a sigh, thankful Ivy had her little family here. Another stroke of envy brushed my heart—I had no friends like this, no family away from family. Our parents had moved to Phoenix when they retired but came when they could. New York was my home, but while Ivy had always had the Bennets and the shop and now Dean, I only had her. I'd had no real time for friends, not with the demands of my job, and while I'd adopted Brock's friends—a collection of doctors, lawyers, and otherwise accomplished professionals—they were proximity friends, nothing more. They weren't the people you texted in the middle of the night or watched old movies with in your pajamas. They were the sort who showed up to dinner and performed, hiding their true nature with predatory skill.

Maybe that was where I'd sharpened my own mask. Maybe it was just the nature of Brock's circle or the circle of the wealthy.

But I longed for something genuine, longed for it in a way I never had before. Not until I'd lost the man I thought I wanted, not realizing how wrong I'd been about what was and wasn't good for me.

I caught a glimpse of it then, a whole other life, like the fluttering of a curtain behind which another world existed. One where my smiles were effortless, where there was no pretense. Only the simple honesty of connection.

It was alien, that world.

It was a dream, that world.

And then the curtain stilled, shutting off the vision, leaving me only with myself and the ghostly glimmer of what I'd seen.

Ivy hooked her arm in mine. "I'm gonna use so much garlic salt, no one will come within five feet of me for a week."

With a laugh, I leaned into her, waving at Tess, then Kash, all dark hair and uncomplicated smiles. And I smiled back, that glimmer flickering again like a shard of glass in the sun.

Ivy tugged me toward the front, chattering about pizza with enough gusto that by the time we reached the door to the shop, my stomach growled like a wild animal. I pressed a hand to it, chuckling.

"God, don't you eat?" she said, pulling her coat as tight as she could around her belly. The seams didn't come close to touching.

"Of course I eat."

"It's just that you're so skinny."

"You just say that because you're so not skinny."

"Hey!" She pinched my arm, eliciting a yelp. "That's two fat jokes in five minutes. Not cool."

"Well, you skinny shamed me, so we're even."

She rolled her eyes.

"By the way, I forgot to thank you for telling Kash all my business. What the hell, Ivy?"

She flushed, lips set. "Well, I was trying to explain to Tess, and she kept defending Brock for not giving you orgasms. I needed a tiebreaker, and Kash always gives the best advice."

I skidded to a halt, pulling her backward with an oof. "You told him about the orgasms?"

"Well, yeah. Isn't that what he said?"

"You think Kash talked to me about orgasms in the greenhouse? Jesus, Ivy! He told me he was sorry about Brock!"

"Oh. Well ... I mean, I'm not sorry."

My mouth popped open, brows stitched together. "You bitch."

"What? I'm not," she said smartly, folding her arms. "He agreed that *zero* missed orgasms was the gold standard for men who aren't assholes."

I groaned, pressing my hands to my face for one brief moment of privacy. "I cannot believe you."

"Really?" she challenged.

Another groan. My hands dropped to my sides, and I straightened up, not taking her traitor arm again. She could waddle on her own.

"Oh, come on, Lila."

I kept walking, knowing she couldn't keep up.

"Wait up. I'm sorry, okay?"

At that, I stopped, turning in wait for the rest, one brow cocked.

"I'm just ... I'm so fucking *mad* at Brock. It's no secret I've always hated him—"

I snorted a laugh at the understatement.

"But Lila, what he did is unforgivable and on so many levels. I'm just mad. And it made me mad that Tess didn't automatically agree with me. I didn't mean to embarrass you. I'm sorry."

I sighed, softening at her expression, which was mushy and looked like she might cry. "It's all right. But if you could maybe refrain from discussing my orgasms with Kash Bennet, that would be great."

She sniffled, smiling. "Deal."

Linking arms again, we started for the pizza window. I could already smell the garlic, and my tastebuds exploded in anticipation.

"Have you thought about a rebound?" she asked carefully.

"I haven't even thought about where I'm going to live, never mind dating."

"Nobody said date," she defended. "But maybe dick is more important right now than a permanent address."

"Oh my God."

"What? You know I'm not wrong. It doesn't have to be serious or anything, just a romp. A frolic. A cavorting rollick with an uncomplicated penis."

"Ivy," I said on a laugh. "Stop it."

She rolled her eyes. "You've always underestimated the power of a good, frisky roll in the hay. I mean, we even have literal hay in storage at the greenhouse."

I gave her a look.

"I'm just *saying*," she insisted innocently, "that you have options."

The look didn't quit.

"And that getting some hot beef could solve a lot of your problems."

"Like what?"

"Like … you could relax. Blow off steam. Loosen up. Live a little. You might even *laugh*. Like, unprompted. It could be a medical miracle: a solid injection of vitamin D, and you're a brand new woman. Take it from a retired floozy—what you need, my dear sister, is a rebound."

Unbidden, the vision of Kash leaning on his shovel with that smirk on his face filled my thoughts. For a moment, I fantasized about him taking off his shirt, imagining the naked truth of his musculature. Imagined him licking those wide lips of his, imagined the scent of him, the warmth of him, the strength of his arms, the breadth of his hands. His lips would be soft and demanding all at once, hot and slick and—

"Oh, they have supreme today!" Ivy cheered, yanking me out of my reverie and into the line. "God, it must be my lucky day. Come on, Lila. You're gonna get the spicy sausage, aren't you?" She waggled her brows, prompting a too-loud laugh from me and a couple of glances for disturbing the pizza peace.

"I'll take all the sausage, please."

At Your Service

LILA

The day was eternal.

Meetings stacked on meetings, including a rush to sit with the Femmes through band auditions, which all five of them had opposing opinions on, resulting in zero choices made. To top it off, fall was in full effect—it had rained all day, resulting in filthy shoes and my ankles dotted with muck despite my constant attention. I'd donned my knee-length peacoat, the deep emerald hiding proof of dirt and protecting the white pencil skirt and tailored shirt I'd decided on today, a risky choice given the weather circumstance.

Four days had passed since I'd seen Kash, my longest stretch away from the shop in weeks. I wondered immediately why I'd kept count. Maybe it was because I was on my way to Longbourne, though I was set to meet Tess—Kash probably wouldn't even be there. I wouldn't admit under duress that I hoped he was, but I did hope. It was stupid and probably irresponsible, but I wanted to see him.

Those days without seeing him had crawled by at the speed of a legless zombie.

I sighed, using a baby wipe from my bag to clean off my shoes and ankles *again*. The cab rumbled along, radio tinny and distant through the little plexiglass window, rain pinging the roof, brushed from the windshield in rhythmic sweeps. The sound lulled me, exhaustion blooming in my chest, creeping down my arms to draw me into sleep.

My fatigue was total, existing well beyond the physical. It necessitated a lot of energy to pretend like I was fine, like my life hadn't been turned inside out like a lonely, errant sock. I longed to have a place where I could be alone just as much as the thought of being alone terrified me. Without the need to hold myself together for the sake of those around me, I worried I'd slip into a state I couldn't control.

The taxi swung toward the curb outside Longbourne, and as I paid, I weighed my options on how to get from the cab to the shop efficiently. My umbrella seemed a silly choice just for the few feet to the door, but my hair would appreciate it, since I'd made a secondary poor choice to leave it down today. Then again, I'd be heading straight for a hot shower from here, and I'd only be inside for a few minutes, just long enough to get Tess to sign the liability forms for a venue and to approve a scope of work agreement we'd finally completed.

Umbrellaless it was.

I gathered my bag and umbrella, taking a breath to brace myself before opening the door and stepping out. As quickly as I could, I got both feet on the curb, turning to shut the door before bolting toward the shop. I was nearly in the inset threshold when a sheet of water overran the gutter and fell like a curtain on me.

I froze in shock, furious and freezing and soaked with filthy rainwater, hair dripping and coat a sponge. One breath, slow and controlled, and I found my wits, stepping into the nook to open the door to the shop, marked with a Closed sign. The sound of rain was muffled when I closed the door, the bell ting-a-linging cheerily, mocking me. Rain patted the tiled floor as I stood in the dark shop in icy indignation.

I headed to the back, frozen to the bone, peering back into the workspace for Tess. My only thought beyond my state of undoing was how desperate I was to put this day to bed and move on. Surely, I'd feel better after a hot shower and a good night's sleep. Surely, tomorrow would be better.

"Hello?" I called, twisting my cold hair into a rope, wringing it out as I walked toward the back.

"Back here," a deep baritone voice that was definitely *not* Tess's called.

I faltered but kept trucking to the back, hoping I could find something to dry my hands off with so I could extract the paperwork from my leather attaché without ruining it. Swiftly and as a diversion, I counted the minutes until I could leave, teeth chattering while I tallied it up. Twelve minutes should do the trick with time to spare.

I didn't know what I expected when I rounded the corner into the workspace. Luke maybe. Jett perhaps. But not Kash Bennet, sitting at a worktable, stuffing buds into plastic water tubes. They were so small, so delicate and feminine in his massive hands, and he handled them with gentle care and attention, as if they were precious. Considering he'd grown them from seeds, I supposed they were precious to him in a way they weren't to anyone else.

Kash glanced up with a crooked smile that immediately faded upon seeing the state I was in. His brows snapped together, and he was on his feet in a flash of motion.

"Lila? What happened?" He moved for a rack stacked with supplies, whipping a white towel and a flannel blanket off a nearby shelf before striding toward me.

"This is just the day I'm having," I said lightly, hands up in display, smart smile on my lips so I didn't cry.

He handed me the towel, tossed the flannel on the table, and stepped behind me. "Here, let's get you out of this." First, he took my bag, which he placed on the table as I dried my hair. Then, his hands closed over my lapels and slid them over the curve of my shoulders.

I stilled but for the tremors of cold, tossing the towel onto the table. Down my arms the coat slid. Instantly, I felt the heat of him behind me and resisted the urge to lean back into him, desperately craving that warmth from the depths of my icy bones. When he stepped away, cold overtook me, my clothes damp and cool to the touch as I curled my shoulders and folded my arms, cupping them to retain as much warmth as possible.

Teeth clicking, I dropped onto a stool and tried to regain composure. I forced myself to sit up straight, dropping my hands to my lap. My eyes found Kash hanging my coat, spreading it over two hooks and shaking it open as best he could so it could dry. When he turned, he looked even more concerned.

"Here," he said, reaching for the flannel. "You're freezing."

He unfurled it as he walked toward me and wrapped the blanket around me.

"Th-thank you," I said once the flannel was in my grip.

As his hands retreated, they lingered on my shoulders, testing the curve with his palm, then the span of my upper arms before falling away.

"I'm sorry your day was shitty."

"That's just status quo these days." I clutched the flannel, grateful for it.

"You need a win."

I huffed a laugh. "I need a win so bad, Kash."

"You drink tea?" he asked, his eyes dark as he looked me over.

I must have looked like I'd been drowned, my hair lank and waving in tendrils, my blouse wet—my white blouse. I gathered the blanket tighter to cover my breasts. "Tea would be w-wonderful," I said.

But he didn't seem to be paying much mind to my appearance. Dutifully, he crossed the room to an electric teapot and flipped the button to start it before rummaging through a box of teabags.

"Chamomile? Green jasmine? Orange rooibos?"

"Jasmine, please." I glanced at the table to the flowers he'd been putting into the flutes. "Are these for the wedding this weekend?"

"For the bouquet, yes."

"Where's Tess? I need her to sign some paperwork f-for me," I said, reaching for my bag, my twelve-minute plan gone but not forgotten.

"She had to get out of here, asked me to stay to meet you."

I frowned at my hands as I pulled the folio of papers out and a pen, setting them in front of Kash's stool. We were alone, which made me uncomfortable. Not because I was afraid of him, but because I could see the line and exactly when and how I might cross it, especially with him looking like he cared so much.

It'd been a long time since a man cared so much. Brock certainly hadn't, simply because he was too self-absorbed. Perhaps he'd bought the facade I'd crafted, the one that broadcasted that I didn't need taking care of.

But Kash saw through it, saw through to me. And the way that made me feel was dangerous.

The teapot rumbled as the water heated up, mug and teabag prepped and waiting. Kash, I realized, was watching me. Our gazes met for only a fraction of a second before he moved across the room again, back to that shelf of supplies.

Steaming mug in hand, he headed over with that smile on his face.

When he handed it to me, I took it, leaning over it like it was a flame. "Thank you so much. Really."

"It's no trouble. Come on, let's get you warm."

Immediately, I imagined him stripping me down and me

stripping him down and our naked limbs tangled together. But he cupped my elbow, jerking his chin toward the greenhouse.

I took his lead and slid off the stool, silently following him through the swinging doors.

Warmth hit me like summertime, humid and thick and tropical. The greenhouse was touched by moonlight, dimmed by the clouds and their deluge, but it was still there, a sweet glow over rows and rows of flowers and greenery and life.

A sigh slipped out of me. "Oh, that is so nice."

"It's climate-controlled, humidity-controlled, warm even in the thick of winter. Come on, we can sit back here."

I brought the mug to my lips, blowing on the surface of the tea to cool it a little before taking a sip. The crisp scent of green tea mixed with fragrant jasmine drew the tension from my shoulders, eliciting another sigh.

He stopped at the table in the back where we'd looked over the florals yesterday. But the buckets were all gone, moved up to the front so Tess could finish the arrangements, the table empty. He took a seat on one of the stools, and I sat next to him, hooking my heels on the bottom rung.

"Feeling any better?"

"I am."

"Tell me why your day sucked." He leaned against the side of the table, propping his head on his fist

"Well," I started, "I had a dozen back-to-back meetings, and my only meal was a hot dog in the back of a cab. I think I've had somewhere in the neighborhood of forty-two cups of coffee, which would explain my heart palpitations. The rain, getting soaked, sitting through hours of the Felix sisters heckling wedding bands. Shall I go on?"

His smile tilted. "They heckled the bands?"

I rolled my eyes at the memory, laughing softly despite my irritation. "Alexandra booed three of them. Sofia insulted one—she stood up, walked to the stage, and spent a solid ten minutes tearing them apart for any and everything she could come up with. I don't know how the saxophone player's mustache had anything to do with the merit of his musical skills, but when she called him a pedophile, he quit on the spot."

"Oh my God," he said on a laugh.

"They're a nightmare. During a cover of a Four Tops song, Natasha hitched up her skirt and twerked for the cameras. To 'Baby, I Need Your Loving,' for God's sake. I would have been impressed if I hadn't been horrified. On TV, her snatch will be blurred out, but in real life, I had a front row seat to two of her orifices I never wanted to see. Which is especially mortifying, given that my ex is intimately familiar with that particular region of her body."

The truth of it stung the second I spoke the words.

Kash's face darkened, his lips uncharacteristically flat, brows serious. "She's got to know what she's doing to you."

"Oh, I'm sure she's aware." I took a sip of my tea.

A noisy, angry breath through his nose. "Why would she do that? Why would she torture you that way?"

"Because that's what she does. She's the youngest of four attention whores. They're a circus, four gorgeous clowns with gags galore. Except instead of squirting flowers and hand buzzers, it's exhibitionism and insults. They're in constant competition with each other, and Natasha is queen. I suppose it's her right as the youngest. And they're rewarded constantly on social media and through their show for their shitty behavior."

"I've never watched it," he admitted. "Just never sounded interesting to me."

"Me neither. I mean, I've watched a few episodes because they're my clients and I thought I should give them a fair shake since everybody knows they're a shitshow. I wanted to judge them on their own merit. But I think the show has created a drama machine. Their audience craves it, and so they keep delivering. I just don't think assholes are funny. It's why I hate *Seinfeld*."

I watched him for a reaction. There was always a reaction—the admittance was blasphemy in some circles.

But Kash only smirked. "Well, they *are* all assholes."

"Thank you," I said, gesturing to him. "I just don't think it's funny to be a jerk. Call me crazy."

"I don't think you're crazy. Not about *Seinfeld* and not about the *Felix Femmes*." He paused. "How's everything else going?"

Brock. He meant Brock, and I let loose another sigh. "I don't know. I've got it all packed up in boxes where I can't see it in the hopes that I'll forget about it."

"And how's that working out?"

"Terrible. But what else can I do? Wallowing won't do any good. I'd rather keep trucking in the hopes that, at some point, it won't hurt so bad."

A flash of emotion shot behind his eyes, there and then gone. "What's been the hardest part?" he asked honestly, so sincere.

I answered instantly, before I had time to think, having already dissected and cataloged the entire affair. "The hardest part is being wrong. I was stupid to trust him. I should have known better. I could have avoided all this if I'd been smarter. If I'd paid more attention."

He waited for me to continue, but when I didn't, he said, "I think it's worth noting that the hardest part isn't losing him."

"It's not," I answered definitively. "I'm more confused about how I dated a guy with calf implants."

A laugh burst out of him, and I smiled at the sound, though my heart twisted.

"It just seemed right, you know? In my grand master plan of life, he was exactly the right man for me." My mind pulled that thread, adding, "Maybe that's been the *real* hard part, the truth under the truth. Realizing that the infallible plan was in fact fallible. That what I thought I wanted isn't what I wanted after all."

"As someone who seems to operate strictly by rule and plan, I can imagine that'd be hard," he said simply.

I was struck by the truth of his statement, a flick of a tether in my heart. It wasn't so much what he'd said, his observance no revelation, but in the way he'd said it. In the soft assurance of his face and his solid presence. For the first time in a very long time, I felt understood and heard, and by a man who didn't know me at all.

It was safety, I realized, and the feeling struck another chord.

"Ivy said I should find myself a rebound." It was a test, a gentle probing for a reaction.

It was offered by way of the warming of his eyes and the ticking up of one corner of his lips. "Did she?"

"She did," was my only answer. I took a sip of my tea, watching him over the rim of my mug.

"Well, they say the best way to get over somebody is to get under somebody."

A laugh, nervous and tittering, jumped out of me.

"You looking for volunteers, Lila?"

My laughter died at his directness. "That's silly," I hedged, certain I misread his meaning.

"Is it?"

I opened my mouth to oppose but closed it again. Then, I snagged a thought. "I'm not really in a place to make pragmatic decisions."

"On a rebound?"

"On much of anything. But yes, that too. How can I willingly involve someone in all of this? It wouldn't be fair."

"The biggest danger is to the reboundee," he said. "And I happen to be immune."

The proposition hung in the air for a moment, simmering between us. There was no mistaking his intention, and a shocking rush of *yes* whispered through me.

"Immune?" I asked quietly. "How?"

A pause. "I already know what things are between us and what they're not. You're not looking for anything serious, and I've never been one for the notion. The reason rebounds exist, why they happen so often, is that when you've been hurt, a distraction makes you forget the pain. And I've been told I'm an excellent distraction."

That smile, tilted and teasing. But his eyes were dark and full of promises.

He stood, closing the space between us with little more than a shift. My mug disappeared from my hand, placed on the table by his. But I hadn't seen the action—there was only Kash, towering and sturdy and *safe*. His smile faded as his gaze hooked on my lips.

"I can make you forget all about him," he promised. His hand, warm and rough, cupped my jaw, thumbed my cheek. "Is that what you want?"

My thoughts were a tangle, jumbled by his proximity. By the heat of him radiating into the chill of my skin, the damp of my hair. The scent of him sliding over me, around me, pulling me into him without thought or permission.

Something in my mind yelled through the fog to stop, to think. To make a pros and cons list, to be rational. But with Kash looking at me like that, holding my face like he was, none of it seemed to matter except for one question, the question he'd asked me.

Did I want to forget Brock? I pulled the thought from the mire, searched for my answer.

And that answer was clear and true as daylight.

"Yes," I whispered.

Deliberately, slowly, he framed my face with both hands, tilted it up to the sky. Moonlight burst around him in a halo, the sound of rain against the glass of the greenhouse, the musky scent of earth and fragrant flowers. The moment held, quiet and still. And just when I thought maybe he'd changed his mind, he shifted, slanted, tilted my face with tender force, and brushed his hot lips to mine.

A sharp, simultaneous intake of breath, the kiss first a brush, then a seam, then a heady tangle of lips and tongues. We twisted together, relief palpable and anticipation tangible as I stood on shaky legs without breaking the kiss. My hands slid up his chest, over his shoulders, around his neck, into the silken depths of his hair. Our bodies were flush, his hand in the small of my back without knowledge of how it'd gotten there, holding me to him as if he couldn't get me close enough.

I was no longer cold. There in the circle of his arms, I was on fire.

Nothing about the kiss was delicate and yet it held a gentility, an exploring tenderness. His fingertips tasted my skin with exquisite demand, precise and deliberate as they trailed the length of my neck, the line of my jaw, the tender space behind my ear. With the slightest squeeze of possession, he tilted my face, angling to delve deeper into my mouth. And with a sharp breath through my nose, I did the same.

How long had I done without this? How long had I been denied wanting and being wanted? Had I ever? Or had I wasted my years with the wrong kind of men, for all the wrong reasons?

It's only that I hadn't known this existed.

That *Kash* existed.

Compliant and yielding, I held on to him, kissed him with feverish lips, with no thought as to what to do and no desire beyond what he could give me. When his hips pressed me against the table, I felt the weight of that desire, hot and hard. I breathed a moan into his mouth, triggering a flex of his hands—one on my jaw, one on my waist—hips shifting at the sound.

The hand on my ass moved to my thigh, gathered my skirt in crawling fingers, hitching it high. His fingertips licked at my skin as he tugged until the fabric was around my waist. Free at last, my thighs parted, making way for his hips to press that solid steel against the seam of my body.

A shock, hot and sharp, shot down my thighs, up my torso, eliciting a gasp that broke the kiss.

When my drunken eyelids parted, they revealed the sight of Kash looking down at me in the moonlight.

His big hand cupped my jaw, thumb stroking my bottom lip in a gesture of ownership, drawing a fluttering flex at my center.

Hot was my desire, pent up and tugging at its chains. And Kash held the key in the palm of his broad hand.

Down my neck that hand moved, down the V of my shirt to unfasten the button between my breasts with a flick of his fingers.

His voice was thick, rough. "When was the last time he made you come?" Flick, and another button undone, along with my composure.

I rolled my hips into his. "A month," I whispered. "Maybe two."

"Unacceptable," he breathed, angling for my lips, his broad hand sliding into my gaping shirt to cup my breast, his calluses snagging on the silk, but I didn't care. He could shred it to bits if he wanted to.

He could do anything he wanted to.

And as if he heard the thought, he did. A frustrated groan preceded him hooking me around the waist. An answering yelp of surprise as my legs wound around his waist. A giggle against his lips before I kissed him, arms circling his neck to hang on, though my grip was useless. He palmed my ass with one hand, which was strong enough to hold me up while he snatched the flannel blanket off the stool with the other. Gravity shifted as he turned, bouncing as he walked me somewhere unknown, and I didn't care where. I was too busy tasting him, too occupied with his lips, too absorbed with cataloging the way he felt against me.

He stopped, tipping me gently, loosening his grip to encourage me to let go of him, but I didn't. I flexed my arms and legs, keeping me resolutely locked around him. Kash laughed into my mouth and popped my bare ass, the snap and sting earning him what he'd asked, though he didn't let me go until my feet were on the ground.

"Stay," he commanded like I was a puppy.

But didn't tell me to be still. I watched him spread the blanket between rows of blush chrysanthemums, undoing my blouse and shucking it. I dropped it without care onto the dirty concrete and shimmied out of my skirt, impatient and aching.

He was right—it was unacceptable that I'd been unattended

for months. That the man I had been with couldn't be bothered with my pleasure, only his own. That I had to take what I needed, frustrated and ignored.

Kash turned and stilled, his eyes dragging down the length of my body, then back up. Hungry appreciation zinged between us. His empowered me. Mine was heavy with the desire to get his clothes off, including that T-shirt, which I only just noticed said, *Gardening Makes Me Thorny*, framed by classic American tattoo roses and thorns.

I drew my bottom lip into my mouth. When it came to Kash, gardening made me thorny too.

"Take that off," I ordered, nodding to his shirt.

His lips flicked into a smile, his eyes locked on mine as he reached over his shoulder to grab a handful of shirt. He pulled it off in what felt like slow motion, first exposing the deep ridges and flats of his abs, the canals of his hips. The breadth of his chest, the discs of his pecs. Down one arm and over his head, his eyes instantly connecting with mine again. And then, the shirt was gone.

"What else do you want, Lila?" he asked, a challenge behind a sideways smile.

Panting. I was panting, too hot, too eager to contain so much heat. "Fuck me up," I said without thought or care beyond that moment.

"Oh, I plan to," he promised, devouring the space between us to scoop me into his arms and kiss me in the same motion.

With a twist, he spun me, backed me toward the blanket, laid me down. Pressed me into the ground with his weight, crushing and restraining and the closest thing to perfect that I could imagine. His skin was on fire, smooth and silken over hard muscle, and my hands learned every curve, every valley. Every ridge and every dip. His kiss deepened, hips rolling, body pinning me, hand sliding from my jaw to my neck, gripping it only strong enough to keep me still. And there his hand stayed, though his lips strayed down, collarbone to breastbone to breast. Hot mouth over peaked nipple, soaking the silk between tongue and flesh. Without permission, my back arched in offering, neck held to the ground, hips grinding his torso, hating the distance between us. But he didn't linger. He released my neck, hand taking the place of his tongue on my breast, teasing my nipple tighter as he moved down my ribs, spending a long moment acquainting himself with the dip of my belly button.

Flashes of what he was about to do burst behind closed lids. Anticipation, the tip of my desire aching in wait for connection. And that wait was excruciating as his nose dragged the flat of my stomach, down the nude silk of my panties, around the peak of my hood, circling the tender flesh before trailing down, down the line of me. The flat of his tongue in the valley of my body, wide lips closing to draw me into his mouth.

My lungs expanded with a tear of pleasure, contracted with a sigh of release. Heavy lids crept open, seeing first the moonlit glass of the greenhouse, smattered and streaked with rain. Down to the lush mum blossoms dotting a thicket of green. Down to the black of Kash's hair, my pale fingers buried in his locks. The draw of his brows in concentration, the crescents of black lashes against his cheeks. The flat of his strong nose.

The pink of his swollen lips. The glimpse of his tongue. The anatomy of my body, every detail visible through the drenched silk.

I whispered his name, and his lids fluttered open, hand hooking my thigh, hitching it wide. His other hand trailed the hem of my panties next to his mouth, slid underneath. Found my heat, spread me open. Slipped inside.

My head lolled, lids too heavy. His hands grazed my breasts, annoyed to find them sheathed. Clumsily, impatiently, I shifted to unhook my bra, sliding it off my arms, tossing it away. And then, Kash was impatient too. He broke away, leaving the wet fabric cool and sensitive without the hot pressure of his mouth. Square fingers hooked in the hips of my panties and tugged them down my thighs, over the bend of my knees, off my feet, gone.

I thought he'd nestle himself where he was but felt the heat of him over me just before he kissed me, lips salty and insistent. But only for a moment—he wanted something else.

My hands were in his hair again, drawn there like they were meant to live in the lush tresses of darkness. I watched through slanted lids as he closed his eyes and paid homage to my breasts, his fingers tracing the curve, cupping their weight, testing it in discovery. Lips closed over my pale nipple, the sweet pinch of his gentle teeth, the sweep of his tongue. And then, down he went again.

I mewled, not wanting foreplay or fingers or tongues. I wanted *him*, every single inch of him inside every space I contained.

He paused at the sound, slowing his pace, teasing my center with one, broad fingertip. "You're impatient," he rasped.

"Please," I whispered as he lowered his torso, settling between my legs. "It's been too long. I don't need all that."

"I disagree," he said, hot breath against my core, palm spread over the flat of my stomach, legs spread and resting on his broad shoulders.

And the moment his lips closed over me, I disagreed too.

My awareness shrank to the point where he was latched to me, my nerves zinging toward the point of contact. Heat in my thighs, pooled low in my belly, a drawing from deep within me with every flick of his tongue, every stroke of his fingers. My hips flexed into him, against him, and he met every move with equal and opposite force.

Equals and opposites.

He gave, and I took. And as he gave, he took his pleasure— the rumble of his moan into me, the tremble of his shoulders, the blind, wild intensity in which he shifted his jaw, gripped my thigh, tasted me as if it were for himself far more than for me. As if he were the lucky one and not me, which was the boldest of lies.

It was a slow worship of my body, exaltation delivered by his tongue and hands. The tight drum of my heart battered my ribs with every second. My lungs locked, neck extending in offering. My back arched, thighs taut and shaking. His mouth—*his mouth*—with its own design, its own directive. The gathering of my senses to the place where we were joined. With a hard, deep draw, I came like thunder, a dark, rumbling division of self, a separation and conjoining at once.

The stop-start of my heart marked the beginning of the fall back to myself, galloping pulse slowing to a trot, then a lazy, deep shuffle as his tongue traced slow circles in my rippling flesh, a savoring. My fingers relaxed in his hair, smoothing toward his ears, settling for his shoulders as I rose, whispering his name. The sound drew him from the place he'd occupied in his mind and between my legs, arms shifting to plant his hands on either side of my hips as he rose, meeting my lips with a crash of desire. My fingers found his face, traced his jaw, splayed the angles, savored the scrape of his stubble against the softness of my palms. And my lips delighted in his, gratified and pliant and desperate for more.

The kiss broke with the roll of his forehead against mine, breath heavy and mingling, eyes closed, my hands on his face, his body hovering before me on hand and knee.

"You were right," I said.

He backed away so he could see me, one brow arched to match his tilted smile. "I usually am."

I laughed, shoving one massive shoulder uselessly.

"You gonna tell me what I was right about?"

"If you're going to tease me, I might make you work for that answer."

That brow climbed higher as he inched closer. "Careful what you wish for."

And when he kissed me again, it was with the determination that he'd get the job done well.

He forged forward, laying me down with the motion, settling between my thighs but keeping his hips away.

A flash of petulance sparked in me—did he not want me as

badly as I wanted him?—before I realized he still had jeans on. And, lips in motion, my hands slid down his body and to his belt.

He shifted into my hands at the jingle of his buckle, then the flick of his button and zip of his pants, and my hands slid into the V, reaching for him until both hands were full. He thrust into my hands, his crown brushing my belly, his body still too far away. One hand stayed where it was, stroking the length of him, testing its size, and the other hand slid around his hip, hooking the waistband to give it a tug.

It barely moved—his ass was too big and round and strong for a casual slipping off of pants. A chuckle from his nose before he broke the kiss, his hand moving to my face, then my collarbone, then my breast in passing. He knelt between my legs, his eyes roaming my body as his hands did their work. And I watched those hands, hands that tilled earth, harnessing it to grow what he wished. Strong, square hands with long fingers and rough palms that rid him of his jeans, but not before he pulled a condom out of his wallet.

And there he was, every naked inch of Kash Bennet. Corded thighs dusted with dark hair. Narrow hips with hard ridges. Those hands tore open the packet, griped his base, rolling the condom down with a swift stroke and an answering pump. My pulse fluttered, breasts rising and falling rapidly, heavy and aching. An echoing ache deep in the very core of me, a drawing of muscles that knew how he would feel in their grip and who needed to feel it.

Needed him.

But not before he descended, pressing the full length of his body against the full length of mine, lips on a track for mine, undeterred. This kiss was different—deeper but not by force. By weight of emotion, of desire. It was reverent anticipation, quiet demand. It was a reckoning, a calculation of map points—mine and his—and the determination to close that space by the quickest means: a line.

And that line between us would be breached, or so help us both.

That kiss was a meeting, a linking of self, a connection of body and of hearts. It was chemistry, alive and deep, the programming unbreakable. And I should have been afraid of it.

Stupidly, I wasn't.

The thought faded with the slip of his tongue and the feel of his fingers in my hair. The weight of his body, the pleasurable helplessness of mine. His immense thigh nudging mine wider, the shift of his hips. The slick press of his crown against the hot center of me. The break of the kiss, the brush of our noses, our foreheads. The sound of our breath, thick with anticipation.

A flex of his hips, and he sank into me.

A gasp from my lips. A trembling breath from his.

Our bodies locked, frozen in a long moment of fullness and completeness.

His body rolled in a knowing, willful wave, pulling out only to fill me up again with a jolt. Another wave, a flex and release, and he pressed the place I needed him so desperately with a slam and a grind. I shifted beneath him, wanting to meet him, match him, but I found immediately that he knew better than I did. That he could do exactly what I needed without my help. And that he didn't *want* my help. Kash fucked me like he had something to prove—not to himself and not *to* me. *For* me. That this was what it should be, that I should settle for nothing less.

And I let him teach me the lesson as he saw fit.

His arms caged me, fingers in my soaked hair, lips on mine. I swallowed his breath, felt the thump of his heart through the drum of his chest. His body waved, and I rode that wave, every crest, every deepening of pressure, every speed of rhythm bringing me closer.

I broke the kiss, turning my face to the sky, hanging on to him like an anchor in a storm. But he was the storm, unbridled in my arms, raw and wild and beautiful. His focus was a devouring of me, a feasting for him, the delivery of my pleasure too great for him to contain. And that consuming pleasure he felt consumed me. He surged in me, and overcome, I surged in answer. And we were both capsized.

We came together, a cry from my lips and a rumbling groan from deep in his chest, our bodies riding those waves until they were slaked, slowing at the shore.

His lips were buried in my neck, kissing sweetly, slowly. But I needed those lips on mine so I could say what I needed without words. So I could explain the depth of my gratitude and appreciation for every second with him in the best way I knew.

I turned, angling for him, and he granted me what I wished, just as I'd known he would. I held his face, kissed him with all my heart, hoped he understood.

When our lips finally slowed, he broke the kiss, backing away to smile down at me. His big hand smoothed my hair.

"Did I earn my answer?" he asked, his voice gruff but the rest of him smooth as a river stone.

"You were right. You are an excellent distraction."

He laughed, wrapping me up in his arms to twist us to our sides. "Like I told you once before—you tell me when and where to be, and I'll be there. Ready and at your service."

"So, tomorrow?"

Another laugh, this one deeper, truer. "Tonight. Tomorrow. Next week. I'm here for you, Lila."

The way he'd said it twisted my chest, that familiar longing. The want to find someone who would *always* be there for me. But I smoothed that twist and smiled at my salvation.

"Tomorrow. But next time, it's on Egyptian cotton."

"What?" he asked teasingly, brushing a lock of hair from my cheek. "Cement and dirt aren't your thing? Never woulda guessed."

"I'm just full of surprises, Kash Bennet."

"Oh, I never doubted that for a second," he said with a smile before kissing every last worry away.

Absolutely Filthy

KASH

"**L**et me help you with that."

I stepped into Lila, taking her skirt's zipper from her hands, pressing a kiss to the curve of her naked shoulder. When she was fastened, my hands slid to her hips, and she turned around.

She wore a smile and not much more, her eyes warm, her hair drying in the softest of tendrils. I'd just spent the better part of an hour with those strands wound around my fingertips and our limbs tangled up, just talking. And I had gotten my wish after all.

Lila Parker, unraveled. Giving and forgiving. Sighing and soft and supple.

I knew she was in there, I thought as I thumbed her chin, raising it so I could kiss her. And I counted myself fortunate for having been able to see it.

I only hoped I'd have the opportunity to see that side of her again.

She sighed when I broke away, her eyes opening lazily. "When can I see you again?"

"Whenever you want."

A slow smile brushed her lips. "Tomorrow?"

I pulled her a little closer. "Whenever you want," I whispered again and kissed that smile off her lips.

Another sigh when I ended the kiss to gather her shirt off the ground and help her into it. I stepped in front of her again to button her up, mourning every sliver of skin as it disappeared. She let me fasten those buttons in a satisfying act of submission, her arms threading around my waist as I reached the top.

"I...I've never really done *this* before," she said with endearing timidity.

"Well, lucky for you, I'm a pro."

"Are there rules?"

"Not really. It's whatever you need it to be, and people don't really...talk to each other. They just fumble around it until something happens. Or doesn't happen for long enough to bail."

A pause. "That sounds exhausting."

"It is," I said on a laugh.

"There are really no rules? Not even like...unspoken things everyone is supposed to know?"

"Would you feel better if there were?"

"Maybe," she answered with a smile.

"All right. Let's start with frequency."

"How about...never more than two days in a row."

"And on the third day, we rest."

She chuckled.

"Spending the night, on or off limits?"

"Hmm. Off. I think? Keeps things more...casual?"

"Okay," I agreed without wanting to. "Dates?"

"Probably not. Flings don't go on dates, do they?"

I shrugged. "Not usually."

"All right, then. No dates."

"Done. Feel better?"

"Much. And I'm suddenly glad you're delivering the flowers for the wedding tomorrow," she said with a wicked smile.

"Why? Already planning your smoke breaks?"

"Maybe one or two. I'll get us a room at the venue."

"With those fancy sheets?"

She nodded, lips together in a smile. "And fancy pillows and an actual mattress."

"Sorry I got you all dirty," I said, fingering the collar of her white shirt where it was smudged with grime from its pile on the greenhouse floor.

"Please, get me dirty anytime you want." She stretched up on her tiptoes to press a swift kiss to my lips, then turned, tucking in her shirt.

I watched, greedy for every detail, every movement as she flipped one heel with her foot and slipped into it, then the other, her legs elongating, calves engaged to keep her upright in those shoes. She twisted her hair self-consciously, looking away.

"God, I must look a mess. Do I have makeup all over my face?"

She swiped under her eyes nervously, endearingly. It was true, she had a little makeup flecked under her eyes, but I'd already thumbed away what she'd have been worried about but for the bit of smoke under her lashes. The rain had washed the rest away, leaving her fresh-faced and gorgeous, maybe more so than I'd ever seen her.

Maybe it was because I'd witnessed her vulnerable, her hair unkempt and natural, the gentle smudge of black under her eyes throwing the pale of her irises into high relief. Those eyes, so big and gray, were all-encompassing, unavoidable. Undeniable.

"You're beautiful," I said without hesitation.

Her laugh was small and self-deprecating, her hands twisting her hair again, this time into a knot that almost immediately slipped loose. She sighed, stuffing the last of her shirt into her skirt.

"Leave it down." In two steps, I was in front of her, smoothing the remnants of the knot, slipping my hands into her hair to shake it loose. "I like it like this."

Her palm rested on my chest, her chin rising to meet my gaze. "That doesn't surprise me."

"Hey, don't get me wrong—I'm a big fan of you all trussed up, your hair all shiny and your suit all white. I've just been wanting to undo you, to see you like this."

A pause, her eyes bright and searching. "And did I disappoint?"

"Never," I whispered against her lips before taking them. I kissed her too long, long enough that I contemplated unwrapping her, undoing her again.

When I ended the kiss, she sighed longingly enough to set a smile on my face.

"Tomorrow night seems a long way away," she said, her fingers twiddling the collar of my shirt.

"I'll see you in the afternoon. And if you want, I can hang around for the event. I'll bring a real shirt with me and everything."

"Wear a tie, and I'll let you tie me up with it."

"Can I get that in writing?" I made the old joke with a pulse in my pants that once again had me considering the ways I might keep her here with me.

But she laughed with a flash of bright teeth and a streak of genuine joy. "Tell me where to sign."

"Right here." I tapped my lips, and she obliged with a kiss.

When she released me, she glanced up at the leaded glass panes of the greenhouse roof. "It stopped raining."

"Good. You won't get pneumonia. Can I walk you home?"

Another happy sigh. "No, I think I'll enjoy a minute alone before I see Ivy. Are you ... are you okay if I tell her? About us?"

"Sure, so long as she doesn't get all nosy about us."

"I can't promise that," she said on a laugh, followed by a pause. "What should I tell her we are?"

My heart lurched. "Whatever you want us to be."

"Easy. Uncomplicated. Casual. No strings, no expectations."

"I can do all those things."

"It's just that I haven't been single in a long time," she continued, her nerves plain and bare despite her efforts to keep them tamped down. "A few weeks ago, I lived with a man. Technically, I sort of still do—I still have a few pieces of furniture there. I don't have my own place, and I'm not even sure how I feel about relationships, never mind—"

"I can do all those things," I repeated a little slower. "You don't need to explain."

She relaxed in my arms. "Thank you."

"Anytime," I said and meant it.

This was my specialty—providing a diversion. I'd trained my whole adult life for this. I could be Lila's soft place to land after falling like she had. I could catch her, give her comfort.

I ignored the fleeting thought that I could give her more, if she wanted it. But the truth rang eternal—I knew what things were and what they weren't. I knew that in this scenario, I could be the one to get hurt if I found myself dumb enough to get my feelings involved. So I'd enjoy Lila when I had her, and I'd let the rest go, for her sake and for my own.

I'd take what I could get.

And I'd keep on pretending it would be enough.

LILA

I kissed him goodbye one final time before he nudged me out the door of Longbourne, his hair perfectly ruffled and his lips swollen from kisses.

As I walked away, I checked my phone, realizing it'd been *hours* of kisses. I felt like I'd blacked out and lost time, unable to parse the passage of time and the state of my person—disheveled, untwisted, loose and lighter than I'd been in a week. A year. More maybe.

Kash had erased my brain like a whiteboard. I could barely remember what I'd been so consumed with a few short hours ago. God, old me was uptight. Past Lila was a drag, and new, improved Lila was bold and wise and happy.

Happy.

After the last few weeks, the sensation shocked me. Intoxicated me. The old adage was right—the best way to get over someone *was* to get under someone else. Preferably someone hotter, with a substantial ass and a smile that turned my ovaries into a toaster oven, who treated me like his sole purpose in life was to give me orgasms. Piles and mounds and dump trucks full of orgasms and kisses and smiles and touching of all the skin, all the muscles.

All the Kash.

I strutted up Bleecker without care that I probably had mascara all over my face and my hair looked like a dirty mop. Because Kash made me feel like a million and one bucks. And tomorrow night, he'd do it again.

And if I was lucky, again and again.

I wasn't even myself, and I couldn't find it in me to care. And why should I? All my life I'd done what I'd thought I should rather than what I wanted—Brock might have been right in that—but that first shot started a war in my heart, and there was no going back. There was no undoing it, no unringing of the bell. I was the new and improved Lila who damned the rules and did what she pleased.

Presently including Kash Bennet.

God, he was perfect. Attentive in ways that had left me flushed, not just for what he'd done to my body, but in the small ways he made me feel like the only woman on the planet. Buttoning my shirt with care. Holding my face like it was porcelain in his palm. That look in his eyes that promised he could be whatever I wanted, whenever I wanted him.

And oh, how I wanted him. After being without for so long, I didn't think my body would be slaked so easily. Already I could see our 'day off' looming, and felt like a hoarder, vowing to stockpile as much Kash as I could tomorrow night to hold me over.

Tomorrow. It seemed like a lifetime until tomorrow.

Up the building's stairs I floated like a loose balloon, and through the front door I went, smiling like I'd just learned how.

At my entrance, Ivy and Dean froze in the kitchen, dumbstruck as they looked me over.

"Hello," I chirped, setting my bag on a dining chair.

Dinner sizzled in a pan, neglected by Dean, whose dark forehead furrowed, spoon midair, head cocked like a bird. Ivy blinked, dishes in hand and blue eyes narrowed in confusion, red hair piled on her head and belly so comically large, she was a marvel of physics. I wasn't entirely sure she wasn't about to tump over.

Her gaze combed over me, head to foot. "What happened to you? You're filthy."

I cleared my throat to stifle a giggle. "I got caught in the rain on my way to Longbourne."

"And?" she prompted, rolling her hand to get me to continue.

"And Tess wasn't there. Kash was."

My face must have said it all because Ivy gasped, hands flying to her open, smiling mouth and auburn brows brushing her hairline.

"Oh my God!" she squealed behind her fingers. "No! You didn't!"

Dean still looked confounded. "Didn't what?"

"Sleep with Kash Bennet," I said archly.

Ivy broke into a stretch of giggles, doing the Flashdance toward me, and I giggled right back, the two of us like a couple of teenagers who'd finally gotten kissed by Billy Mendez.

She stopped, holding her belly and laughing, her cheeks high and flushed. With her free hand, she snagged one of mine and dragged me in the direction of her bedroom.

"You're gonna tell me everything, unabridged."

"Congratulations?" Dean said as we passed, holding up his gigantic hand, which I slapped hard enough to sting in salute of the highest of fives.

"Thanks!" I kicked off my shoes with a thunk, trotting behind my sister, who moved much faster than someone in her state should be able to.

Once in her room, she whipped me like a derby girl toward her bed and closed the door.

"Kash Fucking Bennet!" she squealed, and we broke into giggles again.

I flopped on her bed with a sigh, staring at the ceiling with a stupid grin on my face. "You were right. I needed a rebound."

She climbed onto the bed with an oof. "I like being right. God, you know—Luke was historically the easiest of the Bennets to talk to, to get with. But Kash? I think Kash is hotter. Don't tell Luke I said so."

"I think it's that he seems unattainable. Luke *is* easy, but Kash has another layer to him, you know? What you see with Luke is what you get. But Kash plays it closer to the vest. He's more…I dunno. Mysterious."

Ivy snorted a laugh. "Yeah, Kash is a real international man of mystery with his pun T-shirts and dirty jeans."

I tittered. "Oh my God, seriously, what is wrong with me? I cannot stop giggling."

"You got nailed by a Bennet brother. This is a common side effect."

I rolled onto my side, propping my head on my hand, still fucking giggling. "He's just so …" I sighed, glancing at the ceiling, my cheeks warming at the memory of his hands on me. "Let's just say, I'm no longer upset that you told him about Brock

Bancroft and the Case of the Missing Orgasms. Kash used that information to his advantage."

"He would. He's resourceful like that. Tell me what happened!"

So I did, starting with my shitty day and getting hosed by the gutter to the promise he'd fulfilled of being a great distraction. A perfect distraction. Damn near perfect in general.

"He always was the most easygoing of the Bennets besides Jett, though Jett was too old for me," Ivy said.

I gave her a look. "He's like thirty, Ivy."

She held up her palms in defense. "Thirty-one, and I'm just saying—he had already graduated when I was a freshman. He might as well have been thirty then."

"God, I didn't expect Kash to kiss me like that," I mused, brushing my fingertips to my lips, the ghost of his kiss still there.

"Like what?"

"Like I knew the second his lips touched mine that he was about to ruin me. *Ruined*. I'm going to be ruined for life."

"So … you're not dating?"

"If by *dating* you mean *doing*, then *yes*."

She gave me a look.

"First of all, Kash doesn't *date*. He *does*. And secondly, I don't even have an actual bed to sleep in, never mind being stable enough to get into a relationship."

"Maybe he doesn't date because he hasn't found the right girl."

"Every woman's excuse to date every player ever."

"Kash isn't a player," she insisted, but before I could ask her to tell me why, she said, "And … I don't know. I'm curious. Could you ever see yourself with someone like him?"

I blinked, opening my mouth before I realized I didn't know how to answer. I liked Kash, genuinely and deeply, which I suspected was what'd made our romp so utterly perfect. He made me laugh just as easily as he made me orgasm, which was saying something. Kash made me laugh *a lot*.

But date in a permanent way? I hadn't considered it. He was the polar opposite of Brock—happy to be in the background, comfortable in a T-shirt and jeans, deferential and respectful. And for all those reasons, I wanted to say yes.

Of course, I didn't know him, not really. Not yet. And I wasn't ready to date, not with Brock barely behind me. Really, he was still in front of me and would be for a little while yet.

And so, rather than commit to either, I said, "I need easy and fun, and Kash has offered his services to the cause. Past that? Well, I can't even see past that. All I know is that was the most fun I've had in ages, and I feel like I just won a beauty pageant."

"Which is funny because you look like shit."

I pinched her arm with a laugh. "Hey. Kash said I was beautiful."

She yelped and rubbed the spot. "Well, he was blinded by the afterglow. You look like a high-class hobo. That's not Armani, is it?"

I sighed, not wanting to think about how I'd defiled my clothes. *Worth it.* "Barney's. Definitely could have been worse." I brushed a hand down my scuffed-up thigh. "My dry cleaner is going to make his rent on me now that I'm sleeping with a gardener."

Ivy laughed but watched me—I got the sense to see if I was being snobbish.

"I don't mind it," I clarified, "not even a little. There's something about a man who works with his hands, you know?"

"Oh, I do."

"I'm so used to these … I don't know. Soft, mushy men who have never done a hard day's work in their life. I mean, Brock gets weekly mani-pedis, for God's sake. How many manicures do you think Kash has gotten?"

"Laney's given him at least three, I'm sure. Anyway, there's nothing wrong with guys getting manicures."

"I'm not saying there is. I'm just saying, Brock doesn't even have workout calluses. He specifically uses machines that don't muck up his pretty hands. He sleeps in spa gloves, Ivy. Why didn't I think that was weird?"

"Because he was rich and ambitious and connected, and that made him seem powerful."

I shook my head. "Powerful is watching Kash Bennet shovel dirt with no shirt on."

"Testify." She held up one hand in praise.

"Kash is masculine in ways Brock could never achieve, not with all the muscle implants and all the money and all the power in the world."

"And hair plugs. Don't forget the hair plugs."

I groaned, flopping back on the bed. "I mean, they looked real."

"It's not his fault he got the bald gene," she said, stretching out beside me.

"Or the small-butt gene."

"He really did luck out in the jawline gene though."

"And the smile gene."

"Orthodontics."

I chuckled. "But the shape of his mouth was nice. And he was a good kisser."

"And he loved you once," she added quietly.

"He did," I admitted at an equal decibel.

"But he's a jerk."

"*Such* a jerk!" I said on a laugh. "And Kash isn't a jerk. Kash is goddamn *money*."

Ivy chanted, *Kash money!* over and over, swiping her hand at her palm like she was making it rain invisible Benjamins.

"*So* money," I agreed.

"When are you seeing him again?"

"Tomorrow. He's delivering the flowers for the Cabot wedding, and I'm getting us a room."

"Aww, no more greenhouse banging? Those are the best."

"I want to see what he can do with the comfort of a mattress. The back of my head still hurts from the concrete."

"Next time, just pony up."

"I would have this time, if he'd let me. He was on a mission. I wasn't allowed to do anything but take what he gave me. I've never been so happy to just lie there until it was over. I never wanted it to end."

"Well, you *were* thirsty. You'd been crawling through the Sahara for years."

"Felt like an eternity. And I made it to the oasis."

She lifted a hand for a high five, singing "Wonderwall."

I slapped it and sighed happily. "Thank you. For putting the idea into my head. For talking to Kash. I don't think it would have occurred to me without you teasing me about him."

"As your little sister, it is my joy and pleasure to tease you at leisure."

Dean called us in from the kitchen for dinner, and I hurried to the baby's room to change. I only owned a couple of T-shirts and was thankful for the foresight to have grabbed one, slipping it on with a pair of soft black sleep shorts. My hair I twisted into a messy knot, taking a moment in front of the antique mirror on the wall. I looked relaxed, casual, and not at all like myself. I didn't bother cleaning up my lids or brushing my hair. Not yet. A shower would wash it all away, put me back to myself.

But for now, I wanted to be that happy girl in the mirror. And with a sigh, I trotted out of the room, feeling fresher than I should have for being so filthy.

Blamo

LILA

"**A**re you listening?"

Addison's voice was a cloud in front of the sun, a darkening of my mood, which had, for the past five days, been impossibly happy. Five days capped off by three nights in Kash Bennet's arms, a place where I'd discovered things like time and worries didn't exist.

We'd so far stuck to the rules, but I couldn't pretend like it was easy. It was hard to watch him leave, disheveled and dead on his feet at two in the morning. It was painful not to see him on our days off, and I mean that—it was physically painful to subdue my libido after the drought I'd experienced with Brock. So painful that last night Kash and I spent half the night sexting. Which didn't count.

But the moment I'd stepped out of that elevator and into my office, my mood had dampened with no hope of sunshine until I walked out again.

Addison always had that effect on me.

"Of course I was listening," I lied, recalling the last sentence she'd said easily despite that I'd been daydreaming about Kash. "The Bayard wedding caterer double-booked, and you need me to take care of it."

Which meant money. Money was always the way to *take care of* these problems.

She watched me with jackal eyes. "Tomorrow at four-thirty, I need you to meet with the caterer for the Lennox wedding. I've got an important lunch date that I expect to run over."

A four-hour lunch was excessive, even for her.

But I smiled my best fake smile and said, "No problem."

Never mind that I had an entire day packed with my own event meetings. Never mind that I had less than twenty-four-hours' notice. Never mind that she would run me ragged so she could get day drunk with her *important* lunch date. God help me if that lunch date was with Caroline.

"Anything else?" I asked, desperate to get out of her office and on with my day, which was currently ticking by at an annoying rate from the clock on the shelf behind her.

"Oh, one other thing." She smiled, leaning back in her chair. "St. Patrick's found out about Angelika and Jordan and the confession booth and withdrew their invitation."

My temperature dropped, my skin cold as ice with nothing more than a heartbeat and that sentence. "What?"

"St. Patrick's is off the table for the Felix wedding. You're going to have to find another venue."

My thoughts raced with obstacles and chaos and a string of colorful expletives before landing on a solution. "Skylight. It's already booked for the reception, and they have space."

"You'll have to convince Angelika. You know how she had her heart set on St. Patrick's."

"Then she shouldn't have fucked her fiancé in the confession booth," I snapped. "Are they still airing the footage?"

"Yes. They kept the money in exchange for that indignity."

She watched me shrewdly. Today, her hair was pulled back in a ponytail so sleek and severe, she could have whipped you with it and drawn blood. "Oh, come on—you had to know it wasn't going to be that easy."

"I suppose I did," was all I could concede, too busy with the explosion that had just detonated inside my plans.

"I heard about Natasha."

Even the blood in my veins stilled. I didn't dare speak.

"It's a shame about Brock. What a catch."

The shot hit its mark. A bloom of pain spread in my chest. "She's welcome to him," I said with a wooden smile. "I caught a bigger fish."

Rule number one: never give Addison Lane any personal information, lest she use it to pike your head later.

"Is that so?" she asked with a knife smile.

It was shock and petulance that'd made me admit it. It was fear and regret of the admittance that had me reeling my words back in.

"It is, and thanks *so* much for asking after me," I said smartly, standing to let myself out. "Let me know if anything else comes up, would you?"

"I will."

And then I got the fuck out of her office like my Choos were on fire.

My brain was a flurry of questions and suppositions as I snagged my bag and laptop and headed out of the building for the bakery.

Plans ticked into place for the wedding, the shift not as catastrophic as it could have been. I'd have a thousand calls to make, not to mention the convincing of the Felix women that Skylight would be the right move for the wedding. At this stage in the game, it was the *only* move. I fired off a text to Sorina, asking for a meeting after the tasting, anxious to fix all that had come unraveled.

If they tried to tell me they wanted the Plaza, I swore I'd pitch myself out of a moving cab.

But Addison niggled at my mind. She knew. She knew about Brock and Natasha, and I wanted to know how. The only people who knew on my end were family and Kash. Of course, if one Bennet knew something, they all knew. But it wasn't like Addison hung around the Longbourne water cooler for the latest gossip. And I had no friends at our office, just a host of acquaintances.

It bothered me in the elevator, then in the cab. I hadn't seen Brock since I'd gone to pack a suitcase—when I went to really move my things out, he was gone, as requested. So how did Addison know? Had she seen some of my messages? Had I left something out that would have clued her in? I'd never ask, not willing to give her any more ammunition than she already had. Not willing to admit weakness to the one person I knew would exploit it without a second thought.

But I'd wonder.

In fact, I made it a point to obsess about it until the second I pulled open the door to the bakery and stepped inside.

The Femmes weren't there yet, thankfully and as planned. I shook hands with the owner and the producer of the show, who showed me to the table they'd set up. Beautiful china sat delicately on raw wood, each plate set with slices of cake and little signs noted with each flavor. Tess had sent over small arrangements of peach cabbage roses—I knew them on sight now, thanks to Kash—and they sat on the table in small cut-glass vases, scattered around the creamy, lush cakes.

We barely had time to exchange the minimum before the Felix entourage arrived like a fleet of swans, beautiful and tall and squawking. Instantly, the shop was too small. The crew alone would have filled the bakery. Add in the rest, and there was barely room to turn around, but Jennifer Lawrence had used this bakery for her wedding, and so must Angelika, whether there was space to film a TV show or not.

Four Felix sisters, their matriarch, and Jesus Jordan made their way to me where we greeted each other politely and professionally, air-kissing cheeks. Except Natasha. She barely looked up from her phone, which was just as well.

My gaze caught on her screen, noting she was on Instagram. And that was when it hit me.

Natasha. Addison knew because *Natasha* was probably posting all about him. I'd immediately unfollowed him everywhere the night I caught them together. I didn't follow Natasha because I had enough sense of self-worth not to torture myself. But I swear to God, I wanted to snatch her phone on the fucking spot and find out if I was right.

Of course, I valued my mental health more, and my job most. And so, I silently stewed with a saccharine smile on my face, ushering them to the table.

Cameras rolled, one to our side, one on the other side of the table. The Femmes were dressed fashionably in pink from the palest shade—Angelika—to the deepest fuchsia—Natasha, of course, ever the attention whore.

Things began without incident, the girls oohing and aahing over the beautiful cakes as the baker walked them through the samples. For a brief, wistful moment, I was dumb enough to let myself imagine they'd behave themselves for once.

Irreverently and in the middle of the baker's spiel, Natasha stuck her middle finger in one of the cakes, opening her artificially plump, perfectly lined lips. Her tongue extended just enough to provide a landing for that offensive digit covered in lemon creme, making eye contact with me as she sucked her finger off with a moan.

"God, you are so disgusting," Angelika shot.

Natasha laughed. "And you're so innocent? Who fucked in the confession booth at the church, *Angel*?"

"Girls," Sorina said without a single degree of heat.

Angelika's cheeks flushed dangerously. "And what about you?

Are you going to show your tits at the cake tasting? Everybody saw your bald vagina at the music hall. Don't want to hold out on the baker, do you? Or I guess you could just blow your fingers like a porn star the whole time we're here."

Sofia checked her nails, which were the exact same shade of pink as her dress. "As many sex tapes as she has, she's basically a porn star already. You know, except she doesn't get paid."

Alexandra, the second eldest, rolled her eyes. "Can't we go anywhere without you making a scene?"

Angelika and Natasha turned on her in unison.

"Please, Alex," Natasha said. "You got a waiter fired at lunch two hours ago."

"I have never seen a woman so ugly when she cries," Angelika added, shaking her head. "That's on *you*."

Sofia rolled her eyes and said lazily, "You're all whores, and Natasha is the worst. She thinks if she's enough of an exhibitionist, Drake will call her back."

"It worked for Hailey Baldwin," Natasha answered, deadly serious.

Sofia leaned in, cupped her hand to her mouth dramatically, and yelled, "*He's not gonna call you, skank.*"

Natasha's face wrenched up, nostrils flaring and eyes murderous. Her hand unfisted, reaching for the table.

For the cake, I realized with horror.

Natasha slung a handful of dark chocolate cake, which spun in what felt like slow motion, flicking white icing in a spiral on its track for Sofia's face. It hit its mark with a wet pat and a dark splat against her previously flawless makeup.

The entire room froze for a protracted moment.

When Sofia's eyes opened, they were hot with fury. With a carnal growl, she filled both fists with cake and let them fly, but before they reached their target—Natasha's face—she dodged. Cake splatted against Angelika's face with a one-two plop of red velvet and lemon cake, glued to her face with icing.

A harpy screech. A flash of motion. And the room dissolved into chaos.

Cake flew in streaks across the table, and the rest of us were held hostage by the size of the bakery. The only room was occupied by the Felix sisters, covered in cake and slipping on icing. The baker backed against the wall with her hands over her mouth and eyes tracking the maelstrom. Greedy hands reached for cake, teeth gnashed, faces unrecognizable, covered by dessert. Sofia lunged for Alexandra after a slice of strawberry cake made itself a new home in her ear, the sisters slipping with a squeak and a thud that left them wrestling on the ground. Natasha was on the run from Angelika—who shrieked her rage over her sister ruining her wedding—and with Olympian skill, she vaulted over the counter. She reached into the cooler with a maniacal grin, brows jackknifed in madness, and returned with a massive tiered cake.

Her laughter could only be described as a cackle, a hysterical, evil sound that stopped all three sisters dead. And she plopped the cake on the counter with a thud, reached in with both hands, and fired like a machine gun.

No one was safe from the onslaught, and Natasha had no aim, shooting blind. A slab of cake hit a camera lens. Sorina's cheek, her face whipping away like she'd been slapped. And then me, a thud to the chest, a cool slide of cake between my breasts and down the front of my shirt. When I glanced down, it looked like I'd been shot—red velvet had exploded from the point of impact in a burst.

I looked up with murderous designs, only to get a load square in the face.

The sound of her laughter rang like a fire bell in my ears as I scooped cake from my eyes. But I still saw red. I saw red as I slipped on baked goods, trying to get around the table and out of the way, as if I had somewhere to go. I saw red as I imagined shoving cake down Natasha's throat until she choked. I saw all the red—red fury, red cake, my red hair, which hung lank in my face, sticky with icing.

And I couldn't do one fucking thing about any of it.

My job description was very clear—I was to be a resource, liaison, and director for the Felixes. I was *not* to stop them or interfere with their show. I was not to do anything that might be taken as untoward, opinionated, or unhelpful. And I certainly wasn't allowed to throttle Natasha Felix on the checkered floor of the bakery. It took every iota of willpower that I possessed to endure the shitshow, and though it felt like half of my life, the cake slinging only lasted a few minutes. By the end, all four sisters were laughing, taking final potshots, giggling and swiping fondly at each other's faces.

The last cameraman standing got it all on film. The baker watched on, her face wide with terror and shock but lips in a grim line—she'd known what she signed up for. We all had.

With the glory came the train wreck. And the Felix train had just exploded in a fireball.

Sorina demanded they get up, and Angelika rose first, looking cowed. No one noticed the wad of cake in her hand until it was on a path for Sorina's mouth, then smeared to the chorus of laughter of her sisters and Jordan, who'd been pulled into the fray.

I made my way over to the baker, taking her by the shoulders to steer her away from the carnage. The producer followed, promising damages and a crew to clean it up, and I told her I'd call to reschedule before turning to the Felixes once more.

Sorina was laughing and apologizing, rescheduling our meeting to decide the fate of this cursed wedding while the girls stood and tried to right themselves. I endured it all with that liar's smile on my face, a hundred percent sure I didn't get paid enough for this. At least they got to slide into private cars and go to their penthouses. I had to endure what was sure to be a humiliating cab ride, followed by a humiliating walk through a hotel lobby, and then a humiliating entrance into the hotel room where Kash was waiting for me.

But somehow, I did endure the Felix Femmes' exit, along with their crew and several bodyguards who were smattered comically with cake and seemingly unaffected by the fact. Just another day at the office, I supposed.

I wagered *they* got paid enough for this. They probably made three times my very generous salary just to get slapped with cake and hang around, looking menacing.

The producer hung back, still trying to assuage the baker, who was squeaking her way through her shop, not listening to a word said. And with nothing left to be done, I gathered my things from the back and ventured onto the sidewalk.

The crowd staggered and parted at the sight of me, covered in cake and trying not to slip on whatever was stuck to the bottoms of my shoes. I held a sticky hand up and whistled for a cab, scraping dredge from my pants as best I could as a taxi pulled up to the curb. The cabbie eyed me, offended, as I got in.

Trust me, I am too, buddy.

And with a lurch, we were off.

Because, Reasons

KASH

I looked up from my sketchbook, smile on my face at the sound of the hotel room's door unlocking.

That smile probably should have fallen at the sight of Lila walking through the door, covered in cake and frosting, but it didn't. It spread despite my attempt to smooth it.

"Don't laugh," she warned as the door shut, heavy and loud.

She strode in on those long legs, tossing her bag and coat—which was inside out, I deduced to keep the wool clean of icing—on the desk. I brushed my lips with my fingertips to wipe my smile away and stifle the laugh she'd predicted.

"I wouldn't dare," I said lightly. "Wanna tell me what happened?"

She turned, peeling off her clothes in layers, ruined suit coat first. "The Felix sisters happened. Natasha specifically."

At that, my smile disappeared in earnest. I swung my legs off the side of the massive bed and stood, heading for her. "What did she do?"

Lila sighed, softening as I neared, as if my proximity alone dropped her shields. As if she'd been holding it all together by force and sagged at the knowledge someone was there to help.

"Nothing surprising," she said, looking up at me with those gray eyes of hers, her hair lank with muck. I smoothed it, not caring there was icing on my palm. "The girls got into a battle royale that devolved into disaster. I was caught in the crossfire."

One of my brows rose, and she sighed again.

"Okay, she was aiming for me, I'm sure. But it would have happened one way or another. That shop was too small for four Femmes to chuck cake without there being casualties."

"But still. Fuck her a little."

A chuckle. "Fuck her a little," she echoed. "And that's not the worst of it."

I frowned. "Oh God."

"You can say that again. The church found out about Angelika's exhibition in the confession booth and turned them out. So if you need me for the next month, I'll be dying under a to-do list I'll never complete."

"Don't worry," I said, reaching for her. "Everything will fall into place."

"I hope you're right." She started to slip her arms around my waist but stopped, stepping back instead. "Ugh, I'm filthy. I'm sorry."

"Usually it's me who's filthy. At least you'll taste good."

Another laugh, a flush of her cheeks. I thumbed one, dotted with cake.

Really, she was a mess. Icing had dried in flecks in her eyebrows, little chunks of cake peppering her neck, her cheeks. Her shirtfront was a crimson explosion in the shape of a V, the rest of her shirt, which had been protected by her coat, incongruently pristine.

My hands moved to the buttons, unfastening one with a snap.

"I'm sorry you had a shitty day," I offered, unbuttoning another.

"Knowing you'd be here to make me forget all about it is the only reason I didn't commit homicide in a cake shop today."

With a tug, I freed her shirt from her pants. "Is it always this bad?"

"Cake fight bad? No. Getting permanently banned from a church? Never."

"No, I mean … is it always this hard? It seems too much to ask to work with people like them every day."

"It is. Want to know something?"

"I want to know everything," I answered too honestly, sliding my hands into her shirt, around her waist.

"I hate my clients, and I hate my boss. But I love my job."

"That's confusing."

"I'm very conflicted."

My hands trailed up her ribs, traced the curve of her breasts, slipped over the caps of her shoulders, taking her shirt with them.

"If you hate them, why not quit?"

"I just told you why. I love my job."

"But you don't have to work for assholes."

She paused, seeming to consider. "I've worked my whole adult life for this. To work at this firm, with high-profile clients. We all have to put up with things we hate to be successful."

"True," I said as her shirt fell to the ground in a whisper of silk. "But at what cost?"

Lila frowned up at me. "It's temporary. Someday, I'll be in charge. *That* is the goal. Put in my dues and collect big later."

"But there are other firms. Other kinds of clients."

"But I don't *want* those," she insisted. "I want this."

"Even though you hate it?" My hands paused in the space between her pants and her ass, which sat firmly and roundly in my palms.

Her frown deepened, but she didn't speak.

"If you hate it, change it."

A scoff, coupled with a roll of her eyes. "I can't."

"Sure you can."

"No, I *can't*."

I smirked down at her. "How come?"

An impatient huff. "Because for the last decade, it's all I've dreamed of. Because I've busted my ass to prove myself, put myself through all the bullshit associated with that. Because this is my dream, hard or not. Because *reasons*, Kash, volumes and hoards of reasons."

I kept on smirking despite the pause she expected me to fill.

"All right, Mr. Disapproval, what about you? Is this your dream job? Is working in the greenhouse your calling, or whatever?" She deflected, and I let her.

"Would it offend you if I said I didn't have one?"

"Yes, it would."

I laughed, giving her ass a squeeze.

Her brow quirked. "You really don't have a passion?"

"There are things I enjoy, like sketching and growing things, sure. But passion's a strong word. Are you passionate about getting hit in the face with cake?"

"Not so much that part of it, but the Femmes are a package deal. A smelly, gross package that will end up with me being humiliated weekly on national television, but a package that's good for my career nonetheless. What I'm passionate about is the thrill. Spending months organizing something, bringing it all together to create a perfect moment. The joy of seeing that moment come to fruition and the joy experienced by the people I put it together for. It makes me feel like I did something great, something hard."

"It makes you feel accomplished. But is that your passion? Is it something you'd do if you didn't make a cent doing it?"

She was frowning again. "Is gardening yours?"

I shrugged, taking her arms around my neck for a ride. "Sure."

"That was convincing."

"There are a lot of things I love about it and nothing I hate. Other than getting bawled out by wedding planners."

That earned me a laugh. "You mean to tell me there's not one thing about your job you're loathe to do? I mean, aside from dealing with me."

I gave it the thought it deserved and answered honestly. "No, nothing."

"Even shoveling mulch?"

"Even shoveling mulch. I call it shoulder day and wear a bandana to cover the smell. Makes me feel like a cowboy."

She assessed me, eyes sparkling with amusement. "You know, I could see that. You as a cowboy. You don't belong in this world."

"No?"

"No. You could be a Gallic warrior or a Viking king or a cowboy. Brutish and wild, untamed. Size alone warrants the impossibility that you live in this time and not somewhere long ago, ruled by survival."

The compliment I kept, held it tight, slid it into my pocket to remember later. "I think I'd pick a cowboy. Always did like horses. Although I'd probably be terrible at guns and lassos."

"You'd learn," she assured me, smiling. "There's got to be something about your job you hate."

"Why's it so hard to believe?"

"Because it's impossible."

"Hate's just as strong a word as passion. I don't hate much of anything."

She inspected me, saying after a moment, "Tell me one thing you hate."

I broke my gaze to look over the top of her head at the wall, finally landing on something. "I hate when someone I love is hurt."

"That doesn't count."

I frowned, looking back down at her. "How come?"

"Because it's about other people, not you. Come on, what about something to eat? Like onions. Or mushrooms."

"No, I like both of those. I'm like a raccoon—I'll eat pretty much anything."

She shook her head at me in disbelief. "I cannot fathom this."

"Because you have so many opinions. Is it that hard to believe there could be another end of the spectrum?"

"Sure, but to hate *nothing*? That's just weird, Kash. Everybody has things they love and things they hate, and I aim to figure out yours."

I pulled her a little closer, smirking again. "What do you love to do that's not organizing things and bossing people around?"

She pinched me. "Did you just call me bossy?"

"No, I just called you a boss. It's how you get things done—you take charge. But I'm not letting you slide this time … what's *your* hobby? Something unrelated to your job that you love and hate."

"I don't really have time for much else," she admitted after a beat.

"Ever gardened?"

"Please, I kill everything I touch. Black thumb. I even killed an air plant, and all it needs to survive is air."

I chuckled. "Nobody's good at it until they learn. Come over, and I'll show you at the greenhouse."

A smile, slow and sweet. "All right."

I pushed her pants over the swell of her ass, and they fell, pooling at her ankles. "Don't wear white," I said, angling for her lips.

She started to laugh, but I swallowed it, kissed her deep. Her lips tasted like buttercream, eager and seeking, her hands ruffling my hair as we twisted together. The silk of her bra and panties were slick, catching on my callused fingers, but she didn't care for their well-being, and for that, I was glad. Because that silk in my hands had become one of my favorite sensations.

Deeper I kissed her, lips stretched and seamed, mouths wide, tongues searching. A moan into my mouth, rattling my tongue as it passed. Her thigh hitched, hanging on my hip in an effort to get closer to me, to press against my length. Less than a minute was all it took for the heavy heat between us to turn frantic.

She broke the kiss, lips swollen and breath loud, to look up at me. "I should clean up," she said like she hoped I'd object.

Which I did.

I kissed her again, too impatient to speak. It was a tasting, slow and light, tongues brushing, retreating, teasing and testing. All day, I had waited for this moment, to hold her in my arms, to feel that perilous click of rightness.

I should have run from Lila Parker at the first notice of that feeling. I should have let her go, having done my duty to distract her. But instead, I'd heedlessly indulged.

I hoped it wouldn't be my undoing. And I wished I cared if it was.

Half a step, and her ass was propped on the desk. I broke away to press hurried kisses down her neck, lips closing, tongue sweeping to taste the sweet remnants of cake. The weight of her breast filled my palm as I licked a path to the hem of her bra, to the peak of her nipple, the silk like second skin. Her fingers tightened in my hair, a sigh of pleasure, the link of her thigh around my waist. A thunk as a heel hit the ground.

My fingers trailed all the way down her leg to grasp her heel in my palm. I lifted, spreading her legs wider, fitting myself between them with a promissory grind of my hips. She gasped at the contact, and up I kissed to take those lips again while my hands relieved her of her bra, then, with a shimmy of her hips, her panties.

"Off," she breathed, tugging at my shirt.

Holding her still with my hips, I leaned back and shucked it, tossing it somewhere behind me.

When I looked down, the moment stretched, the details sharpening, collected in a breath that felt like an eternity. Lila stretched back on the desk, elbows propping her up. Her eyes were hot and hungry, scanning the breadth of my chest to my belt and back up, snagging my eyes and holding them. Her neck, white and long, her messy hair, bright as crimson. Her breasts heaving, the curve of her waist beckoning, the circle of her thighs around my waist, that sweet rippling of flesh that awaited my touch.

She was, undoubtedly and without question, the most beautiful woman I had ever laid eyes on, and not for the many ways I'd just cataloged. She was beautiful for the way she looked at me, with adoration and respect, with deference and worship. She was beautiful for the softness she only gave to me, for the slivered crack in her armor she'd shown me with trust.

She was beautiful because she was mine. In that moment, the woman who gave nothing gave herself to me.

To *me*.

And that gift would not be squandered.

Without thought or purpose beyond her body, I dropped to my knees and spread her thighs, tracing the flesh with eager fingertips. A ravenous desire swept through me, and I opened my mouth to appease it, dragging my tongue along the path my fingers had taken, drawing her in with a sweep of salt and sensuality. And with every drag of my tongue, she rose, thighs tight, hips bucking. But I gave her no reprieve. Instead I drove her on, eyes closed, my purpose singular. And I was rewarded in full. With a hard pull of my tongue and the shift of my chin, she came like thunder, a cry on her lips and a tremor of her body against mine.

The moment she eased, I broke the connection to stand and unfastened my belt.

She reached for me, bringing herself to sit with what looked like all her strength, and when I was free of my pants, I filled her arms, met her lips in a kiss of desperation and desire, her tongue sweeping my lips to taste herself there.

Her hand slid down my chest, around her thigh locked to my waist, to close around the length of me and guide me to her heat. The shock of sensation forced an instinctive flex. A second, and I filled her, not stopping until I could go no further.

Forehead to forehead, nose to nose, breath to breath, neither of us moved, not for a long moment stacked with thudding heartbeats. And then she kissed me, and there was no choice to be made.

A roll of my hips, a grinding wave, her lips on mine, her hands on my face. I pulled her thigh until my arm cradled her shin, her knee at my shoulder, opening her up to give me room. And I took that space, filled it up. Everything about her was an exploration, her body, her mind, the enigma of her demanding. Commanding. I didn't want to lose the feeling, the sheer devotion and understanding of her rareness. I wanted to appreciate her with the wholeness I felt, the reckless game we played muted in that moment. There was only her and me and the exotic feeling of discovery.

With every thrust, my awareness shrank, receding like the shoreline before a hurricane. But with the whisper of my name and the pulse of her drawing me deeper, there was no holding on. Only abandon as the storm surged, and I was lost without a care, swept away and erased for a long, weightless moment.

We came down on the wave, bodies and lips and hands slowing but not stopping. Just slipping into a languid, lazy kiss that required the sum of us to complete. And we obliged.

It was me who broke the kiss, leaning back to look down at her. To admire the flush in her cheeks and neck, the shine of her swollen lips. I held her jaw, thumbed the bottom swell, my own lips tingling at the phantom sensation of connection.

Those lips smiled idly as her arms circled my neck, fingers twiddling my hair. "That was maybe the stickiest fuck of my life."

"Then you haven't been living."

The sweetest laugh slipped out of her, quiet and adoring. "I'm filthy."

"I like you filthy. Although ..." I leaned back farther, inspecting her dramatically. "You know, I think I cleaned you up pretty good. Oh, wait," I said, angling for her neck. "Missed a spot."

She giggled, neck arching to cradle my face as I took a moment to taste her neck once more.

When I leaned back again, my eyes traced her face as my hand smoothed her stiff hair, and she sighed happily, the sound hitting me deep in my chest.

"You did it again," she said.

"Did what?"

"Made me forget every bad thing in my life."

"I told you that's my specialty," I said with a sideways smile and a bottomless longing.

"You did. I just didn't expect you to be so good at it."

"I don't do anything halfway, Lila."

"No, you sure don't," she said softly. "Neither do I."

Suddenly the moment was too much, too real. And so, I kissed her, held her face in my hands and washed it away. We didn't need to speak it. I didn't need to know anything beyond that this was good and right, and that the girl beneath me was broken and unready for more than this. And that combination was dangerous as dynamite.

When I backed away, she mewled, her hands trailing my arms as they moved away like she didn't want to let me go.

"Come on," I said, snagging her hand to pull her up. "Let's get you cleaned up."

"If I have to." She pouted, but when I scooped her into my arms, she squeaked, grabbing me around the neck, hanging on like I didn't have her on lock.

"You have to," I insisted as I carried her to the bathroom. "Because I'm about to fuck you in that fancy bed, on those fancy sheets, and nobody wants to sleep on cake."

She chuckled, settling her head into the crook of my neck. I pressed a kiss to her forehead, savoring the moment, not wanting to let her go.

I didn't want to let her go. One day soon, I'd have to.

For the first time in my life, I wished I was something else. Something more. Ambitious and successful and rich. Powerful. I wished I was the kind of man Lila wouldn't just fuck.

I wished I was the kind of man she'd keep.

An Arrangement

KASH

The door to the greenhouse opened, and I glanced up, looking for Lila.

At the sight of my father, my skipping heart tripped and ate it.

"Don't look so disappointed," Dad said with the tilted smile he'd passed down to all the Bennet men.

"I'm not disappointed," I lied, steering my cart of seedlings to the fresh bed we'd turned over.

A noise of dissent was the maximum of his argument. "What time is Lila supposed to be here?"

I paused, a tray of plants in hand, my eyes narrowing on him as he approached. "Who told you? It was Luke, wasn't it?"

"Nobody told me, son. I have two eyes, a couple ears, and something between them, you know. Doesn't take much more."

With a frown, I knelt at the bed and kept my eyes on my hands as they got to work.

"How serious is it?" he asked.

"It's not."

When I noted his stillness, I glanced up at him. His face said he knew better.

"It's not," I insisted. "We have an … arrangement."

"You see each other an awful lot for whatever this is to be just an arrangement." There was no accusation—he stated it as if he were noting the color of marigolds.

And he wasn't wrong.

I'd spent the better part of two weeks pretending like Lila and I had some sort of handle on the rules. Nights apart almost immediately dissolved into hours spent texting. Then sexting. By the beginning of the week, they'd disappeared completely.

And then, there were the dates.

But they *weren't* dates, not technically. Was Chinese takeout a dinner date? Not by my standards. But sitting across the bed from Lila, her hair piled on top of her head, wearing nothing but my Hoeing Ain't Easy T-shirt with duck sauce on her chin *felt* like a date. When I wiped the sauce off and she leaned over her takeout container to kiss me, it *felt* like a date.

And last night, the last rule went straight out the window.

I'd spent the night with Lila.

We'd woken up in a tangle, her body curled into mine, my arms around her like a vise. To see her in the morning light, sleepy and smiling and so goddamn lovely did nothing to convince me this was casual.

It was anything *but* casual.

And I didn't know just what to do about that.

"Your mother knows," Dad said. When my face shot up, he clarified, "Well, she suspects. You haven't been in before midnight in weeks. And last night, you didn't come home. You can't imagine she wouldn't have noticed."

"I'm a grown man. I can sleep where I'd like without having to tell my mother."

"Which is why she hasn't said anything. To you, at least.

Seems to be all she wants to talk about to me. I reckon she knows I know and is fishing. Haven't told her you've been sneaking off with Lila or she'd have already orchestrated a formal dinner to rope you both into."

Sticky discomfort rose within me. "It's not serious. Certainly not serious enough for Mom to get involved."

"Try telling her that."

I snorted a laugh.

"You'll have to tell her at some point. If this keeps on, I mean. She's driving herself crazy trying to figure out who you're seeing and is convinced it's Verdant."

My discomfort was replaced by aversion. "Verdant? Really?"

He shrugged. "She's the last girl you went out with, by your mother's knowledge anyway. You know how she is. It makes her feel better to assume. Gives her comfort in having an answer, even if it's false."

"There's no point in telling her. Let her wonder."

"You say that now. How about when she's snooping around? Or eavesdrops on your siblings? She's gonna find out. If you tell her, you might be able to contain the blast."

At that, I full-on laughed. "Sure. Maybe I could bail out the ocean with a bucket while I'm at it."

We shared a chuckle just as the greenhouse door swung open again. But I wasn't rewarded with Lila like I'd hoped.

Instead, I found Ali Gibson with a smile on her face and a swing of her hips.

I rose slowly as she approached. Dad was still as stone.

"Kash," she said, that smile broadening. "I hope you don't mind my coming straight back. The new girl said it was all right."

"Wendy," I provided. "I didn't know you were in town," was the only other thing I could think to say as she reached me, stretching onto her tiptoes to press a kiss to my cheek.

I resisted the urge to put three feet and my father between us.

"Oh, it's a quick trip, just here for work," she said. "God, how have you been? It's been too long. When was it ... August?"

"July."

She snapped her fingers. "That's right. Just after the Fourth. I can't seem to get away from Boston much these days, what with my caseload. There's always someone needing to be proven innocent," she said, as if being a defense attorney made her an altruist.

"How are things here? I thought I saw Jett on my way back. I didn't know he was back at Longbourne."

"Everyone is, even Luke. They all came to roost when we needed them."

She clutched her designer handbag with a font smile. It was blood red too, that smile, and I wondered how much money she was wearing from toe to top, figuring even that tube of red lipstick cost the equivalent of a decent steak dinner.

"You Bennets always did stick together. Tell me more over dinner." The hopeful note coupled with the slightest curl at the corners of those lips I'd once dreamed would be mine told me all I needed to know. Not that there was any question. Ali only came around in one-night increments.

"Hate to disappoint, but I've got plans tonight."

She pouted, the expression reminding me of a time years ago and the girl she'd once been. She was just as beautiful as she'd always been—tall and blonde and flawless, with a soft, kind face I'd once believed was incapable of anything but virtue. But I noted that beauty and my old familiar feelings with an unfamiliar detachment, a separation I hadn't realized had come to pass. She wasn't quite as tall as Lila, and though their hair wasn't the same color, I compared the two, noting Lila's was a little longer, shinier. Where Ali had velvety-brown doe eyes, Lila's were crisp and bright with wit and determination. But Ali had never made me laugh the way Lila did. I'd never felt seen and appreciated by Ali like Lila did

A cold shock of realization shot up my spine.

My detachment was no fluke. It was simply that Ali wasn't Lila.

My second realization was how very much trouble I was in.

"I leave in the morning, so I can't offer a rain check. Are you sure you can't spare some time tonight?" she insisted quietly, stepping closer to touch my forearm. "Even if it's late. You know I don't mind."

I opened my mouth to decline with my own insistence when the door opened again, revealing the woman I'd been waiting for all day.

Her smile fell, her gait stalling, eyes collecting data from me, then Ali, then Ali's hand on my arm.

My heart climbed up my ribs like a ladder. "I'm sure."

When Ali saw Lila, her face shifted with understanding. "I see," she said with curtness I'd expected and sadness I hadn't, though I wasn't dumb enough to assume that sadness had anything to do with her feelings. Not feelings of her heart at least. "Sorry again for barging in. Maybe next time?"

"Maybe," I answered, unable to reject her so blatantly in front of an audience.

Ali stretched again to brush a harmless kiss to my cheek. Harmless to me, at least.

Lila had come to a stop behind Ali. She was pristine, standing tall and unfazed and smiling that smile she wore at work. Such as to say, it was all a facade, from head to toe.

"I'm sorry. Am I interrupting?" Lila asked in her diplomatic wedding planner's tone. "I thought we had an appointment today, but if we need to reschedule—"

"No need," Ali said. "I was just leaving. Good to see you, Kash."

I couldn't say the same, so I offered a nod and prayed she'd just go already.

With a final assessment of Lila—who endured it with the grace of a goddamn angel—Ali granted my wish.

For a moment, Lila and I stood in silence.

"You have lipstick on your cheek," she noted clinically, but her own cheeks flushed, belying her calm exterior.

"Wish it was yours." I stepped into her, snagged her hand. Pressed a kiss of my own to her rosy cheekbone, encouraged when she let me, though she cut a look to where my father tilled soil, his eyes on his hands with the casual solitude of someone who was blissfully alone.

"Come with me," I whispered, tugging her toward the storage basement.

Down the steps we went, the sound of her heels echoing off the concrete. The moment we were free of them and nestled in the near darkness, I turned her, cupped her face, and descended for a kiss in a single motion. Surprise stiffened her lips, but in a heartbeat, they yielded, softened, opened to meld to mine. We were a knot of arms and legs and heavy breaths before either of us knew it, and for that brief stretch of time, nothing needed to be said or decided or discussed. It was just the simple truth of her and me.

But such moments weren't meant to last, and when that one ended, all the things we hadn't said slid between us once more.

"Lila, I—"

"Please, don't explain," she insisted. "We aren't together. We're not exclusive. You don't owe me anything, not even her name."

It was hurt that came first in a flash of pain, then a sinking sadness. "Maybe not," I said, tucking her hair behind her ear, "but I'm gonna tell you all the same." A flicker of a smile and a warming of her eyes told me all I needed to know. "That was Ali, a girl I used to date."

"An ex-girlfriend?" She frowned, confused. "I didn't know you had any of those."

"I don't. Not many at least. Ali always calls when she comes to town."

She drew a slow, resolute breath that drew her straighter. "I understand."

"No, I don't think you do. She came to ask me to dinner, and I declined."

Bravely, she said, "Kash, you don't have to do that."

"Didn't think you'd ask me to. I declined because I'd rather be with you."

"But … I don't want to stop you from seeing who you want."

It was a lie—I saw it as plainly as she'd offered it.

On a chuckle, I said, "If I didn't know better, I'd think you *wanted* me to go out with Ali."

The color rose in her cheeks again. "No, I can't say that I do."

I tilted her face so I could look her square in the eye. "I'm not seeing anyone else, and I don't want to. Do you?"

"Not in the slightest."

"Good."

When she smiled, it was with genuine relief. But the expression shifted to uncertainty.

"Don't worry," I started, heading off whatever she was about to say. "Nothing's changed. I know just where we stand, what we are. It's just that I'm having too much fun distracting you to be interested in distracting anyone else."

I was rewarded with a laugh, a laugh that I kissed away until she was pliant in my arms.

The click of the light was succeeded by a noise from my mother that landed somewhere between a gasp and a squeal. Lila and I shot apart like polar magnets.

"*Aha*! I knew it! I knew you had a girlfriend, Kassius Bennet, and I cannot believe you didn't tell me!" she scolded with a smile. "But Lila Parker? Of all the wonderful surprises."

Lila and I exchanged a mortified look, hers notably more mortified than mine.

"Mom, hang on—"

She waved me off, beelining for Lila with her hands

outstretched. "My dear, I am just so thrilled. Kassius is such a good boy. Even if he doesn't tell his mother important things like who he's given his heart to—"

"*Mom*—"

"Which seems to be a popular Bennet trait that's cropped up of late. My darling girl, do you have any idea how long I've been trying to find a suitable match for Kassius? *Years*," she answered herself. "Years and years but to no avail. And to think, I thought he was seeing Verdant." Another wave of her hand in my direction, this time coupled with a roll of her eyes.

"*Mom!*"

Studiously, she ignored me, taking Lila's hands. "But Lila? This is just so wonderful. I always have liked her, haven't I, Kassius?" Again, she didn't require an answer, likely guessing—correctly, I might add—that I'd rat her out. My mother most certainly had *not* been a fan of Lila's when she was making a habit of marching in here to tell me off. "Come, come. You'll have dinner with us tonight."

I stepped in, knowing the only way to stop her was to physically intercede. "Maybe Lila has plans tonight."

Mom's bottom lip slipped out. "Do you?"

"I, um—"

Mom clapped. "Good then. You will come to dinner, and we'll all get to know each other better."

Before I could pry my mother's hands from Lila's, she was off, dragging Lila behind her like a carnival toy I'd won her, prattling on about how happy she was. Lila cast a pitiful look in my direction, but underneath it was a shimmer of pride as she let herself be towed up the stairs.

I followed, smiling up behind them, hoping Mom didn't ruin this for me. If her brazen campaign scared Lila off, I swore I'd never forgive her. But Lila seemed more amused than anything, willing to go along with it all for the sake of appeasing my mother.

That alone should have had me proposing on the spot.

We aren't together, she'd said, a statement that was as true as it was false.

I'd promised her I wouldn't see anyone else and she'd done the same, but it was only an incremental step toward something bigger, something that loomed inevitably, impossibly, over us.

The lesson Ali had taught me was fresh as ever, and it wasn't one I was keen to repeat. Especially not now. Especially not with Lila. So I'd keep on lying to myself with the unlikely hope that one day, I'd believe it when I promised her I knew where we stood despite the knowledge that the line had blown away with the wind.

LILA

I probably should have made my excuses and gone.

The first time the thought struck me, I'd just walked into the greenhouse to find a gorgeous, expensively dressed woman with her hand on his arm. I'd felt the obligation to leave once more when Mrs. Bennet finagled me into dinner, particularly upon noting the terrified look on Kash's face. Even now, as I sat at a rowdy table surrounded by Bennets, I felt as if I should leave, as if I didn't belong. It didn't help that I stood out like a match in the toothpicks, too formal and stiff for the likes of the Bennets.

Really, I should have gone. But I was enjoying myself too much to go through with it.

That was, assuming that Mrs. Bennet would have let me get away, which I somehow doubted. I wouldn't put a running tackle past her if she thought it would keep a prospect for one of her children in the room.

"So where are you staying now?" Mrs. Bennet asked before sliding a fork loaded with casserole into her mouth.

It was the umpteenth prying question she'd asked, but I didn't mind. I didn't mind so much, it worried me.

"With Ivy," I answered without hesitation. "I've been looking for a place of my own but haven't found the right one yet."

"The perfect place, the perfect space," she mused. "Of course, I've been known to say that there's no such thing as perfect. Just like there's sometimes no right or wrong answer—only the answer you choose. Yes or no. Door number one or door number two."

I chuckled. "As a hardened perfectionist, that's a difficult thing to convince myself of, though I don't disagree."

"I heard a little about your ex-boyfriend."

I stiffened, as did Kash next to me.

"Pass the peas, please, Mom?" he asked, clearly intending to divert her.

The attempt failed. She passed the peas, picking up right where she'd left off.

"You'll have to understand something very important about the Bennets—there are no secrets here. Chances are, if you think you've got one, at least half the rest of them already know."

A quiet chuckle from the Bennets.

"Forgive me for saying so, but I must say that I think it's terrible what happened. I'm just so glad that you found Kassius. I hope you know he would never be anything but true."

At that, I smiled at Kash, and he smiled back, though it was apologetic.

"No, I don't believe he would."

"You make him sound like a saint," Luke said, shoveling a bite of his own into his mouth.

Mom's nose snapped into the air. "Well, he *was* the only one who stayed here at Longbourne." At the rise of dissent that broke out among her children, she added, "I want you all to follow your dreams, I do, but I missed you all terribly, and I'm not sorry for saying so."

The dissent fizzled into jokes and loving words, and I listened, taking a sip of my wine and enjoying the comforting hum of their family, which was its own living thing.

"Lila, I've been dying to know," Mrs. Bennet started, cutting through the chatter, "what cut diamond do you prefer?"

My wine somehow ended up in my airway, and I coughed to shake it loose as the Bennets almost simultaneously exclaimed some version of her moniker, Kash the loudest.

"You've been wondering?" Kash asked flatly.

"Yes, I have."

"Mother, I would ask you if you have no shame," he said with stern force, "but I already know the answer."

She shrugged innocently, picking up her wine glass. "What? It's a perfectly normal question for one woman to ask another."

"It most certainly is not," Laney said, pinning her with a warning look.

"Lila is a wedding planner. I'd wager she knows the various cuts better than you, Elaine."

This was true, but my napkin was still pressed to my lips as the coughing wound down. Kash's hand patted my back gently, and a brief and befuddling vision of him patting a baby's back just like that flashed in my mind.

Mr. Bennet spoke without looking up from his plate as he loaded his spoon. "We got that shipment of prairie clover in."

Immediately, Mrs. Bennet pounced, the conversation fueled and stoked by Tess, who mercifully steered her through a number of topics, ending up in weddings where I joined in. As we went on about floral arrangements, the rest of the table carried on, the bubbling conversation easy and fluid, just like the Bennets. They might run on high octane, but they didn't seem to quarrel, didn't seem to snipe. The jab here or there, sure, but it was clear without more than a moment with them that they were a unit, a team. Even as an outsider, or perhaps especially as one, there was a feeling of belonging and a desire to belong, to become a part of that unit and hope that your little cog was somehow useful to their machine.

Kash slid his big hand into my lap, palm up, and I filled it with mine. We shared a look, a look that noted the farce as well as the rightness. It was a strange thing, the knowledge that we weren't much more than a fling and the sense that we were so much more.

But I reminded myself of the truth between us. He didn't want a relationship any more than I'd said I did when this all began. It was he who'd proposed we enter into this arrangement, and he'd made it clear that this was nothing more than an affair, a fleeting attachment. *Nothing more*, no matter how it might feel.

And I put that truth on repeat to carry on with the sham, pretending not to enjoy it as much as I did.

By the time dinner was over, I'd been asked only a couple more inappropriate questions, none of which fazed me, simply because I didn't believe Mrs. Bennet would ever do any purposeful harm. I helped the Bennets clear the table and wash the dishes, wearing a hot-pink apron covered in yellow daisies that Mrs. Bennet had me don to protect the integrity of my white suit. But the second things slowed down, Kash made our excuses and swept me out the door with my unending promises to return soon and a hug from his mother that might have dislocated a rib.

As we walked toward our hotel, I slipped my hand into the crook of his elbow, and he flexed his arm to draw me closer.

"I am so sorry about that," he said the moment we were out of earshot of the house.

I imagined Mrs. Bennet rushing to open one of the front facing windows so she wouldn't miss a thing, and the vision made me smile.

"Don't be. I enjoyed being your ... well, if your mother is to be believed, we're to be engaged any day."

He chuckled, but the sound was edged with discomfort.

"Really. It was fine. Your mother is sweet, and your family is ... they're lovely. And very welcoming. Although I shudder to think what would happen if I ever did you wrong."

"A witch hunt."

"I wouldn't expect any less."

We walked in silence for a moment.

"It was a weird night," he said.

"It was definitely that. But I mean it—I enjoyed myself. Other than the whole ex thing. I could have done without that," I teased. But when he didn't laugh or make a joke, I pulled us to a stop. "I never stopped to ask if *you* were all right."

At the question, he looked so deeply into my eyes, I thought for a moment we both might drown from the weight of that long, solitary stare. But just as quickly as it had come, it was gone again, leaving me wondering if I'd imagined it.

With a smile, he said, "As long as I'm with you, everything's all right."

And when he kissed me, it wiped the world away, leaving me to believe the same was true.

Ophelia

LILA

A handful of days passed easily. I'd taken up semi-permanent residence at the hotel where I spent most nights with Kash, still reveling in the newfound pleasure of his company. While my days were crammed with meetings and appointments and the occasional apartment viewing, my nights were rife with Kash.

I'd been swept up like a summer breeze, easy and warm and with promises of endless sunshine.

It was liberating and terrifying, like riding a bike with no hands. I might career out of control before I got my hands on the bars, or I could ride on with the wind in my hair and the sun on my face. It could go either way, and what a thrill that was.

I hummed happily as I checked my reflection in the mirror of my sister's apartment. It was my first day off in nearly two weeks—the reconfiguration of the Felix wedding having eaten every spare minute I had—and my only plans were to meet Kash at the greenhouse. I'd dredged up my only pair of jeans and one of my two T-shirts, a fashionable V-neck in white.

The truth of my addiction to white, black, and the occasional shade of gray was that I didn't have a head for fashion and color, not as it pertained to me. I could choose wedding colors for someone else without a second thought, but my wardrobe was as stark and rigid as I was.

As *old me* was. As I'd looked over my closet, I made it a point to add some color. Any color that couldn't be considered neutral.

I looked fresh and easy, relaxed and happy. I almost didn't recognize myself, my hair loosely braided, my face devoid of makeup beyond a touch of mascara. Regardless of the fact that these were the most casual clothes I owned, they weren't fit for gardening—high-waisted designer jeans, expensive T-shirt half-tucked, a woven Chanel belt—but it was the best I had. Ivy's canvas sneakers were the most authentic thing about me, scuffed with dirt and crinkled in the creases with use.

Kash would tease me in that way of his, a joke that felt more like a compliment than an insult, an endearment rather than an affront. A fluttering in my ribcage flushed my cheeks, just like thinking of him always did.

He gave me what he'd promised—he'd been the best distraction. Since we'd started seeing each other, work had been exponentially more bearable, simply because nothing could touch me. Kash had me floating above it all, too blissed out to be bothered with pithy things like Addison and her shitty attitude. And Brock was largely a thing of the past. Every day that passed with Kash left me wondering why I'd wasted so much time with someone who was so clearly wrong for me. These days, I felt beautiful and appreciated in ways I hadn't in years.

Maybe it was the nature of our relationship. There was a reckless abandon, an untethered freedom I'd found in him. I wished I could have said it was just about sex. I'd come to crave his smile, the lightness I felt when he was near. Of course, I craved his body too, desperately sometimes. Intensely. In moments least expected, like at a wedding venue or signing contracts. He would creep into my mind, the memory of long nights and the feel of his hands, rough and able. Of his body, hot and hard. And just like that, I'd need him with urgency that shocked and electrified me. I was alive with feeling.

I smoothed my shirt once more, ignoring the sharp edge of danger, a sheer drop off a cliff. Because how I felt didn't have to be considered, not now. Not yet. I didn't have to decide what to do or what would come. I was living in the moment just like everyone said you should. It shouldn't matter that every moment was filled with Kash. But it did.

For now, I ignored it with every ounce of willpower I possessed, which was saying something. I had metric tons of willpower at my disposal.

I exited the bathroom, light on my feet, smile on my face. As I passed the couch, I leaned over the back and kissed my sister on the cheek.

"Look at you," she said, craning her neck to see me. "I didn't even know you owned jeans."

"Lucky for me, I didn't have to borrow yours. They would have been high waters on me."

"Maybe you could bring them back in style." At the look on my face, she added, "I'm just saying, if anyone can do it, it's you."

"I'll leave that to Audrey Hepburn."

"I can't believe you're going to work in the dirt. What are you going to do about your manicure?"

"I have an appointment tomorrow during lunch, thank you very much."

She smiled at me, proud and a little smug. "I'm proud of you."

"For what?"

"I don't know. Loosening up. I don't think I've ever seen you this relaxed, not even when we were teenagers. You were too busy planning all the ways to crush someone in debate or working on your student council calendar to actually have fun or relax."

"Hey, prepping for debate *is* fun."

"Says you. But arguing is your love language, so I shouldn't be surprised."

I snorted a laugh and rolled my eyes. "Kash promised to teach me how to grow something."

"You? I've seen your cactus graveyard. Kash doesn't know what he's gotten himself into."

"He really doesn't," I said on a laugh as something in my chest twisted.

A pause while she watched me. "You like him."

An answering sigh from deep in my lungs. "I really do."

She turned, folding her arms on the back of the couch with her brows drawn. "What are you going to do about it?"

"Nothing."

"Nothing?"

"*Nothing*. Not yet. I don't have to decide," I said for the thousandth time that week.

Carefully, she said, "No, you don't. But at some point, you will."

"I know," I answered to my fingernails, not wanting to meet her eyes.

"It's been weeks. I don't mean to rain on your parade—"

"But you're going to."

"—but I'm going to," she confirmed. "Things can be uncomplicated, but not forever. And not unless you're booty calling and don't actually like the other person. Which isn't the case."

"I know."

"And now you're going to the greenhouse on what can only be considered a date—"

"It's not a date," I insisted.

She gave me a look.

"What? We're mucking around in the dirt, for God's sake."

Her look exaggerated. "It's a date, and dates are supposedly *verboten*. Just like spending the night, which was also forbidden, and which you have also disregarded."

"You sound awfully judgy," I snarked.

"I'm not judging, I'm trying to get you to admit the truth. You like him, Lila, and there's nothing wrong with that. You're allowed to have feelings for him."

Shock hit me first, the simple and naked truth of it blinding. For a moment, I was stunned, not realizing something very important.

Ever since Brock, I'd been telling myself I wasn't allowed to feel anything beyond lust, not with Kash and not so soon after the way things ended with Brock.

I hadn't even realized I'd been hiding behind that lie.

The twist in my chest unfurled with the permission to care about him. "I ... I hadn't thought about it like that."

"No, you wouldn't. You seem convinced there's something in the way, but what if there isn't?"

"And what if it's not that easy?"

"And what if shrimp learn to whistle and chickens grow teeth? If you want to really live in the moment, stop worrying so much about what if and just go for it. Living in the moment means damning the consequences. It's about choosing what you want instead of what's safe."

"And what if I'm not ready to choose?" I asked, knowing that if I did, there would be no turning back.

But with a knowing smile, she said, "Pretty sure you already did."

A laughed touched with surprise and relief and a healthy amount of fear shot out of me. Because she was right, and it was a bare and honest truth. I'd already chosen. And I'd chosen Kash.

"When did you get so smart?" I asked.

"When I fell in love and got knocked up. As dumb as pregnancy has made me, I feel super freaking wise. Ask me about preeclampsia or mucus plugs. Go on, ask me."

I made a gagging sound around my laughter. "Mucus is just as bad as moist."

"Worse. At least moist can be associated with happy things like cakes and vaginas. There is nothing happy about mucus."

I turned for the door, shaking my head, scooping up my bag on the way. "I love you, weirdo."

"Love you too. Have fun on your *date*."

With a parting rolling of eyes over my shoulder, I said good-bye and trotted down the stairs, musing over the revelation.

I wondered when it had happened. In the small hours of some long night, wrapped in his arms. Eating takeout in bed for dinner every evening—me in his T-shirt, him in nothing but sweatpants and a smile. The night he'd first kissed me and promised he'd give me all I wanted. Or was it before? Had I known before I'd recognized the feeling? Had I leaned into him instinctively, knowing without knowing that he was good for me?

With some certainty, I realized that I didn't want him to be my rebound or fling or distraction. What I didn't know what whether or not he felt the same.

I'd known Kash for more than a decade, and I'd never seen him with a girlfriend. Girls, sure. But steady relationships? Never. Even now, the only woman I knew of was Ali, and even that was enigmatic. I didn't feel it was my business to ask, as if speaking of serious things, such as past relationships, was oddly intimate, too close to a true relationship status, which we avoided discussing whenever possible. It was clear in the way he'd proposed our arrangement and the history of his relationships—or lack thereof—that he wasn't looking for anything more. Never mind with *me*, the prissy, stiff girl who was so unlike him.

But that didn't change the fact that *I* did.

And now that I knew, there was only one thing to do.

Tell him.

Deep down, I'd known I'd catch feelings, even if I'd insisted in the frivolity of a fling. But I'd thought it'd be easier to manage. Be more clear, how I felt. Take longer to develop.

Brock and I hadn't agreed to be exclusive until we'd been

dating for six months. I love you had come somewhere around a year—*after* we were living together. In college, I'd dated Chad for three full years, and we'd never even discussed living together. Before I'd left LA, Todd and I had seen each other for a year and never even referred to each other in relationship terms like *boyfriend, girlfriend*, or even an *It's Complicated* Facebook status.

I noted then that I'd only dated guys with douchebag names. Not that Kash was much better, though the thought of calling him Kassius was deeply unappealing. I couldn't see myself screaming his full name in bed, but *Kash?* A flush crept over me at the mere thought. That was a name I could whisper all night, and had.

Hopefully I would in the nights to come—once I told him, I might not have the chance.

The instinct was a sweeping tide, a compulsion so strong, it felt as if I wouldn't be able to do or think a single thing until I told him. So I took a breath, honed my focus, and dove into a rationalization.

I couldn't bolt into Longbourne with a declaration on my lips. I had to play it cool, play it smart. The moment had to be right—the right moment could make all the difference. I'd know when, but I had to pay attention. We would spend the better part of our day together, so I'd observe through the lens of my new-found knowledge to determine just how and when I'd let him know.

With that ambition guiding me, I lifted my chin and hoped.

The bell chimed my entrance, the shop buzzing with people. Wendy smiled at me from the wall of tin buckets filled to bursting with market bouquets in chromatic order. Jett jerked his chin in greeting from behind the counter, flashing that brilliant Bennet smile at me.

When I approached, I opened my mouth to explain what I was doing there, but he headed me off.

"He's back there," he said with a flick of his head to the greenhouse.

"Thank you," I answered, my cheeks embarrassingly warm and smiling.

"Try not to get too dirty."

I rolled my eyes and laughed to cover my discomfort, making my way behind the counter and into the workroom. Music played, some happy indie song I'd never heard before, and Tess and Luke were busy in the mini studio they'd set up for Instagram, staging Luke holding a gorgeous bouquet of exotic-looking flowers. Tess fiddled and fussed over the bouquet, and Luke watched her with the deepest, sweetest affection.

Oh, to be adored like that.

It seemed an impossibility, something only a sliver of a percentage of the population found, unattainable by me. I'd always thought that a loving relationship was forged through years of becoming accustomed to someone, of learning them and accepting them. I'd never been much for fairy tales, preferring reality and low expectations. But lately, I'd looked around and found a magic in love I hadn't seen before.

It'd been there all along, and I'd somehow missed it.

Luke looked up and smiled the smile of a man who knew too much, and it left me wondering just what Kash had told him about us.

"Look at what the cat dragged in," he said.

"That cat better not be around," I sassed, smiling. "He hates me."

Tess chuckled, turning to face me. "Don't take it personal. Brutus hates most everybody."

"But does he make it a point to trip everyone he hates?"

"No," Tess noted. "Only you."

Luke's smile tilted a little higher on one side. "He's got a whole setup back there for you. Hope you're ready to get schooled—he's got his chalkboard set and his pencils sharpened."

"I'm pretty sure I'm hopeless, but if anyone can teach me, it's him."

Luke shrugged. "I dunno. He's been trying to teach me for years, but it's just in one ear and out the other."

"That's because you only pay attention to what *you* want to learn," Tess added. "You've learned photography tricks pretty quick from me."

"That's just because *you* were teaching me and not my hairy brother."

She rolled her eyes and laughed, reaching up on her tiptoes to kiss him.

"Well, I'll leave you to it," I teased, heading toward the greenhouse.

"Good luck!" Tess called after me, and I waved, accepting that luck.

I'd need it.

The metal door was cool, but the greenhouse was as warm as summer against the chill of fall. Music played back here too. The Bennets didn't seem to like the quiet much, and with a house that full of people, I doubted it was *ever* quiet. Especially now that all the Bennets had come home to help out.

I should have answered Ivy's plea sooner. I should have helped before now. If I hadn't been so concerned with my own neck, I would have. But ambition wasn't forgiving, and being the best left no room for error.

Lately, that mattered less and less. And I had Kash Bennet to blame.

He didn't see me walking down the wide aisle of the greenhouse, too lost in his work to consider anything beyond his hands or the motion of his body as he cradled small shocks of budding green in his palms, transferring it to the earth where he knelt. Reverent was his care and attention, as if that little plant meant just as much to him as the plants he'd tended for months and years. Or as much as his cat, who sat next to him, flicking his tail, amber eyes locked on me.

I narrowed my eyes at the beast, nose wrinkling as I imagined hissing at him. As if he knew, he stood, arching his back in a long, threatening stretch.

It was then that Kash glanced up, his eyes snapping to me like he'd imagined I'd be there. Thick stubble shaded his jaw, sharpening the line, framing his brilliant smile.

"I thought I told you not to wear white." He dusted his hands on his jeans and stood, still smiling.

"I thought you knew I didn't own anything that wasn't." I smiled back, taking a long moment to appreciate the sight of him.

His T-shirt was heathery gray, tight across his shoulders, straining to contain his biceps and chest, but somehow, it didn't look too small. Instead, it appeared that he was just too strong to adhere to clothing construction of mere mortals. Printed on the front in black was the phrase, *Weed 'em and Reap.*

"Nice shirt," I said with a nod at it.

He looked down as if he'd forgotten what it said. "Got fifty more where that came from."

"Where do you find them?"

"I don't. Don't tell anybody, but I don't even particularly like them. Laney got me one for Christmas one year, and now it's all anyone ever buys me. Figure they make the best work shirts anyhow."

"You're kidding. You don't even like them?"

"Well, I should note that I don't dislike them either. It makes them happy to see me in them, and given that I don't have a real opinion either way ..." He shrugged the rest off, that crooked smile on his face.

I couldn't have told you why it made my heart flutter at the knowledge that he wore those goofy shirts every day for the amusement of his family, but it did.

"Whatcha doin'?" I asked, nodding to the planter box at his feet.

He glanced in the same direction, hooking his hands on his hips. He looked like Paul Bunyan in a novelty T-shirt—all he needed was some buffalo check flannel and a knit cap.

"Planting seedlings. These are black magic cosmos. Planted

them, oh … a month ago? Now that they're ready to move into the ground, we should have blooms in five or six weeks, I figure."

"For the Baker wedding?" I asked with a wondrous smile.

He nodded, smiling back.

I knelt across from him, looking down at the seedlings, the hopeful bursts of green in dark soil.

"Black magics are delicate," he said, lowering to his haunches, big hands hanging between his knees. "Its petals are so deep a red, they're nearly black, but even more interesting—they smell like chocolate. Sometimes vanilla, but I've always only smelled chocolate."

I touched one of the sprouts tenderly. "How strange," I said half to myself.

"Tess is itching to get her hands on the blooms. We haven't planted them here in years, not since I was a kid. I remember coming down here and sitting between the aisles because they smelled so good. Tried to eat one once. I don't recommend it."

I couldn't help but laugh. "Didn't your mother ever teach you not to eat flowers?"

"The opposite—she used to walk me around and make me taste them. Although she was sorry she made me eat a pansy. They taste a little like mint, and forever on, she had to chase me out of the pansy patches. Don't even get me started on marigolds. And when Mom would get shipments of lilac in the spring? Forget about it."

"Lilac? You're kidding."

"I'm not. Some just taste like nothing. Some taste … green. I don't know how else to describe it. But some taste exactly like lilac smells, and it's utter heaven."

"That's my name," I said, suddenly sheepish at the admission.

His brows flicked together. "Lilac?"

"My grandmother's favorite flower was lilac, and my parents were married in her garden at the end of May when they were in bloom. So, they named me Lilac, and my sister Ivy because they must have known she'd be wild and clingy."

That earned me a laugh, and I smiled.

"I'm surprised she didn't tell you. She loves to embarrass me by telling everyone I don't want to know."

"I take it you're not a fan?"

"It's just so … I don't know. Whimsical? It was a name for a fairy, not a practical girl who got perfect scores in penmanship. It felt patently unlike me. So I rejected it on principle. And the color purple too. It was all they put me in before I was old enough to have an opinion."

He smiled at me across the planter box. "And how old was that?"

"Second grade. It didn't help that I was teased mercilessly about it."

"Kids are cruel."

"And I didn't want to give them any more ammunition."

He paused. "Was it bad?"

"Remember Ashley Sanders?"

His scoff told me he did.

"She lived in our building. When we were home, she was my best friend, *the* best friend. But at school? She was queen of the mean girls."

"I don't think I knew a single person who wasn't terrified of her."

"There's another side to her. Or maybe she's a sociopath."

"I'd vote for the latter."

"Anyway, I ended up in her sights. She spent her time either rejecting me or pretending to be my friend so she could trick me—lock me in the bathroom, humiliate me in front of everyone, whatever her fancy was that day. And then we'd get home, and she'd knock on my door, apologize, and stay over for hours. All weekend. Sleepovers. The works."

Kash watched me with those depthless eyes of his. "Your parents didn't put a stop to it?"

"They didn't know. Not really. They thought it was just the typical old girl drama, not noticing that I withdrew, that I was anxious about going to school. Even when I was having melt-downs in class. Like once, when my teacher interrupted me, I crawled under my desk and cried because no one ever listened to me. The teacher just sent me to the counselor, my parents thought I was just overreacting, and everyone went on their merry way." I sighed. "But it wasn't their fault. I should have learned my lesson when it came to Ashley sooner."

"When did you?"

"Middle school. I didn't have many friends—in hindsight, that was probably her doing too—and I was lonely enough to play right into her hand. When we were at home, she was honest and giving and funny and cool. I looked up to her, wanted to *be* her. But she was a liar, and I eventually gave up trying to make her happy."

"There was no lesson to learn, Lila. She should have known better."

"No, it was an important lesson, the most important lesson I've ever learned—people will manipulate you, if you let them. And no one will save you but yourself."

Sadness touched his face, smoothing his lips, his eyes, his brow. But he didn't disagree, didn't pity me or tell me I was wrong. He just watched me for a long moment before finally saying with a quirk of his lips, "Think I can prove you wrong?"

A relieved laugh slipped out of me, along with the phrase of the hour, one I meant more deeply than he knew. "If anyone can, it's you."

He smiled fully then, turning to the plastic tray of seedlings. "Wanna plant one?"

"I don't know," I hedged, eyeing them like they'd turned into live explosives.

"Here, it's easy." His hands stretched out, pausing expectantly with a little seedling in his palms.

I reached out, cupping my hands like his. Mine looked so soft and small and pale next to his, which he lowered, his knuckles brushing my palm. Slowly, he opened them, transferring the cool pile to my hands with a long stroke of connection. I held the plant like it might electrocute me if I moved too suddenly, but Kash's fingers dug into the earth, spreading the dirt to make a space.

"Go ahead, set it in here."

I did as he'd said, lowering my hands, nestling them in the dirt before opening them up. "Now what?"

"Press the dirt down with your fingers, not too hard," he warned, and I backed off from packing it down. "Good. Now, just brush a little dirt over the top to level it out. Don't leave any space around the ... yup, just like that. You just planted your first flower."

I dusted off my hands. "You grew that from a tiny seed. All I did was dump it in the dirt."

He shrugged, smirking at me. "You just put that little flower in the home it'll know its whole life. So I'd wager it appreciates your effort."

There, in that quiet, mundane moment, the desire to tell him all the ways I wanted him surged in my chest, up my throat, my lips parting to speak. But he'd already stood to move the seedlings out of the way, the moment fading with the motion.

"You ready to become a crazy plant lady?" he asked.

I laughed to cover my nerves. "If you can show me how to keep a plant alive for more than a month, I'll buy you a commemorative cake."

"Deal," he said over his shoulder as he rounded the aisle. "Come on, I set us up back here."

I followed him, admiring that broad back, his rolling shoulders, the luxurious, dark hair curling gently at his nape. And with every step, I gathered my courage.

I was a girl who knew what she wanted and went out and got it. But when it came to Kash, I was as delicate as those seedlings, roots fresh and seeking purchase in uncertain ground. He was uncharted territory—why exactly, I couldn't say. Not beyond the simple newness, the unexpected truth of him.

He stopped in front of the big table butted up against the end of the greenhouse, the same table he'd nearly nailed me on just a few weeks ago. Sitting on top was a variety of supplies, organized in neat, orderly rows—a plastic pot brimming with ivy, a tin of gravel, a pitcher of dirt, a pair of gloves, and a hand spade.

"I present to you one of the easiest plants to keep alive—pothos ivy."

I leaned in, curious.

"This little guy can stay alive with minimal sunlight, although the more it gets, the more it grows. All you have to do is water it once a week. Wednesdays, if you can manage it."

"Why Wednesdays?"

"So you don't forget. Watering Wednesdays."

"That might actually work." I stepped closer, thumbing a waxy, spade-shaped leaf. "How much water?"

"More than a sip, less than a drenching."

"I see it's an exact science."

He shrugged. "You'll get the hang of it."

"Says you," I teased.

"That's right, says me. If you can run the Felix wedding, you can keep ivy alive."

Kash reached for an old, square tin covered in nouveau art. Swirls and swoops shaped like smoke built a frame around a beautiful girl sitting among lilies, brushing her long auburn hair. The details of the frame were shimmering gold, and written in a crisp deco font were the words *Gilded Lily* with the description of the face powder and manufacturer beneath.

He set it down without ceremony, reaching for the container of gravel, but I scooped the tin up, inspecting it with wide eyes.

"This is beautiful," I breathed, turning it over in my hands, imagining the woman this had belonged to in some era long ago. "Where did it come from?"

"We have about a million of them in storage. This was probably one of my great-grandma's, once upon a time."

"Oh, it's too valuable," I insisted, shaking my head. "I can't accept this."

He snorted a laugh. "If you saw how many we had, you'd disagree. Trust me when I say you'd be doing me a favor. And anyway, she reminds me of you," he said half to himself, eyes on the tin. "Her hair. The curve of her nose. The gilded lily—beautiful and perfect without any adornment but adorned all the same. Almost to frivolity."

The feeling of rightness struck me again, a deep thrum that set an admission rising within me.

"Keep it," he said. "It was meant to be yours."

What about your heart? I thought. *Was that meant to be mine too?*

I clutched the tin to my chest hopefully. "Are you sure?"

"I'm sure. In fact, I'll take you down there when we're finished, and you can fill up a wheelbarrow with anything you want. Just run it by Tess," he added. "She'd kill me if I got rid of something she needed for a window installation."

I beamed at him, my mind tripping over what treasures I might find there. What I might find in him. "Thank you."

"You're welcome." He paused, watching me for a beat. "You'll have to set it down if you want to plant in it."

"Oh." I laughed. "Sorry."

Once it was on the table, Kash handed me the gloves.

But I waved him off. "I'm not afraid of a little dirt."

With one brow cocked, he reached for a canvas apron. "Guess you won't be needing this then."

I snatched it from him. "*That* I will take, thank you."

He stepped behind me as I looped the strap over my neck, his hands finding the strings to tie around my waist. As his fingers did their work, he closed the small gap between us, his chest against my back, his lips against my neck for the briefest of kisses.

"All right," he said against my skin, kissing me once more before stepping back up to the table. "First, the gravel."

At that, he launched into his instructional with Brutus watching me from across the table. When he hopped up and took a seat, I half expected him to make hard eye contact while he knocked things off the table, one by one. But instead, he sat silently, tail flicking judgmentally as Kash directed me to pour in a few inches of gravel for drainage, then a couple small pieces of concrete to discourage the roots from growing into the drainage. Then a little bit of fresh soil, mixed with the ivy's topsoil when I turned the pot to empty its contents into my hand. I squeezed the pot-shaped soil to break up the roots as he instructed, then set the little plant inside and filled it with the remainder of the dirt in the pot, just like I had the cosmos.

Proudly, he handed me a watering can. "Go ahead. Give him a little drink."

I smiled and did as I'd been told. "Why's it gotta be a he?"

"It's whatever you want it to be. You should name it."

I set down the watering can and held up the tin for inspection, the ivy's leaves bobbing with the motion. I traced the visage of the girl basking in the sunshine, combing her hair surrounded by lilies. "Ophelia," I said, utterly certain that it was most definitely a she, and her name was a fact that had been waiting to be uncovered, in that moment, by me.

"Ophelia it is," he said, leaning on the table to watch me.

And I watched him right back.

He was immovable, a pillar of solidarity and strength. An unwavering truth clung to him, the air of safety and certainty. A worthiness of trust.

I trusted him. He had nothing to gain by deceiving me.

I didn't even think him capable of deceit.

"Thank you," I said quietly, from the very depths of my heart. Because that moment of truth was upon me, and I wouldn't waste it.

"For what?" he asked honestly. As if everything he gave wasn't a gift and privilege.

"For this. For everything."

He reached for my hand, that tilted smile on his face as he pulled me into his chest, wrapped me in his arms.

"I told you I was an excellent distraction," he said.

"You did," I agreed on a gentle laugh.

"Next time you need a rebound, I'm your guy."

"And what if I don't need another rebound?"

Something shifted behind his eyes, but the rest of him maintained that cavalier air he always had about him. "Then I'd say whoever locked you down was a lucky guy. You're going to make somebody really happy one day, Lila. And I'm glad you picked me for your rebound. It's been fun while it lasted."

My admission died in my throat. "It has," I admitted with a thin smile to cover the sting of those words.

You knew this was temporary. Deep down you knew. Let it be what it is. Because he'll never want more, not from you.

"Kiss me," I commanded gently, wanting nothing more than to hide, to seal away my wishes, to kiss them goodbye.

And with the brush of his fingers on my cheek, he did.

Acute was the pain, fading into a dull ache in my ribs, the word rebound a barb that struck me mercilessly.

Because who would help me get over Kash when he was gone?

Deeper we kissed, and I only hoped he attributed my desperation to desire, not the loss of what I'd wished for—that we could be more.

But if this was all I could have, I'd take it.

I'd take whatever I could get.

When the kiss slowed, then stopped, he leaned back. A curious, amused look colored his face. "You okay?" he asked.

And there was nothing to do but smile and lie.

Sex Palace

KASH

"**C**ome with me," I said, snagging her hand to tow her toward the shop.

She laughed, trotting behind me. "Where are we going?"

"There's something I want to show you," was all I said, and she took the hint that I wanted it to be as much of a surprise as possible.

I wanted to leave the moment that passed between us in the greenhouse, but it followed us silently. Because if she'd been about to tell me she was ready to move on, I wasn't ready to hear. I wasn't ready to end this or let her go. I'd pretend like it was all fun and games if it meant I get to keep her a little while longer.

But that ticking clock was a bomb waiting to detonate. And I was beginning to lose hope that I'd defuse it in time.

I hurried her out of the greenhouse and on to our destination. There was a space in Longbourne I had long ago claimed for my own, one that no one bothered with beyond the occasional perusal by my father. I'd never taken a girl to this place, not ever. In fact, I never willingly invited *anyone* to this place. Inexplicably, I wanted to show Lila.

I *needed* to, the compulsion overwhelming as I dragged her through the workroom under the watchful gaze of Tess, Luke, and Wendy, then around the corner of the brick wall and to the narrow stairs only I ever used.

"Was your house expanded over the shop?" she asked, brushing the brick with her fingertips.

"It was, about a billion years ago. We used to own half the block until my grandmother sold our other properties. But she had the property lines redrawn so we could keep the greenhouse in the back."

"Clever."

"We have a genetic predisposition to resourcefulness," I said as we reached the top, and I pushed open the door to the roof.

The moment we were clear of the threshold, she gasped at what she found—the small roof greenhouse I'd claimed a decade ago, a place to grow projects just for me. Her face was full of wonder, her red hair shining like a penny in the sun as she approached the structure, which was stuffed to the gills with greenery.

"I didn't know there was another greenhouse at Longbourne."

"Oh, this one's not for the public. It's strictly mine." I moved for the door, and she followed, stepping into the space made warm by trapped sunlight and an abundance of plants nestled together, shoulder to shoulder.

Dirt crunched underfoot as we wound our way in. Every wall was lined with shelves, and from the rafters hung a dozen planters, all teeming with life. In the center stood my workspace, capped on each end with yet more shelves. Below the table was a cacophony of tools, pots, bags of soil and pH tests and fertilizer and enough spiders to ward off almost anybody—with the exception of Dad. He'd stick his hand in there willy-nilly, but then again, he never was afraid of much. Other than Mom, I figured.

I leaned a hip on the worktable, folding my arms with pride as Lila wandered around with her mouth open and eyes wide.

She reached out to touch an orange flower head. She'd picked one of my favorite breeds, with clusters of orange that made a trio of perfect petals that reached up to the sunlight as if in prayer. "I've never seen a flower like this before. What is it?"

"Astragalus. That one is a hybrid of a buffalo plum and Russian milk vetch. See," I said, pushing off the table to stride to her side, "one of its parents is this one." I thumbed the leaf of the peach flowers, which also had three petals, but less blossoms on each cluster. "And this one is its grandparent." I pointed to the next one, which was closer to pink but had only two petals. "And this is its great-grandparent. I've been breeding this one for a few years. See the other side?"

She glanced to the space on the other side of the plant where we'd started. "Look at that. It's yellow, and its petals look like … pistachio shells."

I chuckled. "That's the milk vetch."

"This is wild. How … how did you learn how to do this?"

I rolled a shoulder. "Just messing around really. Dad showed me how once, and I just sort of…ran with it. All you need is a paintbrush and the knowledge of flower genitalia."

"You make these flowers have sex? So you're basically a flower pimp?"

"Think I should put that on my business cards?"

I was rewarded with a laugh as she turned her attention back to the flowers. "These are incredible. Have you thought about selling them?"

"Oh, yeah—I sell them all the time. Over the years, I've met enough enthusiasts that I have a good, solid customer base."

"How much do you charge?"

"Why, need me to make you a new strain of flower?"

"Just curious, is all."

"I don't charge, just tell them they can tip me. Marcus set me up on some app thing they pay me on and it goes straight into my bank account. But I don't think about it all that much, to be honest—I'd do it for free, if they didn't insist on paying. And if Marcus would let me get away with it. He set it up as a business and everything, said I had to or I'd get thrown in jail for tax evasion."

"That's an overstatement, but I see the point," she said on a chuckle.

"Sometimes I wonder how much is in the account, but I figured if it was substantial, Marcus would be hounding me about investing it or something."

Lila made a face I wasn't sure how to read. "You don't know how much is in your business account?"

"No. Why?"

Her face flushed, lashes fluttering as she blinked. "Because … because, I mean, how could you not know your profits?" she stammered. "Don't you have to, like … buy supplies?"

"I've got everything I need in the greenhouse."

"But what if you could make good money? What if you could expand? Start selling them in Longbourne? What if you—"

"I don't do it for money. I just like growing things."

"But what if you could monetize?" she started, excited now, bright with ideas and ingenuity.

"I don't need the money."

"Everybody needs the money."

"I make my salary at the greenhouse, and I live here rent-free. What do I need money for?"

She huffed, scoffed, and rolled her eyes, but for all her stalling, she couldn't seem to come up with an answer.

"I don't want to monetize something I enjoy, Lila. I don't want something I love to become a job. A chore. I just want to play up here in my botanical sex dungeon and create." When she pouted, I asked, "Why do I get the feeling that offends your sensibilities?"

"Because it does," she said without hesitating. "Why not do something you love for a living?"

"Because once you ask your passion to make you money, I imagine it would lose its luster."

"But that's what I did, and I love my job."

I gave her a look.

Her cheeks flushed brighter, and she frowned. "I do."

"You do your job strictly for the joy of the thing? Every Felix sister is endured because it's fun?"

Lila's mouth opened, then closed. Her frown deepened.

"Tell me, what is it you love so much again? Is it the lying to nuns or being humiliated by the people who pay you?"

My tone was light, but I was defensive of that truth, of that stark difference between us. And she matched me for it, folding her arms across her chest.

"There are moments of joy, or I wouldn't put up with all the bullshit."

"Do you love it as much as you did when you first started?" I pressed.

"No. But isn't that every job? Doesn't everyone have an illusion of what things could be? And isn't that illusion *always* wrong? Nothing is what it seems. Life is never what you think it's going to be."

The shift in her meaning didn't go unnoticed by me. I didn't think she was referring to our jobs anymore.

"Fair enough," I admitted. "But that doesn't mean you have to accept where you end up without fighting for your own happiness."

Something tightened her face, a pain she didn't want me to see. The memory of accepting less than she was worthy of, I hoped. Because I never wanted her to accept anything less than absolute happiness. I wanted her to fight for the things she wanted and abandon what she didn't.

Even if that meant she abandoned me.

Not wanting to get any closer to that truth, I turned for another wall of the greenhouse where I kept my lilies, grabbing her hand along the way.

"What are these?" she asked as we neared a cluster of lilies between shelves, the plants waist high and branches heavy with flowers. They hung in arches, the petals extending back to the stem, making it look like a paper lantern of white, speckled with deep purple.

"Lilium duchartrei. Exotic, difficult to grow. I've had this plant, oh … five years or so. You can see I've been breeding it, but I can't ever seem to get it to hold the shape. It always unfurls when the flowers bloom."

She must have noted the disappointment in my voice and squeezed my hands gently. "What are you trying to accomplish?"

"Beyond getting it to keep their shape, I'd like the petals to be a different color. I've tried my hand at breeding it with dozens of species, but I have yet to do it. This plant is about to bloom though, see?"

I brought her closer to my latest experiment, brushing back the leaves to expose a pod that had begun to form.

"Maybe this one will be it," she said hopefully. "And Kash, I'm sorry. For pushing you. I just don't know any other way to be. I mean, look at me. I decided at sixteen that I was going to be a wedding planner, and every single thing I've done since then has been to move me in that direction. My goal in life has been to make a living—a *good* living—working in events. I'm just wired this way, I think. To decide something and chase it with all the tenacity I have. Which is a lot, by the way."

"Who, you?" I teased.

"Anyway," she said with a smile, "when you're that intense about something, it's hard to understand someone's lack of intensity, if that makes sense."

"It does. And there's nothing to be sorry for. Last I checked, two people could disagree without someone needing to apologize for it."

"Force of habit. Ivy thinks I show love by arguing, so I feel like I apologize a lot."

"Well, don't. Not to me. You can save your apologies for your sister."

With a soft laugh, she stepped into me, winding her arms around my neck. "So how often do people come up here to bother you?"

"Never," I said, sliding my hands down her back.

"Good. Because all these pistils and stamens in your sex palace have me all kinds of worked up." Her thigh rose to hitch on my waist. "So are you gonna pollenate me or what?"

And like the pimp I was, I did just that.

Hours later, I trotted down the stairs of my childhood home, smiling to myself, just like I'd been all day, the ghost of my memories replaying on a loop. Lila naked in my greenhouse. The smell of wet earth and sunshine. Her words and her way and the ineffable happiness she gave me.

Everything else, particularly anything regarding our permanence, I ignored like it was my duty.

I just rounded the staircase to the second floor when I heard Mom's voice floating up the stairwell.

"I will *not* sign for that. I've told your kind before, and I'll do it again—I refuse to accept that sanctimonious scrap of paper, and you can't make me," she said, ironically sanctimonious.

I sped up, wondering whose face I needed to turn inside out.

"Ma'am," the weary voice on the porch said as I hurried into the entryway, "you can't avoid this, so just do us all a favor and *take the damn letter.*"

"I won't!" she said petulantly as I approached. "Now, if you'll excuse me—" She started to shut the door, but the courier stuck her boot in the doorjamb.

"Take the letter, Mrs. Bennet, for God's sake!"

I stepped in front of my mother to open the door, glaring down at the sullen girl who looked just as unhappy as my mother did.

"What's this all about?" I asked the girl, ignoring my mother, who tugged uselessly at my arm.

"Kassius, it's nothing. Come, come, it's almost dinner. Aren't you hungry? Jett is making a nice—"

I shot her a look over my shoulder. "Mom …"

She flushed. "I'm not taking that letter!" she spouted. "I'm not!"

"What is it, and *why* won't you take it?"

"Because," the courier said, "it's from Bower Bouquets."

The blood in my veins went cold at the mention of their name.

"Marcus," I called into the house. Then, to my mother, I said, "Sign for that letter. Now."

"B-but—"

"*Mother*. You cannot run away from whatever this is. So sign the letter, let this poor girl go, and let's see what's inside."

She pursed her lips, shaking her head emphatically as she took a step back.

"Ah, ah, ah," Marcus said, hands on her shoulders as he steered her toward the door. "Sign it."

Her unadulterated fury at being handled was matched only by our insistence. But it was her knowledge that there was no way in hell she was getting out of it that finally broke her.

With an illegible sweep of the pen, she practically threw said pen at the courier. "There. Are you quite happy now?"

"Yes, thank you," the girl said flatly, extending her hand with the letter in it.

Mom reached out to take it, but I snatched it first.

"Give that back, Kassius," she scolded, jumping to scramble at my arm as I held the letter far out of her reach.

"Oh, now you want it." I kicked the door closed, my face grim and Marcus's set to match.

"What have you done, Mom?" he asked, sounding exhausted.

"I've … done … nothing …" she said between hops, arms outstretched.

Marcus and I made eye contact, and with the slightest of nods, I grabbed Mom with my free arm and set the other in Marcus's direction for the handoff.

He snatched the letter as Mom began to screech unintelligibly. I made a few words and phrases, including a variety of uses of *don't, grounded, your father, I didn't,* and *don't you dare.* Otherwise, I couldn't make anything out, just a garbled string of dissent by a seemingly mad woman.

With every word he read, Marcus's face drew tighter. Our entire family flooded the entryway, asking questions and trying to figure out why Mom had turned into a howler monkey, but when Marcus lowered his hands and laid his cool eyes on Mom, the entire room went silent as a tomb.

"This is a cease and desist," he said. "From Bower. They say that *you*, Mother, are in breach of contract."

The boom of shouting was instantaneous, every mouth in the room on fire except for Marcus, Dad, and Mom, who went half-limp in my arms.

"*Stop*," I finally shouted, loud enough that they actually listened, chests heaving and hands on their hips and glaring eyes on Mom.

I put her firmly on her feet and took a step back. She looked smaller, older than she had only a moment before, her blue eyes shimmering and chin bent and wobbling.

"You took out a contract with Bower?" I asked carefully, quietly.

"I had no choice," she said resolutely, albeit with a weak undertone and a sniffle. "Things were in disrepair before you all came home. When I put out word that we were filling wholesale orders, Bower signed on with the promise to overpay. What was I supposed to do, refuse? We couldn't afford to refuse, Bower or not."

Marcus drew a long, loud breath through his nose, his gaze heavy on her. "Where is the contract?"

"In storage. Give me a second and I'll get it." She patted her pockets until the jingle of keys sounded, then headed out the front door.

We all shared a look, and I figured we all were imagining her running for the Christopher Street station.

"I'll go," Laney offered, heading out on Mom's heels.

A collective sigh sounded before all our gazes turned to Dad.

His hand framed his chin, fingers testing the consistency of his snowy white stubble, his unfocused gaze on the parquet.

"You knew," Marcus said.

A nod. "Not until after she signed the cursed thing, but yes. I knew."

The hot flash of betrayal washed over me. "How could you not tell *me*?"

"Because your mother asked me not to, and my loyalty is to her above all. Even you, son. We were determined to finish out the contract and be done with the whole thing, but it seems things are more complicated than we realized."

"Who read over the contract? Marty?" Marcus asked after their old incompetent lawyer, his brain firing behind his eyes like a machine gun.

At that, Dad flinched. "Your mother."

This time, we all groaned.

"Oh my God," Luke breathed. "We are so screwed."

Marcus scrubbed a hand over his weary face. "We are. This letter says something about a noncompete. Why would she sign a noncompete with *Bower*?"

"Because she believed she had no choice," Dad said, defeated.

"We could have helped," Marcus shot. "All you had to do was ask, and we would have."

The door opened again, marking the entrance of Mom, a banker box overflowing with papers nestled in her arms. Her face bent in pain, eyes accusing when they met Marcus's.

"This wasn't your responsibility. It was my fault, and I

wouldn't drag you, my children, into the mess I made. I know I'm not smart, and I have no head for business, as evidenced by my gratuitous mismanagement of the business that is my legacy. I have enough regrets without drowning you all with me. If you hadn't discovered it, Marcus, if you all hadn't insisted on taking over, I would have just let Longbourne die. It might have put me into the ground to do it, but there is no world that exists in which I would willingly put my children in danger, financial or otherwise."

But Marcus shook his head at her tearful plea. "Don't you understand the position this puts us in? If you had just told us from the beginning, all of this could have been avoided. Every time you keep a secret from us, the danger multiplies. Running away from it only makes things worse. Case in point." He held up the letter in display.

Mom's chin rose, nose in the air as she strode toward him. "It must be very fulfilling to look down at me from up there on your high horse, Marcus Bennet." She shoved the box into his hands.

"Nothing about this fulfills me, Mother," was his reply. "I'll start with the contract, figure out what we're dealing with. Until then, it's business as usual. No more surprises," he said with a hard look around the room. "As your investor and the current owner of Longbourne, that's not a suggestion."

And with that, he headed for the door, opening and closing it with more force than was necessary.

Mom sniffed again, nose still up but her eyes full of tears as she moved for my father. He opened his arms, and she curled into him gently, her defenses gone slack as her spine.

"I can't believe you kept this from us," I said quietly, locking eyes with my father again. "How long has it been going on?"

"A year," he admitted. "You have to understand, your mother was just trying to help. To save things as best she could."

"She should have come to us," Laney insisted. "Marcus is right. This all could have been avoided."

"How bad is it?" Jett asked carefully.

Dad's eyes grew sad. "There are quite a few more surprises waiting in that box, I'm afraid."

"Did you even read the letters, Mom?" Laney asked. "Did you know what you signed? How could they make Longbourne cease business?"

"The noncompete," Dad answered for her, his arm around her shoulders protectively but his face apologetic and heavy with remorse. "If the shop made over a certain amount of money, we would be in breach. They've been sending requests for our financials, and those requests have been ignored."

"Have we exceeded their terms?" I asked, not wanting the answer.

With a sigh, Dad nodded. "I think it's likely."

"Everything we've worked for," Luke said, half to himself. "Everything we've done to save Longbourne, and now they're going to shut us down? I can't believe this. I cannot believe you didn't tell us."

Mom hiccuped a sob into Dad's chest. "I'm so s-sorry," she said miserably, the sound muffled by his shirt. "You have a right to be a-ashamed of me. My mother turned over in her grave when my pen touched that contract. And n-now I've r-ruined everything." The word dissolved into a wail.

And that was just about all I could take.

I stepped toward them, cupping Mom's shoulder. At the gesture, she spun into my arms, launching herself at me as a fresh trail of sobbing escaped her. Her fists, gnarled from arthritis, twisted my shirt.

One by one, my siblings joined until we were a knot of arms and torsos, Mom in the middle.

"We'll fix this," I promised. "We'll figure it out."

And I hoped with all my heart that I could make good on it.

Birthday Bitch

KASH

A week passed in a whirl. Days in the greenhouse, after-noons with Marcus as he sifted through the unholy amount of paperwork our mother had dutifully ignored for months. Nights in Lila's arms, the distance between us always slim.

It had become impossible, in fact, to maintain any form of detachment. I'd become accustomed to ignoring our looming end, a constant presence that took up a dark space in my heart. But I happily pretended as if it wasn't silently waiting to be acknowledged.

Pretending felt good.

Being with me had proven to be as easy as I'd promised, and she was happy. And her happiness made me happy, the infectious feeling fuel for my denial. Neither of us had broached the sub-ject of our status, maintaining the front that there were still no strings, exclusive or not. But both of us knew we were in trouble. Whether it was because she had feelings for me or because she was worried I did remained to be seen. And I'd rather live in ignorance in order to keep her than to uncover that particular truth.

It was a trait I shared with my mother, it seemed.

The uncovering of my mother's secret turned into a massive excavation, resulting in horrifying discoveries. The noncompete in the wholesale contract she'd signed was a five year deal, one that Dad had been filling from the greenhouse unbeknownst to any of us. I'd thought it strange he'd taken to the occasional delivery, citing back or knee pain as a reason to drive rather than dig. But I couldn't have guessed he was delivering our crops to Bower. Of course, I'd never had a reason to be suspicious before now. Per the contracts, the shop could not gross two hundred thousand dollars in a calendar year, or we would have to either cease business or give the remaining profit to Bower. There was an escape hatch, a clause that said we could buy ourselves out of the contract.

The purchase amount: two million dollars.

Marcus might have been able to pay it had he not sunk all his money into saving the shop. The clause didn't specify *profit*, of which there was none—all of the money we'd made in the last few months went straight back in to pay off the debts accrued during the shop's downturn, with no small thanks to our horrible old accountant. Marcus had a lawyer friend, Ben, who'd taken us on, and the two of them were knee deep in the process of determining the legitimacy of the claim and running through our finances—a complex process involving a decade of improperly filed paperwork, invoices, and tax returns.

Either way, we had a minute before we had to close Longbourne's doors or turn over every penny we'd made. Which, as noted, was already gone.

In the meantime, it was business as usual. But we'd have some big decisions to make soon, and none of us had a good feeling about it.

I pulled the delivery van to a stop in the service bay of the Plaza, chatting with Charlie, one of the dock managers, about the event everyone was talking about—Natasha Felix's twenty-first birthday party.

Longbourne had put together the centerpieces, a few garlands, and the table display for the banquet portion of the evening, the "family" dinner that consisted of a cool three hundred guests at five hundred per head. Lila had planned this event, plus transportation for a hundred of those people to Noir, one of the hot nightclubs in town, which the Felix estate had rented out for the night. And it only cost them half a million dollars.

Chump change.

Charlie and I shook hands before I got to work, hauling arrangements out of the back and onto carts, which the staff transported into the venue. Lila's interns waited with instructions to set up the centerpieces, and I would get the table display and garlands in place. A couple hours was plenty of time, thanks to Tess's stellar organizational skills. She'd boxed, labeled, and color-coded everything, leaving me instruction sheets in triplicate.

The second I walked into the banquet hall, I saw her. As was her custom for evening events, she was in all black, the deepest, darkest of blacks against the cream of her skin. The pantsuit was tailored to fit her body in exact proportions—the V of her lapels, the bend of her waist, the flare of her jacket, the long, straight length of her pants that made her legs impossibly long. Her hair, which she usually wore up at events, was down and shining in waves like a starlet from the golden age.

When she saw me, she smiled in a stretch of red lips, sending an intern off with a word and striding in my direction. Without thought, I moved to meet her. There was nowhere else to go.

She kissed me, or I kissed her—I couldn't tell and didn't care. All that mattered was that we were kissing, brief and delicate as it was. When she leaned back, her gray eyes sparked like flint, bright and hot and lovely.

"What can I do for you?" I asked, my voice low and rough.

She hummed, watching her hand as it trailed down my shirt.

"So many ways to answer that question. But let's start with the flowers."

I kissed her nose. "If we must."

"Sadly, we must. But if you're up for a late night—" She froze, her eyes flicking behind me.

I heard her laughter and knew exactly who was there. Turning confirmed that Natasha Felix stood behind me, tall and blonde and beautiful in that contrived way only achieved by makeup artists and plastic surgeons.

Judging by the way the man at her side looked at Lila and the proprietary way Natasha hooked his arm, I could only assume this was Brock.

He was handsome, I'd give him that. Strong jaw, cool eyes, easy smile. Rich and confident, the kind of guy who walked into a room and drew the attention of everyone in it.

Stupid fuckbag. He had no idea what he'd had in her—and bully for me.

I turned fully, straightening my spine and drawing back my shoulders to flex the extent of my height and breadth on him. I wasn't even ashamed to posture so blatantly.

I wanted him to know who the bigger man was. The better man.

But Natasha laughed again, a disdainful sound, drawing herself a little closer to Brock the Cock.

"Wait, you're not telling me you're fucking the *gardener*, are you?" Cruel was her laugh as she glanced up at Brock.

He eyed me with challenge and an air of disbelief as he took stock of my appearance. Size aside, I was dressed in a T-shirt and jeans, not willing to mess up my good clothes, which were in a garment bag in the van, to haul up centerpieces.

Brock didn't seem impressed.

But Lila, ever the professional, smiled and stepped around me. "Not that it's any of your business, but yes. The bar is over here, already set up and ready. Shall we?"

She swept her hand in the direction of said bar, behind which was waiting a bored bartender on his phone. The minute he saw her glaring in his direction, he straightened up, tugging his coat to straighten it.

But neither Brock nor Natasha moved. Their gazes fixed on me.

"Kash Bennet," I said shortly, extending my hand to Brock in a gesture of good will, for Lila's sake.

They looked down in unison. He hesitated, and I didn't know if it was because he thought me beneath him or because he was just so fucking amused at the circumstance that he figured me for a joke.

I wondered if he'd think a black eye was funny. I sure as hell would.

Brock shrugged Natasha off and took my hand in an exaggerated clap and a squeeze that was too hard. I returned the gesture forcefully enough to feel his bones gather.

"Not every day I get to meet the guy fucking my ex," he said with a false smile and hard eyes.

Lila stiffened next to me, insult on her lips—I could feel it. But for the sake of her job, she kept her mouth shut. Fortunately, I wasn't bound by the same laws.

"Not every day I get to meet the guy who fucked her over." His face flashed with offense, but before he could speak, I said, "If you'll excuse me, I have some work to do."

"Dick," Natasha shot, slithering up next to Brock again.

"Nice to meet you too, Miss Felix." When I turned, I caught Lila's gaze.

Fuck them. Don't let them get to you, I told her without speaking. *I'm here.*

The tension in her eased, a ghost of a smile on her lips.

And with every ounce of my power, I left her there with those sharks, knowing she could hold her own and hating that she had to do it alone all the same.

My mind whirred with fury and spite as I worked on the table. The only way I survived was a continuous reminder that I wasn't going to make this table look spectacular for Natasha Felix. But for Lila, I'd do anything. Even make that eel's birthday look good.

I watched her move around the room, never still for longer than necessary. She greeted the Felix Femmes as they arrived with entourages in tow, directed her interns, fielded interruptions from the caterer, the DJ, hotel employees. And she did it all with that cool confidence, the control and command she ruled her environment with.

When the banquet table was set up and the garlands hung, I made my way around the room under the guise of double-checking the centerpieces. With Lila directing her interns, I had no doubt that they'd been done to the letter. But it gave me the opportunity to get closer to the Felixes and that fucking asshole Natasha had brought to parade in front of Lila like a prized pony.

I hated him, deeply and unreasonably. I didn't even know the guy, and the honest truth was that I had no place to call him an asshole. All he'd ever done was hurt her.

But by that measure, he was irredeemable.

The Felix women quieted when I neared, shifting things on a nearby table without purpose. The men excused themselves for the bar, and the second they were gone, rustling whispers fluttered at my back.

"Excuse me," one of them said. "I think this one's wrong."

When I turned, three-fourths of the Felix sisters eyed me hungrily, along with their mother, who I'd been sure I was going to marry when I was a kid, and I had a stack of *Sports Illustrated* with a bikini-clad Sorina Felix on the cover to prove it. The men of the pack gathered near the bar, sipping amber liquid from crystal glasses with flat, bored faces that said nothing short of, *If we're here, we might as well drink.*

Sure enough, it looked like the centerpiece was missing one of its candles.

"I see," I said with the smile I used to get women to smile back, belying my annoyance. No way had that candle not made it onto the table. Which meant one of the Femmes had taken it.

"I wonder if it's back there," Sofia said with a flick of her hand. "Maybe one of those interns lost it in the green stuff."

The "green stuff" was fern, a spray of it large enough to hide a candle, it was true. Nestled in its fronds were three lanterns—one of them devoid of its lighting—filled with flowers and moss.

"Mind if I have a look?" I asked.

"Be my guest," Angelika answered, recrossing her legs too widely to be considered modest by even the loosest definition.

Natasha glared, folding her arms as I tried to approach the table-top. I say *tried* because Sofia and Alexandra didn't budge, blocking my path with their crossed legs, elbows propped on the table in identical poses.

"Go ahead," Alexandra said with a devil's smile that made me regret my cheek in coming over here.

I'd thought I'd get some gossip. Instead, I had a feeling I was about to get my ass grabbed.

Sorina, their mother, leaned on the table with hot eyes and a salacious smile. "These are just so beautiful. You did a *wonderful* job."

"Oh, I can't take credit," I said lightly, leaning over their laps to delve my hands into the fern, rooting around for the rogue candle. "I just grow them."

"He works with his hands, Alex," Sofia said.

"I'll bet he does," Alexandra agreed. "Bet he plants his seeds all over the place too."

One of my brows rose, and I gave her a look. She returned it with an expression that belonged in a porno.

"God, it's like no one has standards anymore," Natasha barked.

Alexandra snapped back, "Fucking a doctor instead of a DJ doesn't make you suddenly enlightened. You're the same old slut you always were. Only difference is that *now* you're with a guy who can prescribe you penicillin for your STDs."

"Girls," Sorina said apathetically.

"You're the worst, you know that?" Natasha asked, standing in a huff, the action punctuated by a stamp of her foot and a bounce of her perfectly coiffed hair. "You'd think you'd at least be nice to me on my birthday."

But Alexandra laughed. "I'm sorry. I love you even though you're a desperate hag."

Natasha's cheeks flushed, her face screwed up with rage. "Whatever. I'm going to find Brock."

This time, all of them chuckled.

"She's so cute when she's mad," Sofia said.

"I hate you," Natasha shot over her shoulder as she strutted away in a glide that defied physics, given the height of her heels.

"But we love you," her sisters sang in unison, as if they'd had this exchange a thousand times.

She flipped them off without breaking her stride.

With a sigh, Alexandra stood. "I'll go get her."

"She'll feel better once she opens the Chanel ring I got her," Angelika said.

"Ugh, you bitch. I was going to get that for her too, but I wanted it for myself." Sofia pouted. "I got her Gucci instead."

Angelika perked up. "The sunglasses or the watch?"

"Both," Sofia answered with a smirk.

Angelika's eyes widened, her mouth opening up in wonder. "She's going to *die*."

"I know!" Sofia said on a giggle.

I'd moved out of the way a few minutes before, not wanting—or able—to interrupt as I waited to probe them for clues as to where the candle had gone. Their dynamic was as uncomfortable as it was understandable—if anyone got the sibling relationship and all its vicious colors, it was a Bennet. But they were spiteful and venomous while somehow also seeming to care for each other very much. It was astonishing really, just how godawful they were to each other by typical standards. And yet, they somehow kept on loving each other, despite their outbursts and jealously and general dreadful behavior.

I cleared my throat, and their attention swiveled to me again. "Any idea what could have happened to it?"

Sofia batted her lashes, playing at coy. "Have you checked under the table?"

"Oh, good idea," Alexandra added.

Sorina just smiled, her blank eyes locked on a patch of nothing in the distance. I wondered how often she ran away to some sanctuary in her mind, going vacant just to endure the snipes she'd bred.

I reached for the tablecloth, gathering it up to check the very edge, taking the bait. But I found nothing.

"You should get under there," Sofia insisted. "I'm sure it just fell, rolled underneath. I'd do it myself but …" She laughed rather than finish as if I could deduce the reasons myself.

"You know what?" I started, dropping the tablecloth and backing away. "I've got extras. I'll grab one."

Their faces fell into petulance.

"You're no fun," Alexandra said.

"No, he's just banging Lila," Sofia corrected. "Can you imagine what she'd do to him if he fucked around on her?"

"Well, all she did to Brock was leave him to Natasha. She didn't even put up a fight. Tash can't even get a reaction out of her. Doesn't matter what she does—cake to the face, insults … nothing. She's unflappable. If Natasha doesn't break her, this whole subplot for the show is going to be *so boring*."

At that, my jaw clamped shut. "She didn't put up a fight because she realized he was an asshole. And Natasha won't ever break her. I'm surprised you haven't already figured out she's indestructible."

They turned to look at me like they'd forgotten I was there, mouths gaping at the slight.

"Be right back with that candle," I said, smiling amiably before turning on my heels. That smile melted into a scowl the second I gave them my back.

Of course I knew she was anything but indestructible. Underneath her armor, she was soft and forgiving, easily bruised. But how could they know? To discover what was underneath, her trust had to be earned.

And once lost, I didn't think it could be regained.

I scanned the room for her, finding her next to the bar with a wax smile on her face, clipboard hooked in her elbow. And in front of her was Natasha in that ridiculous sparkly minidress, knife smile on her face as she fondled Brock's tie. A cameraman flanked them silently.

I made a hard turn, weaving around tables with a single objective—save her from whatever torture Natasha had devised.

"And if the scallops are cold, I swear to God, I'm going to be pissed," Natasha said as I approached. "Brock's a vegetarian, and if his favorite food isn't *perfect*, I'm holding *you* responsible."

"I'll double-check them myself," was Lila's answer.

Brock watched her with an intensity that had me fantasizing about how well my fist would fit into his eye socket.

"Good," she snapped. "How many cars do you have coming after dinner?"

"Twenty, as requested."

Her smile twisted. "Twenty? We'll need at *least* thirty."

Lila's smile didn't waver, but I saw the almost imperceptible tightening of her posture and eyes. "Are more guests coming to the club than originally planned?"

"I sent you a list," Natasha said, her innocent tone more bait than concealment. "Don't tell me you didn't get it."

"It's no problem," Lila answered lightly. "I'll have them waiting for you at ten."

Natasha apparently didn't possess much of a poker face. Or at least no ability to put it on when she was disappointed. "You'd better."

"Excuse me," I interjected, saying to Lila. "I need you to sign off on a few things, and I had a question for you."

"Of course," she said, smiling genuinely even if it was schooled for the sake of our audience. "If you'll excuse me," she addressed Natasha before turning without waiting for her response.

And together, we trucked away from them.

Once out of earshot, she let out a breath. "Thank you. I was imagining I was in Bora-Bora or London or Tokyo. Even an iron maiden. Honestly, I'd prefer an iron maiden to that, whatever it was."

"Fuck them," I said, gesturing to the service door in the same motion I laid a hand on the small of her back. "The sisters just admitted in front of me that Natasha's trying to get you to break on camera. She said you were a ... subplot?"

"Oh, I know."

I frowned, reaching out to hold the swinging door open for her. "You do?"

"Of course I do," she said as I followed. "You see, this is where my extraordinary stubbornness comes in handy. She wants me to cry and thrash and get mad, on camera if she can manage it. Or worse—she wants me to grovel. It's driving her nuts that I won't give her what she wants."

"The audacity," I said with a sideways smile touched with admiration.

"She's not going to goad me, no matter how painful it is to endure. The only thing I want to come of this is my complete ownership of my reactions, so at the end of the day, my job will be safe, along with my dignity."

I watched her as we wound our way past workers against the stream and into the kitchen. "You're no match for them."

She tossed me a smile over her shoulder. "I know. I only have a second, what did you need me to sign off on?"

I snagged her hand, towing her into a dark inlet packed with racks that would be filled with food any minute.

Lila gasped, laughing as I pulled her into my chest, one arm around her waist like a vise, the other steering my hand to her face.

"Just this," I said against her lips before I took them.

Too brief was the kiss, edged with the distance of her distraction. But still, she sighed happily when I let her lips go.

"You," she started, "are truly the best distraction a girl could ever ask for."

My heart flinched at the word, the one we brandished like cold steel to defend against the truth.

"I know." I smiled down at her. "And tonight, when this is all over, I'm gonna distract you again. And again. And again."

"I hope so," she said before kissing me again, this time with heat that betrayed her agenda for the promise of me. When she leaned back, she asked, "Did you have a question for me? Or was that a lie too?"

"I *did* need you to sign something, just not with a pen."

A chuckle, a fond slide of her hand from my neck to my chest. "What's the question?"

Without warning, questions rose in my mind, commandeered my heart. *Can we be more? Will you be mine? If I promise you something, will you do the same? If I fall in love with you, could you love me too?*

But I flashed that smile again, brandished it as I did that cursed word. "Are you wearing panties?"

She laughed from deep in her belly, her teeth bright and perfect, framed by crimson lips. "Are you?" she countered.

"Never," I answered, my hand moving to cup her ass, testing its weight and shape with my palm. "And I don't have underwear on either."

With a laugh and the swiftest of kisses, she backed away. And with a suggestive smile, she said, "Neither am I."

Two steps, and she disappeared around the corner, leaving me panting in the dark.

And for new and happy reasons, I couldn't wait for this night to end.

Heartless

LILA

The second Natasha's guests began to arrive in earnest, the night got easier by half.

I wasn't sure how I survived seeing Brock, here, with her. He watched me all night from her side, face unreadable, drink in one hand, the other on her waist as she flitted around the ballroom. It was almost unbearable to watch, a shocking alternate universe—or universal joke—that I had to witness my ex on the arm of the biggest client of my career.

And I couldn't get mad. I couldn't be sad. I couldn't be bitter, and I couldn't be petty. So I packed each emotion in its own little box and stuffed it in the basement of my heart so I could do my job.

And I did the shit out of my job.

Every course was perfectly timed, flawlessly cooked, and the exact temperature it was supposed to be, which I was sure Natasha triple-checked. The DJ's set went off without a hitch or a hiccup. The speeches were made in her honor, and the champagne flowed with effervescent ease. And by the end of dinner, Natasha seemed to have forgotten all about me.

My only respite was Kash.

He'd changed into slacks and a button-down, both straining to contain his massive form. His tie was perfectly knotted, which I'd never realized was a turn on. But it was. I imagined his big, rough hands tying that knot and decided I'd have him put it back on after he tied me up with it.

As reassuring as I'd been about the hired cars, I'd immediately known it was going to be a problem, and it was. Saturday night in Manhattan was the first strike. I'd booked the cars months ago in order to reserve enough to cart every person she knew—and their agents, producers, or groupies—to the club. As predicted, they had no extra cars, but somehow, we found a fleet in New Jersey, thanks to some strong words, a few phone calls, and the promise of an inflated rate.

With the chaos of the cars, I wouldn't get to the club in advance of the caravan to make sure everything was ready. So I sent my best intern to make sure Noir was in place, as nervous as that made me.

And so at two-after-ten, I found myself waiting at the curb under the awning, staring down Fifth, looking for thirty Escalades, ten of which were, by my estimation, going to be late.

I heard the birthday crowd before the doors opened, and people flooded out. Drunken, obscenely rich people led by none other than Natasha Felix.

"I knew she wouldn't get the cars," she said too loudly. Her toadies laughed. "I never thought I'd see the day that Lila Parker actually fucked up."

As if on cue, the first of a line of black SUVs rolled up.

"Aw, man," Natasha whined when she saw them.

Smile firmly in place, I breathed my relief and walked down the line, counting. My phone, which was clutched in my fist, vibrated with an alert that the other cars were three minutes away. And then my smile was genuine.

Guests filed into car after car, taking their drunken time, and by the time the first twenty had made their way around the block, filled up with people like clown cars, the final ten had arrived.

Sorina and her husband, Adrien, were last to leave, having waited to say goodbye to their guests.

Adrien climbed in with nothing more than a sullen nod in my direction, but Sorina stopped, smiling that dazzling smile of hers, to take my hands.

"You were wonderful, Lila. Thank you for making my baby's birthday party so utterly flawless."

"It was my pleasure," I lied.

"We never could tell her no," she said fondly. "I'm afraid to her detriment."

Unsure how to respond, I landed on, "I'm sure she's perfectly lovely. Just not to me."

"That's kind of you to lie, Lila. You might know," she started, stilling and softening with the remembrance I'd read of in a dozen magazines, "when I was a girl, we had nothing. We were refugees, hungry and running from war and into France. When I was discovered in Paris, it was more than a job I was given. It was a way to save my family, save myself."

A pause, pregnant with memories before she continued, "I shouldn't spoil the girls as I do, but I never … I never wanted them to know what it was like. To be without." With a breath, she straightened up, smiling. "Plus, with three older, ambitious sisters, Natasha has to fight for attention. Good attention or bad, it doesn't matter. The show doesn't help—so much of their behavior is for the cameras, for the drama of it all. But my girls have always been very"—she hesitated, searching for the word—"*emotional* and opinionated. They rarely make it easy, but you have managed them exquisitely."

"Thank you, Sorina," I said, not needing to pretend this time.

Another pause, her smile fading. If her brows had been able to move, I had the feeling they would have gathered with concern.

"I realize the position you're in. With Brock and Natasha. And I want you to know that I admire your grace. You are a diamond, Lila Parker—brilliantly shining and completely unbreakable."

I would have been suspicious had she not been so earnest. And though her eyes were a little glassy, she didn't seem overtly drunk. It was an admission, nothing more. And I appreciated it.

"If only we could be truly unbreakable," I said with a smile to disguise the truth of that wish. "But I appreciate your support. There's no need to worry for me."

"Oh, I don't. If there's one thing I won't ever have to worry about, it's you." With a smile, she turned for the car and climbed in.

I watched that last SUV drive away, taking a moment to collect myself, to let the sense of understanding—and I couldn't call it forgiveness, but acceptance, maybe?—sink in. It was emotional distance, as if observing them from behind a glass wall. A moment of objectivity. It was easier to think of Natasha as a wild honey badger, hissing at me with a threat she couldn't act on. Because there was nothing she could do to me that hadn't already been done, other than get me fired. But so long as I didn't take the bait and open her cage, everything would be fine.

With the draw of a long, heavy breath, I turned for the doors to check on vendor load-out before heading to the club. Walking the plush hallways of the Plaza, Brock was on my mind.

Natasha I could accept. But Brock I could not. Considering he was in his mid-thirties, I figured it could be a midlife crisis. Or maybe some Peter Pan complex. He was vain, and on that merit alone, I could see the appeal of someone like Natasha. And he was arrogant, which he'd found a likeness with in her. Really, they had so much more in common than he and I did. She offered him youth, power, and the combined pride that made them nearly bulletproof.

I wondered if either of them had feelings, real, honest feelings. Natasha definitely felt rage and jealousy. Brock felt entitlement. But beyond that, what did they care for other than themselves?

And how had I gone on so long with someone so deeply selfish?

As much as I hated seeing him, he just kept making it easy for me to walk away. Oh, how much harder it would have been had he told me all the things I'd once wanted to hear, professed his love, begged me for forever. Don't get me wrong, I still would have walked away. It just would have been harder, that was all.

I had to admit my satisfaction when Brock had seen Kash and me together. When Kash snarked at him with that easy smile on his face, defended me when he didn't need to, saved me when I could have saved myself, just because he could. Just because he wanted to.

A hot ache bloomed in my chest. Kash was my safe place, my refuge. He was the best part of my life, which at present was dominated by the pack of starving hyenas known as the Felix Femmes and the fact that I was on the rebound and homeless. He gave me respite. But what had started off as a distraction had turned into something more. Something deeper.

I didn't want it to end. I didn't want it to go away, though I'd done my best to put a modicum of space between us, thin as it was. There was nothing else I could do since realizing my feelings and the subsequent awareness that they probably weren't returned. Except to tell him the truth.

But if I lost my safe place now, I'd come unraveled.

I closed my eyes and hung on to Kash with all my strength, solidly in denial where I would remain until I had no other choice.

The ballroom was pandemonium. Racks of chairs were being filled noisily. The kitchen crew rid tables of remaining glasses and flatware. Table linens were stripped and dumped into rolling bins. My two remaining interns were helping Kash pack up the centerpieces and displays, and by the look of it, they were nearly done. Sadly, Tess's organization didn't work in reverse—everything had been shoved willy-nilly in boxes and loaded onto carts, which hotel employees were already rolling out the back to be moved into his van. He directed it all with that cool, collected way he had about him, commanding attention while somehow remaining affable and undemanding. And everyone listened because everyone loved him.

I, on the other hand, ruled by fear. Not on purpose—it was just my nature. A byproduct of my incessant suspicion and general mistrust that someone else could do any given job to my requirements. Especially when the results of their work reflected directly on me.

As I checked in with the various crews, I watched Kash out of my periphery, wishing I could be so relaxed while being that productive. People said I was unflappable when in fact I got ruffled rather easily. Kash Bennet was *truly* unflappable. He remained unperturbed under the most stressful and chaotic of circumstances. When faced with a challenge, he kept a confident calm, assumed that everything would work out, and vowed to help however he could to make it so.

If he could bottle that up and sell it, I'd buy a truckload.

When I made it around to him, his arms were buried to the shoulders as he lowered the wound-up garland into a huge box.

"Looks like you're almost done," I said. "I think that's the fastest floral load-out I've ever seen."

"Well," he said as he stood, "I figured I'd better get to it if I'm going with you to the club."

I flushed with gratitude. "Are you sure? It's going to be nothing but rich, drunk celebrities and socialites for hours."

"If you think I'm letting you walk into that snake pit alone, you don't know me at all."

"Thank you," I said, relieved that I'd have backup. "I have to get going. Meet me there?"

A nod and a smile. "I'll be right behind you."

The depth of that statement didn't escape me. He had my back, and I didn't take that for granted.

With a brief kiss and last-minute instructions to my interns, I was on my way out, carrying out phase two of the night that wouldn't end. There was very little for me to do at the club. The venue had been rented out and would run as it always did. They had their own security and amenities, and as such, there wasn't much for me to coordinate. But I couldn't leave until the last guest was gone. Part of my job was to be on hand in case something went wrong. I was the fixer, the person whose sole purpose was to make sure everything went exactly as planned. But once we hit the balloon drop, the champagne distribution, the giant cake, and the birthday singing, I would have nothing to do but be present for the last two hours of the night.

Hopefully, Natasha would be too busy to bother with me. Thank goodness I'd have Kash to keep me company. And then, when it was all said and done, we could go back to the hotel and climb into bed, and he could make me forget tonight ever happened.

I held onto that thought as I slipped into a cab and rushed to the club. It was a gorgeous building, everything black and gold, the sign reading *Noir* in an art deco font. In fact, everything was deco, from the geometric bursts and slashes in glimmering gold to the finger curls and shimmering fringe of the aerial dancers suspended from the ceiling.

Everything was exactly in order, the club beginning to fill up. The hundred people we'd carted over were the tip of the iceberg—she'd invited eight hundred of her closest friends, and I suspected with their dates and people attempting to sneak in, we would hit the venue's capacity.

As promised, Kash was right behind me. He took up post at the smaller bar off the dance floor, sipping on whiskey and serving as a silent presence, a touchstone in the madness of the club while I floated from post to post, making sure everything was running smoothly. Although the party was full of celebrities and invite only, there was still a VIP section upstairs, and I made my way up on my circuit with no real intention other than to keep moving.

Brock stood at the bar, long body stretched out as he leaned against the surface, elbow on the glossy onyx trimmed with gold, drink hanging in the circle of his fingers. Natasha was nowhere to be seen, and for that, I was grateful. Although the space was barely lit and full of people, his eyes snapped to me, just like they'd done all night.

Discomfort wriggled in me, and I straightened myself up to banish it, heading for the other end of the bar where one of the managers stood.

A brief conversation with her confirmed that everything was up to scratch, and with a word of thanks, I turned to get out of there before Natasha came back. I'd successfully avoided her all night, and though I was sure my luck would run out at some point, I wasn't planning on knocking on its door.

Brock, it seemed, had other plans.

He pushed off the bar, striding toward me like a bullet. Pretending I didn't see him, I kept moving for the stairs.

"Lila," he called.

But it was loud, so I kept walking as if I hadn't heard.

His hand on my arm was unfortunately unavoidable.

I stopped. Turned. Looked down at his hand, which he removed with a slide, his fingers tasting the shape of my forearm before dropping away.

"Are you all right?" he asked, brows drawn.

"What do you care?" I asked back with a calm I didn't feel.

"A lot actually." A pause. "Listen, I know this isn't easy—"

"Don't pretend to understand how I feel. Now, if you'll excuse me—"

"No, I won't excuse you. Because I *know* you're not okay, Lila."

"Then why did you ask?"

"Because contrary to your belief, I do care."

A humorless laugh shot out of me.

At least he had the decency to look remorseful. "I'm sorry for this. For all of it. I just wanted you to know."

"You mean you wanted me to let you off the hook." I stared at the stranger before me, finding the truth of that accusation all over his face. "I can't believe you. You really expect me to clear *your* conscience? Because I may be a lot of things, but a liar isn't one of them."

Rather than flinching like I'd hoped, he drew himself up to his full height, eyes narrowing. "This ... none of this is what I thought it would be."

"I can't say I'm surprised."

"When she came to me—" He caught himself, pausing to re-orient what he'd been planning to say. "None of the reasons make sense to me anymore, Lila. I can't seem to understand how we got here."

"I'd be happy to remind you. I'm sure Natasha wouldn't mind either."

His eyes narrowed. "Do you always have to be such a bitch? Jesus, Lila, I'm trying to apologize."

"And I've already told you, it's not accepted." I tried to turn, but he hooked my arm.

"I didn't mean to hurt you. I wouldn't have even come to-night if I could have avoided it. But then again, I didn't realize your fuckboy would be here, or I wouldn't have felt so bad."

For a moment, I stared at him with a storm brewing in my chest, knowing full well that if that storm came to fruition, I was going to get myself in trouble, more trouble than I was already in. "Are we done here? I need to go check on the cake and balloons for your *girlfriend*."

His jaw locked, the muscles bouncing as he watched me for a handful of heartbeats. "Yeah, we're done here."

"Good. If there's a problem, do me a favor and tell anyone but me."

With a dizzying turn, I headed for the stairs, hands shaking as I made my way down to the main floor. The crowd was thick and bouncing, the music thumping at such a decibel, I felt it in my chest, in the air. I saw Kash from across the club, his smile fading as he looked me over. He straightened up as if to move for me, and that reassurance would have made me smile had Natasha Felix not stepped in front of me with murderous eyes.

I stopped, jolting back a little from the shock and velocity of my pace.

"Is everything to your liking?" I asked, praying to God that there was a problem I could actually solve.

"As a matter of fact, it's not. I saw you talking to Brock."

I stiffened, feeling the presence of a cameraman at my elbow. *It's a setup.* "Then you also saw that he chased me down to talk to me. I have no intention of speaking to him again, if that makes you feel better."

"It doesn't," she shot with enough force that she listed. I realized just how drunk she was, and my worry deepened. "It doesn't make me feel better. You are not to speak to him."

Rebellion flared. "Nowhere in my contract does it state that you can dictate who I speak to and who I don't."

But she smiled that wicked, cruel smile. "Rumor is, you don't get along with Addison Lane. Wonder what she'd think if she heard you flirted with my boyfriend all night."

That got my attention. My lips flattened, face stiff. "Maybe you should worry more about your *boyfriend* and less about me. He stopped me, Natasha, not the other way around. If you honestly think I want to even lay eyes on him again, you haven't been paying attention. But really, I should be thanking you. If it wasn't for you, I never would have realized what a pathetic shitbag he is."

She pulled in a breath that heaved her chest, and then she breathed fire. "You really don't feel anything, do you? He said you were cold and heartless, but I didn't really believe it until just now. You don't care about anything but yourself, do you? You're a robot, just like he said. And a terrible lay. *That,*" she said, hatefully looking down my body, "I believed."

"Takes one to know one," I answered, forcing a smile. "It's almost time for your cake."

She glared, shoulders square, blocking my path.

"If you don't let me go, we won't be able to start," I reasoned with a single desire—to get as far away from her as I could.

"Stay away from him," she said through her teeth.

"My pleasure."

I clipped away on shaky legs, making my way through the crowd and backstage. The crew didn't need anything from me but a point to my watch, and in seconds, the music stopped so the DJ could announce her birthday. The cake would roll onto the dance floor, one of Katy Perry's dancers would pop out, "Happy Birthday" would be sung, and the balloons would drop.

On autopilot, I watched the cake come out, finding my intern up on the catwalk with a crew member holding the rope to the balloons. The happenings went on around me, and I observed with clinical detachment, my mind somehow both present and a thousand miles away.

You really don't feel anything, do you?

How I wished she were right. The sting of her salt burned to my bones. But it wasn't just the words she'd spoken. It was the truth in them. Maybe this was all my fault. Maybe I'd pushed him away, or maybe I'd been too bold. Maybe I was cold. Heartless. Unlovable and unable to love.

Maybe it had been me all along.

I felt Kash near with a gathering of my senses, of my nerves, as if they were reaching for him. When I turned, I found worry written all over him—in the line between his brows, in the flattening of his lips, in the draw of his shoulders and the tightness of his fists at his sides.

And I cracked under the pressure, the scaffolding crumbling just because he was here, and he was safe, and he was strong enough to carry my burden with me.

He said nothing, just wrapped me up in his arms, slipped a hand into my hair to cup my head, holding me to his chest like a precious thing. And I breathed him in, the scent of earth and soap and musk.

They started singing when he leaned back to inspect my face as if for wounds. "Who do I need to kill?"

My laughter surprised me. "They're not worth a felony."

A flicker of a smile. "Tell me."

"Brock caught me upstairs."

Kash tensed.

"It was fine. He wanted me to make him feel better about this whole thing, and I refused."

"Attagirl," he said, that corner of his lips ticking up again.

"But Natasha saw and cornered me. Or blockaded me. She threatened my job, pressed my bruises. She wants to hurt me. In fact, I think she's planning to make a career out of it."

"Can't imagine there'd be much money in it."

I wished I could laugh.

"Do you think she's just doing it for the cameras?"

"Maybe."

He paused, seeming unnerved by my silence. "What did she say?"

"That ... that I didn't care about anyone but myself. That Brock was right—I'm emotionless, heartless. Passionless. Maybe they're right." Anything else I might have said jammed in my throat, squeezed tight with emotion.

"They're not." Kash cupped my face, held it delicately in his wide palm, tilted it up to his. "Do you hear me? They're wrong. You care more than anyone I've ever known, and I'm a Bennet."

The smallest of laughs eased my heart.

"I mean it," he insisted with quiet demand. " I have seen your passion, and it has left me changed."

I stared up at him, at the fervency in his face and the honesty of his words. "Kash ..."

"They want to hurt you, Natasha strictly for sport. Don't let them. Don't give them that. Because they are wrong about you. Trust me when I promise you that."

"I do," I said, believing him with my whole heart.

A soft, sweet smile brushed his lips. "I also promised I'd make you forget him, and I don't break my promises."

"It worked," I admitted with reckless courage. "It worked too well."

He stilled.

For a protracted moment, we hung in that limbo, watching each other as we stood at the edge I'd been so afraid of for so long. And there was nothing left to do, no ground left to rely on.

It was time to jump.

"Kash, nothing about this feels like a rebound. This isn't a fling, not for me. I don't know when it happened, when things changed. Maybe it was there from the start. Maybe I've just been too afraid to admit it."

"Don't be afraid. Don't ever be afraid, not of me."

"No, never of you. Afraid of losing you." I swallowed a dry knot, meeting his gaze with all the strength I had in me. "I understand this isn't what you proposed. You said the only risk was to the re-boundee, but it's not. You've told me time and again that this is a distraction, nothing more. So I understand if you say no, but I need to know. If I asked you for more, would you give it?"

A thundering heartbeat marked the time for him to draw a breath. "Lila, I'd give you anything you asked. I think you know that."

Tears pricked the corners of my eyes. "Even this? Even your heart?"

At that, he bestowed the full extent of his smile on me. "Especially that. All I ever wanted was you, any way I could get you. I wasn't foolish enough to imagine you'd ever want anything more from me."

"But why?" I asked, confused.

"Because ..." He paused, eyes flicking beyond us to the crowd. "Because I'm not like you. I'm not like them." He nodded to the dance floor. "I'm just a filthy, uneducated gardener who lives with his parents."

"You think that's all I care about?" I breathed, the echo of Natasha's words in my ears.

"No, I know it's not. But you date guys like Brock. He represents a life I can't give you, a person I can never be."

"But Kash, that's *exactly* why I want you. Because you are nothing like them."

For a moment, he watched me, something uncertain behind his eyes as he searched mine. "What do you want, Lila? What do you want us to be?"

The question jolted me, simple and straightforward as it was, and it gave me pause, pause that deepened the uncertainty in his eyes. So I said what was in my head without reservation.

"I don't know what we are, what I want us to be, not exactly. All I know is that I want *you*, all of you."

He stroked my hair, traced my face. "I didn't think we'd ever get here, to this moment. I've wanted to tell you for so long, but I didn't want to lose you. I didn't know if you were ready for this. For me. For more."

"I was. I am." A pause. "I was going to, you know. I was going to tell you the day we planted Ophelia, but you said you'd be my rebound guy, and it broke my heart."

"I wish you had."

I watched him, thinking through all the missed opportunities, all the wasted time. "What do you want, Kash? Tell me so I can give it to you."

"For you to be happy. That's all."

Sweet were those words, selfless and true, and I felt every one. "I am," I said before kissing him to prove it.

The crowd behind us cheered. The balloons fell. The music started again.

But we didn't notice and didn't care as we kissed in a dark alcove.

And I didn't let him go until I was certain he knew he was mine.

A Certain Rightness

KASH

I could have kissed her forever.

    We hung there in time, suspended and oblivious to anything beyond our hearts and our wishes. But despite what we wanted, the clock began to tick once more. She was called away, and I was left there to consider my luck as the night went on.

    Fortunately for all of us, without incident.

    Natasha was too hammered and busy with her friends to bother with Lila, and Brock stuck close enough to her that it bordered on lewd. And I mean that honestly—there was a point when they were grinding on the dance floor that I couldn't be certain he wasn't actually fucking her.

    But with the lion's share of her duties done, I did mine—I kept her back to the peep show and her eyes on me.

    The clock mercifully struck two, and the house lights glared everyone toward the exit. As the stumbling, chattering crowd moved in that direction, Natasha climbed into the DJ booth, stole his mic, and instructed everyone to meet them at an afterhours club a few blocks away. When she dropped the microphone, the feedback nearly deafened us all, but she was unfazed, strutting her way to the exit with surprising grace for someone so tanked.

As she and Brock passed, she caught sight of Lila and shifted, beelining in our direction, her face darkening. She was looking for a fight and had Lila in her crosshairs. I moved to put myself in her path, prepared to throw her over my shoulder if I had to, but fortunately, I didn't. To his credit, Brock kept ahold of her, whispering something in her ear that made her laugh. That laugh was at Lila's expense—I knew strictly through observation. With a spiteful glance in our direction, they walked away.

When Lila exhaled, it was a thousand years of relief she let go. She brightened by increment, giving me a fleeting kiss before bounding off to wrap up her last duties. And I leaned back on the bar and watched her go, my foot hooked on the barstool rung and my heart on fire.

All I'd wished for, all I'd wanted, she'd delivered with the deepest affection. The admission had released me, the truth of her feelings sunshine on the fog of my doubt.

She wanted more. She wanted me. And this wouldn't end. At least not because we didn't try.

And I hoped beyond hope that we could find a way to make that work.

Find a way, I vowed as she strode toward me.

The smile on her face shouldn't have been as fresh as it was for two in the morning. "You ready?" she asked.

With a nod, I stood, offering my arm. And out the door we went, into the cold New York night. I stepped to the curb, hand in the air and whistle on my lips. And within a minute, we were sliding into the warm cab, closing the night out behind us.

I gave him the address as Lila slid across the bench to nestle into my side with another sigh, this one lazy, sleepy.

"You finally run out of energy?" I asked, kissing the top of her head where it rested on my shoulder.

"Maybe a little," she admitted. "This always happens—the let-down after a long night. It feels so good to not have to wear that mask anymore."

"I don't know how you do it."

"Sometimes, I don't either. I just turn it on when it needs to be on, and I leave it on without regard for how much electricity it takes. That is, until I get the bill." She shifted to stretch her legs a little, rolling her ankles.

"Feet hurt?"

"Nope."

I leaned back to look at her.

"I can't feel them."

A laugh slipped out of me. "Well, I'll get you out of them soon enough. And the rest of this."

She mock pouted. "What, you don't like the rest of this?"

"Oh, trust me, I do. I just like you out of them even more."

A happy sigh left her. "Thank you. For coming with me. I thought it would never end."

"Psh, please. That was the most fun people-watching I've had in ages."

"The rich and ridiculous *are* entertaining, if not a nightmare to work for. Did you see Ariana Grande trying to climb onto the aerial setup?"

"When she was on Shawn Mendes's shoulders, trying to reach one of the girls? I don't know if she was sober enough to realize she was short by at least fifteen feet."

She laughed. "No, when she climbed up on the catwalk. It took three security guards to get her down."

"Thank God she didn't fall. What about when Katy Perry came out in that pineapple costume?"

"Her hat was a paper umbrella! I don't even know why she did it, but watching her dance in it the rest of the night was the highlight of the whole ordeal."

"Better than having to clean up Gwyneth Paltrow's sick?" I asked.

She groaned, still laughing. "I have never seen so much vomit come out of a single human being in my life."

"Ninety percent kale, ten percent gin."

Another groan, this one coupled with a swat to my chest. "I mean, it was awfully green."

I shuddered. "File under Things I'd Never Like to See. I totally had a thing for her when I was a kid."

She twisted in my arms to give me a look. "You. A fan of Gwyneth Paltrow movies."

"I'll have you know, I have a very diverse movie repertoire."

Her look intensified.

"I have an older sister, you know," I admitted, which only eased the look by a hair. "And we take turns distracting my mother by watching period dramas with her. Emma is one of her favorites."

"Distracting her from what?"

"Oh, you know. Sneaking out. Sneaking people *in*." I paused. "Actually, that's pretty much it."

"Emma, huh?"

"And Shakespeare in Love. But Sliding Doors is my favorite."

"That's not a historical."

"No, but it *is* a great movie. That Scottish dork ending up with Gwyneth Paltrow gave me hope that I had a shot."

"With Gwyneth?" she asked on a laugh.

"Nah. Just in general."

"Please. I can't believe you ever doubted you could get any girl you wanted. Most guys too, I'd wager."

"Believe it or not, I wasn't always this *dashing*," I said with a British accent.

"Impossible. You forget I knew you as a teenager."

"Ask any of my siblings. Or my mom, but be prepared to spend the next three hours looking through photo albums. I was the runt of the litter, Laney not included."

"You're six-two."

"Not until I was eighteen," I noted.

"Kassius Bennet," she said, leaning away with a stern look on her face, "I personally know at least five girls in high school who you ruined for life."

I frowned. "You're thinking of Luke."

"Brenna Jacobs, Leah Fairview, Portia Chambers"—she ticked off on her fingers—"Evelyn Morley, and Cassie Argyle. Should I go on?"

"None of those girls actually liked me," I insisted.

"That's not what Evelyn said after prom. *She* said she was in love with you, but you brutally dumped her *in the middle of the dance.*"

"Because I caught her making out with Brian Sears under the bleachers."

Her mouth popped open. "No."

"Yup. Right behind the punch bowl. I saw her dress between the slats. Couldn't miss it."

"No one could. She looked like a safety cone."

"Those girls didn't like me, trust me. In fact, most of them were more interested in getting close to Luke than being with me."

"Why?" she asked, face screwed up.

"I think you could ask your sister that question," I joked, seeing as how Ivy and Luke had been friends with benefits through high school and then some.

"I never got the appeal. He was too …"

"Uninhibited?"

"Exactly. How'd you guess?"

"You like rules too much for a guy like Luke."

"That's true. But really, I just didn't think he was as hot as everybody made him out to be."

"Everybody says we look alike," I said with a brow arched.

"You don't. He looks like trouble."

"And what do I look like?"

She considered the question with a smile on her face, which tilted back and forth as she inspected me. "Safety."

I reached for her, drawing her to my arms, into my chest where the word had struck like an arrow. "I am, you know."

"I do," she said, her hand on my face and her eyes bright with honesty.

I kissed her so she wouldn't say more, a tender seam of our lips. And I wondered how to stop myself from falling. Once in motion, was there anything I could do? Would I be too late to throw out my hands, to minimize the damage? Or was I already doomed?

I knew the answer without fully acknowledging it, glancing over it, through it, anywhere but directly in the eye. There was no way to separate myself from the truth—I was in over my head. I was at her mercy. And I couldn't turn back if I wanted to. Which I didn't.

So I kissed her until our breaths were heavy, until the function of my brain quieted to only the most necessary of functions necessary to hold her. I kissed her until the car had been still long enough for the cabbie to clear his throat. And the second we were through the lobby and into the elevator of the hotel, I kissed her again. I kissed her down the hallway in a blind stumble for our room, swallowed her sighs and her laughter. I kissed her into our room, the one we'd shared for weeks, long enough that the suite was filled with us—our memories, our nights, all the whispers and all the laughter.

And all I wanted, all I wanted in the world, was for her to be mine.

And she finally was.

The room was dark, unfathomably black. I could see nothing in the infinite darkness, but I could feel her. Hear her breath, the shuffle of fabric and abandoned shoes and bare feet on carpet, and the sound of our lips as they met, parted, met again. Electric was the feeling, and I imagined that if I opened my eyes, I would catch sight of a spark when fingertips brushed skin, where our bodies met, skating over our lips in a crackling web.

Her hands. They were all I could consider as they held my face, the scratch of my stubble loud against her soft palms. Down my chest they roamed with fire in their wake, down to the buckle of my pants.

Her lips disappeared, but her breath puffed against mine, a noisy pant that I matched as she tugged my belt loose with a jingle. The vibration of my zipper zinged against my cock, and once freed, the silken warmth of her hand wrapped itself around me, stroking as if her fingertips wanted a taste strictly for their own pleasure. Blindly, I reached for her face, cupped her jaw, found her nose with mine, then her lips for a kiss. But her hands didn't stop their slow path up my shaft, cupping my crown before sliding down once more. Her fingers fanned each time they finished the circuit, brushing my sack with gentle authority.

My fingers slipped into her hair and tightened, tugging to tilt her face, to moan around her tongue, into her mouth, down her throat. But still, she didn't stop. My feet were planted, knees locked—if they hadn't been, I feared they would have buckled. Her mouth moved in time with her fist and fingers, drawing that feeling from deep in my belly, from low in my base.

Again, her mouth disappeared, this time with the lowering of her body too fast to be considered anything but desperate. As if she needed me, every inch of me, for herself. A tug of my pants, and they slid down my thighs, one hand still clutching my shaft, angling it toward her lips—I could feel her breath against my crown, a pulse of desire flexing through me at the sensation. Anticipation was thick, my hands smoothing her hair, sweeping it over her shoulder, gathering it in my fist to keep it out of the way. Without sight, I waited with anxious breath tight in my lungs for the moment of contact. But the truth of the feeling was beyond my imagination—a wet, warm taste. The flat of her tongue in the ridge of my crown. The very tip of me in the humid chamber of her mouth before it closed around me. And when I could breathe again, it was with a shaky sigh.

My senses exploded, raw and attuned and humming. The hot

hollow of her mouth, the feel of her tongue, the soft pull of suction, her hand fisted at my base, shifting in time to the motion of her neck. Her silky hair in my hand, the curve of her neck under my palm, the line of her jaw against my thumb. The sound of her breath and of mine, the wet kiss of her mouth, the hum from deep in her throat, an answering hum of my own.

It was an eternity. It was a heartbeat. And I would wait for her no longer.

With a flex, I retreated, surprising a gasp out of her. I urged her to stand with my hands on her face, taking her lips the second I could find them in the darkness. Tasted the salt of my body until it mingled into the taste of *us*. Threaded an arm around her waist, moving blindly for the bed. Delicately, I laid her down, slipping my thigh between hers to pin her hips. But they wouldn't stay still whether I desired it or not, shifting slow circles and waves to use the weight of my body to apply pressure where she wanted it, needed it. I propped on my elbow, my free hand worked her clothes, and her hands joined the task. First the suit coat, shrugged off and disappearing into the void of blackness. Then the small buttons of her shirt, too dainty for my big, clumsy fingers. I kissed her as she made easy work of them, taking the opportunity to unbutton her pants, to slip my fingers into the space between her hip and the fabric, to drag them over the swell and down her thighs. With a shimmy, they were gone, as was her shirt. And on inspection by my hungry hands, her bra was gone too.

Naked before me in the utter darkness. Filling my palm with soft flesh. Breathing her breath, the drum of her heart against my fingertips.

My lips parted with hers in favor of her jaw. Her neck. The hollow of her throat. Her breast in my palm, tight peak brushing my lips. A flick of my tongue. Then a sweep. Then a deep draw. A sigh, her fingers in my hair as I paid my homage to her body by way of her breasts. Down the valley of her breastbone. Over the soft swell of her stomach.

I spread her legs, settled my chest between them, found her heat first with my fingertips, then with my tongue, the taste, the sweetness of her flooding me with desire. My tongue did the job that my cock wanted, but with more finesse, a long, languid lapping. A silken, scandalous sucking. A shift of my face, never releasing my latch, a draw of my tongue that set her thighs trembling against my shoulders and back arching. A tightening of her body around my finger. Another, with a shift of her hips into my mouth. A sharp gasp, the lock of her body for a single, frozen moment, and she came with a hot burst and a galloping pulse from the very depths of her.

Swiftly, before she came down, I climbed up to meet her. And knowing, she reached for me, made room for me, room that I filled with my body, pressing her into the bed, slipping into her with a flex and a sigh of relief. As if I had been waiting for this moment always. As if this was the place I was most right. Stripped bare and laid before her, plain as day in the darkest of night.

A roll of my hips, and she pulsed around me. Another thrust, teasing her orgasm, coaxing it to life again. The embers flamed with a cry from her lips, the sound stoking the fire in me. My name. She whispered my name, the sound dissolving into a moan as my awareness slipped away, drawing toward the place where our bodies met. Unbound, without control, my restraint falling away like shackles, I slammed into her, my body curling around her, holding her in place, where she belonged. With me.

The orgasm shuddered through me, quaking and trembling as my hips and hands and outstretched neck acted on their own, the reins gone and my pleasure careening away.

I sagged, burying my face in the curve of her neck as her arms wound around mine, her breath noisy in my ear and mine smothered by her skin, which I kissed with devoted tenderness. Our bodies were locked in a twist of limbs and necks and hands, and though our bodies languished, we didn't let go.

We *couldn't* let go.

And I foolishly hoped we'd never have to.

Biohazard

LILA

Morning came too soon.

A sliver of daylight carved its name on the wall, the only light to enter the room since yesterday, I supposed. Even though it was the slimmest illumination, it seemed to touch every corner of the room. After so much darkness, the light almost blazed, casting a halo on his sleeping profile. The strong nose, flat ridge. The angle and swell of his lips. The jaw made of stone, his chest made of brick. Sheets twisted around his narrow waist, the fabric thin enough to make out the shape of his hips and corded muscles of his legs, as well as the bulge that made my thighs clench around its ghost.

He woke with a noisy intake of breath through his nose and a simultaneous shift to his side, arm stretching out to hook my waist and pull me into his chest. And I curled into him, smiling at nothing, covering his hand with my own.

His lips brushed my bare shoulder. "Morning."

I hummed like a cat in the sun. "Can it be night again?"

A chuckle as he nosed my hair from my neck and kissed me again. "In about nine hours, it sure can."

My day would be long, and I didn't want to do any of it. Not the paperwork or dealing with Addison or putting the finishing touches on Angelika's wedding. Two weeks, and this whole ordeal would be over. I hoped last night would be the worst of it, that abominable birthday party plaguing my calendar for weeks. Now there was only one thing left to do—I'd get through this wedding, make it the best goddamn event the Felixes had ever seen, and be on my merry way.

"That bad?" Kash asked. I could hear him smirking.

"What gave it away?" I turned around in his arms, our legs scissoring together.

"You sighed."

"Did I?"

"It's how I know you're worrying over something. You'll sigh in forty-five-second intervals until I distract you."

A smile pulled at my lips. "Well, you've always said you were an excellent distraction. How lucky am I that you're mine?"

"Yours," he said, testing the word. "I think I like that."

"I think I do too."

I angled for his lips, and he met me halfway, as he always did.

I only let myself get a little carried away before I slid out of bed, heading for the bathroom.

A long, slow whistle sounded at my back. When I turned, Kash was propped up on one arm, head on his hammer fist.

"Now, that is a sight I'll be thinking about all day."

As my gaze swept over his visage, I said, "You and me both." And with a promising smile, I turned and strutted away.

When the door slid closed behind me, I clicked on the light around the sinks, surprised for a moment by my reflection. But only for a moment—the girl in the mirror had become familiar to me over the weeks with Kash. I liked her, liked being her. Wished for her life, which I fantasized about more often than I'd ever admit, and did again as I stepped into the shower.

Only now it wasn't just a daydream. Now it was a possibility.

Her life was simple, slower. Lazy afternoons on the couch with a book in my lap and my feet in his while he sketched. We'd have a dog—he just seemed like the kind of man who should have a dog, and while I didn't have some personal drive to be a pet owner, I wanted him to be with a deep desire that surprised me. I imagined trotting down the stairs of some nearby brownstone and into Longbourne, floating into the greenhouse just to give him a kiss and hear how the dahlias were doing. Maybe I owned my own firm, something smaller, with more room for fun and less room for demand. In this fantasy, we lived together, with regular family dinners with the Bennets and my sister.

I imagined many things, things that set a fire in my heart. It was a fire that scared me, raging brightly enough to threaten my other dream, the one I'd been chasing for what felt like my whole life. Already the edges were singed and smoking, curling away from the heat to save itself.

Already I dreaded every part of my life that wasn't that bright and sunny dream full of love and belonging and home.

It was madness to consider, a lavish, decadent dream that could never be real. It could never be mine.

Not if I kept moving in the direction I found myself headed. But more and more, I believed Kash was right—my life was not as satisfying as it could be. Somehow, I'd denied myself the knowledge, so entrenched in what was *supposed* to make me happy that I didn't realize I was miserable instead.

And the only way out was to make a change so drastic, I couldn't even speak it aloud. Daydream, sure. But in practice?

That unmentionable thought wrinkled my brow as I exited the shower, and with it, the circle was complete. I'd ridden it around and around like a carousel, and though there was a beginning and an end, there was no getting off. In a few hours, when faced with Addison and the Femmes, I'd start at the beginning. That was probably an ambitious estimate—I was likely to consider it when we kissed goodbye ad it in the elevator and in the cab too.

But I let myself have that little daydream all the same. It was my favorite way to pass time these days. And now that things had shifted, I suspected my musings would get worse.

We got ready for our day as we always did, kissing our goodbyes in an impolite and irreverent display of affection at the curb before he deposited me into a cab. I smiled to myself the whole way to the office and through the lobby. But at some point before the elevator doors opened on the Archer floor, that smile died a cruel death, forgotten as if it had never been.

I stiffened, steely and cool as I greeted the receptionists and nodded to my coworkers as I passed. Addison was as dark as ever, grilling me on my schedule and the status of the events in my docket. She didn't micromanage me per se, but she demanded to know everything—literally everything, down to napkin colors and plate patterns—and expected me to relay it to her in every mundane, meticulous detail.

Once that lengthy and unpleasant business was out of the way, I went along with my day in a blur of efficiency and coordination. Everything went perfectly, and I made the mistake of praising myself too soon.

I was at the bakery going over the details of Angelika's cake when my phone rang.

There was only one person my phone actually rang out loud for, and it was my very pregnant sister. And my sister did not use her phone for phone calls.

I excused myself, heart thundering. "You okay?" I said the second we connected.

A siren sounded in the background of the call, followed by a low groan from my sister.

"No, I am not okay. I'm on the way to the hospital." The

words quaked. "My water broke and I'm in labor and Dean is stuck in Long Island trying to get back and I—*oooooooophhhh*," she breathed.

I was already heading back to the table to gather my things. "I'll meet you there."

"Thank you," she wept, actually wept the words. "I can't do this alone, Lila. Don't make me do this alone."

"You won't have to do it alone, Ivy," I soothed, belying the rush of adrenaline that currently sped through me. "I'll be right there, okay?"

"O-okay."

"Want me to stay on the phone with you?"

"Yes, please."

"Give me one second."

I muted my phone, explaining the circumstance to the baker, who, overjoyed, made me wait for a box of celebratory cupcakes to take with me. And I ran out of the shop with full hands and my sister huffing into the phone, hailing a cab as best I could before promising him fifty bucks to get me there fast.

By the time I got to the hospital, Ivy'd had to disconnect in order to register. The nurses at the station directed me to her room, which was already buzzing with activity.

The second she saw me, her face cracked open and her tears flowed easily. "Oh thank God you're here—*ah*!" she squeaked, glaring at the nurse attempting to put in her IV.

Ivy's auburn hair was a pile on top of her head, and she'd donned her hospital gown, which was that unflattering shade of sea-foam green that made everyone look sea*sick*. Her legs were covered with a scratchy-looking blanket that smelled like bleach, and I schooled my face to keep my nose from wrinkling.

I made a mental note to search for the fanciest hospital where celebrities had their babies to ensure down pillows and high thread counts.

I dropped my things in what looked like a wildly

uncomfortable mauve chair and offered her my most reassuring smile. "I'm here," I said, taking her free hand when I reached her.

"Dean won't be here for an hour and—*ooooooooh.*" Her face bunched up as she leaned forward, knees spreading under the blanket.

I glanced at the nurse as Ivy squeezed my hand hard enough that I felt something pop. The nurse looked concerned. Too concerned.

My coordinator hat was instantly on. Birth coordinator—I wondered if that was a thing. If not, it should be.

"How dilated is she?" I asked in that tone that got answers.

"Nine centimeters. The doctor is on her way."

One look at my sister told me Dean wasn't going to make it in time. Unless the doctor was parking her car, I didn't think she was going to make it either.

"Is the anesthesiologist coming soon?" Ivy asked hopefully, miserably.

The nurse's face melted into pity. "The doctor will be here in a few minutes—she'll tell you everything, okay?"

"So that's a yes? I'm getting drugs, right?" Ivy's voice rose, the pitch edging on shrill.

"Ivy, look at me," I commanded, and the wide, scared eyes of my sister fixed on me. "You don't need drugs. You've already made it through the worst part, the really grueling, terrible, never-ending hours of contractions. All you have to do is push."

"But not yet!" a nurse chimed from across the room.

Ivy began to weep.

"Your body knows what to do," I insisted. "All you have to do is go along with it, and it'll be over soon."

"B-b-but Dean's not here," she wailed. "I want Dean. I want Mom. I can't do this," she said frantically, trying to get out of the bed. She barely made it to sitting before another contraction came. "*Ahhhhhh—I have to poop,*" she announced to the room, clutching her belly like she could squeeze out the pain.

A nurse ran up, palms out. "*Nonononono*—No pooping!"

"But the book said pooping is normal," Ivy whined.

"Honey," the nurse said gently as a fleet of women began stripping off blankets and breaking down the bed, "you don't have to poop. You have to push."

"No, I'm sure I have to poop," she insisted. "I haven't pooped in at least three days!"

"Ivy"—the nurse's face hardened with authority—"if you try to poop, you're going to have a baby. You don't want me to deliver it, do you?"

Her chin wobbled. "N-no, thank you."

"I didn't think so," she said, returning to her task.

"Just hold on for a few minutes, Ivy," I said.

Her shoulders shook with sobs she tried desperately to keep in. "T-this wasn't supposed to be how it went," she said. "Dean's not here, I have no drugs, I—" Ivy sucked in a breath and curled in on herself. When the contraction passed, she flopped back in bed, panting and sobbing.

"Ivy," I said in that commanding voice again, "I am going to get you through this. Okay? Do you trust me to get you through this?"

She blinked tears from her eyes, nodding. "More than anyone. You do everything you ever say you're going to do. Could you tell me you're having my baby for me?"

"I wish I could," I lied, "but I'll be here the whole time. I will make sure every nurse does her job, that the doctor is here, that every single detail goes off without a hitch. All you have to do— the only thing you have to do—is lie right here and do what the nurses tell you. Can you do that?"

Hope lit in her eyes. "I think so."

"That's right. You can." I turned to the nurse. "I need two more pillows, cool washcloths, and"—I picked up the pitcher on the rolling table, shaking it to find it empty—"ice chips. Where is the crib?"

The nurse managed to look both annoyed and afraid. "It's on its way." She scooped up the pitcher. "Be right back," she said sweetly to my sister but shot me a look on her way past.

I ignored her, instead helping Ivy sit so I could rearrange the sawdust pillows at her back. Then holding her hand, wiping the sweat from her brow, soothing her when she came unraveled, which was about every third contraction. Texting Dean updates, overseeing the nurses, feeding Ivy ice chips.

The doctor ran in—literally ran, snapping gloves on as she entered—rolling up on a stool to acquaint herself with the state of my sister's vagina. Minutes later, Ivy's thigh was in the crook of my elbow as she bore down, teeth bared and face crimson. When the doctor announced the crown of the baby's head, I made the mistake of glancing down to find her vagina made unrecognizable—first by that poor, elastic orifice's size and shape, then by a mushed-up purple face covered in muck—and with a scream, a rush of fluids, and a strangled cry, the space in my heart grew to accommodate another person.

Ivy sagged, crying and peering through the gap between her knees as the doctor held up her baby, wailing and wrinkled and shining with gore and absolutely, life-changingly perfect. Tears welled in my eyes, emotion jamming my throat as I leaned into my sister, kissing her damp forehead.

"You did it," I whispered. "She's perfect."

Nurses flocked, huddling around the baby for a cursory cleanup.

"Do you want to cut the cord?" the doctor asked.

It took me a moment to realize she was talking to me.

"I … yes," I answered, the weight of the honor overriding my overall disgust at cutting an organ still attached to my sister.

I approached the table, taking the scissors as they held the wiggling purple baby, her mouth open and screaming and a shocking shade of red against ashy skin. The doctor held the cord between pinched fingers, which was already clamped at the baby's belly button, indicating where I should cut. So I did, cringing, trying not to think about the gamey texture or strength at which I had to saw at it to disconnect the baby.

Frankly, it was one of the most disturbing and meaningful moments of my life.

From there, everything happened in a blur. The baby was placed in my sister's arms, and the elation in the room as she met her child left me shaken. Too soon, they took her again, moving her across the room to a station to bathe her and weigh her and run tests.

"Go with her," Ivy commanded, and all I could do was obey.

I pulled up to the counter, too struck to speak, which the nurses seemed grateful for. They were a finely tuned machine, moving around the baby as they slapped her foot, pricked her heel, and called out numbers. Took her hand and footprints, washed her with gentle care. Put her in the tiniest diaper I'd ever seen, then the tiniest long-sleeved shirt I'd ever seen. It had little pockets on the end that flipped over to cover her hands, so she wouldn't scratch herself, the nurse told me when I'd asked. Tiny socks, tiny hat, and then she was wrapped up like a burrito in an ugly, scratchy blanket and carted back to my sister.

The doctor and a nurse had something red and slick in a metal bowl. Curious, I leaned in, trying to figure out what it was.

"Want to see the placenta?" the doctor asked when she noticed me lurking.

I spun away from her like a tornado. "Nope. No, thanks. I'm good."

Ivy laughed, looking up from the bundle in her arms. "I'm gonna keep it. Put it in the freezer and fry it up with some onions."

I gagged, swallowing back my lunch. "That has to be a biohazard or a CDC violation or ... you cannot take that home, Ivy."

"I'm kidding," she said. "I don't even want to see it, never mind eat it. You're welcome to it if you want it though." Laughing again when I shook my head, she looked to the doctor. "Could you make sure that's gone before my boyfriend gets here? As much as I hate that he wasn't here, seeing that without the context of the rest of it just feels wrong." She bounced the baby in her arms. "That's right. Because Daddy will be here soon. Won't he, Lila?"

I checked my phone. "He's in the building," I promised with a smile, leaning over the baby.

She was beautiful, even all smooshed up. Under her cap, which was pulled down to her eyebrows, her hair was dark and curly. Her lashes were thick, and when her eyes occasionally cracked open, the irises were a deep, strange shade of blue. Her toothless mouth sometimes opened to mewl, but since finding her way back to Ivy, she was mostly quiet, wiggling every once in a while.

Dean burst into the room like there was a fire, his eyes wild and gigantic chest heaving. With a swipe of his hand, his beanie was clutched in his fist, his gaze fixing on Ivy and the baby. His dark eyes filled with tears, and his lips curled in the most reverent of smiles.

A happy sob burst out of Ivy as he floated toward her, and I stepped out of the way, fingertips to smiling lips and tears sliding down my cheeks.

They cried and laughed and hovered over their child. They kissed and held each other, and when Ivy passed the baby to him, he cradled his daughter in his arms with more care and wonder than I'd ever seen a person possess.

They were three, their love creating another, a bond between them that couldn't be broken. Their lives would forever be full of love, full of joy. Full of pain too, because that was the nature of life, after all. But I knew without a doubt that they would cling to each other just as they did now, with all the hope and love they held in their hearts. Which was a lot.

I was struck again with a longing, a moment of wishing for

that other life, the one with the easy Sundays and the abundance of kisses. I added a new daydream to the reel, one just like this.

And there was only one man I could imagine it with.

I felt myself approach a moment, a precipice. A cliff face where I was given a choice. The wind of change whipped my face, beckoning me closer to the edge where I'd have to decide—fly or flee. The life I had or the one I dreamed of.

I knew what I wanted to do, but what would I sacrifice to do it? Could I have it all, the life I wanted and the one I was living? Was there an in-between, a middle ground, or was I destined to have one or the other?

And how much did I even want what I had?

I didn't know the answer, not yet.

But the wind carried me closer to the edge all the same.

Girls Like Her

KASH

I smiled down at my phone where a picture of Ivy and her baby smiled back at me.

"Lemme see," Luke said impatiently, reaching across the worktable where we'd perched that night, the display I'd been helping him build finally ready for Tess's finishing touches.

When I passed my phone over, his face went all gooey.

"Man, would you look at that? A baby. Ivy has a baby."

I laughed. "She's been pregnant for a year or something. Didn't you ever figure that was going to happen someday?"

"I mean, theoretically, sure. She's just the first person I've ever known to actually *have* one. It's wild—a few hours ago, that baby was *inside* her. All this time, that little baby has been *right there*." He shook his head at the screen.

"That's usually how it works." I held out my hand for my phone, amused.

He sighed and passed it back. "Someday, that's gonna be us. Someday, Tess is going to have a baby—my baby, if I play my cards right."

"And that doesn't scare you?"

"No, it really doesn't. Because it's Tess. Things that should scare me just don't anymore." He shrugged. "I don't know. I can't explain it. But I figure if I have her with me, I can do just about anything."

My smile tilted as I leaned against the table across from him, folding my arms. "Never thought you'd commit, Lucas."

"Everybody's got to grow up sometime. Isn't that what they say?"

"That's what Mom says. I dunno about anybody else."

"How about you?" he asked. "Things going good with Lila?"

"They are. So good. Probably too good."

His brow quirked. "What's that mean?"

"We came clean last night and it went well. It went so well, in fact, that I woke up this morning terrified something will go wrong."

"How doomsday of you."

"Yeah, well, you've seen my track record," I joked.

But he didn't laugh. "Come on. You don't actually believe she's anything like the rest of them."

I didn't—in fact, I knew she was nothing like the women I'd dated. But I couldn't explain to my brother that when I'd woken up with her in my arms, my unbound joy was immediately dashed at the thought of losing her.

That fear rose swiftly and without warning, and I'd struggled to contain it ever since.

"I know she's not," I answered, defaulting to levity. "But you've gotta admit, things like this happen to you, not me. I'm not the one who gets the girl and rides off into the sunset. I'm the one who has the girl for a minute before she rides off with a guy like *you*. Or in this case, a guy like Brock Fucking Bancroft."

"Fuck that guy," Luke shot. "And if she doesn't want a guy like you, then fuck her too."

My brows drew together. "Watch it."

"I'm just saying. If she's going to be a snob, she doesn't deserve you."

"I wouldn't know a Gucci bag if it hit me in the face. She lives a life full of things I can't even wrap my tiny little brain around."

"A life she affords just fine on her own. She's not looking for a meal ticket, Kash."

I shook my head. "I know. I really do. But it's Pavlovian. I keep doing the same thing, over and over again. It'd be naive to expect new results. I can hope. But I can't expect. This could be the best thing to ever happen to me, and I hope it is. But I'm not wrong to be scared."

"Lila isn't Ali." He called me out quietly, sternly.

"No, she isn't. But this is the first time I've involved my heart since Ali, and we all know how that turned out."

"I know you've been conditioned to think you're not worth more than a night, but have you ever stopped to consider they never wanted more because *you* were so sure it couldn't be?"

"Maybe," was all I was willing to concede. "I want to be the one to make Lila happy, and I finally have the chance. We're together, *really* together after all our skirting around our feelings. Trust me when I say that I am relieved. Relieved and hopeful and finally happy, happier than I've been since…well, since I don't know when. It's just not so easy to believe my luck won't run out, that's all. But I won't let her go without a fight."

"No, I don't think you will. I'm only saying all this is in your head. Who knows—maybe you're soulmates and everything will be a cakewalk."

"We've been official for less than twenty-four hours. I hardly think that constitutes being soulmates." I shook my head at him, laughing. "I might be dumb, but I wasn't born yesterday."

"Why do you keep saying that?"

"Saying what?"

"That you're dumb."

"Because what do I know? I'm just a gardener who lives with his mother."

"And I'm just a fuckup who couldn't hold down a job. Oh, and who *also* lived with his mother."

"Lived, past tense. Plus, you went to college *and* moved away and lived on your own."

He pinned me with a look. "You could have if you'd wanted to. Why not just own the fact that you didn't want to?"

"Because it doesn't matter what I want. It matters how it looks."

"To who?"

"To people."

"To Lila?"

"You know how it is, Luke," was all I said.

"I don't get it. I don't get why you think you're not good enough," he fired off in challenge. "It can't be money—you have that just as much as the rest of us. It can't be your job because you fucking love your job, and don't lie to me and say you don't. And you don't live with your mother because you can't take care of yourself. You live with your mother because she can't take care of herself. There's a big difference, and anybody who doesn't see that is an asshole."

"Guess I have a thing for assholes," I fired back in defense.

"Man, you assume a whole lot, considering."

"Considering what?"

"Considering you think you're so dumb."

I opened my mouth to argue when Marcus busted into the workroom with Jett and Laney in his wake.

"We have a problem," he said, his face dark as a storm cloud. And the pressure in the room changed to match.

The five of us gathered around one of the tables, Marcus at the head, looking grim.

"We're being sued by Bower."

Luke and I were too stunned to speak. Marcus didn't require a response.

"They've requested immediate turnover of the financial statements, which aren't ready. But we're easily over the noncompete limitations. If we comply, Longbourne won't open its doors tomorrow."

"But our contracts," I started, thinking immediately of Lila, the risk she'd taken on us, the events we had lined up. "What about our contracts?"

Marcus shook his head. "I said, *if* we comply."

"What do you mean, if?" Laney asked.

"Ben and I have been trying to build a case that the clause is unconscionable. If we can, it would mean the contract won't stand in court. In fact, we could get the whole thing thrown out before it goes far. Theoretically. With enough money and weight to throw around, anyone can take a case like this all the way to the end."

"And Bower won't back down," Jett noted darkly.

"There's another thing to consider. If Bower makes all the right moves, the cost of litigation alone would bankrupt us."

The room fell silent.

"What do we do?" I asked.

Marcus paused, scrubbing his hand over his mouth as he thought. "My instinct is to tear up the contract and throw it in the fire. I don't think they can prove that Longbourne's success would in any way threaten their own. And I don't believe they can win."

"Of all the Bennets' gut feelings, yours is the one we'd follow without question," I said to a chorus of nods. "But is there any danger for Lila? Will her contracts be caught in the crossfire?"

"I don't know," he admitted, offering nothing more.

"If there's any risk, I won't put her anywhere near it." I scrambled for a moment. Until an idea struck me like a bell. "Can we transfer them to me?"

Marcus paused, then lit up, his mind whirring behind his eyes. "You know, I think maybe we can. Why didn't I think of that?" He was practically pouting.

"Think of what?" Laney asked, her gaze bouncing between us.

"I own a business. We can transfer the contracts to me, and I can fill them."

Three-fourths of my siblings blinked at me.

"You own a business?" Luke echoed.

"Selling his hybrids," Marcus added. "I made him set it up years ago. Seriously, why didn't I think of this?"

I chuckled. "It's all right. I forget about it too."

"No, I mean … you have all that money to work with. You can get whatever you need. You could even lease Longbourne from me and keep it running, if it came to that."

His words climbed their way through my thoughts, leaving me confused. "All what money?"

Marcus stared at me. "What do you mean, *all what money*? You have almost two hundred thousand in that account." He kept staring as I stilled. "You mean to tell me you haven't even looked?"

"No," I breathed. "I didn't ever need to. Didn't even think to."

He ran a hand over his mouth, glancing up at the ceiling as if to ask for deliverance from my idiocy. "Kash, you're hopeless."

"How about you berate me later," I suggested. "Are we sure this is legal? They won't see it like, I don't know, like we set up a shell to evade paying them?"

"I think there's a way to do it, but let me talk to Ben. Whatever we do, it's got to be by the letter. If we don't, Bower will burn us to the ground. Talk to Lila, see if you can get new contracts drawn up under your name. The rest of you, help Kash with whatever he needs to switch gears and get himself going. And maybe brainstorm a new name for his business, would you?"

"What, Kash Bennet Hybrid Flowers not catchy enough for you?" I joked, not at all feeling funny.

"*That's* your business name?" Laney said in disbelief.

"It's not like I ever thought I'd put it on a sign," I defended.

"We'll come up with something," she promised Marcus.

"Good," he said. "And I'll figure out how to get us the rest of the way out of this mess. Kash," he started, turning to me with earnest, grateful eyes, "thank you. I really wish I'd thought of that."

I chuckled, but the flame in my chest fanned brighter. "I'm just thankful you forced me to do it in the first place. And that there's some way I can help. Though I hope it doesn't come to me taking over Longbourne. I don't know the first thing about running the shop."

"If it does, you won't be alone," Luke said.

And looking around that table, I took comfort in that fact, believing it with so much conviction, I knew without a doubt that if there was a way to save the shop, we'd find it.

We dispersed, chattering our way out of the shop, but I wandered into the greenhouse looking for I don't know what. Clarity. Answers. Comfort. And in many ways, I found it as soon as I stepped through the doors.

It was quiet and still, the darkness dotted with flower heads in rows. My worry eased to a bubbling whisper, one that spoke Lila's name.

I thought of my past, of the things I'd run from, the things I'd feared. Things I never thought of, things dredged up by the depth of my feelings for her. It was easy to want her when I thought she didn't want me. But now that I'd been given hope, the stakes had risen to dangerous heights.

The door opened behind me, and the familiar sound of expensive heels on concrete had me smiling, smiling and turning to find Lila walking toward me.

She glowed, floating down the aisle with a blissful, tired smile. And I met her, sweeping her into my arms.

When I'd kissed her well, she sighed, looking up at me with adoration.

"The baby is perfect. Everything is absolutely perfect, and I cannot believe my sister created that sweet, tiny thing. I've never been so terrified as I was holding her. I kept thinking I was doing it wrong, or worrying I'd drop her. Isn't that silly?"

"Oh, I dunno," I said, drawing her closer. "I think it's natural to worry when you've got something precious in your arms."

Her face tilted to inspect mine. "Are you worried, Kash?"

"I'd be crazy not to be."

"But why?"

"Because I don't want to lose you."

She softened, her hand moving to cup my jaw. "Why would you think you would?"

I turned to press a kiss into her palm. "You didn't do flings? Well, I don't do serious. And I've realized I am very serious where you're concerned."

"Well, lucky for you, I'm a pro," she teased, giving me the words I'd given to her what seemed like ages ago. "And for the record, I'm very serious where you're concerned too. I'm not going anywhere, Kash—I'm afraid you're stuck with me."

"Promise?" I asked with a sideways smile.

"Promise," she echoed, stretching up to seal it with a kiss that washed my worry away, leaving only my trust and faith in her. In us.

And I sank into it without another thought.

Gravity

LILA

It took us a solid week, but we got my wedding contracts moved to Kash's business, and I found myself unendingly grateful that through all of this—the tumult for his family and the uncertainty of their future—he'd been at all worried about me. They decided to give Bower the bird, keeping Longbourne open and welcoming the lawsuit like Bruce Lee stepping into a circle of drug lords.

There was much to be said for the single-minded determination and perseverance of the Bennet family.

They had already delivered on their promises to keep my position safe. In fact, at that moment, Kash and I were ambling down Fifth in the delivery van on the way to the Felix wedding.

My excitement was electric, the rush that came with the day I'd been working for, the dash of anxiety in wondering what kind of obstacles would be thrown at me, the thrill of knowing that after today, I would largely be done with the Felix family. And by proxy, Brock.

It was everything I'd been waiting for, and I was only one very long, hectic day away from it.

I'd planned a whole celebration for Kash and me to mark the occasion. Tonight felt like the beginning, the real beginning when we could be together without any Felix-sized obstructions. No more cameras, no more humiliation, and most importantly, no more Brock. Just me and Kash and whatever our future held.

And tonight, I was going to surprise him with the news.

I'd bought an apartment.

It had fallen into place a few weeks ago when I found an apartment near Longbourne within hours of it listing. My real estate agent showed it before lunch, and by mid-afternoon, I made an offer. It was a once-in-a-lifetime deal, and the second I'd walked through that front door, a feeling of kismet had struck me. The apartment so close to the imagined space of my daydreams, it was uncanny, though it needed to be renovated. Gutted, really, which was the only reason it was listed at such a price—still an insane amount of money, but a steal for the Village. Walking through that apartment, its windows tall and the light buttery and brilliant, I could see those lazy Sundays take shape, blossoming and blooming in the empty space.

Things moved quickly from there. I had the down payment in hand, and I'd been preapproved for the rest, including a home improvement loan to handle the renovations. My agent was connected well enough to expedite the inspection process, and she provided a strict list of paperwork that I supplied nearly on signing the contract. As difficult as it had been to find time in my already hectic days for all the extra running around—faxes and notaries and meetings galore—everything had gone off without a hitch. And yesterday, I'd picked up my keys.

It was a prime location, just around the corner from Longbourne and Ivy, and after renovations, I could not only sell it with ease, but make a good bit of money too. The perfect location and perfect apartment, with two bedrooms to grow into. I'd always heard that buying a house was one of the most stressful things one could do. But the truth was, I hadn't felt it, not beyond the frenetic pace and the constantly growing checklist of things to do. I processed it all, absorbing the tasks with a businesslike detachment and the certainty that the investment was not only sound, but a boon. Of course, I felt that bit of buyer's remorse that hit everyone when they made a major purchase—there was no way to walk away from a deal that large and feel like you unquestionably did the right thing.

But the most stressful part of the process was keeping it from Kash.

I couldn't have said why, not exactly. In fact, I hadn't told anyone, not even my sister. It all happened so fast, and there was, of course, the fear that it would fall through. The process was more like a strange, stressful dream than any kind of reality. And if it did fall through, I didn't really want an audience for the disappointment. It was a secret, one I guarded with the quiet solitude of a miser, holding my dream in the dark like a golden coin. It was *my* secret, one I didn't want to have to defend or answer for, one I'd made strictly because I could, autonomously and decisively.

But it'd been harder to keep it from Kash than anyone. In part, the thought of involving him in such a decision felt too familiar, as if that knowledge would apply some pressure I couldn't foresee, pressure that would change things. Or maybe it was that I'd chosen a place so close to him, and I didn't want to spook him by invading his space despite the fact that we spent every spare minute together. But perhaps most of all was the admission that I'd bought this place with him in my mind, with that daydream on my lips, ready to be spoken. It was the intent I found myself denying most. Because I couldn't pretend as if I hadn't made this purchase in large part for us.

Even thinking it made my stomach and heart trade places. I knew it was crazy. It was too soon and I was jumping the gun and blah, blah, blah. But even if he didn't move in right away, I had a feeling he would eventually. He was sick of sleeping in the bunk bed at his parents' house, and I somehow doubted that once I had a place of my own, he wouldn't become a regular fixture. The next natural step was cohabitation. It would be convenient above all— or at least, that was the reason I gave for allowing myself such a frivolous musing. It wasn't like we could ever stay at his place, although I'd suggested it once as a novelty. Apparently, he drew the line at hooking up with his mother under the same roof.

When he put it that way, I saw his point.

It'd made me wish I'd been as carefree as Ivy was when we were teenagers. If I'd accepted her many invitations to hang out with the Bennet brothers, Kash and I might have dated then. I would have snuck into his room while one of his brothers distracted their mom with *Jane Eyre*. Kissed him in the greenhouse when life was still shining with promise on the horizon. Been part of a hundred Bennet dinners and the undeniable feeling of belonging that clung to them like summer. I mourned the years we hadn't had together. I wondered what my life would have been like if we'd gotten together all those years ago. If I would have gone to LA or stayed in New York, if I would have even ended up being a wedding planner.

The thought shocked me, left me flapping in the wind like a luffing sail. I couldn't imagine another profession for myself, not even under duress. But for Kash, I might have.

I'd do just about anything for him.

The delivery van pulled to a stop at the service entrance to Skylight, and Kash smiled over at me as he put it in park.

"You ready for this?" he asked, concern flickering over his otherwise affable face.

"Ready as I'll ever be. And just think—tonight, we will be through with the Felixes."

"What if they have another event?"

"They do, an anniversary party for Alexandra. But Addison has already taken it over—she *informed* me this morning. I'd like to think it wasn't to throw me today, of all days, but I know better. But want to hear something funny?"

"Always."

"I've never been so happy to have a client stolen out from under me."

He chuckled, leaning over the wide space between the captain's chairs for a kiss, which I happily provided. And with that, we stepped out of the van.

I could already feel the hum of action that waited for me inside, but there was also a buzzing anxiety—my interns weren't waiting for me and weren't answering my texts. So once Kash had the first cart loaded, we headed inside to see what the holdup was. The elevator ride was quiet, which was unlike us on its own. But he seemed to know I needed to roll through a string of paranoid fantasies about what had gone wrong just to get it out of my system. Like maybe there was a fire. Or a salmonella outbreak. Or the cake had exploded. Or a flock of pigeons had kamikazeed into the skylight and busted it into a trillion irreparable pieces.

But what I found when the elevator doors opened was far, far worse.

Addison Lane wore that cruel smile of hers, the superior one she liked to don when I was in trouble. Her dark eyes shifted from me to Kash, taking a moment to look down the length of him slowly enough that I fantasized about flying at her like a bat to scratch her eyes out.

"Look at you, riding the service elevator like a plumber."

"What are you doing here?" I said with a false smile as I strode toward her, back straight and the facade of confidence firmly in place.

"You didn't actually think I'd let you do this alone, did you? This is one of the biggest accounts at Archer, and I'm not about to sit back and wait for you to screw it up."

Kash stiffened beside me, cart in his big hands and his brows holding back thunder.

But I just kept smiling, my concern clutched in a headlock. "Do what you have to do. Where are my interns?"

"I've got them directing the staff as they set up the tables in the ballroom."

"Thank you. Now, if you'll excuse me—"

"I mean it, Lila. This event reflects on me just as much as it does you. I've already found discrepancies with the linens"— she glanced at Kash's cart—"and I'll need to have a look at those centerpieces."

I drew a breath that did nothing to calm me. "Do what you have to, Addison," I repeated, not willing to engage.

Discrepancies, my ass. I'd gone over everything last night for the fortieth time. If she'd actually found a problem, I would have handed over my gun and badge on the spot.

Addison gave Kash a final look, one mixed with appreciation and suspicion, but he only glared back before following me toward the atrium.

My hands shook, not from fear, but adrenaline. The pressure was palpable—Addison was going to breathe down my neck all night, inspect everything I did with kid gloves, looking for something, anything, to hold over me. She'd see me screw up or die trying.

I could only hope for the latter. Maybe one of those fictional dive-bombing pigeons would attack her like a Hitchcock movie. Or maybe she'd be within the cake's blast range. Or she would eat the fish and shit her pants all night. I'd take any disaster if it rid me of Addison.

Once in the ballroom, I beelined for my interns, directing them to help Kash unload rather than uselessly watch half a dozen hotel crew lay out tablecloths. All five of them headed for the door, looking grateful for something to do, but before Kash followed, he stepped into me. His hand slid into the notch of my waist like it belonged there, the other capturing my chin, tilting it so the full weight of his gaze would be felt. And it was.

"It doesn't matter that she's here or what she says. Everything is going to be perfect—you know that deep down. Because *you* have orchestrated this event, and you don't do anything halfway. You don't even do it all the way. You don't settle for anything but above and beyond, and she'll see it. Even if she doesn't acknowledge it, she'll see it."

The twist in my chest eased with a release of breath. "Thank you."

"You're welcome," he answered with a sideways smile. "Now, go do what you came here to do so we can get the fuck out of here."

With a laugh, I pushed up on my tiptoes to kiss him.

And then I went and did the hell out of my job.

Five hours—that was how long it took us to get set up. All hands were busy and full with the exception of Addison, who made it her job to triple-check everything I did, floating behind me like a ghost. Kash kept his distance, his eyes forever darting in her direction, watching her like a great black cat. And the jackal watched him right back, promising ruin should he even try to intervene.

It felt like no time had passed—there never seemed to be enough when setting these things up—before the wedding party began to arrive. The Felix sisters arrived first, bridesmaids and groomsmen and immediate families. A fleet of makeup artists and hairdressers were already waiting in the bridal suite, and the bartender in the groom's quarters was stocked up and ready to pour.

Other than escorting them to their suites, I was too busy with final preparations to even notice Addison's hovering or Kash's absence or anything beyond the checklist occupying the majority of space in my brain.

I stood at the back of the atrium room where the ceremony would take place, the city stretching up in the night around me as I enjoyed the moment of relative calm before the guests began to arrive. Interns were still fooling with the arrangements at the ends of the rows of chairs, and a crew member ran final tests with the microphones wired into the arbor. The wedding was about to go off, and the only hitch would happen at the end of this aisle.

"Lila …"

A flash of recognition, then disappointment as I turned to find Brock standing behind me.

His was not the male voice I wanted to hear.

My shoulders drew back, chin leveling. I started to turn away. "I'm sorry. I'm very busy—"

"Hang on. Please."

There was something about the way he'd said the word, a sincerity so unlike him that I paused, uncertain what to do.

He took the window, saying softly, "I hate this, Lila. All of it."

"So do I, but I don't suspect for the same reasons," I answered at equal decibel.

Standing there with him, his face touched with regret and sadness, something in me softened. It was that space in my heart he used to occupy, the one I'd bricked over to pretend it had never existed. And for the first time since I'd walked away, I remembered what it was like to know him.

His smile was sheepish. Boyish. "I've been watching you, you know."

"I do, and it's creepy," I teased.

"Oh, don't act like you don't command it. You always did. I just keep wondering when I forgot."

"Forgot what?"

"How much I loved you."

The words were a bucket of ice water down my back. "Brock, I—"

"Just … just let me say this. Please."

There it was again, that earnest word from a liar's lips. Only I didn't think he was false. Not this time.

"I've been watching you, trying to figure out what's different. Something about the way you walk. A softness to you that wasn't there before. But I've realized it's worse than all that. I think it was there all along, but I didn't see it. And I've been trying to recon-cile just how I can live with that."

I took a step back, needing out. Out of this conversation. Out of this room. "Thank you," I started. "Thank you for saying so. But I should really—"

"This is what I always wanted, you know."

At that, I stopped my retreat. "What you can't have?"

His lips parted, breath drawn to speak, but whatever he was going to say died. "This wasn't what I signed up for. She wasn't what I expected. None of it was." A pause. "I can't help but feel like I've made a terrible mistake. We had a life together, a future, and I threw it away. I threw it away, and I can't seem to remember why. But seeing you like this, with that ... *gardener*?" He said the word like an insult. "Everything feels crystal clear for the first time in a long time. If I asked you to give me another chance, would you do it? If you were with me, would you be this ... effortless? Undemanding? Would you give me what you've given him?"

What I'd given Kash he had earned simply by loving me. What I'd become was because of that love. And that could never be duplicated, least of all by the man standing before me.

Before I could tell him no in ten languages, slap him hard enough to leave a mark, knee him in the groin, or all of the above and in no particular order, a door at my back squeaked open and closed. Guests. Guests were coming, walking through the door, and here I had Brock groveling.

We stepped aside, and I glared at him, furious and sad and anxious to get away.

"We cannot discuss this here and now. I have work to do."

"Later. Can we talk later?"

I paused, weighing my options. Saying no would delay me. Telling him all the ways he could go to hell wouldn't do well for my future at Archer. Saying yes would be a lie.

"Text me tomorrow," I dodged, turning to go.

"Maybe we can get coffee. Talk things over."

I opened my mouth to let him know there was zero chance of that, but before I could speak, one of my interns approached with salvation on her wings.

And it was sweet enough, I could have given her a raise.

KASH

My hand slammed into the door, pushing it open hard enough to ping off the wall and rebound. I stopped it without looking, storming down the service hall.

I'd heard the whole thing, the acoustics in the atrium too good to have avoided it, which I desperately wished I had. When I'd come into the room looking for her, I'd seen her with him and paused. He was too close, too familiar with her as he waxed poetic about her beauty and grace like he hadn't neglected her. As if he hadn't betrayed her so cruelly. Unforgivably.

The only pleasure I took was that he was jealous, and spitefully, I believed he should be.

But what fueled my fury was her response. Or more accurately, her lack of response. She didn't tell him all the ways she'd disavowed him. She didn't tell him she'd chosen me, nor did she regale all the ways he had been wrong.

Instead, she'd agreed to speak to him again. And all the joy I'd felt on Brock's jealousy shifted into a deep, unsettling rage at my own.

Maybe I'd been a rebound all along. Maybe I'd only convinced myself because she was so convincing.

I'd believed her, every word that she said. But I knew other truths to be certain, too. She hadn't dealt with her breakup, the humiliation, the truth of how it hurt her. Instead, she'd packed it all up and put it away, pretending to forget. Pretending to move on. And along came Brock to crack that door open again. What if she decides she made a mistake? Would I be realized as replacement rather than a relationship? Would those feelings we'd both believed were honest be tarnished by the knowledge?

I should have known Brock's presence would bite me in the ass. It was inescapable, a cruel inconvenience, and one that kept him firmly in his line of sight. How could she forget him when he—and more notably, Natasha—were so present? When Natasha insisted on parading it in front of her, flag in hand?

There has to be an explanation. It wasn't what you think it was.

I drew a deep breath to steady myself, fearing it would only flame the inferno in my chest.

Trust her, I told myself. *There's nothing he has that she wants.*

Except money. Power. Status. He's everything you're not, another merciless voice said.

She doesn't want that. I know she doesn't.

That ruthless other self only smiled like it knew better.

I made it back to the reception hall, and when the interns caught sight of me, there was a light of concern in their eyes. So I did my best to smooth my face, to calm myself, to offer a smile and relax my coiled shoulders and clenched fists, still poised to make Brock Bancroft eat his own teeth.

The visceral fury surprised and confused me. Not that I could have knocked Brock out—I'd been in enough fights with and behind my brothers that I held no issue with expressing myself with my fists, if necessary. But the depth of the potential betrayal tore open a part of me I rarely saw, one without ration.

What has she done to me?

I was changed, and at present, that change was not pretty. I sought to know why and realized it was simple.

I loved her. And the thought of her leaving me for that son of a bitch had turned me into a monster.

Lila wouldn't entertain him, I was sure. So sure that I watched the doors of the ballroom, waiting for her to rush in and tell me everything, moving things around without purpose just to stop myself from going crazy. But the minutes ticked by, and still, there was no Lila.

She's busy, I assured myself. *She's in charge of this whole operation, and Addison is here, looking for an excuse to hurt her.*

The thought redirected my rage to Addison, a protective flare overpowering my jealousy and fear over Brock.

When I couldn't stand Lila's absence anymore, I exited the ballroom, heading through the grand hallway to the atrium, buttoning the top button of my suit coat on my way. I slid into the room with the stream of the wealthy, chattering guests, splitting off once I entered to snake around the back. Lila stood in the corner, visible enough that anyone who needed her could find her but discreetly enough that she almost blended in. When she saw me, her eyes lit up, her red lips smiling her relief that was cool rain on that fire in me.

She dismissed an intern as I approached, and I put all my energy into playing it cool.

"Look at you," she said with an admiring sweep of my form. "I love this suit."

"Same goes. The Armani?" I guessed, the twin black suit to her white one.

"It's a special occasion," she said with a smile.

"The wedding?"

"Only in that it marks the end of the whole ordeal."

I couldn't help but smile back, even with worry niggling at my heart. The conversation halted with an uneasy pause.

"So," I started, hoping an opening would lead to an admission, "how's everything going? Hit any snags?"

I could see it behind her eyes, the desire to tell me flitting around like a moth in a jar. But she shuttered it away, smiling instead.

"So far, so good, though not for lack of Addison's digging."

Disappointed but unwilling to push, I said, "She found anything?"

"Nothing. But the night is young. How about you? Everything going okay?"

"Fine," I answered, unnerved by the stunted silence and superficial chitchat so unlike us. "Well, I'd better get back. Just wanted to check on you."

"I'm glad you did," she said with a smile, genuine and warm and reassuring. But it wasn't enough to quell my doubts.

The two of us were caught in a dance, a farce. Only I couldn't do what needed to be done to dispel it. I couldn't kiss her, couldn't sweep her away. Couldn't make a space safe enough for her honesty. Because this, her keeping something from me, was uncommon and unfamiliar. She'd never hesitated to tell me anything, even at events, even under the gun. She always found a quick moment to make a joke or admit her worry.

And that made it feel like she was hiding something.

As I strode away to find refuge in the ballroom, my thoughts seesawed, taking turns kicking off and floating down. She would tell me. But she'd kept something from me. She cared about me. But she'd cared about him for longer. She'd said she didn't want that life. But she'd chased that life for most of hers. Every positive had a negative to pull it back to the ground like gravity. But I kept pushing, hoping at some point that other, worried part of me would tire out and leave me on the high.

Trust her, I told myself.

And that was the thought I held on to, no matter how terrified I was of gravity.

Best Laid Plans

LILA

The ceremony came and went in a rush of silk and heels and flowers, the procession perfect, the vows exchanged, the rings slid onto waiting fingers. The best and worst thing about the Felix sisters was this—their entire lives might be orchestrated for television, but their love wasn't. Or at least in the case of Angelika and Jordan, who wrote beautiful, if not a little vapid, vows, his voice trembling with emotion and her tears streaking her face.

I oversaw every step, anticipated every pitfall, of which there were several. No exploding cake, though I'd rounded up a last-minute contingency plan for that too, just in case. I did, however, save Angelika from tripping over and-or ripping her dress, stopped a potentially violent spat between Sofia and Alexandra about whose bouquet was better, salvaged a minor microphone issue seconds before the ceremony began, and straightened out a carpet issue. Literally, I straightened it so the wrinkle didn't break somebody's leg. With the heels on the Felix gams, it wasn't a possibility. It was an eventuality.

In fact, everything had been so intense and so fast, I hadn't had time to consider Kash or the fact that I'd kept something from him. I'd wanted to tell him everything Brock had said, but I didn't. In that painfully distant conversation, I'd said nothing, unwilling to dig into any of it now, tonight. But Kash saw through me as he always did. The brief look of mistrust stung bitterly, and I'd vowed to tell him the second this night was over. At this rate, it seemed like it might be a flash.

At least, a girl could hope.

With a flurry of action, the bride and groom walked back up the aisle and out the doors, only to be swept away by the photographer. Guests were directed to the ballroom for drinks and to find their tables, and I flitted from the ballroom to the kitchen to my interns to the photographer and back again. Before I knew it, we were lining up for the processional's entry into the reception.

It wasn't until dinner had been served and cleared, the speeches had been made, the first dances said and done and the DJ rolling out his setlist that I had a moment to pause. I ate cold chicken in what felt like a long inhale, standing at a metal prep table in the back as the kitchen crew cleaned up. I hadn't seen Kash since that moment before the ceremony, not a glimpse or a glimmer, and his uncommon absence worried me. In my anxiety, I imagined the worst. Maybe he was angry, my dishonesty still sitting sour in my chest. Maybe he'd gone home, left me here. Heaven knew he didn't have to stay, but he always did, always had, and the thought that he was gone left a streak of concern in my chest.

I brushed it away, counting myself silly. Even if he had gone, he wouldn't have left without a word, especially tonight, of all nights.

Through the event, Addison lurked, jumping in at intervals to micromanage or criticize me. There was nothing to be done except take it with a smile, the same one I wore while trying to ignore Brock, who eyeballed me from Natasha's side. I couldn't make sense of it, couldn't understand why he'd declare himself to me, then spend the whole night with her on his arm. The lowdown, dirty bastard. Coming on to me at his girlfriend's sister's wedding, no less. His girlfriend who I worked for. The one he'd cheated on me with.

It was too much to comprehend. Though I couldn't pretend his honesty hadn't struck me. I'd replayed the conversation, dissected it. He'd said this wasn't what he'd signed up for, and I wondered what he'd thought it would be. The entire *country* could imagine what dating Natasha Felix would be like.

He was obtuse, but he wasn't so dense to be shocked or surprised by her.

I was bone-tired, worn out from keeping the wall of false indifference up for this long. It was crumbling from exhaustion, bolstered by my will, sandbagged by determination.

A few more hours, I thought, shoveling the last bite of chicken into my mouth, following it with a swipe of my napkin as I chewed.

I figured I had another half hour before I'd start getting the wedding exit together, so I went on the hunt for Kash. I searched the service spaces without finding him, and with my heart in my throat, I rode down to see if the van was still there, relieved to the point of weak knees on finding it there. Back upstairs I went, into the dimly lit ballroom, scanning the faces of guests and searching the fringes for Kash.

But I found Addison instead.

She stood at the edge of the dance floor, arms folded and gaze hard, focused on the guests as they laughed and danced and drank. I didn't know why I stopped at her side, struck with some familiarity, a still, unexpected moment of equality. For that brief stretch, I saw us from a distance, good and evil, side by side, her darkness to my light. Or perhaps just a couple of stone-cold bitches ready to rip each other's throats out.

"I have to admit," she said, watching the crowd jump around to a Calvin Harris song, "you didn't do a completely terrible job."

"Look at you, being all sentimental."

"Don't get used to it," she said without making eye contact.

I spent a moment inspecting her profile, finding her cold and beautiful, the exemplification of power. We should have been friends, I realized. We had more in common than not, but somehow, we'd ended up in this vicious circle, one that ended and began with me pinned at the neck.

"Why do you hate me so much?" It was bravery or foolery that inspired me to ask the question I'd never asked before, struck with a brief, regrettable streak of sentimentality myself.

She turned those hard eyes on me, her expression flat and unchanged. But with my question, she opened the veil, answering with all the cold honesty and unshakable pride I knew her to possess. "Because I've worked for a decade for what you've gotten in half as many years. I've worked my whole life for what is handed to you. Because you're good enough that someday, my position will be threatened by you. And I didn't come all this way for that."

The plain fact and blatant threat hung between us. And in my surprise, I made the mistake of reacting, my face softening and opening.

"And that. That look right there. You, Lila, are by the book. You don't have a knack for deceit, no skill for deception. What you don't realize is that good guys finish last."

I schooled my face, nudging my mask back into place. "I guess we'll see, won't we?"

"Oh, we will." Her gaze shifted to the dance floor again. But the honest moment was gone, wiped away with the curl of her level lips. The expression was her equivalent to putting up her dukes. "So, you and the gardener, huh? You said you caught yourself a bigger fish, but I didn't think you meant physically."

I looked in the direction she'd indicated, finding Kash standing in the shadows in that glorious suit, watching me with his brow low and lips level. It changed his face, darkened it to menace, the expression foreign to me on a face I'd come to know so well.

I met her eyes again and found challenge there. Challenge and ruin.

"It's no wonder you wanted to use Longbourne," she continued, turning to face me fully, shoulders square and eyes black.

"Why does it matter where we get flowers?"

"It doesn't matter to me beyond the fact that it matters to you."

A flash of danger, a siren of warning. It was all a game to her. The Felixes. Brock. Kash.

Kash.

If she knew what he meant to me, he'd be cannon fodder. If she saw my feelings, she'd exploit them.

She'd exploit him.

"He's pretty, I'll give you that," she said, still smiling that horrid smile. "I don't know if I'd risk wedding contracts on him, but if that's what you had to do to get him into bed, who am I to judge?"

Don't take the bait. Don't let her know. Bury it, hide it so she can't find it.

Let her think she's right.

"Well, that's all they're good for, right?" I lied, the words sour and thick in my mouth. "You know how it is. After Brock, I needed to blow off some steam. He's a useful distraction."

"You're a shitty liar, Lila," she said, amused. "You forget I've seen you together. If you think I'd believe he's nothing more than a distraction, you don't know me at all."

I laughed, the sound easy and carefree, my heart sick. "And if you think I'd go from Brock to a gardener, you don't know me either. He's a rebound, Addison. He means nothing to me."

"Oh, I think he might disagree," she said, her lips twisting and cruel and triumphant.

Horror, absolute and complete horror, overtook me as she glanced behind me, still smiling that knife smile.

Kash loomed at my back, dark and fierce, his eyes blue shards of glass, glittering under the low lights. For a long, still moment, he laid the weight of the betrayal on me, the full extent of what I'd said, of what he'd heard, and I buckled under the pressure. The second I reached for him was the second he turned and walked away.

"Oh God," I breathed, following him swiftly. "Kash, wait," I called after him, weaving through people in a useless attempt to catch him.

He broke out of the crowd like a bullet, heading for the service exit.

"Kash, please," I begged, trotting carefully behind him.

But he didn't stop, didn't slow, didn't even acknowledge me. And I was so fixated on him, I didn't see Brock flank us.

"What did you do to her?" Brock shot, his eyes fixed on Kash.

This was what finally brought Kash to a halt. He turned, dangerously deliberate, his face black with rage. "Excuse me?"

The words were a threat.

"Kash—"

He cut a look in my direction that stopped me cold.

"I said, what the fuck did you do to her?" Brock stepped into Kash, close enough that fury crackled between them, raising the fine hairs on my arms.

"What happens between Lila and me is none of your fucking business," he said with quiet force. "And you leave her alone. You've done enough."

"What do you know?" Brock snapped, and I realized he was drunk.

And that these two men were about to fight.

Over me.

In the biggest event of my career.

I braced myself and moved to put myself between them, to beg them to stop, for all our sake. But I never got to. Because a very drunk and shoeless Natasha Felix came teetering toward us.

A camera followed behind her, and on a glance, I discovered one behind me, not knowing how long he'd been there.

"You don't get to dump me!" she screamed, waving her champagne glass toward Brock.

"You don't care," Brock fired over his shoulder at her. "You never fucking cared, Tash. This whole thing was *your* idea. I never should have done it."

I froze. Every molecule stopped and turned and listened.

"You were already going to dump her," Natasha volleyed. "Like *you're* some hero. God, you're so fucking dumb. All of you are so. Fucking. Dumb." With every word, she pointed at us with her champagne, landing on me last. "Especially you. It was a setup, the whole thing. You'd shit your pretty white pants if you knew how much money I paid Brock to frame this up. And everybody knew except you and your little piece of ass. Even your fucking boss is in on it!" Laughter burst out of her. "My fans are going to *die* when they watch this season. Didn't you know, boyjacking is my thing? I coined that," she noted before turning to Brock, her lips twisting in disgust. "Ugh, you are so pretty, but you are literally the worst lay of my life. And *you* do not get to dump *me*. Especially not for *her*."

Time slowed, stretching out like a rubber band as the knowledge washed over me. I'd been a toy, manipulated and maneuvered against my knowledge. I'd been tricked. Trapped by Brock. Addison. Goddamn Natasha Felix.

They'd done this to me. Used me. Humiliated me. And for what? Ratings? Sport? To make a fool of me?

In this entire room, there was only one person I could trust. The one person I'd betrayed with a lie meant to save him.

Kash.

I didn't realize what he was doing until it was too late to stop him, as if I could have halted the freight train that was his massive arm as it coiled and sprang almost too fast to see. His fist hit Brock's nose with a crunch and a spurt of blood.

Brock crumpled, clutching his face as gore dribbled down his chin and over his hands. "You broke my nose!"

"You broke her heart," he said with conviction I felt in my marrow. "Fuck you. Fuck you for doing this to her. And fuck you too," he spat at Natasha.

"You stupid motherfucker," she said coolly, striding toward him. "Dumb, just like her. You just lost your job. Your business. Whatever you have, you just fucking lost, all because you were too stupid to mind your own business."

My breath labored, my vision dimming, the shallow sips I dragged into tight lungs not enough. There wasn't enough air.

You're hyperventilating, I thought clinically.

I held a painful breath and let it out slow. Commotion went on somewhere outside of me, followed by a scream from the gathering peanut gallery when they saw Brock's face, which was disgusting. Addison materialized, somehow managing to look both horrified and pleased with the chaos.

"You need to leave," she said, and I looked to Kash.

But he was looking at me.

And so was Addison.

The gravity of the situation dawned on me slowly. The Felix wedding had come to a grinding halt, the massive guest list gawking and whispering, phones out and recording. Natasha ranting, swinging her champagne around. Brock dabbing at his nose with a napkin. Kash with raw knuckles, face grim. This was not only my fault, but my responsibility. I hadn't just breached every line of professionalism, I'd sullied the name of the company I'd worked so hard for.

And then there was Kash. Somehow, I thought he might pay the steepest price of all.

But in that moment, he didn't seem to care. As I nodded at nothing and no one, Kash moved to my side, his hand in the small of my back, applying the gentlest pressure to guide me toward the door. I complied on numb, shaking legs, drifting by his side without knowing where he'd gotten my bag or how we got in the service elevator. Only that we were in it, then out of it, then into the cold winter night.

He opened the door to the van and helped me in, and for a moment, I sat in the silence and tried to parse what had just happened. I was fired—that was clear. Addison would get what she wanted after all. I'd been controlled in a ruse orchestrated by at least half a dozen people, strictly for their amusement.

And I'd hurt Kash, the one person who mattered.

I swallowed the lump in my throat as he climbed in and started the van.

"I … I'm—"

"Please," he clipped, pulling out of the service parking lot. "Don't try to explain. I don't know if I can bear it."

I paused, unsure as he took a shaky breath.

"Lila, I am sorry—so sorry—that they did this to you." His teeth ground together, the steering wheel squeaking under his grip. But he wasn't soft, and he sounded anything but forgiving. "Of all they could have done, this is too much, too far. If I could have ruined every one of those useless skinbags, I would have. I don't care what they do to me. Fuck them. Fuck every last one of them."

"Your job," I breathed. "I won't let them hurt you. I won't let them hurt Longbourne."

"I don't think you have any choice in the matter. But even if you did, it's not your concern."

"What do you mean, it's not my concern? Everything having to do with you is my concern."

"I heard what you said to Addison," he answered after a pause, his voice somehow both soft and hard. "And I'm not surprised. I hate it, but I'm not surprised. I can't pretend I didn't know you were out of my league."

"What? No, it's not about that," I insisted. "You can't honestly believe I meant that."

He said nothing.

"Kash, I was trying to protect you. Protect *us*."

"From what?"

"From Addison. She wanted me gone, any way she could get it. She would have used you to get to me."

He shot me a look. "You sure you were worried about protecting *me?*"

I drew a breath sharp enough to sting. "Yes, *you.* And Longbourne."

"I'm not afraid of them—especially not Addison Lane—and I don't give a goddamn what they think. But you seem to."

"Stop it. Stop saying that. I don't care about them, how could I?" My breath hitched and hiccuped. "After ... after w-what they've done to me, I hope every last one of them goes to hell."

"You know," he said as if to himself, "I didn't think you were anything like them, but you proved me wrong, as you tend to do. They're a den of snakes, a nest of liars, and I thought you were honest. But you lied to her about me. And you lied to me about Brock."

I stilled.

"I saw you with him. I heard what he said. I heard him tell you how he loved you, and I heard him tell you how wrong he was. What I didn't hear was you argue."

"I was at work," I countered. "I was standing at work while he bowed and scraped, his girlfriend in the next room and a pack of cameramen roaming around. With my boss trying to find any reason—*any* reason—to fire me. Did you really expect me to tell him what I thought right then, standing in the middle of the event I'd been charged with?"

"No, Lila. I guess I couldn't," he shot, the fire in him flaring. "But you didn't tell me. You were going to. But you didn't, and that left me wondering why. Why would you hide it from me? Haven't I earned your trust?"

"Haven't I earned yours?" On his silence, I pressed on, "How could I explain? In that moment, surrounded by socialites, how in the world could I have explained it all to you? You have to know I was going to tell you. And if you'd wanted to know so bad, if you'd seen the whole thing, then why not ask me? Why did you test me instead? I don't expect subterfuge, not from you."

"I don't know," he said, the heat gone, replaced by weariness and finality. "I guess I don't trust you like I thought I did."

I flinched from the pain of those words. "I have never given you any reason not to trust me, not one. And yet, you are so quick to assume I would turn my back on you." Blocks. A few short blocks was all I had. I could feel the end approaching and shrank in its shadow. "That says more about you than it does about me. And if you honestly believe anything you just said, then I was wrong about you. Wrong about us."

We fell silent as he turned the corner, my eyes on the hotel awning as it grew closer.

"Let's face it," he said with quiet detachment. "It was always going to end like this—we knew it from the start. My job was to be a distraction, and I think my work here is done."

He pulled to a stop, not bothering to put it in park. But he looked at me with infinite sadness behind the blue of his eyes.

Something inside me came unraveled and collapsed. Tears, sharp and hot, stung my eyes, blurred my vision. I knew the end when I saw it. And so, I memorized his face for a long moment before opening the door and stepping into the cold.

I didn't know if I'd ever be warm again.

Scorched Earth

KASH

I watched the colors in my room shift from blues to purples to buttery yellows as the sun rose, the shadows shrinking away with every tick of the clock.

My room felt foreign after spending so many nights away. It was a place I'd left behind, a place of memory. A limbo, the space between the boy I'd been and the man I'd become. That limbo had stretched on far too long, years where every day was the same and nothing ever changed.

Until her.

I'd captured sleep in wisps and fluttering moments through the night, plagued by what she'd said. What I'd said. What I'd so willingly stepped into and what had been inevitable from the start. Acceptance set a quiet resolve upon me, a heaviness that settled in my chest, immovable. This had always been our fate.

I'd just been reckless enough to hope.

I'd been careless enough to fall in love with her.

I knew it now in hindsight, the path to this moment laid out plainly behind me. I'd realized it last night when she stepped out of the van. When she'd broken, so had I, and what had spilled out was my love for her. But there was nothing to catch it. So it'd slipped away, disappearing in the cracks, lost but for the remnants.

Those, I feared, would stain me for the rest of my days.

My alarm went off uselessly, and I found that heaviness weighed down my arms, my legs, my weary eyelids. But I slid out of bed, mindlessly pulled on jeans and a T-shirt, shoved my feet into my boots, and carried myself down the stairs. There was nothing else to do. Not with myself, not with my day, and not for Lila and me.

Lila. The pain on her face, the shock at discovering she'd been betrayed, was etched in my mind. In that moment, I could have burned that place to the ground. I would have scorched the earth to save her, to serve vengeance, to end it all.

But she wasn't the only one who had been betrayed.

The words I'd spoken that very first night haunted me. It was true—the only danger in a rebound was to the reboundee. And here I thought I'd known what I was getting myself into.

Silly me.

The greenhouse awaited, the earthy musk comforting in its familiarity. Dad glanced at me from behind the dahlias with a flicker of concern in his eyes. But he said nothing, as was his custom, and for that, I was grateful. The last thing I wanted to do was regale him with the story of my dashed and foolish hope.

So I picked up my shovel and worked. The shuck of the spade against the wheelbarrow brought me back to center, hypnotized me into forgetting.

No, not forgetting, but burying.

I buried my wishes and the things I'd believed under the growing mound of mulch that would feed the flowers. Something beautiful would come out of the shit I piled on top—that was just science. But that didn't make it stink any less.

It wasn't long before I was sweating, reveling in the ache

of my shoulders and arms. When I finished mulching, it wasn't enough to have burned off my thoughts. I needed to exhaust every ounce of energy I had, burn it down until I was empty. So I made my way down to storage, deciding I'd rearrange the heaviest stuff I could find.

Bags of dirt and mulch and fertilizer were piled haphazardly along one wall, and that seemed the best place to start. Silently, I got to work, picking up bags and dumping them with a slap onto each other. I had just moved forty bags to the middle of the room so I could start organizing them when I heard someone on the stairs.

Luke smiled to cover his worry, but I saw it all the same.

"Need some help?" he asked, nodding to the pile.

"I got it," I answered, picking up a bag of dirt and slinging it over my shoulder, giving him my back, though I knew better than to hope he'd actually take the hint and leave.

He was quiet for the length of time it took me to drop the first bag with a satisfying thump.

"What happened?"

I turned, avoiding his eyes as I grabbed another bag and headed off again. "It's over." I couldn't bring myself to say her name.

Unfortunately, Luke didn't have that problem. "Lila? But I thought—"

Thunk went the bag. "Yeah, me too. But I was wrong."

"About what, specifically?"

"Everything. All of it. I told you our differences mattered, and I was right."

Thunk went another bag. I hadn't stopped moving, hadn't looked my brother in the eye. As resolute as I was, I was still hurt. I was still heartsick and lovesick and just fucking sick.

"What happened last night?"

I contemplated picking up two bags at a time just to punish myself but stuck with one. It'd take longer this way, and I wanted to kill all the time I could. Briefly, I recounted the night, leaving it cool and uncolored by how I felt. Because how I felt was too much to speak. Betrayed and unworthy. Resolved and despairing. Foolish and misguided by my own instinct, my own heart.

Luke listened silently, his face drawing tighter, though not with anger. With concern. When I finished, a pause stretched between us.

"Kash, I'm sorry."

"Not your fault." *Thunk.* I swept the back of my hand across my forehead and grabbed another bag.

"God, what a mess. But I've got to say, I can't imagine she meant to hurt you."

"Of course she didn't. Doesn't change the fact that she did. But there are two important things to remember." *Slip* went the bag off the pile. "One—I am a rebound, and I never should have expected to be anything more. And two—her life and mine will never, ever be compatible."

Thunk.

"Have I ever told you that you assume a whole lot?"

At that, I paused, arms akimbo as I laid a hard look on my brother. "It's my own fault. I shouldn't have jumped in so fast, should have kept some space between us, but I thought I knew better. Selfishly, I got myself all wrapped up in her, and she did the same. There hasn't been a breath between us for weeks. How can I know without question that what she feels for me is real and not a byproduct of being ignored by that fucking asshole?" I dragged a hand through my damp hair. "And then there are those people—though *people* seems like too generous a word. They lied, manipulated her, set her up, humiliated her for some fucking ratings. For money. Those *people* are predators, and despite that, she lied to them, told them I meant nothing to her. Because despite it *all*, she cares enough about what they think to throw me under the bus the second she was under fire. I don't want that life, Luke. I won't be a part of that, no matter how much I love her."

The word visibly jolted Luke, but I was still as stone on the outside. Inside, I split open like the earth in a quake.

He folded his arms, schooled his face. "She lied, which on its own is one of your cardinal sins. But that lie pressed your deepest bruise, *your* favorite lie—that you're just a dumb gardener and good for nothing but a lay."

"You might think it's not a lie, but *they* believe it. The way they talk about me, like my profession offends them. As if who I am is so far beneath them, it doesn't even warrant a second look. I'm as good as a hot bartender or UPS guy—disposable. Luke, I can't even be fucking mad about it. I *told* her I was disposable then expected something different. It's on me, not her."

"Whatever happened to not giving up without a fight?"

"Believe me—if I thought there was a chance I could win, I would."

"Since when do you only fight wars you know you'll win?"

"Since today, I guess," I snapped, turning on my heel for the pile.

He didn't argue, just sighed.

"Oh, don't give me that," I muttered, hastily grabbing a bag.

"Someday, you'll realize your worth, and on that day, I hope you put your pride aside." He paused, weighing what he was about to say. "Did you know she bought an apartment?"

I stopped and turned, bag still on my shoulder. "What?" I asked quietly, another betrayal flaming in my ribs.

"Around the corner. She asked me if I'd help her renovate it, asked me not to say anything. She said she was waiting until after that godforsaken wedding to tell you. I know it's not much, but Kash—the way she talked about you was not like you were disposable. Weirdly, she asked me if you liked dogs. She might as well have asked how many kids you wanted to have."

I tossed the bag on its mates and shook my head to clear it.

"Do you honestly think she bought a place right here, right around the corner just for Ivy? Because she never once mentioned her sister's name, but yours found its way into every sentence." He watched me, and I didn't speak, parsing what he'd said. "Listen, I'm not going to tell you what to do or how to feel. But I'll say this—if you truly love her, don't just walk away. Give her a chance."

"I already gave her my hope. How much more can I give?"

"You can give her your trust."

I stilled.

"All of this, all these things you're afraid of, they have nothing to do with her and everything to do with *you*. But Lila isn't Ali. No amount of worrying will make it so. But if you're not careful, you'll lose her. And I have a feeling this time, you won't move on." With another sigh, he straightened up to leave. "I hope you change your mind."

A dozen smart responses fired in my mind, but my heart stung with the truth, with the future he'd painted, the one without her. I grabbed another bag, unsure what to say, how to defend myself when he was right. But when I'd unloaded my haul, he was gone.

My pain stayed right where it was.

Hey, Dummy

LILA

The baby's room had been plagued by daylight for hours, chasing me under my pillow, burying me deep in the covers where it was cool and dark and lonely.

I hadn't slept, but I didn't toss and turn either. Instead, I'd lay there in the dark as still and quiet as a tomb, counting my mistakes in tens and twenties.

Ivy had welcomed me in late last night, shepherded me to the baby's room—currently unoccupied, as baby Olive had taken residence in Ivy's room—and there we sat until the baby woke to eat. She held me when I cried and listened to me recount and sort what had happened. We'd uncovered no solutions, only an infinite sadness.

The simplest loss was my job. No doubt it was gone, the spectacle last night so outrageous, I would not only be fired, but it would be difficult for me to find another job. Impossible really, especially if Natasha got involved.

When it came to vengeance, I trusted her at her word. It was perhaps the only thing I trusted her on.

The betrayal was beyond the pale. A wriggling, writhing discomfort slithered through me, and on its tail was adrenaline, sharp and cold. They had manipulated me, controlled me, used me. And the knowledge was a shrinking cage, sparking an anxiety I hadn't known in years but on a scale so grand, there was no escaping it. It would affect every corner of my life.

Especially once the show aired.

And underscoring it all was that I'd lost the one good thing in my life. The best thing in my life.

It was too much to bear, the burden too heavy. I could have handled the betrayal if I still had him.

I could have handled anything if I still had him.

Tears sprang fresh, sliding into the creases of my nose before being absorbed by the pillow I hid beneath.

The doorknob jiggled just before I heard the creak of the door opening.

"Hey," Ivy said softly, closing the door behind her. "You in there?"

I scooted over so she could sit, but I didn't emerge from my cocoon.

Her hand rested on my leg, gave it a squeeze. "Are you hungry? It's almost two."

"No," I said, the sound muffled by down.

"Do you want to talk about it?"

I unshielded enough of my face to squint at her with one eye. "What else can I say?"

"I don't know. I was hoping sleep would help. That maybe you'd wake with some kind of clarity."

"If I'd slept, maybe that would be true."

Acclimated a little to the light, I moved the pillow, propping my head on it so I could blink at her through the sunshine. Stupid sun, all bright and cheerful. All I wanted was an unending night to mourn. It didn't seem like too much to ask.

My gaze hung on Ophelia where she sat on the windowsill,

her leaves green and vibrant, the new shoots of growth filling me a sense of pride, then a deep and relentless sadness at what I'd lost.

"Did you hear from Mom?" I asked, hoping we could avoid talking about me.

"She called yesterday, asking for more pictures. I can't believe I got her to agree to wait to come see us for a few weeks. I think she's had a suitcase packed for a month."

I chuckled halfheartedly, trying to think of something else to say. But I was too slow.

"Are you going to talk to him?"

I drew a painful breath and let it out slow. "He doesn't want to talk to me, Ivy."

"He didn't say that," she said with a brow up.

"It was implied."

"He was upset and hurt. He punched Brock. You lied to him and about him. You found out about what those assholes did to you. There was a lot to process, Lila."

"He doesn't want to talk to me, especially not today. It's been like twelve hours."

"Why don't you say what you really mean? You're scared to talk to him."

A flash of pain cut through me. "Yes. And that."

"Well, that's not a good enough reason to give up. He's too important to you."

"You didn't hear what he said last night. I don't know how to convince him of what he means to me. I don't know what to say to make him understand." I stopped myself with a shaky breath, my eyes filling with tears.

"The Lila I know would march down there and argue with him until he agreed with you."

"Yeah, well, that Lila was hit by a bus. She doesn't have any fight left in her—she's in traction."

For a second, she just watched me. "You are not allowed to give up," she insisted again.

A sad chuckle. "Ivy—"

"Don't you *Ivy* me. You love him, dummy."

The cut of that word carved my heart. I did love him, fiercely and desperately. I'd known it without acknowledging it, and now that it was spoken, I feared I would never unhear it.

But Ivy kept on, her face hard. "When have you ever not fought for what you want? The people you love? You know when you're wrong, and you own it. You challenge everything head-on. Why not Kash?"

"Because ... because I deserve this," I said around a sob. "I love him and I ruined him and I ruined everything."

"You cannot possibly believe you're wrong."

"I did everything he said I did."

"Because you were trying to save him from *them*." She spat the word. "Your intentions were good."

"And I paved the road to hell with them."

"Stop that. I'm right, and you know it. You deserve to be heard if nothing else, and he deserves to hear the whole of it before he decides to walk away once and for all. Yes, you hurt him. But there are reasons. And if you don't defend yourself, so help me God, Lila, I will never, ever in a trillion years let you live it down. You love him. So put on some fucking pants and go tell him."

I wanted to just as much as I was terrified at the prospect. She wasn't wrong—I could feel the desire to convince him of my feelings for him niggling at the wall of despair I'd built. At some point, it would chip away and bust through. But now? So soon?

"If I go talk to him now, he'll never hear me. And even then ... Ivy, he doesn't believe this is what I want. That I'd choose him."

"Then prove it to him."

"How? He doesn't trust my word. My job is forfeit. If he won't listen, if he doesn't trust me, then what do we have anyway?" I caught my breath, swiped at my nose. "I don't even know what I'm going to do with my life. Natasha and Addison will make sure I can't get a job with any New York firm. And I just bought an apartment." Tears sprang again. "I'll just flip it. I already have loans in place for renovations. Maybe I can make enough money to live off until I figure things out. But Kash is going to have to wait. I just wish it felt like he was the least of my problems. He feels like my *only* problem."

"Do you think Natasha will go after Longbourne?"

"I don't think Natasha bullshits when it comes to revenge." Worry tightened my heart as I imagined the fall of the Bennets' legacy. "This is all my fault. I never should have dragged him into it, and now, everything we worked for is ashes."

Ivy reached for my hand. "I know it doesn't feel like it right now, but everything is going to be okay. One day, this will be behind you. It's hard to see when you're down in the dirt, I know. But I promise, it's all going to work out."

"I hope you're right."

"It's common enough that I think you can count on it."

With a quiet laugh, the baby cried, the sound moving closer with every one of Dean's footfalls. I watched them as they made the handoff, the purest adoration on their sleepy faces.

For a moment, I'd naively thought that could be me. But maybe Kash was right. Maybe we were too different, from different worlds, with different dreams.

Even if for that beautiful moment, he'd been my only dream.

All You Ever Wanted

LILA

I tugged at the hem of my Armani suit coat as I stepped into the elevator to meet my fate.

Anxiety scratched at me, knowing how unpleasant the confrontation would be. I'd be chastised, made to feel wrong. And in many ways, they wouldn't be mistaken.

In all the other ways, fuck them.

Of course, if I was to have any hope of getting even a mild referral, I wouldn't be able to burn this place down like I wanted to. I'd have to sit there and take the reprimand, ignore the scald of the scolding, endure what was sure to be a brutal lashing without defense.

They made the Felix Femmes look like a basket of kittens.

The doors opened to Archer, and I could practically hear the screech of tires as eyes shifted to me. The girls at the desk gave me a quiet hello. The faces beyond turned to me. And I did the only thing I could—I straightened up, lifted my chin, and strode into the galley with all the confidence I had left.

I was so focused on keeping it together that I didn't see Addison until I was nearly upon her office. The sight brought me to a halt, my stomach climbing up my esophagus in shock and confusion.

Addison Lane stood behind her desk in a suit of black, her hair in that stern ponytail she was partial to. But her dark eyes were ringed with dark circles, her face without a stitch of makeup, swollen from crying.

The shock that the devil not only had working tear ducts, but emotions deep enough to engage them, was total.

The utter disbelief that she was haphazardly shoving the contents of her office into boxes nearly brought me down in a faint.

Slowly, I entered our offices, my eyes locked on her. When she looked up, those eyes were hard and hurt and hot.

"Come to gloat?" She tossed an award into the box without care.

"You ... you got fired?"

"What gave it away?" she snarked, dumping a stack of files on top of the award.

"What happened?"

"I did my job. I did everything they asked, and they still fired me. I was supposed to get *promoted*." Her chest heaved, fanning the rage in her. "This is all your fault. You and Natasha. I never should have agreed when she came to me, but I thought it would be the thing to break you. That you'd crack, falter, and I'd be rid of you. When I pitched it to Caroline, all I had to do was say *publicity*, and she was in. She thought you could take it, the indestructible Lila Parker. I hoped differently. But none of us saw last night coming." She snatched the box off her desk and dropped it on the floor with a clang and a thump. "I ended up the villain, and I've lost my job for it. So will Brock. It's all in a day's work for Natasha, but you? You ended up the hero. Lucky fucking you."

I stood there mutely as she picked up an empty box and

started throwing things in. The world tilted sideways and stuck there. Nothing made sense, and nothing was recognizable.

I'd pictured this moment a thousand times, imagining how triumphant I'd feel. But despite all she'd done, I didn't feel vindication or spite. Only sadness and pity and a deep aversion for the woman who had played me like she had.

After a moment of me standing there like an idiot, her eyes snapped to me. "Would you mind getting the fuck out of my office? It's bad enough that they can all see. But I can't do this in front of you." Her gaze moved back to her hands, which shook gently as she picked up a paperweight and pen holder. "Caroline wants to see you."

I didn't move, feeling like I should say something. But I couldn't apologize, not even offer an empty *I'm sorry* to fill the dead space between us. I couldn't wish her good luck, couldn't provide even the most meaningless of well wishing. I forgave her in that moment, but I wouldn't put either of us in the position to discuss her absolution.

We'd been humiliated enough as it was.

So I turned and walked away. Felt the eyes on me as I crossed the length of the floor to Caroline's office. Her assistant said nothing, just gave me a nod and delivered me into Caroline's hands.

She looked up with a smile as if nothing had happened. "I've got to call you back, Patrick. No, no. We'll get it sorted out. Okay. Buh-bye." When the phone had been returned to its cradle, she turned her full attention on me. "Please, sit."

I did as I'd been told, folding my damp hands in my lap, back straight as a ruler.

She smiled, and for the first time, I noted how foxish the expression was on her otherwise temperate face. "I wanted to formally apologize for what happened with the show. When Addison came to me with the idea, I thought it would be excellent for the firm and for you. I had planned on moving Addison up and giving you her job once it was all said and done. What with your being a sympathetic character on the show, I knew you'd end up booked out for a year. But ..." A sigh. "Well, things rarely ever go as planned, do they?"

That betrayal rose in me, tightening every muscle with the urge to fight, not fly. Quietly, I answered, "No, I don't suppose they do."

Caroline leaned back, that mild, carefree smile still on her traitor face. "Sorina Felix called me yesterday to tell me how disappointed she was in Addison and Natasha. We thought she knew—Natasha assured us she did. We probably should have known not to trust her." She laughed, a flippant sound. "But she demanded Addison's job, recommended that you not only take her place, but handle their events from now on, if you want the job."

I opened my mouth to tell her to go to hell, and she saw it, cutting me off before I could speak.

"There's more. The producer wants to offer you your own show. After the display at the wedding, she's planning to paint you as the underdog, the unknowing heroine."

"What had they expected to paint me as? A fool?"

But she laughed, making a mockery of my pain. "Really, it couldn't have worked out better for you."

"I'm afraid I'd have to disagree," I noted.

Dutifully, she ignored me. "They'll spin off into a show featuring you as the celebrity wedding planner. Think of it, Lila— think of what it could mean for your career. And not just for you ... if you keep using that little flower shop you're so fond of, it could help them too."

And that was it. That was where she knew she had me. I could see it on her face, that superior confidence, softened by a gentle face and easy words.

I thought I'd ruined Longbourne. But I could save it.

I could save them all.

They'd easily make the money to either buy out their Bower

contract or pay for what was sure to be an unconscionable amount of money.

All I had to do was sell out.

I sat in the opulent leather chair across from the most powerful woman in my sphere who offered me everything I'd dreamed of for so long, and then some. It was all right there, waiting in her expectant palm. I only had to reach out and take it.

So I drew a breath that I knew would change everything and did what I had to do.

Both Ways

KASH

I'd never thought Mondays were the worst until today.

My days usually blurred together, Saturdays the same as Wednesdays in the greenhouse. But today I woke with heavy dread. I was not where I thought I'd be. Not today. Not in life.

Luke's words had shaken my certainty, my resolve, and as a result, I spent the rest of that day holding on for her to text or call. I shouldn't have expected to see her walking through the greenhouse door, not after everything. But I did. And she hadn't.

All night, I'd thought about us. About her.

About the hellfire she'd endure when she walked into work today.

After everything she'd been through, to get fired. Fired and dumped. The knowledge that I'd added to her pain made me heartsick. But the thought of seeing her didn't make me feel much better. And all of it left me wishing I could roll everything back, put things where they used to be. I wished for the simple comfort of her, that elemental thread that bound us. But it had been stretched to its limit, tight and creaking and ready to snap. I tried to tell myself it was broken, but that was a lie. I still felt that thread and was exhausted from fighting the urge to tug, to pull her back to me.

But this was the right thing, the inevitable thing. This was where I'd known it would end.

It didn't stop me from worrying about her all morning, wondering what had happened when she walked through the doors of Archer. Wondering if Addison had gotten her licks in before, during, or after she'd gotten fired. Had they humiliated her even more? Had Natasha called for her head? Either way, they'd delivered. Of that, I was certain.

It was my fault. I shouldn't have hit that son of a bitch. Or at least not there, in the middle of her event. But the location was the only thing I regretted. The punch itself was perhaps the most satisfying thing I'd ever done, besides being with Lila.

I was on my knees in the dirt, a tall bucket at my side brimming with mums in shades of fall. Mustard yellow, deep amber, rich crimson. Mindlessly, my hands moved, snipping where I knew to snip, filling the bucket with my thoughts circling about Lila. Maybe Ivy would know. I could ask her.

That, at least, gave me a sliver of hope.

My eyes shot up, looking for Lila when the door to the greenhouse opened.

This time, they found their mark.

She was beautiful, too beautiful, a thing made perfect by nature and gilded with Armani and Louboutin. Her eyes, cool and gray, were touched with hurt and hope.

I knew that feeling. I knew it too well.

Chest aching with the same pain that lived in the lines of her face, I rose.

She slowed as she approached, and for a moment, we stood there, breathing the same air, cataloging the sight of each other as if it were the first time and the last.

I tried to be mad, tried to remember all the ways she'd hurt me, all the reasons why we couldn't. Why we shouldn't. But I couldn't think of a single one.

"Are you all right?" was all I could think to say, the thing I wanted most to know.

A smile, small and tinged with regret. "I will be."

"I'm sorry, Lila. I'm so sorry you lost your job over this."

"That's the thing. They didn't fire me."

Shock and relief dashed through me, one behind the other. "How? What happened?"

"Caroline fired Addison and offered me her job. Sorina demanded it."

A smile flickered on my lips. "You're kidding."

When she smiled back, it set a fire in my heart. "She didn't know what Natasha had done, was blind to the setup and appalled by it. She wanted Addison's head on a platter and her job given to me. She also requested that all of their events go through me, if I wanted it."

"It's all you've ever wanted," I said with sadness.

"But that wasn't even what shocked me. They offered me my own reality show."

An uncertain pause, unsure that I'd heard her right. "Your what?"

"My own reality show. My 'subplot' on the show was so engrossing, they're sure viewers would gobble it up. She even mentioned Longbourne and how much it could help the shop."

That warmth in my heart flared into an inferno. After everything, she would drag me—drag my family—into that world of deceit.

It was low, lower than I'd thought she'd go.

"Like I said," I snapped, "that's what you wanted, isn't it? Fame and glory and money. You wanted power, and you got it. But leave Longbourne out of this. Take your contracts somewhere else."

She staggered from surprise that shifted into fury. "Excuse me?"

I shook my head, turning to the flower bed, needing something to do, some way to dismiss her. "Congratulations," I shot, unable to be kind, unable to be civil. "It's all you've always dreamed of—to be one of them. But you won't use my family's legacy to boost ratings for your new show."

"Kash, if you'll let me explain—"

My gaze snapped to her. "Why, so you can justify your choices like you did last night? You're the one who has to live with them, not me."

Tears sparkled, clinging to her lashes, but her face was bent with hurt and anger. "You know, you never figured me for a liar. But I never figured you for an asshole."

"Guess we were both wrong."

With the smallest, sharpest of breaths, she flinched, though our gaze never broke. But she didn't shrink away—she grew, drawing herself up to her full height, squaring her shoulders, lifting her quivering chin.

"I guess we were." One step back. Another. "Then I guess that's that," she said with resilience and force and bottomless sadness.

But I said nothing back. Only turned to my flowers with my heart clenched in my throat. And I listened to the sound of her heels on the concrete as she walked away.

This time, I feared it would be for good.

And good riddance, I told myself without faith.

She might have sold her soul, but I'd be goddamned if she took my family with her on the road to hell. She'd gotten in bed with lie-eating snakes, and there was nowhere to go but to become one of them. I wouldn't watch her do it to herself. I couldn't watch her demean herself any more than she already had.

And I wouldn't become a part of that lie factory with her. Not when my family was at stake.

Not when I knew there was no way to save her.

Blindly, I worked in the flower bed for a dozen painful heart-beats. Until my father cleared his throat.

He stood on the other side of the flower bed, looking sheepish.

"How much of that did you hear?" I asked carefully.

"Well, once she started talking, I couldn't exactly walk out. If my knees were young enough to crawl, I might have."

"Don't worry. I won't let her take us to hell with her."

"That's not what I'm worried about, son."

I drew a noisy breath and shifted my gaze to my hands in the dirt. "Don't worry about me either. I'm fine."

"You're not, but why should you be?"

"It doesn't matter. I shouldn't have gotten involved with her in the first place."

"And why not?"

"Because we're different," I said to the mums.

"Since when does that hurt?"

"Since I was stupid enough to think I could be with someone who puts herself above everyone else."

"But that's not all."

"No," I huffed. "It's not. Girls like her aren't interested in simple lives. They want some asshole with a PhD and a penthouse, not a man who plays with flowers in the dirt. We're different, Dad. There's no getting past that."

"I dunno. Seems like you're the one with the problem, not her."

I paused, glaring up at him. "You can't be serious. She cares so much what *they* think of her, she lied *about* me. She wants to sell our family out for a fucking television show. How am I the one with the problem?"

"Well, for starters, you didn't even hear her out. You're so convinced you're right, you decided for the both of you."

"I heard enough the other night to have good reason."

"Son, listen to me." He watched me until I met his gaze, silver brows drawn. "I know it feels safer to run—you got that gene from me—but think about what you'll lose. And for what? Fear? Pride? Lila Parker does not strike me as the kind of woman to be anything short of a straight-shooter. And I suspect you care very deeply for her."

"I do," I said around the lump in my throat.

"When I met your mother, she was the heiress to a fortune, and I was the son of a plumber. She ran in society, and I ran snakes through drainpipes. Never in a million years did I think she'd want someone so beneath her. But what you don't seem to understand is that love doesn't care where you come from, only who you are. That, and snobbery works both ways. You thumbing your nose at the things she wants is no better than her thumbing her nose at yours."

"So, what … I should hear her out? Give her a chance to make it right?" I shook my head at the question he never asked, the same one Luke had suggested. The one that just one hour ago, I was willing to take. "If it were just about the other night, that'd be one thing. But a reality show? That's too big for me to look past."

"She didn't exactly say she accepted the offer. Only that she got one."

I frowned. "No, she said—"

"That she got an offer. That was all. I won't tell you what to do, but I will say this—I'd hate to see you let love go for the sake of vanity, Kash."

Before I could argue, he turned and headed back to his post in the zinnias, leaving me with his words ringing in my ears.

Mostly because he wasn't wrong.

I was running away, so convinced I wasn't enough that I'd doomed us from the start, turned us into a self-fulfilling prophecy. I'd turned my nose up to the life she wanted, what she'd worked for, partly because I hated—*desperately* hated—seeing her be demeaned. But also because all the things her life represented were patently opposite of mine. And that comparison made me feel less than, even though this life made me happy. It was all I wanted, besides her.

But the show. The thought of her participating in a reality show made my stomach turn, and my heart sank into its waiting arms. She might not have come out and said it, but she'd taken that offer. Everything she'd ever wanted had been handed to her on a silver platter, tarnished with lies and deceit. The devil had made her an offer, and I couldn't imagine a world in which she'd refuse. I also couldn't imagine a world in which she wouldn't have told me right then and there that I was wrong if she'd turned it down.

She *had* called me an asshole, which wasn't off base.

As I watered the beds, my thoughts swirled in brackish eddies like the water running through the dirt at my feet. Time. I needed time to sort through it all, to take stock and reconvene when I would be objective—a trait which I generally embraced. But not when it came to my heart. Not when it came to Lila.

With her, all bets were off.

All Hail the Dumbassador

KASH

Dusk had fallen, painting the greenhouse in golden pinks and blues as the winter sun inched toward the horizon. It was still, quiet, the shop far away from my solitude. Dad had gone up hours ago, leaving me to withdraw in peace. As peaceful as my mind was at least, which was not very.

My hands stayed busy. Stupidly, I'd thought going to my greenhouse on the roof would cheer me, but instead I found traces of her. I found them everywhere I looked—in the potted plants she'd admired, the lilies that were on the verge of opening up to show me if I'd successfully bred them. Even in the main greenhouse, even old Brutus. The black-eyed Susans where she'd fallen what felt like a lifetime ago. The table where I'd shown her how to plant ivy.

She was everywhere, in the air, under my skin, living in my heart. But every thought was tainted with a fear, the see-saw once again in motion. And this time, I didn't have a truth to hold on to beyond that I loved her, I feared her, and I desperately needed to talk to her.

In my most relieving imaginings, she explained everything away with words I couldn't deny. In the most terrifying, she told me all my fears were warranted. In all of them, I had a resolution. But only a few ended happily.

I was lost in that thought when the door to the greenhouse opened hard enough to slap the wall. When I looked up, I didn't know who I expected to find. But it wasn't Ivy Parker with hell on her heels and an infant strapped to her chest.

She flew toward me with her face screwed up in fury. "Hey, stupid."

One of my brows rose. I glanced behind me in an attempt at a joke.

It didn't land.

"You dumb, stupid son of a bitch," she said, trucking to me. "I cannot believe you. I'd expect this from Luke or Marcus, but I never thought you'd be so goddamn brainless."

At that, I frowned. "What are you talking about?"

"See? That. Cretin. What do you think I'm talking about?"

"Lila," I chanced.

"*Lila*," she said in a dumb boy voice. "Yes, Lila, you dirtbag." She screeched to a halt in front of me, red-faced. The bundle snuggled to her chest wiggled, and a tiny fist popped out of its confines before disappearing again. "You didn't even listen. You didn't even hear her out, you simpleminded moron."

"That's a little redundant."

She pointed her skinny finger in my face. "Don't you back-talk me, Kash Bennet. I'd expect Luke to jump to conclusions. I'd expect Marcus to chase paranoid delusions. But I thought you'd give her a chance."

"Ivy, could you stop insulting me for long enough to tell me what's going on?"

"I'm sorry," she yelled, poking me in the chest. "I'm just really, really mad at you!" Every really earned me another poke. "She quit her job, you witless jerk."

A jolt of adrenaline cooled my palms, dampening them. "What?"

"She. Quit. Her. Job." She poked her punctuation hard enough to leave a bruise. "But you were too much of a dumdum to listen, and she was too proud to tell you, especially if you thought it was to change your mind. She quit her job, told Caroline Archer to go to hell, and refused to do their stupid, idiotic show. And you know why?" She didn't wait for me to answer. "Because she loves you, ding-dong. She loves your stupid, thick head—God knows why."

"Oh my God," I breathed, dropping to a stool.

"All that with Addison, the wedding—all she ever did was try to protect you from those monsters, and all *you* did was punish her. You don't even deserve her," she shot, amending, "Okay, that's a lie, you do, but *God,* you are so dumb! Her whole life—her whole goddamn life—everything she's worked for, she threw it away. And you know why? Because she chose you. She chose *herself*. You wanted proof she really wanted this life? Well, you were about to get it until you berated her. And then you let her walk away without even putting up a fight. You are just so—"

"Dumb. Yeah, I got it." I raked a hand through my hair. "She really quit?"

She rolled her eyes so hard, I was pretty sure she saw the sunset. "No, she fake quit. *Of course* she quit, mouth-breather. She doesn't ever want to step foot in that place, never mind work with all of them. Never mind put herself on television. She almost did, you know, but not for herself. For you. For Longbourne. She thought it could help you make the money you needed to buy out Bower. Not for personal gain." Her steam finally ran out, and she sighed, breathing out the last of it. One hand moved to the lump I assumed was the baby's butt. "Come on, Kash," she said wearily. "You know her better than to believe that."

"Maybe I don't." Regret, heavy and thick, filled my ribs. "I was so sure she'd taken it."

"Just like you were sure she would sneak around with Brock? Or that she would ever tell Addison Lane the truth of her feelings?"

When she put it like that, my regret turned to shame.

"You're smarter than that," she said.

"I dunno. I think your little speech convinced me I have the IQ of a worm," I joked, not at all feeling funny.

"Well, you *are* a worm right now, but usually you're at least a beetle. Or a gopher."

"Graduated to mammal? I'll take it."

She chuckled, but my half-smile fell.

"I was wrong."

"You were *so* wrong. About everything, except punching Brock. Man, I wish I'd been there. Thank God for the internet—that video has been going around social media on a loop since you hit him."

I held up my hand, knuckles out, to show her the damage. "Worth it."

"I bet it was. And it meant a lot to her too. You were the only person who didn't lie to her."

"And then I dumped her for lying to me."

She gave me a look that said, *Yeah, dummy.*

"What do I have to do?" I asked half to myself. "Will it even matter? Have I ruined everything?"

"Of course not," she said gently. "She loves you, Kash. All you have to do is tell her you love her too. Oh, and apologize for being a soft-headed ass monkey."

"Ass monkey?" I said on a laugh.

"Dingus. Dickasaurus. Asshat. Dumbassador. I can go on."

"I think I've got it."

"Good." The baby mewled, and Ivy bounced gently, her hand on the baby butt patting in time. "Now, figure out how to make it right. And if you ever hurt her again—and I mean *ever*—I will not just call you names. There are a lot of things in this green-house that can be used as a weapon."

"I dunno, Ivy—your name calling is no joke. And your mom voice is scary."

"I know, right? It's exciting to wield this kind of power."

"Don't let it go to your head."

"Too late."

For a moment, we were silent as I tugged that thread between Lila and me at last, figured out how to reel it in, pull her to me.

I should have trusted her. And I vowed never to make that mistake again.

I only hoped I had the chance to prove it to her.

As a plan unfurled in my mind, a smile spread on my face.

An answering smile spread on Ivy's. "You have an idea."

"Maybe. Will you help?"

And that smile split until I could see her molars. "Of course, dummy."

First and Always

LILA

"That's it. Get out of bed," Ivy said just before my comforter was ripped away with a snap and a rush of cold air.

"Hey!" I squinted at her, blindly patting for it so I could pull it back over my head. "Give that back!"

"Nope." She rolled it up in her arms and tossed it out the door. "Up."

I curled into a ball and groaned.

"You smell like a dumpster, and all this sulky, sad panda business is freaking me out. So get up. Shower. We're meeting Luke at your apartment in an hour to talk about construction."

I groaned again, but this time it came out closer to a whimper.

"Don't gimme that. You've had your allotted moping time, and in forty-eight hours, I'll allow another wallowing session. I'll even climb in bed with you for as long as you want."

I lifted my head so I could see her. "As long as I want?"

"Days even. I'll bring the takeout and John Hughes movies."

"And *Dirty Dancing*."

"Sure. *Dirty Dancing, Sixteen Candles, Pride and Prejudice*—whatever you want."

"Not the Colin Firth one," I warned.

She rolled her eyes long enough that one of her eyelids fluttered. "Fine, we'll watch the wrong *Pride and Prejudice*, but only because you're sad."

"Fine," I huffed, hauling myself to sit.

When I sighed, the triumphant look on her face faded. She took a seat next to me. "I'm sorry, Lila. For all of this."

That heaviness that had taken up residence in my chest sank lower. I curled around it protectively. "It's my own fault. All of it."

"Hang on—I know you're sad, but let's not be delusional. Natasha Felix was not your fault. Brock was not your fault. Kash … well, that one is more complicated, but frankly, he's being an asshole."

"I was the harbinger of every fear he possesses. I fulfilled every prophecy. Lived up to the worst version of myself. He thought he wasn't good enough for me when it was the other way around. He thinks he's unaccomplished, but not by my definition of the word. He thinks he's not smart enough—"

"Well, he *is* being a stupid dummy right now."

I chuckled, but the sound was sad. "I don't care. I don't care about any of it. I love him. I didn't realize the life I wanted wasn't the life I'd been working for, not until him. And now he's all I want. That life is all I want. But if I can't have him, at least I walked away from the rest of it. I can start over. Work toward a new life, the one grown-up me has figured out she wants instead of the one teenage me imagined she wanted."

"Have you figured out your next move?"

"Open my own firm. I just have to come up with a good name and I can get started on the rest."

"Well, once the Femme's show airs, you shouldn't be lacking for clients."

I humphed. "I'm not sure if I want the clientele that will

attract. But that'll be the best part—I can cherry-pick who I want to work with. I have enough in savings to float me, and when I flip the apartment—"

"You can't flip the apartment," she said with such authority, I frowned.

"I can't afford to keep it. I'll have to rent something smaller, tighten the belt. Don't look at me like that. Dreaming might be free, but getting there is most certainly not." I paused. Sighed. "Trust me, the last thing I want is to give up that apartment. It's the first piece of my new dream, and I won't even get to keep it."

"Well, let's just see. Who knows? Maybe things will turn around faster than you think." She rose and moved for the door. "Now, come on, sad sack. Let's get you out of the house before you wither up like a raisin, which is the most offensive member of the fruit family. Nobody wants to be a raisin."

"They're so wrinkly."

"And gummy." A shudder rolled through her.

"Wouldn't want to be gummy. I'd best get up."

"That's the spirit," she said cheerily, bouncing into the living room to plop down next to Dean.

I gathered my things and shuffled to the bathroom, smiling at them on my way. The baby was tiny and fair in his dark arms, his face soft as he smiled down at her. Ivy peered over his massive bicep, resting her cheek on the curve. The two of them were colored in hopes and dreams, realized in their child, their love.

I could only hope that someday, I'd find that too.

Kash's face flashed in my mind, a streak of pain on its wake. That dream I'd had of the apartment and the dog and the long, lazy days hadn't died. It hadn't even quieted. If anything, it had flared, a bright and shining beacon in my heart, the most tangible form of my dream. Because it wasn't about my job or where I lived or what I did on Sundays.

It was him.

The shower was hot enough to burn, the sting siphoning my

other hurts, drawing them away to distraction. I prided myself in not crying as I dried myself off and pulled on my clothes. I'd done enough of that over the last few days. On average, I cried once per quarter, usually instigated by something stupid like my lipliner breaking, endured in solitude where no one could see.

Over the last few days, I'd cried enough to fill my quota for three years—and a few times in front of Ivy, to boot.

I didn't know what Kash had done to me, but I didn't think I could ever reverse it. He had changed me elementally. There was no going back.

Only forward, I supposed.

When I'd left Archer yesterday, it was with a year's severance and a glowing recommendation from Caroline in exchange for not suing Archer for damages, of which there were many. I walked out feeling like I'd won. And then I walked into Longbourne and lost it all again.

He hadn't believed me. He didn't trust me, that mistrust so deep, he assumed I would get in bed with the devil just to save my own skin.

That was perhaps the worst part of all. He'd thought so little of me that he believed me capable of so much selfishness.

Part of me wanted to wallow still, starting with the refusal to blow dry my hair. I could braid it, tie it back, something fast and easy and utterly unlike me. But I had a forty-eight-hour wallowing ban to comply to. So I rallied. I blew out my hair. Used a silly, expensive, probably useless oil on my face, leaving it dewy and fresh. Dashed on mascara, dusted a touch of color on my eyebrows. With a little lip gloss, I was presentable. And better—I didn't feel like a bridge troll anymore.

There was something to be said for a few minutes of self-care and a little mascara.

When I exited the bathroom, it was with more cheer than I'd had since before that cursed wedding, and for that, I was grateful. It gave me hope that maybe, just maybe, I wouldn't be miserable forever.

Ivy was ready and waiting for me, and together, we ventured out. The closer we got to the apartment, the more excited I got, thinking about renovations. I had thoughts and plans and a notebook in my bag, teeming with lists that I hoped wouldn't drive Luke crazy. Ivy distracted me by brainstorming names for my new event company, but the best we came up with was Parker Planners, which was not only boring, but sounded like I made organizational tools. Granted, helping people organize their lives wouldn't be a terrible second career, but I wasn't ready to throw in the towel on events. Not yet.

When we reached the foot of the brownstone, my smile was broad and genuine. My mind skipped with possibilities as we climbed the stairs, and I slipped my key into the door of my home that would never be mine and turned the knob.

I stepped inside thinking I'd find what I'd found before—an echoing, empty, slightly dirty, completely perfect space. But it was more perfect than I could have imagined.

Because it wasn't empty at all.

Standing in the bay window was Kash Bennet.

He was resplendent, so tall and broad-shouldered, he seemed to take up all the space in the room, all the space in my heart. His jaw was darkened by stubble, framing wide, smiling lips. But it was his eyes that nearly brought me to my knees, deep and blue and regretful. Loving and longing and hopeful.

Slowly, I moved toward him, taking in every detail. He stood before a shelf of lilies, the lilies I'd admired in his little greenhouse on the roof. But one stood apart from the rest at his side, its blooms opening to reveal lilies the color of marigold, speckled with golden flecks. It was the strain he'd been working toward for so long. He'd done it.

"You're here," I said, disbelieving my eyes.

"I'm here. And I'm sorry."

Hope zinged through me, emotion gripping my throat, closing it tight. His fervent eyes held me still as he spoke.

"All my life, I've worked at putting two things together to make one. At a glance, they seem so different, from petal to leaf, from texture to color. But somehow, they not only work. They *thrive*. They don't care whether they're different or the same—they come together and make something new, something unexpected. All this time, I've bred flowers to wash away their differences, and all this time, I've cataloged ours. But what I didn't count on was that it wouldn't matter to you any more than it would to a lily. And it shouldn't have mattered to me at all." Something in his eyes deepened, his brows drawing with his regret. "There are so many things I wish I'd done differently, so many things I wish I'd said. But more than anything, I wish I'd realized just how much I love you."

A shaky breath, a shock that brought my fingertips to my lips.

He glanced at his hands, swallowed hard, met my eyes again. "Love doesn't wonder. It doesn't question. It trusts with its whole self, as I should have. And when I looked past the things I feared, I uncovered the truth—I was afraid, and I was a fool. Can you forgive me for my pride? Can you absolve me for all the ways I hurt you? Because of all the things I want, your happiness is first and always."

I took a step toward him. Toward us. "Only if you'll forgive me. I made you feel like you weren't enough when you were the only thing I wanted. I dragged you into a world you wanted no part in because I wasn't ready to choose, convinced I could have it both ways. But in the end, there was no choice to be made. Because my perfect life isn't perfect, not without you." I took another step, closing the gap between us.

A hitch in his chest, a bob of his Adam's apple, his hand sliding into the curve of my waist and eyes searching mine. "Tell me you love me, Lila."

"I've loved you since the start," I said without hesitation. "I loved you before I should have and before I even knew." I shook my head at him in wonder. "You don't even know what a gift you are. You have no idea how you've changed me."

"I didn't want to change you."

"Neither of us had a choice in the matter. You saved me simply by being. You showed me another life, another way, when I thought I was on a one-way street. It's because of you that I had the courage to quit my job. I could walk away because I was walking to you."

"Then it's settled."

"What's settled?"

That smile, clever and bright. "You're mine."

"I'm yours," I promised with a smile of my own.

"Can I get that in writing?" he asked archly, angling for my lips.

"Where do I sign?"

"Right here."

Our lips brushed, melded, the seam hard within a breath and a fluttering heartbeat. We wound together, my arms around his neck, his around my waist, our bodies twisting and tightening to bring us flush. Chest to chest, hip to hip, fingers splayed as if to hold as much of the other as we could. I breathed him in, reveled in the safety found in his arms, the weightlessness of relief. The scent of him, earthy and so wonderfully masculine. The silken strands of his hair in my fingers, the stony landscape of his body surrounding me. And I surrendered myself to the sensation, to him, knowing he would honor the sacrifice with all the reverence and adoration I would give to him.

A burst of clapping snapped us apart, and we turned to find Ivy in the doorway, smiling and crying and clapping.

"I swear I left," she said through her tears. "But I had to sneak back in to make sure you were okay, and you are. Right?" She hiccuped a sob, swiping at her cheeks.

Kash and I shared a smile before I made my way to console my sister. "Yes, we're okay. Are *you* okay?"

"I think it's my hormones. Yesterday I cried because Olive pooped for the first time in twenty-four hours. I'm a mess." She drew a breath, straightened up, and dried her eyes. "I'm sorry. I really did only mean to peek but then … well, I saw you kissing, and before I realized what was happening, I was clapping."

"It's okay," I said around a laugh.

She raised her hands, waving them palms out. "I'm going. I'm sorry. I love you two and I'm so happy for you and goodbye!" she rambled, still waving as she backed out the door, closing it behind her.

With that smile on his face, he crossed the room to take me in his arms again. "I love the apartment, by the way."

I threaded my arms around his neck, smiling back up at him. "I'm sorry I didn't tell you. I was going to after the wedding, but …"

"But all hell broke loose. You're not mad Luke let me in?"

I shook my head, glancing to the bay window with eternal longing. "Not at all. I'm glad you love it. I just wish I could keep it."

"Why can't you?"

"I have no job. Luckily, I secured my loans *before* I quit. And fortunately, I finagled a year's severance out of Caroline before I walked out."

"You're kidding."

"Well, she couldn't very well let me sue her, could she?"

He laughed, face tilting back in his surprise. "That's my girl."

"But even with that, I shouldn't take on the mortgage. I'll need to find a place half this price so I can start my own firm."

A slow smile spread on his lips. "You're starting your own firm?"

"With my own terms, including the right to refuse service. If I'm going to make the life for myself that I want, I'm afraid that's nonnegotiable."

"What else is part of that life?"

"You. Past that, I couldn't care less."

He scanned the room, lifting his eyes to the high ceiling. "Not this apartment?"

"In a perfect world, yes. But I'd rather live in a studio and be able to run my own business than lose my shirt on my dream apartment."

A pause. "What if you could have it all?"

My brows quirked. "How?"

"I don't know if you remember, but I've recently discovered I'm in possession of a hefty sum of money."

"I couldn't let you pay for my apartment, Kash."

"Not even if I lived here?"

I frowned. "You want to rent the apartment from me?"

A laugh, soft and amused. "I want to live here *with you*."

Surprise opened my face, my lids shuttering.

"I know it's soon," he said. "I know it's crazy. But I have the money and means to make your dream come true. And in doing that, my dream can come true too—every morning, I can wake up to you. This place can be yours, Lila, if you want it."

"Ours," I breathed. "It can be ours."

"It can be ours," he echoed. "If that's what you want."

I was so overcome, I couldn't answer.

"It's too much," he backpedaled, suddenly nervous and reassuring at once. "I don't want to rush you, Lila. I don't want to lose you. I only thought—"

"Kash, I have done everything in my life by the book until you. I'm tired of playing it safe. I'm sick of denying myself the things I want just because it isn't part of my ten-step plan. I'm over all the rules. From now on, I'm going to do what I want."

"And what do you want?"

I peered up at him with a shyness only he brought on. "What I wanted the first time I walked through that door. I want you here with me."

Without a word, he kissed me to accept, but in every breath was a simple truth, the deepest truth of my life—he was mine, and I was his.

Not for the first time, I believed it would be forever.

And this time, I'd be right.

Sign For It

KASH

"**J**ust put it right there, against the wall." Lila pointed at said wall, which touted exposed brick and faced the bay windows in our bedroom.

Luke and I shuffled in that direction, setting the box spring on the floor.

With a smile, she hung her hands on her hips, appraising her domain with pride and hope.

It had only been a week since we decided to move in together, and if it'd been up to me, I'd have stayed here with her that night and every night after. But we had to have some plumbing work done, and although we could have stayed here through that, she insisted on having the floors refinished afterward, correctly assessing that it'd be the only thing we couldn't live around during renovations. We could eat takeout while the kitchen was being gutted. We could add the second bathroom, then renovate the other. But the floors had to be done, and there was no way around it.

I'd have agreed with her, had I not been so impatient.

Over the course of that week, we'd slowly purchased and moved over the things we could put away—clothes and dishes and glasses and flatware. Toiletries and towels and linens and shower curtains. We'd even hung curtains after painting the walls a crisp white that reflected sunshine like it was its full-time job.

Lila carried in bed linens as we brought in the mattress, thunking it on the box spring.

"I still can't believe you're going to sleep on a bed on the floor," Luke said with a sidelong smile at Lila.

"Please, I'm not as prissy as you all make me out to be," she said, ironically prim, nose up just enough.

Luke chuckled. "Anything else you need?"

"Nope," I answered. "I think we can manage putting the sheets on the one piece of furniture we own, but thanks."

"Couch tomorrow?" he asked.

"And breakfast table," she answered. "We can empty out my storage unit too, right?"

"Works for me," Luke said with a shrug. "And the day after, we'll start framing for the new bathroom."

"Right on schedule." She smiled the smile she wore when checking something off a list.

"All right. Then I'll see you guys tomorrow. Try not to party too hard," he joked, glancing around the empty, echoing apartment.

"We'll do our best." Lila unfurled a fitted sheet with a snap.

Luke said final goodbyes and left the apartment, and as the door closed, I made my way to the opposite side of the bed and grabbed one corner of the sheet.

"It looks so lonely in here," she said as she stretched the sheet over the curve. "But I don't even care. I'm so glad to be out of a hotel."

"And out of the baby's room," I noted.

"And out of a bunk bed."

I laughed. "Yes, and that."

Once the fitted sheet was on, she unfolded the flat sheet and shook it out like a billowing sail. I caught the other side.

"How was the office space?" I asked, curious as to how the tour had gone.

"Oh, it's perfect. And the price is right. Luke really does have all the hook-ups, doesn't he?"

"I think he's on a first-name basis with half of Manhattan."

Lila chuckled, folding and tucking the corners like in a hospital. "It'll do nicely until I have my office set up here. Are you sure you're okay with me taking that space? Couldn't you use it for growing?"

"Why would I do that when I have a whole greenhouse around the corner?"

She flushed, laughing again as she smoothed the sheets and turned for the comforter. "Oh, I don't know. But it feels selfish somehow."

"Well, it *is* your house," I reminded her. "Technically, you're my landlady."

She hummed with appreciation. "There are so many ways I could collect my rent."

"Oh, I'll pay you in that currency, rent or not."

The pillows went *thump*, followed by Lila, who flopped onto the bed on her back. "Come here and sign for that promise."

Smirking, I kicked off my shoes and climbed onto the bed, crawling toward her. The second she was within reach, she was in my arms, my lips signing on the line. I leaned back, looking down at her.

The shiny crimson of her hair against the clean white sheets. The flush of her porcelain cheeks. The steely gray of her eyes and pink of her smiling lips.

"I love you," I said, dragging a thumb across her cheek.

"Good, because I love you too."

"Are you scared? About all of this? About me?"

One of her brows rose with the corner of her lips. "Why? Should I be?"

"Not as far as I know. But your plans for life aren't what you thought they'd be. Two months ago, you hated me."

"Oh, I don't know if I'd say *hate*," she said with a smile, her fingers twiddling in my hair. "But old me was a little uptight, if you'll remember."

"I remember. I remember wanting to undo you like this. I wondered then if it'd just take the right man."

"I suppose I did—I needed you. I needed your love, because no one ever had loved before, not like this. Not like you."

I kissed her softly, briefly. And she gazed up at me.

"But you're right," she said. "Life didn't turn out like I thought it would. It's better."

My gaze skimmed the planes and angles of her face. "Is it? Because in my whole life, I could never have imagined the truth of this feeling. Of moments like this. Of the depth of how I love you."

"Me neither," she said quietly. "And to think, if I'd spent more time in the greenhouse in high school, I could have felt this way for so long."

"Don't worry. We have the rest of our lives for that, if you want."

Her cheek under my hand warmed, and the sparkle of a tear shone in the corner of her eye. "It's all I want."

"Then that's what you'll get," I said against her lips before I took them for what they were.

Mine.

Epilogue

LILA

"**A**re you ready?" Kash asked with that smile on his face, the one I loved so well.

The puppy answered for me with a bark, his dusky gray hair flopping.

I laughed, scooping him up as best I could, big as he already was. "He didn't ask you, Georgie."

But Georgie only aggressively licked my face, wriggling in my arms.

"Oh, you're impossible," I said, setting him down, the two of us laughing when he jumped at the door, tail wagging and paws on the wood in wait.

Three months had passed since we moved in. Three months of renovations and half-finished projects around the house. Three months with Georgie, the Labradoodle puppy who was the perfect mix of priss and filthy.

Three months of working on putting together my new company, Revelry.

Once the new season of *Felix Femmes* had aired, I'd found that I didn't have to look for work. Work found me.

Kash and I watched every episode with sick stomachs and cringes affixed for forty-two of the longest minutes of my week. They played the subplot all right, and it was brutal. Unconscionably brutal. My only consolation was the lovely financial package they'd offered me for damages and the villainization of Brock and Natasha.

The producers had painted them in the most unkind and unflattering of lights. The plotting and plans had gone so far beyond what I'd realized. Addison's long lunches were with producers of the show to discuss me. In fact, that was how she'd known about Brock all along—she'd been in on it. The internet turned on her in the most brutal and despicable ways. So despicable that it left me empty and sick. And so, the last time I met with the network with my lawyer, I pulled one of the producers aside who I knew from the *Femmes* and suggested they give *her* the show I'd refused. They could make it like *Dance Moms* but for weddings.

Last I heard, she'd accepted. And it made me sleep just a little better at night, knowing I wasn't the end of her career.

No matter how awful she was, no one deserved that. In some ways, she'd been played too—they'd let her do their dirty work, then cut her loose the second she was a liability.

On the airing of the first episode, my social media exploded overnight, the client requests coming in like a rogue wave. I interviewed brides, chose my favorites, and had not only a stable of wealthy, respectful, kind clients, but I was booked out for the next year. A *year*. The thought alone was staggering, the need requiring an upgraded office space, the hiring of two assistants, and the acquirement of a handful of interns. The only price had been my humiliation. Kash's too, although GIFs of him popping Brock in the nose had been circulating the internet since the wedding episode aired. Unsurprisingly, on the public meeting

Kash on television, the flower shop found themselves in the midst of a boom. A boom and a lawsuit.

But that was Marcus's story to tell.

Through it all, Kash had maintained the calm power with which he handled everything. Including me. The upheaval of our lives had been taken in stride because, despite all the chaos and uncertainty before us, one thing was undeniably clear and true— we had each met our match. We knew it in our marrow, but so did everyone who loved us. Mrs. Bennet had officially inducted me into the family with zeal and fervor. She inspected and assessed me too, don't get me wrong. But she'd seen it from the first, noted the rightness, the clicking together of two pieces to make one, and had already provided lists of old family names we could use for a baby and made it a habit of asking me about my ovulation cycle.

But every night, we came here, came home. Curled up on the couch where I'd read and he'd sketch and we'd listen to old records. Every night was thick with I love you's. Every morning, his was the first face I saw, the first thought in my mind, the first name on my lips. And that perfect life I'd abandoned seemed so empty, so vain.

The perfect life was the one I had.

Georgie barked again, and I met Kash's gaze. He'd asked me if I was ready. And I gave him the answer I'd always give.

"Yes."

His big hand closed over the doorknob to our apartment and turned, Georgie dashing in the second there was enough space to wiggle through. Three days ago, we'd headed to the Plaza with Georgie as the finishing touches were put on our home. It'd been Kash's idea to splurge in celebration of our renovation completion and our successes, citing the anticipation would make the reveal that much sweeter.

And as usual, he wasn't wrong.

The apartment was lit by candles, golden and flickering in the dark. Someone—Tess, I was certain—had staged everything. The last of our furniture had been delivered, the art finally hung, every detail, every corner pristine and perfect.

But I barely saw any of it. Because in the bay window stood an archway of flowers.

White and cream, layers on layers of soft petals. Feathery grasses, roses, orchids and lilies and a wealth of perfumed florals, all in a spotless shade of snow, lit from below by candles all over the floor.

A brief concern regarding fire hazards blitzed through my thoughts, but when I looked at Kash, my worry fell away. Nothing bad could happen when he smiled like that.

He took my hand and guided me toward the arch.

"What is all this?" I asked, eyes above me as we stepped beneath the curve.

"This," he started, drawing my gaze, "is forever."

Kash glanced above us, his smile fond as he looked over the flowers he'd likely grown, knowing each by name.

"Arches and doorways have their own magic, their own mystery. Moving through them, standing beneath them, we are in the in-between, the twilight, the passage. There's an unspoken danger, the threat of being lost or forgotten. It's why a husband carries his bride over the threshold—so he can protect her from any harm, any pain. It's all I want—to shelter you from harm, to give you the happiness you've given me. I want to step into that life with you. Because together, we can survive anything. I promise to carry you through life, to comfort and protect you. To keep you safe. You asked me once what my passion was, and I've finally found it. It's you." He lowered to one knee, stopping my heart. "Will you marry me, Lila?"

He opened a small velvet box, his face alight with hope and a tremor of fear. Candlelight caught the diamond, and it winked and twinkled, beckoning me.

But that ring wasn't the offering. The offering was his heart.

Breathlessly, I nodded. "Yes," I whispered, that word that belonged to him.

With shaking hands, he slid that ring on the finger tied to my heart, and when he stood, it was to pull me into his arms and kiss me like I was his, truly and forever.

But I already had been. I'd been waiting for him my whole life, it seemed, as if every step and every choice had brought me closer to him. To this moment. To all the moments ahead of us.

Because of all the dreams and wishes I had, he was the greatest of all.

thank you

Dear Village,

Through nineteen books, you have cheered me through the finish line, held back my hair when I was sick from it all, and held me when everything felt like too much. Each and every one of you is vital to me, and I hope you know that I could never do this without you. That's right, you. I love you. Thank you will never, ever be enough.

Dear Bloggers,

Each of you works a tireless, thankless job, and for nothing beyond the joy of reading. It's you who we have to truly thank for our success, for reading, for sharing, for spreading the word about our stories. You are perhaps the most important part of this great machine, and I hope you know how much you mean to us.

Dear Readers,

Thank you for letting me into your heart and soul for a few hours. I hope you enjoyed the little glimpse into mine.

Until next time, friends

also by
STACI HART

CONTEMPORARY STANDALONES

Bad Habits

With a Twist (Bad Habits 1)
A ballerina living out her fantasies about her high school crush realizes real love is right in front of her in this slow-burn friends-to-lovers romantic comedy.

Chaser (Bad Habits 2)
He'd trade his entire fortune for a real chance with his best friend's little sister.

Last Call (Bad Habits 3)
All he's ever wanted was a second chance, but she'll resist him at every turn, no matter how much she misses him.

The Austens

Wasted Words (Inspired by Emma)
She's just an adorable, matchmaking book nerd who could never have a shot with her gorgeous best friend and roommate.

A Thousand Letters (Inspired by Persuasion)
Fate brings them together after seven years for a second chance they never thought they'd have in this lyrical story about love, loss, and moving on.

A Little Too Late (Follow up to A Thousand Letters)
A story of finding love when all seems lost and finding home when you're far away from everything you've known.

Living Out Loud (Inspired by *Sense & Sensibility*)
Annie wants to live while she can, as fully as she can, not knowing how deeply her heart could break.

The Tonic Series
Tonic (Book 1)
The reality show she's filming in his tattoo parlor is the last thing he wants, but if he can have her, he'll be satisfied in this enemies-to-lovers-comedy.

Bad Penny (Book 2)
She knows she's boy crazy, which is why she follows strict rules, but this hot nerd will do his best to convince her to break every single one.

The Red Lipstick Coalition
Piece of Work
Her cocky boss is out to ruin her internship, and maybe her heart, too.

Player
He's just a player, so who better to teach her how to date? All she has to do is not fall in love with him.

Work in Progress
She never thought her first kiss would be on her wedding day. Rule number one: Don't fall in love with her fake husband.

Well Suited
She's convinced love is nothing more than brain chemicals, and her baby daddy's determined to prove her wrong.

The Bennet Brothers

Coming Up Roses
Everyone hates something about their job, and she hates Luke Bennet. Because if she doesn't, she'll fall in love with him.

The Hardcore Serials
Hardcore: Complete Collection
A parkour thief gets herself into trouble when she falls for the man who forces her to choose between right and wrong.

HEARTS AND ARROWS
Greek mythology meets Gossip Girl in a contemporary paranormal series where love is the ultimate game and Aphrodite never loses.

Paper Fools (Book 1)
Shift (Book 2)
From Darkness (Book 3)

.

meet staci

Staci has been a lot of things up to this point in her life: a graphic designer, an entrepreneur, a seamstress, a clothing and handbag designer, a waitress. Can't forget that. She's also been a mom to three little girls who are sure to grow up to break a number of hearts. She's been a wife, even though she's certainly not the cleanest, or the best cook. She's also super, duper fun at a party, especially if she's been drinking whiskey, and her favorite word starts with f, ends with k.

From roots in Houston, to a seven year stint in Southern California, Staci and her family ended up settling somewhere in between and equally north in Denver, until they grew a wild hair and moved to Holland. It's the perfect place to overdose on cheese and ride bicycles, especially along the canals, and especially in summertime. When she's not writing, she's reading, gaming, or designing graphics.

www.stacihartnovels.com

Made in the USA
Monee, IL
28 July 2021